The Ravages of Time

Pat McDonald

Strategic Book Publishing and Rights Co.

Strategic Book Publishing and Rights Co., LLC
USA | Singapore
www.sbpra.net

For information about special discounts for bulk purchases, please contact Strategic Book Publishing and Rights Co., LLC. Special Sales, at bookorder@sbpra.net.

ISBN: 978-1-950015-58-0

Dedicated to:

The real 'Mary Mundy' whose name I never knew

Acknowledgements:

To the real 'Mary Mundy' whom I met only briefly during a placement in an Old People's Homes where she lived having spent most of her adult life in a Mental Asylum admitted because she got pregnant as a child and therefore felt to be mentally deficient. She spoke very little, kept her room immaculate and her tiny animal figures she displayed in the bay window of her room. She inspired me to write this book.

PROLOGUE:

"Mundy!" I heard the rasping voice with the underlying dryness he gets from smoking a lot of cigarettes. I could hear the harshness in the sound and knew the straw hat I wear to work in the gardens gives me away when I day dream.

Just for a minute I stop working, kneeling amongst the rows of pea plants, listening. I can't help running my fingers through the fineness of the grains of rich soil where the peas grow. I love the feel of the warm earth letting it slip between my fingers, it makes me feel alive, that earthy smell. Oh, how I love that smell. It's so much better than the carbolic soap stench in the laundry. There I can only smell strong bleach drifting upwards when I rub the coarse fabrics over the washboards, rinsing them in the 'dolly blue.'

It's lovely being outside, away from the darkness of the dimly lit wash house. It's hot today, even with this breeze and with the sun shining down as I pick the pea pods now they are ready. I borrowed this straw hat because of sunstroke, they say my skull is thin just like all the other 'mental defectives', without it I would get sunstroke with nothing on my head, so I wear it even though it gives me away.

I got the hat from one of the old women who no longer works in the gardens. I haven't seen her since they took her to the place next to the laundry. It's a place no one talks about and I daren't ask anyone, it's not wise to ask questions or talk to people too much.

I learnt this when I came here. I was just a girl back then, so I didn't have much to say anyway. Early on I saw a group of women chattering in the laundry, they were laughing and making saucy talk to each other. One of the women called Phyllis laughed so loud she couldn't stop. They took her away because of 'hysteria', gave her the *cold bath treatment 'til she calmed down and went quiet again. You learn from things like that.*

Like I say, the hat gives me away when I stop working and start to daydream. It's why I try hard to keep my head bobbing up and down because I'm tiny for my age and the pea plants almost hide me, though not quite enough, so I keep my head moving even when I'm not working.

When I peer under the brim of the 'coolly' hat I can see the man standing on top of the bank above the rows of vegetables. He's watching me picking the peas and putting them in the raffia basket the clever people make in the basket weaving room. They sell most of them at the market to make money for the Asylum.

You see, I got distracted by the white butterfly flitting down the row of peas, it has such delicate wings and I can't help but watch it lightly fluttering from one flower to another. I'm careful never to smile even though the butterfly makes me want to, just in case the man watching sees me doing it. Smiling to myself is a sign you're......well I'm not really sure what it means....so I make a serious face being mindful not to look too melancholy because sadness would, I've been told, make them give you the electric to jolt you back to normal.

The problem is I have no idea what 'normal' is either.

CHAPTER 1

"Miss!" The boy at the counter shouted interrupting her thoughts. No "Mundy!" or "Mary Mundy" as she remembered the harsh nurse shouting at her when she found herself day dreaming.

The boy held out her change from the money she gave him for the shopping. She looked up at his irritated face as he waved the coins in a clenched hand in front of him. She took it out of his hand moving away towards the out-door, head bowed, placing it into the old worn out brown leather purse which she then dropped into the plastic carrier bag containing her meagre shopping. She nearly collided with a young girl coming into the shop who scooted around her where she stood making her money safe. On pension day she worried about carrying so much money on her person.

She scurried along with the shuffling gait of the elderly woman she had become, her hips painfully stiff from a life time working in the gardens at the Asylum, scrubbing the floors on hands and knees with cloth, scrubbing brush and blocks of carbolic soap. Her hands and arms bear the red scars from endless hours immersing them alternately in hot or cold water and rubbing the coarse fabrics against the wash boards which rubbed away the skin on her fingers.

She hurried with an urgent need to get back home where she knew she would be safe, making sure she looked at no one she passed or spoke to anyone, even if they bid her good day.

Mary Mundy lived in a one bedroom flat in a sheltered complex they found for her at the halfway hostel where she stayed briefly to learn how to cook and make tea in a pot. She learnt a lot of other things, some of which were long since forgotten. She didn't mind because she loved her flat where she lived alone not having to share it with anyone else.

She could sit all day, dream as much as she wanted and if she wanted to she could even smile to herself when she thought about how Mary Mundy, the 'mental defective' could sit reading books she fetched from the library each week. She no longer needed to hide them or find a secret place to read. The ever present wobbling of her head, as well as her scarred hands, were the only reminders of earlier times, although a comfort nonetheless.

She felt sure they would believe it a sign of something if they knew she could read. 'Mental defectives' didn't have the capacity to read, so they would think she pretended, a sure sign she needed some kind of dreadful treatment and there were so many of those, some of which she knew about.

Mary Mundy learnt to read and write at school where she did really well early on in her childhood, always keeping a journal, writing about everything she did on a daily basis. It was much easier no longer having to hide the fact. Here she wrote every day using writing books she bought in the post office shop. The early ones of her life were on scraps of paper or flimsy exercise books she borrowed or stole whenever she could get them from the clever people.

Tonight she would read her latest book from the library about a young girl sent away to school for being wilful and stubborn. She recognised herself in this girl, in as much as she had been locked away just like her a long time ago.

First she made her tea like they showed her at the other place, putting the beans into a saucepan, two slices of bread under the grill making sure she didn't forget to turn them over when they got brown. She sometimes thought she might do an egg on top, but the eggs were for breakfast, they showed her at the hostel. Anyway it would take too long to make and she really wanted to get back to find out how Jane Eyre fared at Lowood School where Mr Brocklehurst took her.

CHAPTER 2

I heard the baby crying again echoing down the length of the long dimly lit corridor with the faded lime green floor that's covered in all those scuff marks from the tramping feet. It sounds like the cry of a new born baby wanting to be fed.

My baby, I recognised it, even though I only heard it the once when the nurse swaddled it with a sheet before she took it away. I could just see as I raised myself on my elbows, barely able to sit up I felt so weak I had to strain hard against the straps they tied me to the table with.

I saw the precious pink arm flail out at one corner of the sheet trying to reach for me as I watched the nurse move quickly through the door. I heard the sharp cry the baby made, holding the one note without stopping for breath – then they were gone.

They didn't even let me hold my baby. I never knew if it was a boy or a girl, though in my many recurring dreams I feel the pain again, followed by the release in my body, then the rush of something slippery between my legs. I kept my eyes tightly closed until the moment when the nurse took it away.

They didn't tell me, but I imagined her – my very own daughter. Afterwards those endless days of searching, following the sound I always heard of my baby crying, calling to me from one corridor or another in this, my sprawling prison.

What mother wouldn't recognise the sound of her own baby? Even though I heard it just the once that day, the echo could never be wrong. My baby girl wants me, because I am Mary, her rightful mother. I promise myself that one day I will find my baby and we will be together again.

*   *   *   *

Joselyn parked the coach built pram outside the co-op supermarket just to the left of the shop's main door, leaving the pram's handle sticking out so that she could see it from inside the shop. Her face showed all of her pent up frustrations at having to bring the baby out to do this bit of shopping to slow her down on her day off.

"Once you get me these things," Mrs Devonshire told her, "then you can go!" She sounded a bit irritable, not like her usual self. Making Joselyn run errands on her day off, was unfair when it meant she would be late meeting Dorian, he wouldn't like that. Now she would be anxious in case he resented it happening again and he might get angry, his temper was unpredictable.

He told her to put her foot down, insist she be given the time off owed to her, "they are taking advantage!" He scolded forcefully. Of course, he didn't seem to have a job like she did. He pleased himself what he did with his time.

She hurried into the co-op with the list of shopping items hoping it wouldn't take her too long to find everything her employer wanted for her dinner party that evening. She left the baby in the pram because it would be quicker, then nearly collided with an old woman shuffling out of the shop not looking where she was going, fumbling with her purse and shopping bags. She managed to swerve around her at the last minute without stopping, grab the basket from the pile inside the door in one easy movement.

It took her no more than ten minutes to fill her basket and instead of searching amongst all the spices as there were so many, she asked the girl on the counter "do you have paprika?" The girl sniffed grudgingly going off to find her a small jar of the red powdered spice to add to her basket. The spotty youth on the next till stared at her making her feel uncomfortable while she waited.

Back outside once again she slipped the bag under the pram on a special rack beneath the pram's body, took the brake off hurriedly pushing the pram back to the house. Fiona Devonshire lived in the tree-lined Blackheath Avenue in one of the large detached elaborate homes with an ornamental covered porch with flamboyant pillars, one each side of the door holding up the porch roof where a vast array of climbing roses clung against ornate trellis giving off a wonderful perfume.

Fiona wasn't much older than her Nanny, married to Bernard twice her age and 'something' in the city. She didn't care much how he earnt his money, just that he did, giving her this privileged comfortable life of leisure. In exchange she put up with him, entertained his business clients and fairly recently produced him the child, a daughter Phoebe, he said he always wanted.

Today, however, Fiona felt aggrieved, Bernie having sprung this dinner party on her at the last minute before he left for the city. She craved a less fraught day with a leisurely lunch at the Golf Club to give her the opportunity to observe the new golf pro everyone spoke about. The fact of her Nanny's day off hit her at the same time as the dinner party news, delivered by Bernie before he left home, made her doubly irritated.

When she got back, she found Fiona outside clipping roses from the intertwined climbing stems she supposed to make a centrepiece for her dining table. Joselyn tried not to look too annoyed. At least the electric gate stood open which meant she didn't have to wait for it; it took ages to open. Joselyn needed this job as Nanny to fulfil her ambition to move away, perhaps somewhere abroad as Nanny to some well to do family who travelled taking their Nanny with them.

She needed good references to be able to achieve this. Not that she told Dorian about it, he wouldn't have approved. He really didn't understand the concept of having to work for a living or the need to ingratiate himself with anyone. Money didn't seem to be a problem whilst he pompously declared himself to be a "free spirit" with no intention of ever being at the beck and call of anyone. His life, as far as she could tell, seemed to be as a member of a rock band and as Josie (he insisted on calling it her) saw it, not a very good rock band. It surprised her once when she heard the band rehearsing in the back room as she left the house after meeting Dorian on another day off.

"Did you get everything?" Fiona Devonshire asked catching sight of Jocelyn bustling up the drive, from where she stood cutting flowers. She moved through the front door without waiting for a reply, leaving her Nanny to manoeuvre the large coach built pram up the porch steps into the house. Fiona purchased the pram because she thought it looked classy having seen one like it on a news reel clip of the latest Royal baby being pushed around the grounds at Buckingham Palace.

"I think I have what you asked for," Joselyn bent down taking the bag from the rack beneath the pram now standing in the hall, handed it to her employer who took it and peered inside. "Can I go please?" She hurriedly begged hoping to get off without further delay.

Fiona Devonshire twirled around heading with her flower basket and the shopping bag towards the kitchen. "Bring Phoebe through will you?" She said calmly over her shoulder ignoring her request. Fiona made it as far as the kitchen door before she heard the piercing scream Joselyn let out.

Fiona came back at the sound staring at Joselyn whose face was now as white as a sheet, "The baby's gone!" she cried bursting into floods of tears.

CHAPTER 3

I found the secret room today when I went out to search for my baby. I must have walked past it many times without seeing it. I found it when I dropped my book. I bent down to pick it up looking into the alcove I found it wasn't what I thought. It didn't occur to me to wonder why the alcove is there, as it seems to serve no purpose.

I 'borrowed' the book from the room in the physician's house, it's a sort of library with so many volumes and papers, mostly about sickness treatments except for a few other books like this one someone must have left behind. When I bent down I felt a draught of air coming from the alcove, yet there is no window to let it in. Moving closer I saw a door left slightly open, it just looks like part of the wall when you close it.

I felt the crack with my fingers pulling it open. It's clever, with a concealed handle, covered so you wouldn't think it was a handle at all. Once open there are stairs leading down into the dark. At first I was scared, then I had the urge to go down those stairs even though I know there are places, all kinds of rooms in here they take the patients to, especially the violent ones.

I saw one once as I hid from some men in white coats pushing a bed with a man on it. Those wild staring eyes caught my attention, as did his shaven head with a jagged cut roughly sewn together on his scalp, still oozing bright red blood across his face. I will never forget those eyes staring, fixed in space, empty because he locked them on me from where I kept mostly hidden, he showed no recognition I was there. When his head turned towards me, I knew he did see me although the others didn't; he showed no emotion just a fixed staring gaze.

At first I thought it could be one of those rooms they took the man to, but it didn't stop me. I felt my way downwards into the blackness, needing, wanting to find out where it went. I was so afraid I felt my heart fluttering in my chest.

I had to see if this is the place they took my baby to. I mean to search every part of it to be sure. I listened for the cries but none came from below. When I got to the bottom of the stairs, I found a small dingy window high up on one of the walls letting in a strong beam of light, it fell across the room. I could see dancing dust motes even though everything looked still.

There was no one there. Just a room full of all kinds of broken things, beds, tables, chairs now derelict or discarded as if they are no longer used. I found a long cord hanging from the ceiling which gave off a very dim light when I pulled it. Such a good place I think, although long forgotten (like me), just the right sort of place to come to read or where I am writing this entry in my journal.

I can leave my books here, all my writing things where I think no one will find them if I keep them well hidden; a sanctuary where no one will find me.

*   *   *   *

Ten o'clock already and Brendon showed signs of acute boredom as he sat at his desk in the CID room playing a game of solitaire on his computer. The novelty of being a CID detective wore off years ago. These days the simple programme he installed on his computer represented a countdown calculation, when he logged on each morning, of how many working days he needed to serve until his retirement. Only everyone knew it as pension day.

If he were truthful he was already the wrong side of his fortieth birthday, going on 'flabby' having succumbed to this more sedentary life. Walking the beat as a uniform officer kept him trimmer for a number of years until the advent of 'new policing'. There are fewer coppers nowadays all riding around in cars covering a bigger patch. The boundaries having been recalculated to take account of the percentage reduction in front line officers due to the year on year savings in policing, a requirement of the Home Office, hence governmental cuts across all police services.

Moving to criminal investigation accelerated the aging process. His once youthful baby face matured into a doughy rounder version of his former self not even his wife seemed to find remotely attractive and which he had long since given up trying to change.

"Flannery!" The sharp yell interrupted his idle thoughts with an urgent need to camouflage the game he was playing. He ducked his head down quickly changing the screen, bringing up the force notice board of unflattering I.D pictures, where wanted local villains were listed together with the crimes they were wanted for.

He glanced over at the Chief Inspector's office expecting him to be standing at his office door summoning him. He wasn't there, the door being firmly closed. The bright spark Taylor-Smythe sat grinning his toothy mocking grin having mimicked the yell of their Chief Inspector.

"Funny man!" Brendon retaliated. As if his life wasn't bad enough without being surrounded by the new breed of detectives, all vying for promotion with their upwardly mobile lives. He particularly resented Taylor with his pretentious double barrelled name, expensive tailored suits, sharp shirts and silk ties. Rumour had it his parents were loaded. A rumour Taylor put about himself, but nobody knew, just a whisper here a word there and round it went, the grapevine could always be trusted.

The new breed wouldn't appreciate 'real' detective work if they tripped over it, Brendon thought. They were all statistics, criminal profiling and any short cuts they could make to get a fast result, all from the vantage point of their desks. It didn't matter to them whether they got the right perpetrator as long as they got one. He, Brendon, was used to traditional methods of hard foot slogging door to door, endless interviews, cross-checking facts with old style analysis relying on collecting intelligence and matching up the evidence. There didn't seem to be much in the way of common sense amongst the lot of them.

The door of the chief Inspector's office opened revealing a stern looking old school detective who scowled as he surveyed the room. Mike Harvey had a deeply wrinkled face which only a combination of too many cigarettes, too much whisky and endless sleepless nights from too many serious cases could produce.

His voice, when he called "Flannery" to gain Brendon's attention held a husky quality, not so much bass tone as smoke damaged.

"Gov?" Brendon acknowledged him.

"With me," he merely said. "We've got a baby snatch." He walked off expecting Brendon to follow him. The others watched as he got up, grabbed his crumpled suit jacket following him out of the door.

"What have we got so far?" Brendon asked his superior as they drove through the centre of town and out towards the suburbs.

"Taken from outside the local village co-op whilst the Nanny went inside for ten minutes," Harvey related.

"She came out and found the baby gone?" Brendon could relate to the Nanny's alarm as he once misplaced one of his own children on a trip to the children's playground, his wife Nancy never let him forget it. He often thought it was perhaps the time when their marriage cooled somewhat, although not really certain.

"What about the mother?" He asked thinking about Nancy's anger when she found out he'd lost sight of his four year old daughter who wandered off on her own.

"At home, she doesn't work," Harvey emphasised as if something out of the ordinary.

"She has a Nanny?" He said incredulously. Brendon thought of his own circumstances with endless arrangements at nurseries and childminders because Nancy kept her job with the Council expecting him to do his share to cover the childcare arrangements.

"The mother is Fiona Devonshire," Harvey revealed glancing over to assess for recognition of the name. He got none so added, "Wife of Bernard Devonshire?"

"Isn't he something in Property Development?" Brendon queried.

"It is certainly his officially recognised occupation," the implied sneer hit home.

"Dodgy?" Brendon asked.

"Well he is reputed to be worth a considerable amount. Tip of the iceberg," he said. "What lies beneath is anybody's guess."

"Do we have anything on him?" Brendon asked expectantly.

He shook his head slowly, "Oh, Bernard Devonshire is way too slippery to let himself get caught," he added scathingly.

"Is this likely to be a ransom snatch then, Gov?"

"Now that remains to be seen," he offered as he pulled up outside a large sprawling detached property. "Here we are then." He parked behind a marked police car and got out. "Uniform called us. I believe there is a female police officer trying to comfort a very distressed mother and young Nanny."

The front door opened as they approached. The female police officer looked relieved to see them; being new to family liaison she already felt the strain of the mother's distress as well as the Nanny's guilt.

She updated them on the situation. It was forty five minutes since they discovered the baby missing. When they entered the spacious hallway they could see the coach built pram standing there. They were both surprised to see the pram. Harvey glanced at Brendon who shrugged.

"Mr. Devonshire?" Chief Inspector Harvey asked the P.C.

"He's on his way back," she informed them. "He works in the City so has a way to travel."

"Okay," Harvey said. "Where are they?"

The P.C lowered her voice, "They're in the lounge, Sir. Mrs. Devonshire seemed very distressed when she told her husband."

"Well of course she's distressed….." he began eyeing the police woman critically.

"No, Sir," she lowered her voice even more. "I mean she became quite agitated, like she might be afraid to tell him."

"Only natural," Brendon Flannery chipped in remembering how he felt at having to confess his slip up to Nancy knowing how she would react.

"It's just a feeling I got as I watched her, Sir." The P.C. wanted to redeem herself for stating what seemed perfectly obvious. "I think she is genuinely scared of him." *'There, she'd said it, let them think her naïve, but she knew what she knew'.*

"How's the Nanny bearing up?" Brendon asked assuming she would take the brunt of any anger.

"She's beside herself Sir, she didn't realise the baby was missing until she pushed the pram back here….."

Harvey walked over to the pram peering into the interior, empty now except for the pram covers and an elastic string stretching across the front the hood, threaded with an assortment of brightly coloured plastic animals containing small beads that rattled when Harvey flicked them with the nail on his finger.

The P.C followed the two detectives standing beside them, "The hood was up with the front piece of the cover attached each side to keep out the cold or rain. You couldn't actually see the baby unless you lowered it, obscured by those toys." She already established these things from the Nanny who had been eager to defend herself for not noticing, she thought the baby was asleep. "Oh, and there's a small teddy bear missing." She added. The two detectives seemed to frown in unison. "The baby always has the small teddy bear at the side of her." She explained.

Odd, thought Brendon, *how would a kidnapper have the time to take it?*

"The baby's name?" Harvey asked.

"Phoebe, Sir."

"Okay, let's talk to the mother," Harvey said. "Perhaps you could take the Nanny to the kitchen, make some tea, constable?"

P.C Terri Wilson stifled a sigh, it seemed to her this family liaison malarkey was more like an unpaid tea masher than a serious support role – they were already awash with tea.

CHAPTER 4

After P.C Terri Wilson reluctantly took the Nanny to make yet another pot of tea, Chief Inspector Mike Harvey with his Detective Sergeant Brendon Flannery introduced themselves to a very fragile Fiona Devonshire. He apologised for having to ask her questions seeing her distress, "It's important we get as much information as soon as possible whilst we search for.....Phoebe..... it is your daughter's name, Mrs Devonshire, I believe?" Mike asked.

Fiona nodded tearfully.

"How old is Phoebe?" Mike Harvey asked gently.

"She's three months...." Fiona's voice cracked. "Who would take a baby?" she asked through her sobs.

"That's what we need to find out," he offered. "But in these cases we find it is someone who will take care of the child let me assure you." Mike always felt a little patronising when he told the distraught parents this, even though he knew it to be true in most cases. "Can you tell me what happened Mrs Devonshire?"

Fiona Devonshire retold the events of the morning she'd already related to Terri Wilson, starting with the news of the unexpected dinner party making it necessary for her to send her Nanny out shopping.

"Does your Nanny usually do your shopping?" Harvey asked to try to establish if she was in the habit of leaving the baby outside shops for someone to notice.

Fiona Devonshire scrutinised him for a moment to see if he was being critical of her. He could see she felt uncomfortable with the question.

"Well actually no, she doesn't….." she said as though realising the fact herself for the first time. "I usually do my shopping on line, have it delivered, it saves time." She added the latter because she thought she needed to justify herself.

"I see," Harvey said. "So it's not a routine thing your Nanny would do, to take Phoebe shopping?"

Fiona had felt so peeved that her day would be ruined by the impromptu dinner party, she needed to take it out on someone. She chose Joselyn because, even without the sudden burden of the dinner party, it was her Nanny's day off which meant she wouldn't have the day to herself anyway.

"No, she takes her out for walks of course, I believe they go to the park. It's a country park down the road a way with a lake, wild life, birds and such like."

Brendon knew it well, as the place where his own daughter Rosie went missing some time ago. "I've been there," he admitted, more for his bosses benefit than hers. He didn't welcome the reminder.

"So today was a one off?" Harvey felt uncomfortable talking to Fiona Devonshire although he couldn't place why. He instantly began formulating all kinds of thoughts related to her apparent detachment from her baby. She didn't seem to be showing a level of distress he normally expected in these cases. He felt her sobs were more of self-pity at having the dinner party than the loss of her child. Now, he felt guilty thinking it.

A knock on the lounge door brought P.C Wilson's head as it opened.

"Sir, can I have a word?"

Harvey got up leaving the room for a couple of minutes before returning to resume his interview. He sat back down on one of the large couches. Fiona Devonshire sat up on a matching armchair; straight backed and attentive.

"Sorry about that," he apologised. "But I've got a forensic team to look at the pram - we will have to take it away." He explained, omitting they would also be doing a thorough search of the house at the same time because he didn't want to alarm her by telling her if he could help it. Instead to distract her he asked, "Can you tell me what Phoebe was wearing today Mrs Devonshire?"

Fiona Devonshire looked shocked. She frowned and began to stutter, "I'm not really sure."

"Did your Nanny get her ready to go out?" he suggested helping her.

"Yes, she did," she sounded relieved by the expression on her face. "I got a bit distracted like I told you by my husband's sudden announcement he wanted a dinner party for some of Jed's clients, he's his financial advisor," she said looking instantly irritated.

"So.....an impromptu evening you were planning?" Harvey could see Fiona Devonshire seemed more put out by that than her missing daughter. Perhaps his gut feeling had been right.

"Yes it wasn't something I welcomed on a Tuesday – it did rather annoy me given my shopping order is delivered on a Friday," she searched their faces for support, some understanding of the inconvenience of it all.

"Made worse, I suspect, by it being your Nanny's day off," Brendon suggested.

"Quite!" Fiona glared at him seething, all thoughts of her lost baby momentarily forgotten. Then her face took on a worried look, "I hope he doesn't still want...." She began to say then stopped when she realised what she implied.

What husband would expect it under such circumstances? Harvey stared at her in amazement.

"Mr Devonshire is on his way back home I understand," Harvey prompted.

She nodded, failing to meet his eye contact looking suddenly afraid. She began to sob shaking her head as though denying it.

"He's really angry," her whispered gasps between sobs.

The two men sat staring at her sudden delayed distress. Harvey had never met Bernard Devonshire although he knew of his reputation, a thoroughly bombastic character, someone revealed to him once. "I'm sure he'll realise how distressing all this is Mrs Devonshire, he's hardly going to blame you...."

"He's angry because his schedule is being disrupted," Fiona Devonshire interrupted showing momentary signs of contempt that swiftly faded. "The dinner party being with important clients, he hoped to close on a deal I think." She explained. The two detectives were somewhat taken aback at the lack of mention of her baby.

At this point they could all hear raised voices coming from the hallway. The look on Fiona Devonshire's face turning grave, she shook violently giving away a frightened recognition as the lounge door suddenly burst open with some force hitting the wall behind it.

Bernard Devonshire appeared through the door, a large overweight middle-aged man in a business suit, his countenance formidable, with a doughy pale face, double chins and bulbous red nose giving away his penchant for business luncheons, an addiction to fine whisky with an obvious abstention from any form of physical exercise.

"Who are all those people?! What the hell are they doing in my house?!" He demanded loudly at all three startled people but particularly his quaking wife.

Mike Harvey stood up offering him his hand in a friendly gesture meant to reassure him. "I'm Detective Chief Inspector Mike Harvey, Mr Devonshire; I'm here to find out about the circumstances around the taking of your daughter Phoebe."

"Are you now?" He sneered. "I asked about those people crawling around my house!" He pointed towards the hallway; he'd obviously seen the forensic team searching the house.

"They're looking at Phoebe's pram Bernie," explained Fiona trying to pacify him. "She was taken from it - they are checking for fingerprints." Fiona looked at Mike Harvey for some kind of backup.

"Yes, for any forensic evidence left behind," Brendon Flannery chipped in to try to quell any further objections.

"They are doing a damn sight more than that, Chief Inspector!" He hollered. "I saw them loading the pram into their van as I came in.....they appear to be searching my house!"

"It's purely routine I assure you, Mr. Devonshire, we have to check the home where a child lives in these cases...." Mike began as he watched Bernard Devonshire move over to his wife who almost cringed as he joined her. How could he tell this irate man they always checked the baby's home first to see if the baby was somewhere here, or if there were any signs of foul play. They had no evidence the baby was taken from the pram.

"What has been going on?" He rounded on Fiona accusingly.

"Someone took Phoebe from her pram outside the co-op when Joselyn went inside for ten minutes getting some shopping for me."

"She left her on her own outside!" he yelled his face turning bright red with anger. "Where the hell were you?"

"If we could just calm down a little Mr Devonshire your wife is very upset," Harvey suggested beginning to feel sorry for Fiona Devonshire who looked so frail at the side of this loud aggressive overbearing man.

Fiona took this moment to completely lose control, "Here trying to sort out what I could give your bloody guests this evening!" She yelled back furiously. "I blame you for this – obviously someone holding a grudge against you has taken my baby!" She poked a finger at his chest as if to emphasise 'you' which neither of the Detectives thought wise.

Whether Bernard Devonshire temporarily forgot the two police officers were there, or didn't care anyway, he hit his wife across the face with sufficient force to knock her back into the arm chair she stood up from when he entered the room.

Brendon Flannery, who held a particular moral stance against anyone who struck women, rushed over caught Bernard Devonshire's arm mid-air as he swung it in order to follow his wife to hit her again. He stopped the blow with his forearm, caught it with his other hand wrenching it behind his back roughly and promptly arrested him, marching him out of the room.

CHAPTER 5

"Was that absolutely necessary, Flannery?" Mike Harvey demanded once back at the station, now looking deflated.

Brendon stuck to his principles as he marched Bernard Devonshire from the room. He then called upon the assistance of two of the uniformed officers searching the property to take him back to the station where he booked him in at the custody suite for ABH on his wife. He left him in one of the cells to stew. The one thing Brendon hated more than anything else in the world happened to be violence against women. He saw enough of it as the child of a drunken violent father and an abused subservient mother whom he knew took some of the beatings he would have been given if she hadn't intervened.

"You witnessed it Gov I don't care if his daughter is missing, it's no excuse to hit a woman," he declared defiantly. "He shows no empathy for his wife - cares more about having his house searched than about his baby. I find it strange." Harvey never having seen Flannery quite so animated had to concede.

"Well just go easy," Harvey warned. "He's a slippery customer by all accounts. He has some important contacts in high places."

"Point taken, Gov," he said. "How's his wife?"

"She's not badly hurt," he left P.C Wilson with her whilst he went to talk to the Nanny. "According to the Nanny she only went in the shop for ten minutes, it's always fairly empty early on except for one old lady she noticed as she went inside. I've sent Taylor to the shop to see if we can identify her to talk to her, see if she saw anything." Harvey frowned, "This is an odd one," he suddenly declared, it not being his first baby snatch case. On the other occasions he successfully found the babies quickly, thanks to the help from obliging public and very co-operative parents. He felt extremely lucky given just how badly some of these cases could go.

"Why, Gov?" Brendon knew babies were often taken from outside of a shop in the area; warnings were continuously being given to young mothers to take their babies in with them.

"Well, it's a narrow window, ten minutes. It couldn't be planned given taking the baby shopping wasn't a routine thing, it has to be a chance snatch don't you think?"

"Would have been easier to just wheel the pram away wouldn't it?" Brendon observed.

"Well yes, although it is rather a distinctive type of pram, someone would surely have noticed it," Harvey suggested. "Easier to disguise the fact you are carrying a baby."

"Whoever did it had to release the pram cover, take the baby out, then replace it before they walked away," Brendon tried to imagine someone going to all that trouble.

"Yes, it's one of the puzzling things, although it did give them a lot of time to get away with the baby before they discovered her missing," Harvey was intrigued by the discrepancy in time scales he'd heard between Fiona Devonshire and Joselyn the Nanny's accounts. Joselyn saying the whole shopping trip only took twenty minutes whilst Fiona thought it well over half an hour. "We need to get P.C Wilson to walk it, Flannery, could you sort it?"

"Yes, Gov," Brendon said gleefully, only too pleased to leave Bernard Devonshire longer in his cell to calm down whilst he actioned Harvey's request. Just as he put the receiver down from speaking to Wilson, it rang immediately. The Custody Sergeant requested Brendon to come down, Bernard Devonshire's solicitor having arrived, insisted on the immediate release of his client, threatening all kinds of things.

With a sigh Brendon reluctantly left the CID office to find Bernard Devonshire hadn't calmed down by any means and his solicitor seemed equally abrasive.

"I insist you let my client go!" The demand made by the solicitor met him the moment he arrived in the custody suite just as the Custody Sergeant brought Bernard Devonshire from the cells into the interview room.

"I can't, he's charged with ABH as witnessed by myself and Chief Inspector Harvey," Brendon announced. "He hit his wife and without my restraint would have further assaulted her." Brendon absently rubbed his arm where Devonshire's blow impacted.

"His baby daughter has been taken for heaven's sake, I'm sure the shock of it caused the moment of aberration." The solicitor Brendon noted wasted no time in inventing mitigating circumstances.

"It's only my word against yours," Devonshire sneered showing absolutely no remorse. "You are exaggerating somewhat."

"I think two police officers together with your wife's statement far outweigh whatever you wish to describe," Brendon hated a bully especially one prepared to lie his way out of the consequences of his actions.

"Has Mrs Devonshire made a statement officer?" The solicitor queried. "Or even made a complaint against her husband?" His question came with a smirk.

Brendon hadn't given a thought to Fiona Devonshire's wishes or considered maybe she might be too afraid to make one.

"I don't need Mrs Devonshire to make a statement," he countered. "What we witnessed is sufficient to proceed." He thought they would be in trouble if she actually denied it happening.

"My client also wishes to make a complaint officer," the solicitor replied having heard Brendon admit to having to constrain him. "He wishes to make a complaint against you for attacking him in his own house as well as for injuries sustained from the said attack."

Bernard Devonshire couldn't resist a matching smirk as he also rubbed his right arm to emphasise the solicitor's point. "He wishes to see a doctor to document and attend to his injuries." The fact of a doctor attending, they all knew, would be recorded in the prisoner records.

Brendon felt sure Devonshire regularly played these games. Harvey's words of warning that he was 'slippery' echoed in his thoughts. He rose from his chair, left the room seeking the custody sergeant. He requested him to call for the duty doctor for his prisoner. "Put him in the observation cell, continuous observation until he gets here." Brendon face now livid, he didn't want him left unattended in case he self-inflicted any 'actual' injuries in the meantime.

He went off to find Harvey to update him on the situation.

CHAPTER 6

DC Trevor Taylor-Smythe suffered from a lack of patience at the best of times. When faced with the kind of person the shop assistant turned out to be, he became doubly so. Clearly by the way the lad spoke about Joselyn the Nanny he remained smitten by her. He drooled unnecessarily about her in the way young lads did with girls they fancied. Taylor doubted whether he would have noticed an invasion of alien life forms if they entered the shop at the same time she did. He admitted he didn't serve her but "Oh, yeah," he did remember her, grinning suggestively.

Of other customers he had no recollection save for one old biddy. She always came in on a Tuesday at that time, being pension day she bought the same things every week.

"It always includes a loaf of bread, the weird round one 'Slimcea' my Nan buys, three tins of baked beans, half a dozen eggs, a packet of tea bags, milk and one of those packets of assorted jam tarts." He reeled off much to Taylor's surprise.

"What the same every week?" Trevor was more astonished that he remembered than the composition of the actual list. His memory relating to the lady stopped short her groceries however, admitting he neither knew her name nor where she lived. Why would he know her name, he said, she always paid in cash from her pension. Taylor's patience grew shorter faced with such arrogance; it being the one thing he noticed about people, but never the trait in himself.

The absence of the shop manager irked him as he thought he might recall a regular customer like this one. It left him with an abortive trip to the co-op store. He stood outside the shop just where the pram had been, scanning the immediate vicinity of the small shopping precinct to establish who might have a clear view of the spot. It consisted of a row of mostly takeout shops; an Indian takeaway, next to a fish and chip shop, a pizza takeaway nestling alongside a funeral director, Taylor thought ironically.

"Just about right," He mumbled under his breath, especially with all those takeout shops. Taylor was fussy about what he ate being more into a healthier life style inherited not from a privileged background, quite the opposite.

Situated at the end of the row, next to a flower shop (*advantageous to a funeral director* he thought), the village post office resembled a small add-on hut starkly different to the other shops in the rest of the row. Across the top of the line of shops a row of flats looked to be independently occupied.

Not wishing to be found wanting by his boss or colleagues, Taylor decided to try his luck with the post office, although he knew pensions were no longer administered over the counter these days, being paid directly into bank accounts. Old ladies he knew frequented post offices because they were more likely to write letters, thus needing postage stamps. The problem he knew was the absence of any real description of the old woman beyond 'small with grey hair' it hardly picked her out in a crowd.

The post office turned out to sell a curious mixture of greetings cards, a sad looking array of cheap plastic children's toys, a selection of handbags and leather purses he thought a quaint misguided attempt to bolster a living beyond one of a mere post office. As if an afterthought, a large old fashioned photocopier, tucked into one corner, complete with a notice cello-taped amateurishly to the wall with old yellow brittle peeling tape, showed faded instructions on how to use it. He let words like 'antiquated' and 'anachronistic' buzz around his head, he loved long words learning them at every opportunity.

Taylor waited, although impatiently, in the small queue until it was his turn. The man behind the counter wearing a turban he guessed must be the Sikh postmaster, Amar Sandhu, the name he picked up from the sign over the door as he came in. He flashed his I.D card explaining what occurred outside the Co-op store.

"I heard something happened," the man replied in perfect English with a slight colloquial lilt to it. "I'm afraid I didn't see anything."

"I'm trying to establish the identity of one potential witness who did some shopping at the Co-op at the time," Taylor explained. "An elderly grey-haired lady, small about five feet is all I have to go on."

"Ah, about half past ten," the man declared. "You mean Mary."

"You know her?" It surprised Taylor with so little to go on.

"Mary Mundy is a regular," he explained. "Always the same time every Tuesday, you could set your clock by her – still draws her pension using a giro."

"I thought they did away with the over-the-counter payments and it's all done by bank transfer," Taylor commented.

"Yes, it is unless you don't have one, then you can't," the slight inflection in the words to indicate 'isn't it obvious' Taylor found a bit patronising.

"I suppose not," Taylor conceded. "So you think her name is Mary Monday?"

The way he pronounced it made Amar Sandhu spell it out to be sure he got it right, "That is M U N D Y," he wondered at this policeman common sense for all his smart suit and silk tie. "Sounds like her. She would do her shopping once she cashed her giro wouldn't she?" Taylor saw the frown appear on his face. "I wouldn't expect too much from her though." He added trying to be helpful.

"Oh, why not?"

"Mary isn't a great talker," he grinned. "I can't say I've heard her speak more than a passing grunt of thanks, but I wouldn't swear to it!" He laughed noting the lack of a sense of humour as the policeman kept frowning.

Taylor thought he might be pushing his luck when he added, "I don't suppose you have any idea where she lives do you?"

"Not her actual address, but I do know from the postman she lives in one of those single person flats on North Road as you go out of the village; they are part of a sheltered housing complex."

"What kind of 'sheltered housing complex'?" Taylor didn't want to sound ignorant, although he didn't normally admit to not knowing something, but on this occasion he waived his usual tendency to feign knowledge.

"It's where they put a lot of the most vulnerable people," he added chirpily. "Like the elderly infirm or like Mary discharged from long stay facilities," he added, "warden assisted," he said to make sure he understood.

"What kind of facilities?" Taylor remained intrigued by the man's knowledge of the community especially as he'd already made up his mind he must be an immigrant to the country. He realised as a police officer - a detective police officer – he ought to have more of an understanding of the locale.

"I believe she was once an inpatient at the old Asylum," he said. "It closed down some years ago."

Taylor knew nothing about the Asylum only there used to be one somewhere out in the countryside.

"What did they do with all the patients?" he asked rather naively.

"I'm not really sure other than one or two have flats in the 'sheltered', what they did with the rest is any one's guess."

Taylor saw Amar Sandhu lean to one side glancing around behind him. He turned to see a small queue forming all waiting to be served and felt embarrassed at holding it up as he could see one or two people giving him a hard look.

"I expect she'll be in the telephone directory," he muttered at the postmaster.

"Don't count on it," he sounded affable almost amused. "I can't imagine Mary talking on the telephone." He said simply as Taylor gave up his place at the counter almost getting elbowed out of the way by one impatient elderly gentleman with a walking stick.

CHAPTER 7

The pram, as Harvey suspected, yielded few useful fingerprints, those partials lifted from the handle and other smooth surfaces matched with Fiona Devonshire or Joselyn Phipps elimination prints. The pram cover being made of a ridged waterproof fabric rendered any prints obsolete. When matched with his prints taken in custody, they found none of Bernard Devonshire confirming Harvey's suspicion he had little contact with his own child. Harvey supposed he left all child-rearing to his wife or Nanny.

Harvey heard Flannery's account of Bernard Devonshire's first interview followed by the complaint against him for excessive use of restraint on arrest. He looked at him for a long time before he spoke assessing his mood.

"We're going to have to let him go," he said quietly. He saw Flannery's face turning red as his anger rose once again. "The media will have a field day...." He began.

Brendon interrupted him, "But you saw what he did and just about to attack her for a second time."

"Even so," he returned ignoring his plea. "If Fiona Devonshire doesn't corroborate the charge we don't stand a chance, the C.P.S will blow it out of the water as a non-starter."

"Why?" he squeezed out through his teeth. "He doesn't seem one bit concerned about his daughter being snatched, he hasn't even asked what we're doing about it, or if we're found her."

He knew Flannery had a point, convinced Devonshire would plead mitigating circumstances, telling a different story in his own defence whilst making it sound convincing.

"You were right to protect her Flannery, but charging him I think is a non-starter." Harvey knew he would be relying on the child's parents to go on air to plead for their daughter's return. In these cases they relied on information from the public whilst giving them a chance to assess the parents' reactions.

"Let's go do his interview, see what he was doing when Phoebe was taken," he stood up expecting Brendon to follow him out.

*   *   *   *

Settled in the interview room Mike Harvey asked Bernard Devonshire to go over the events of the morning before he went off to work.

"What has this got to do with the charges?" The solicitor asked.

"It has nothing to do with your assault on your wife Mr Devonshire," he replied calmly. "It's related to our investigation into the kidnap of your daughter, Phoebe."

Bernard Devonshire glanced at his solicitor for a moment unsure whether to respond, his face a mask of defiance. The solicitor nodded to indicate he could proceed. Harvey saw no concern shown by him for his daughter's disappearance, like he had forgotten altogether about her.

"What do you want to know Chief Inspector?" He suddenly looked more relaxed than they had witnessed so far.

"Start with what time you got up?" Harvey asked.

"Just after seven o'clock when I always get up take a shower and get ready for work."

"Did you see Phoebe at any time before you left the house?" Harvey asked.

He watched Bernard Devonshire trying to recall, his face grey in pallor except for his bulbous red nose which Harvey couldn't help staring at fascinated by the array of open pores. He shook his head to indicate no, "I heard her briefly when she woke, heard the Nanny talking to her as I went downstairs," he said.

Harvey recalled his own habit in those early days of making sure he always looked in on his daughters before he went off to work and last thing at night when he came home whilst they were sleeping; always long hours and snatched moments which he came to regret. *They grow up fast*, he thought. *Before you realise it they're gone, just like his marriage.*

He could see Devonshire watching him waiting for his next question as his thoughts played over the memories during the silence whilst everyone stared.

"Where was Mrs Devonshire?"

"Already up, making coffee in the kitchen," he took a sip of water from the plastic beaker in front of him. "Where I told her I'd invited people for dinner this evening.... she got cross." He coughed as he remembered how Fiona reacted. "My wife didn't much take to the idea." His voice changed to hard done by husband, "She can be difficult....." he added by way of explanation taking exception to her attitude. Brendon Flannery sat mystified by him acting the aggrieved.

He tried to bite back his comment but it escaped his mouth nonetheless, "What woman would welcome a dinner party sprung on her the same morning....?"

Bernard Devonshire glared at this obvious condemnation. "What else has she got to do all day?" he demanded leaning into the table between them, managing to convey threat.

Harvey caught Flannery's arm in a quieting gesture, "So you had words this morning Mr Devonshire?"

"Not for long," he replied nonplussed. "I told her just to get on with it.... then left for work," he said.

"Did you see your daughter before you left?" Harvey asked; even his own disastrous marriage seemed warmer than this one.

"No officer I'm always in a hurry to catch my train in a morning," he replied.

Harvey stood up abruptly much to Brendon's surprise, "Okay you may go," he announced tersely. He turned leaving the room much to everyone's surprise.

His sudden termination of the interview before he departed left Brendon shocked. The solicitor appeared equally surprised although he nudged a bemused Bernard Devonshire to get moving and they both hurriedly vacated the interview room.

He felt let down by his boss, now fearful for Fiona Devonshire whom he believed would get the full force of her husband's temper when he got back home. He took out his mobile, dialled a number.

"Harvey has just released Bernard Devonshire," he told P.C Terri Wilson. "You might want to warn Mrs. Devonshire," he said simply following them all from the room.

He watched as the custody sergeant formally released him, giving him back his possessions. Bernard Devonshire spotted Brendon standing observing him, a smirk played about his doughy face. He could see the visible signs of Brendon's frustration at having to let him go.

His solicitor ushered him out of the custody suite not wanting any more confrontations, but Bernard Devonshire looked back at Brendon glaring, nodding his head in a knowing gesture. There was no doubt he would remember him.

CHAPTER 8

Today I found the big king's chair in my secret place, just by accident. I went to the corner to fetch my books from the broken cabinet. I pushed too hard on the door to shut the cupboard. It's got one broken leg, making it look wonky so it slipped over a bit further. I could see the big chair hidden behind it in the corner of the basement room where I go now as often as I can get away.

I need to be careful not to stay away too long. Nurse Bryony scolded me the other day because she couldn't find me. She needed me to look after a new girl. The poor mite looked terrified, it reminded me what it was like when my parents left me here.

This girl looks like a child with the swollen belly of a 'mental defective'. I tried to comfort her I could see the fear in her eyes, so I sang to her. I couldn't remember all the words of the song. I hummed the lullaby my mother used to sing to me when I was little. It worked. She fell asleep with her thumb in her mouth. It meant I couldn't come here for a few hours until they took her away to the room where they took my baby from me.

The big chair doesn't seem to be broken like all the other things. I managed to push the cabinet a bit further to squeeze through the gap. It's wonderful to sit in it. It has a padded seat like they have on the walls in the quiet room. I made it extra nice with some old threadbare blankets I found to cover up the hard wooden arms with the dangling leather straps.

When I climb on it, it's so big I can curl up with my feet tucked under me. I don't know why it's here or what it's for, not that I really mind as long as I don't fall asleep sitting in it.

That would be dreadful!

          *   *   *   *

Mary stood in the kitchen making her eleven o'clock cup of tea. She held the tea bag, cutting the top with a pair of scissors from the kitchen draw, to empty the tea leaves into the pot, throwing the empty tea bag into the bin. When they showed her at the hostel the tealeaves came in a tin caddy and she could spoon two heaped teaspoons from it into the pot. Two tea bags just about made two heaped spoons, she measured it, didn't even mind having to do this as it always tasted right.

Just as she was pouring the boiling water from the kettle into the pot, she heard the knock on the flat door. She stopped, standing rigid with the kettle in her hand, she listened hoping they would think there was no one in and go away.

Mary didn't like visitors especially ones who upset her usual routine. She knew she didn't have to answer the door if she didn't want to. In her flat, she could do what she liked without being told what to do. Nobody would know as she saw no one anyway.

The knock came again, a little louder this time. She quietly crept from the kitchen along the passageway to the door peering through the spy hole on tiptoes. She found it just a little too high up to be able to focus through it, keeping her balance whilst stretching up on tiptoes.

She saw the back of someone's head as they turned to face away looking down the short corridor outside of her flat. It was a man. He suddenly turned his face as he leaned into the door placing his ear against the wood. She pulled back sharply as he seemed to lunge at her; her heart pounding in her chest. Then came the sharp rap of his knuckles against the wood for the third time.

There was no window so she knew he couldn't see inside. She was used to hiding having spent a lot of time avoiding meeting people face to face. When she dared, she placed her eye once more over the spy hole watching the tall man dressed in a dark suit slowly walking away down the corridor. He opened the fire door disappearing through it.

Happy he had gone away she went back into the kitchen, put the tea strainer over her tea cup and poured herself a cup of tea putting a splash of milk into the cup. She took two arrowroot biscuits from a tin with a scuffed picture of a quaint old thatched cottage with roses around the door, placed them onto her saucer then she carried her tea into her sitting room.

She settled into an old battered armchair with her feet up on the worn foot stool covered in fabric rubbed bare from many years of other people's feet; only too grateful for inheriting all these pieces of furniture when she moved in. Sitting comfortably, she began to read her library book occasionally dunking her biscuits into the hot liquid, content to just be in the quietness of her own home.

She could hear the faint sound of music through the ceiling, coming down from above where someone else lived on the top floor. She knew no one and liked it like that. She learnt to trust no one thinking it better to avoid the others as someone would always make it difficult for her. If you trusted someone, told them your thoughts they would tell the doctors, make it sound like a sign of something she couldn't pronounce. It was when they did the treatment to you; awful things to make you hurt.

You could trust no one with your thoughts because if you did they would do their treatment which meant you couldn't remember your thoughts. 'Treatment' made you forget and the one thing Mary didn't want above all else was to forget because all she had out of her long life so far were her memories - a tiny pink arm waving to her, disappearing through the door.

Yes, you could trust no one; which was one reason why Mary never answered the door to anyone.

CHAPTER 9

When Joselyn heard the female police officer telling Fiona Devonshire her husband was on his way back home, she suddenly felt alarm for her own safety. After all she left the baby outside the shop; he would see it as her fault. Why wouldn't he? If only she'd taken her inside none of this would be happening. All because of her need to hurry to go to meet Dorian on her day off.

Even after all the drama kicked off she still felt guilty for being late, for letting Fiona take advantage of her, well that's how he would see it. He would have urged her to say no, put her foot down and left her to do her own shopping. Maybe then it wouldn't have happened either. She texted him to tell him about the baby going missing hours ago, why didn't he reply?

P.C Wilson left Fiona Devonshire in the lounge closing the door. Joselyn didn't disguise the fact she overheard her warning Fiona.

"What happens now?" Joselyn asked anxiously. "He's going to be in a bad mood....." she already knew just how threatening he could be, not only seeing Fiona Devonshire's face after he hit her; she witnessed his temper on previous occasions.

Terri Wilson could see the same fear Fiona Devonshire showed, her dilemma one of what to do about it. "Is there anywhere you could go for a while?" Terri asked. "Maybe whilst Mr and Mrs Devonshire can talk it through."

Joselyn thought the idea worth considering; she really didn't want to be here when he got back, he must know by now it was her fault for leaving his daughter outside in her pram.

"Well, it is meant to be my day off," she reminded herself. "I'm meant to be seeing my boyfriend Dorian. Maybe I could still go to his place, see if I could stay there."

The more she thought about it the more she liked the idea. She could see the police woman nodding approval.

Family liaison was a new role for Terri Wilson and under the circumstances she felt quite relieved when the Nanny disappeared upstairs to get her things before she left the house, it would be one less person to worry about when Bernard Devonshire got back. She watched him as he arrived earlier seeing his reaction to the police presence searching the house had disturbed him sufficiently to send him into a rage.

She saw Sergeant Flannery manhandle him out of the lounge having assaulted his wife, she heard him cautioning him. Terri applied some first aid where he'd broken the skin on his wife's face, probably with a ring or something he held in his hand. The bruise on Mrs Devonshire's face immediately began to darken and swell under her left eye. She offered to take her to A&E to get it checked out properly, only Fiona Devonshire wouldn't go saying she didn't need it.

"This sort of injury can affect your eye sight if it isn't treated properly," she told her wisely.

Fiona assured her she was fine and that her husband wouldn't like it if she went to the hospital *because the injury would be documented* although she didn't say it.

Terri informed her she could make an official complaint. They could do a statement maybe have him charged or get a restraining order.

Fiona Devonshire became quite hysterical at this point, "Are you mad?" she yelled. "How do you think he would react to that?"

It took Terri a while to calm her down afterwards so didn't mention it again. It was all very well Harvey and especially Brendon

Flannery, making things worse by arresting him, having let him go it left her alone to deal with the aftermath.

After seeing the Nanny off, Terri went back into the lounge to talk to Mrs Devonshire who sat crying as she ripped the paper tissue she kept dabbing her eyes with into strips.

"Is there anyone you would like me to call to come over to be with you, family or friends?" Terri asked.

Fiona glared at her then shook her head. "Having more people here would make him even angrier." She sobbed.

"Well if there is anywhere I could take you, just for a little while maybe, give your husband time to calm down." With Terri's shift rapidly coming to an end it was the last thing she needed. Her conscience pricked at the thought of leaving Fiona Devonshire alone with her bully of a husband, not that she expected him to let her stay there anyway.

Fiona Devonshire suddenly gasped as if she'd just seen a ghost. "Joselyn!" she said. "He'll go crazy when he sees her, especially if he knows....."

"It's okay, Mrs Devonshire," Terri consoled her. "Your Nanny has gone to stay with her boyfriend to be out of the way."

"Boyfriend?" Fiona looked puzzled. "I didn't know she had a boyfriend."

"Yes, she was meant to meet him as it's her day off." Fiona looked back at her blankly. It surprised her Fiona Devonshire didn't know.

"Oh, I see," she sank into her own thoughts.

"What do you think Mrs Devonshire?" Terri prompted.

"About what?"

"Maybe going to stay with someone, whilst we look for your baby."

"I suppose I could go to stay with one of my friends," she admitted thinking it over.

"Do you have family, a mother perhaps or someone close?" Terri felt sure Fiona would want her mother after having her baby kidnapped; she knew she definitely would want hers.

"Not local," she replied not elaborating further.

"I think we ought to do something soon," Terri urged looking at her watch trying to work out how long it would take to get from the station back to the house. Time moved on and she needed to comply with the sergeant's request about timing the walk to the shops and back.

Eventually, she convinced Fiona to seek refuge with one of her golfing friends. Although she offered to drive her, Fiona said she would make her own way. It only fleetingly occurred to Terri Wilson she ought to have insisted on driving her.

At the time Fiona made the decision she could only think about walking the distance back to the precinct so she could finish her shift at a reasonable time. Mostly she overran her shifts and today after such a stressful one, she needed to get home at a reasonable time for once.

CHAPTER 10

For once finishing at a reasonable time, Terri changed her clothes in the women's locker room back at the station. The events of the day left her uneasy, which still bothered her, as she thought that maybe she had forgotten to do something. Instead of leaving for home straight away, she went up to the next floor into the almost deserted CID office where she found only a couple of detectives still sitting at their desks.

The Chief Inspector bustled out of his office nearly running into her.

"Sorry sir," she apologised although not really her fault as Harvey wasn't looking where he was going.

"Ah, Wilson isn't it?"

"Yes, sir," she said.

"Shouldn't you be at the Devonshire's?" he snapped irritated having just taken a telephone call from one of the Assistant Chief Constables who wanted him immediately on the Command Suite. Harvey knew it meant trouble to be summoned up to the top floor.

"No, sir," Terri replied. "Well, strictly yes, but there's no one there." The house looked deserted when she got back from the precinct to pick up her car to drive back to the station, although she felt a little guilty for not actually checking for certain there was no one there. She just didn't want to meet Bernard Devonshire again or tell him his wife and Nanny had left to find a place of safety. She drove straight back to the station.

"Where are they?" he asked mindful any conversation would delay him from reporting to Command.

"The Nanny left to meet her boyfriend, sir, because of Mr. Devonshire's imminent arrival," she could still see the fear in her eyes when Joselyn heard her tell Fiona they had released her husband.

"What about Mrs. Devonshire?"

"Too afraid to stay also, sir, she went to stay with a friend she plays golf with." Terri began to worry now that she should have stayed or at least checked on Bernard Devonshire before she left. "I didn't think he would want me there, sir, you saw him earlier with the police in his house."

Harvey thought it a valid point. Saying no more he hurried out of the CID office leaving her standing there.

Spotting Brendon Flannery at his desk she wandered over to him. She filled him in on the events since he left the Devonshire house, got out her black police note book where she wrote down her timings to tell him her findings emphasising how she paced herself in keeping with pushing an imaginary pram.

"It's quicker coming back, Sarge, because it's downhill." She had no idea of the times from the Nanny's interview, "I did wait ten minutes outside the shop to allow for a quick purchasing of items."

"The Nanny did say it only took her ten minutes," Brendon agreed.

"It's not long really to look for a lot of things if you aren't familiar with where they are," she pointed out. "Fiona Devonshire does her grocery shopping on line," she added.

"Fiona Devonshire says she was gone longer anyway, but then she wasn't really timing it either."

"It took me fifteen minutes at a reasonable pace going – it's a hill, with that large coach built pram it would take some pushing," Terri said. "Mind you when you're in a hurry to get off to see your boyfriend, who knows?"

"We're getting the CCTV from inside the shop," Brendon informed her. "At least we'll be able to see how long she it did take inside."

"Your timings fit better with Fiona Devonshire's anyway," Brendon confirmed.

Terri finished her report and left for the day just as Mike Harvey was receiving a dressing down on Command from a not too happy ACC Ackroyd.

As predicted Bernard Devonshire lodged a formal complaint for being arrested in his own home after having his baby daughter kidnapped. To make matters worse arriving home after being released, he found his wife and his Nanny both missing.

Mike Harvey knew his day was going to get much longer.

CHAPTER 11

When Bernard Devonshire arrived back home he found the house completely empty. He retained a certain level of rage as he travelled there expecting the same amount of intrusion as before he left it disgruntled by being manhandled in the most undignified way in front of so many people.

The activity this time concentrated on the outside of his house, in front of his private electric gates in the guise of the news media congregating there. It stirred his anger even more finding himself besieged by people pushing microphones, mobile phones and other devices at him as well as a barrage of questions.

"What do you think has happened to your baby?" over shouts of "Who do you think took her?" Others were asking, "Have they asked for a ransom?" all this accompanied by flashing cameras.

A couple of traffic police constables were busily trying to usher the press back from the gate, giving commands to move vehicles, large TV mobile units and assorted cars which were blocking the tree-lined avenue with tail backs as far as two streets away. This melee of activity delayed Bernard Devonshire's return home, allowing his wife and Nanny sufficient time to leave. The once quiet leafy suburban road gave way to a chaotic nightmare for other residents.

Bernard's blood pressure soared, his head throbbed with the blood surging through his veins, and from yelling, "No comment!" He had abandoned the taxi he used to get home a couple of streets away walking the rest of the way home. The two traffic officers helped him gain entrance through the ornate gates, then once through he quickly ran up the steps of his porch.

Once inside, the quietness of the house hit him as he moved from room to room looking for his wife. Touring the entire house he found no one and began to panic as being alone wasn't something he ever felt comfortable with.

He fixed himself a whisky from the assortment of drinks sitting on a sideboard in the lounge, took it into his study to sit down behind his desk. As he sat he spotted evidence suggesting someone had been searching through his desk draws which he never left open like they now were.

His anger flared at the thought of nosey coppers searching his desk. What did they expect to find, his daughter Phoebe shut up in one of the draws? He leaned over his computer keyboard, pressed the return, seeing it spring into life, it showed the 'password denied' statement on the front screen. He always left it switched off, so he knew someone tried to access it. Luckily there was plenty of security installed with a password hard to guess at. Anything else incriminating he had securely locked away in a hidden safe.

He knew it went well beyond acceptable for a kidnapped baby unless, of course, they suspected he kidnapped his own child. What a preposterous notion.

He swallowed the whisky in one gulp, hoping it might settle his jaded nerves he took his glass over to a cabinet containing a further selection of drinks and poured himself a second measure from a decanter. His face was now suffused with a feverish rage. So far he'd heard nothing from the police about what they were doing to find his daughter or whether they had any leads.

As he sat thinking the face of the copper who stopped him hitting Fiona flashed through his memory. Something about his disapproving expression riled him all over again. Had Fiona been there at that moment she would have got the full force of his anger. But she wasn't there and neither was his Nanny, that stupid girl who left his child outside a shop to be taken by anyone passing, his anger settled on her.

He picked up the telephone pressing in the number of one of his acquaintances from the Rotary Club.

"I want to speak to the Chief Constable," he told the woman who answered. "I wish to make a complaint about the way I have been treated by the police."

When the Chief Constable came on the line, Bernard Devonshire did complain. He also reported his wife and Nanny missing from home, even though he felt sure there was some conspiracy involved due to police interference.

The call from Bernard Devonshire to the Chief caused a chain reaction which led to the ACC calling Mike Harvey up to Command. It placed him in an awkward position caught between the obvious need to satisfy the Chief's irritation at his justifiable complaint and the needs of a serious investigation.

"The press would have a field day if they heard we arrested the father of a baby snatch, not to mention one with Bernard Devonshire's standing in the community!" The Chief instructed his ACC to immediately look into the claims of the wife and Nanny missing from home.

Whilst the ACC didn't necessarily share the Chief's view of Bernard Devonshire, he did want to get the police take on the events of his arrest for assaulting his wife before her subsequent disappearance. As it stood the priority of a missing baby took precedence over any domestic squabble.

When Mike Harvey informed him quite calmly he understood Mrs Devonshire went to stay with a golfing friend, whilst her Nanny went to visit her boyfriend as both of them were justifiably afraid of Bernard Devonshire, it seemed a reasonable explanation. His wife, Mike Harvey reported, in particular having already sustained facial injuries that led to Devonshire being arrested and removed from the house. He believed that Joselyn Phipps, their Nanny to also be afraid of him.

"Bernard Devonshire is a violent man, sir," Harvey informed him. "His actions were witnessed by me and DS Flannery who interceded stopping him before he struck Mrs Devonshire again."

"Tell me, do we have any leads on the missing child?" ACC Ackroyd asked.

"It's early days, sir," Mike replied. "Or rather hours – had it not been for Mr. Devonshire's actions we would probably be further on with our enquiries. He seems to be more concerned about the police presence in his house than his missing daughter. In fact, he hasn't once asked about the child or our enquiries."

His lack of concern didn't go unnoticed; the observation being noted by several people he came into contact with. PC Terri Wilson for example recorded it in her police note book, whilst a similar impression formed part of the Custody record. The on duty Solicitor made the exact comment on his yellow legal pad.

Of course, Bernard Devonshire could barely contain his grief over his missing daughter. It was this grief, mainly responsible for unleashing his rage that threatened to launch his blood pressure completely off the chart.

Phoebe was the child he waited years for, through two disastrous previous marriages and the reason he deliberately pursued Fiona to secure. He had no illusions about her feelings for him. He knew she fell in love with his bank balance and in exchange for the production of a child she secured herself a comfortable life style.

She wanted for nothing. All he asked of her was a favourable public performance as his wife; someone who would appear to be the doting little lady to entertain his important clients. To this end he wheeled her on to encourage them in securing a lucrative contract or two. She didn't need to understand anything about what they were, which didn't bother her, as long as he kept his end of the bargain. She didn't seem to mind producing Phoebe, having none of the problems other women did, being a young fit healthy woman.

He now regretted more than anything letting her talk him into getting a Nanny. He blamed her for leaving Phoebe alone allowing her to be taken. After a couple more drinks his temper began to settle a little into a cold determination to make someone pay for his missing daughter. At the moment he directed his anger towards the Nanny, although he felt sure it would shift when he found out who had taken her.

CHAPTER 12

Next day, on her long awaited days off, Terri Wilson received a telephone call from one of the DCs. The one with a hyphenated name no one particularly liked for being a bit loud and very arrogant, she mostly avoided getting into conversation with.

Here he was telephoning her on her personal mobile, something most people in the job avoided. She always looked forward to switching off her police mobile so that she wouldn't be disturbed, days off were sacrosanct. To contact her on her personal telephones it had to be an emergency, an understanding observed by everyone.

Not so Taylor, he wasted no time in getting to the point, "Is that PC Wilson?" He demanded in his usual brusque manner which she instantly recognised and took exception to.

"Who's calling?" She asked even though she knew him by the tone of his voice. He always managed to make her feel inferior. She was never sure whether it was because she wasn't a detective like him, just a uniformed cop, or because she was a woman and even a mixed race one at that. Whichever, she heard the disapproval in his voice whenever he spoke to her.

"Taylor-Smythe," he answered sounding pompous.

"What do you want, it's my days off," she resented the intrusion.

"I need to know where the Devonshire's Nanny is staying," he sounded irritated at having to call her at all. "I understand you let her go off to stay with her boyfriend?" The criticism unmistakeably yelled out from the phone. The way he spoke to her made Terri immediately angry at his implication.

"I didn't, as you say 'let her' do anything," she snapped. "She wasn't under house arrest so free to go wherever she pleases, DC Taylor."

"She is our key witness who you didn't think to ask for an address of her boyfriend?" Taylor's anger increased.

For a fraction of a second Terri felt guilty, if not a little embarrassed she hadn't asked her. Always wanting to say 'sorry' had plagued her all her life, being part of her character to apologise. Her thoughts played around with her own failings. Maybe she was too keen to finish her shift at a reasonable time making her less cautious? She heard Taylor's tone of voice once again condemning her encouraging her own anger.

"Look!" She raised her voice, "They were both frightened because Mr Devonshire had been released," she remembered Fiona's face, the cut under her eye, wanting to take her to get it checked out at the hospital. "Joselyn went upstairs to get her things. She disappeared whilst I tried to persuade Mrs Devonshire to let me take her to hospital."

"So you know where Fiona Devonshire is PC Wilson?" Taylor interrupted sounding scornful emphasising yet another failure.

"Gone to stay with a golfing friend ...... before you ask, she wouldn't let me drive her there either." She was almost yelling down the phone now. "I had to check the timings to the precinct for DS Flannery....."

"The what!?"

"The walk from the house to the Co-op in the precinct, then back again to allow time to go inside, do the shopping like Joselyn described." Terri felt exasperated after all with only her to protect them both and run errands what could she do?

She hung up on him before she told him something she would regret later; after all he had no business telling her what she should or shouldn't do.

She sat for a while mulling over the events of yesterday, trying to work out whether she should have dealt with it differently. All thoughts of what she intended to do with her time off vanished.

She picked up her work mobile, pressed it back into life, looking up Brendon Flannery's number, hoping he would answer and understand her predicament. After all he saw Bernard Devonshire assault his wife, never mind tasking her with timing the Nanny's journey.

When he answered, she retold the call from Taylor – now close to tears.

"Bernard Devonshire is a very violent man, Terri," he reassured her. "You were right to safeguard them I have no doubt he would do it again." She heard him pause for thought choosing his words carefully so as not to upset her further. "Can you remember anything from either of them that might help find out where they've gone?" She thought she heard a hint of desperation hidden behind his words.

At this stage he didn't tell her Bernard Devonshire reported them both missing.

"Only Joselyn Phipps called her boyfriend, Dorian....." she tried to recall if she mentioned his last name. The initial's DD coming back to her, "Yes, Dorian Drover, I'm sure is what she said." She had a thing about names and what people called their children, at the time she thought it sounded posh.

"What about Mrs Devonshire?" he asked.

"I remember being worried, thinking her husband would know who she plays golf with," Terri did briefly consider he might go looking for her, which made her choice a bit risky. "She just said she could go to stay with a golfing friend. I think she said something like....*he wouldn't think to look for me up there*....I only just caught it as she seemed to whisper it to herself. For some reason I took it she meant 'up' at the golf club. There are some houses on the drive leading up to the clubhouse." Terri noticed the houses along the approach road when she attended a call out of a disturbance, thinking at the time they looked extremely expensive with their view across the golf course. "Maybe one of her girlfriends lives up there." She knew it wouldn't have been a relative or her mother as she made the point she wasn't local.

Terri knew deep down she should have asked her, although her main concern at this point had been to get them both away before he came home which she achieved. She couldn't help thinking perhaps more to enable herself to finish her shift on time. She felt like she failed in her liaison role?

"I thought they would go back when he'd calmed down a bit," she offered in justification. They were both so scared of Bernard Devonshire it didn't occur to her what might happen next. "Why are you asking, Sarge?" The silence on the end of the line made her repeat, "Sarge?"

"Devonshire has reported them both missing," he said simply.

"But they aren't missing, what a preposterous idea. Why would he do that?"

"Who knows with him," Brendon Flannery felt sure it was a deliberate ploy to get his own back for being arrested. "He's also complained about me arresting him."

"For assaulting his wife! I saw her face, Sarge, she was quite badly injured. I thought she needed to go to hospital to be checked out.....a blow near your eye can dislodge your retina."

"You may have to make a statement," Brendon suddenly thought if they couldn't find her, Terri Wilson witnessed her actual injuries.

"You're joking..!"

"No, I wish I was – apparently he's got friends in high places....."

"Even so, Chief Inspector Harvey is also a witness...." Terri recognised the seriousness of her failures. "This is all my fault...." She began slipping back into self-deprecation.

He did his best to reassure her none of it was her fault, then he sat going over the events of the previous day trying to reassess whether he should have dealt with it differently and came up with the same conclusion. He knew his childhood played a large part in his reactions; no longer the small boy who let his bully of a father carry on hitting his mother because he was neither strong enough nor brave enough to intervene.

Bernard Devonshire reminded him of his father. When he saw Fiona Devonshire flinch, the fear in her eyes, made him react like he wanted to all those years ago, how he should have done then. He knew Bernard Devonshire intended to make his life as uncomfortable as possible which made him feel like years ago – powerless.

CHAPTER 13

As a consequence of sleeping in a communal facility and a by-product of other people's nightmares, Mary always woke up early. Now she lived alone, she would lie in her bed listening to the sounds around her as she had done all those years in the Asylum. It was dark outside so there wouldn't be many people about. Sometimes she heard the distinctive whoosh of the early morning milk float or catch a flash of the lights as it drove past. Maybe too early for the milkman, not that he stopped to deliver her any milk, it would have meant answering her door to him to pay for it. She preferred to get her milk from the Co-op once a week with the rest of her shopping and she always kept a tin of condensed milk for a special treat in case she ran out.

Mary listened to the faint cry of her baby echo from the ceiling. It was a long time since she'd heard her baby crying; it sounded like a hunger cry making Mary want to go to her. She couldn't understand why she heard her here when she'd not heard the cries since she left the Asylum. Her baby wouldn't know to come here to find her. The echo died and silence took over followed by the faint sound of lullaby music coming down through the floor.

A flash of headlights moved across the curtains at the window – five o'clock – you could count on the milkman, even set a clock by him. She didn't move as she never got up before six o'clock; another habit from the asylum. In those days she slept in what they called a large dormitory with lots of other women.

The baby's cry came again briefly reverberating around the walls of her tiny bedroom, only big enough for the single bed, a small tallboy wardrobe alongside a dressing table with the slightly damaged mirror at the top corner where the reflective backing had been scraped off. Mary didn't mind the old furniture they gave her when she came here. Furniture no doubt discarded by someone years ago who could buy new things. She got used to being surrounded by old broken things taking comfort from its familiarity.

All these things belonged to her now, the very first she'd ever owned. She polished the damaged wood, like furniture in the hospital for all those years, making some of the wood shine where it kept its varnish and wasn't worn away over time.

Here she loved the bay windows the most with their deep windowsills where she laid out all her treasures, the tiny animals she gradually collected since she could have possessions of her own. They were made of china or chalk or some such thing in bright colours that were glazed to a shine. Penguins, sheep, cats, mice, a duck with an orange beak, each one she found and brought home to sit on the collection of old fabric doilies with crocheted lace edges she got at a jumble sale. They were a slightly dingy grey 'seconds' that no amount of scrubbing would remove the old rust spots from. She kept the penguins, the swan and the duck together making it look like they were standing in a pond on the doily just like the pond in the country park down the road she visited occasionally.

Every week she dusted each one standing them in exactly the same place pointing outwards into the room. Most pension days she would find one, a new addition to her collection, the post office sold a vast amount of things. It being the first time, in her long life she had something of her own, other than her journal books she managed to keep hidden in her secret place with the big chair where she sat writing her thoughts about those rare events that happened within the world she stayed in for so long.

As she lay listening, looking at her special things, she pondered on the day ahead. Once again she must be brave to face the world outside. In this she prepared herself in readiness to do all the things she must, as swiftly as possible to avoid any unnecessary contact with anyone else. If she prepared herself for what she needed to do each day she could get back here to her sanctuary as fast as she could make it.

Another two minutes by the clock on her dressing table. It was made from plastic painted to look metallic silver. She loved it because of the white swan inside a glass window to one side of the clock face that looked real set against a water scene with bulrushes and lily pads just like the one in the park.

Another minute as the silver second hand ticked around the numbers; in one more minute she would get up to face the day.

CHAPTER 14

Brendon knew he'd taken his eye off the game letting the events of early morning mar his concentration. Life at home had become quite fraught of late especially since his children reached the difficult teenage years. His eldest, his son swiftly moved from a self-reliant happy yet cheeky boy into a surly teenager almost overnight. The once positive chirpy youngster evolved into a negative, often aggressive, stranger.

To Brendon his antagonistic behaviour towards his mother was too reminiscent of his own father, something he found unacceptable, coupled with his sudden growth spurt, making him taller than Brendon, he became a threatening adversary to have.

This morning Nancy innocently raised the state of her son's bedroom which prompted Michael to launch verbal abuse at his mother. The alarming thing for Brendon, he saw the fear in his wife's eyes whilst Michael's barely disguised surge of aggression resulted in him lashing out by kicking the bathroom door as his temper flared.

The door sported a foot sized hole exposing the inner cavity in the wood which now required replacing. It wasn't so much the cost of the door, more a visual reminder of his son's loss of control, prompting images of the old days of his own childhood symbolising his failure to protect his mother.

He was unsure how he would react if Michael physically attacked his mother – he knew he could protect Nancy, being old enough and strong enough. It scared him in case he lost control in the heat of the moment, he always dreaded the thought he might one day turn out to be violent like his father.

With all this constantly playing in his head, it sparked a reaction the moment Bernard Devonshire attacked his wife. A kind of reflex action with the events of the morning still vivid; he jumped up instantly to stop the hand descending, blocking it with his forearm he took the full force of the potential hit. Fiona Devonshire fell back into the armchair otherwise Bernard Devonshire's fist would have made contact again.

He knew exactly how hard the punch would have been against her face, which later made him take a picture of the resulting bruised arm. His other hand grabbed the striking arm forcing it up the back of its owner, instantly marching him out of the room and leaving Chief Inspector Harvey to pacify Fiona Devonshire.

When he arrived home later after Bernard Devonshire's release, he felt totally frustrated by the events of his day. He knew he failed ultimately to protect Mrs Devonshire because Bernard would he knew go straight home to finish what he started.

Once home again the incident with Michael played itself back like a rewound video, the bathroom door testament to his son's aggression. He found Nancy peeling potatoes at the kitchen sink. She seemed withdrawn and silent and unable to pose a greeting when he asked if she was all right. She barely spoke more than a grunt.

"Where's Michael?" He asked her back as she carried on peeling without looking round.

At that moment loud heavy metal music filtered through the ceiling. Nancy looked upwards without a word.

"Right!" Brendon declared swiftly moving upstairs, he glanced at the bathroom door in passing, bursting into his son's room where the noise level bellowed out. He rushed over to the iPlayer flicking it off he silenced it.

"Hey!" Michael yelled fiercely, alarmed at the intrusion into his personal space.

Brendon yelled back he was grounded, took the iPlayer, making for the door where Michael intercepted him raising his fist in a threatening gesture which reminded Brendon instantly of Bernard Devonshire. His arm automatically shot out moving upwards as Michael's fist descended; he stopped the trajectory of the blow using his own body force upwards against Michael's arm.

It caught Brendon in the exact place Bernard Devonshire's hand hit earlier sending a reverberation of pain up his arm into his shoulder blade. As Brendon grabbed his painful arm, Michael stood back in alarm at the resultant howl that escaped from his father. Nancy rushed into the room having followed her determined looking husband just as Brendon fell back onto Michael's bed clutching his arm.

"What have you done?" she shouted at her son.

"I didn't mean to....." Michael began once again becoming the young child frightened by the consequences of his temper. ".....Mum?" He queried as he saw how much pain his father looked to be in.

Brendon gingerly rolled up the sleeve of his shirt to examine his arm, saw the darkening of the bruise he sustained earlier only this time his arm began to swell. Nancy looked on aghast.

They left their children at home whilst Nancy drove Brendon to the A&E department to check out his arm where they found a hairline fracture of his radius and put it in a plaster cast to immobilise it. After reconciliation with his son, some paracetamol to help with the pain, Brendon sat quietly pondering on the events of the day and his misfortune in receiving two damaging blows to the same arm in two day.

When he fell asleep in the armchair his last thought was of Bernard Devonshire's face as he left the Custody Suite, feeling instinctively he had gained himself an enemy.

CHAPTER 15

Although set back from the road, the public library sat directly across from the row of shops along the precinct giving a fine view of the police activity undertaking door to door enquiries. Mary watched the officers, from where she stood, halfway down one of the bookcase aisles. She saw them, systematically moving between each of the premises, mostly hidden from anyone else inside the library or situated behind the librarian's counter.

A small group of children from a nearby playgroup sat on rubber matting in the juvenile section of the library, listening to a young woman reading to them from one of the library books. Her face twisting and contorting, she imitated the animals within the story, mimicking their imaginary voices that only young children believed to be a credible representation of how they would speak, should they be able to.

Occasionally Mary heard childlike laughter coming from them, whilst her attention fixed on the external activity. She stood stock still absently holding a selection of books in her hands.

Mary was well practiced in the art of observation having spent many years of her life assimilating information about her surroundings, watching for any changes that might indicate danger to her, not only from other patients but also from the people who ran the institution – nurses, doctors, administrators alike. Only latterly in her long stay and before her release into the community, these new types of people came – the business Managers. They took over running the Asylum from the doctors; white coats giving way to smart suits. They changed the name of the Asylum to Mental Hospital and she began to notice the doctors looking worried, sometimes even afraid, with the loss of their power having been transferred into other hands.

Well-practiced in listening whilst assessing danger over the long years, she noticed them voicing their concerns about losing their second office to yet another administrator.

Once a week she came to exchange her library books, a task which usually took her no time at all on a normal day, it being her habit to systematically work her way down the rows starting at the A's. She felt it the simplest way to avoid overlooking any of the books as they were always kept in order. It didn't matter what the book was about, she loved them all, quite liking each story to be a surprise to her.

Mary watched the tall young man wearing a smart suit enter the post office on the end of the row of shops. She noticed him particularly because even at this distance she remembered seeing him through the spy hole in her flat door when he thrust his face into the door as if he were trying to squeeze through the tiny glass spy hole. She knew he had to be one of the Managers who took over up at the Asylum.

*   *   *   *

The nurse led Mary into an office with a big oak desk in front of one of the large bay windows in the administration block. Years ago this end of the hospital was a house where the Head Psychiatrist lived, now given over to the many people it took to maintain the new ways of working. Here she discovered the books in one of the rooms full of shelves stacked with them. Taking one away to her secret place to read, she always made sure the gap she took it from didn't show.

The man behind the desk, wearing a suit, had a severe frown as he peered at her over his spectacles.

"Sit down Mary!" he ordered in his serious baritone voice.

Mary obeyed as she always did, placing herself in front of his desk in the one chair set out for the purpose. She quaked inwardly at the sound of him believing they may have discovered her secret place or found her writing books that meant they would give her the 'treatment' she always expected would come if they ever did.

She heard him talking without taking in any of what he said. She blinked knowing she looked like the mental defective they thought her to be.

"Do you understand?" she heard him ask. Mary shook her head because she heard nothing; she was never very good at thinking and listening at the same time and her mind chose to think about her secret place where she escaped to for a while whenever she could.

"We have found you a place in the community, however we will first send you to a half-way house to learn how to look after yourself," he repeated. "After that to sheltered accommodation......."

"What's that?" Mary dared to ask not understanding all of the words.

"It's where you will have your own flat, somewhere of your own to live in." He watched as Mary tried to assimilate the idea of having somewhere of her own, like her secret place, where only she would be allowed to go. "It is 'sheltered' because it will have a warden who will check on you occasionally to see if you need any help with anything, they are there to help you".

Mary stared in disbelief trying to assess the dangers of what he was telling her.

"Of course, if you should be unable to look after yourself, then there are other alternatives....." he went on.

"Will you make me come back here?" Mary asked.

"No, not here," he said coughing. "This hospital won't always be here...." He didn't elaborate further or attempt to explain any of it to her. Mary didn't ask him what he meant. Something as old and solid as the Asylum would always be here she thought.

Of course Mary didn't hear anything else after that. She began to think of the future without this place, although it was difficult and way beyond her imagining. She knew she couldn't listen as well as think at the same time so she decided she preferred to think about the endless possibilities of having a place she didn't have to share with anyone else.

*   *   *   *

Watching the man in the suit moving about with the others across the road made her suspect they must be searching the shops to try to find her. She could only think about her flat with all the space being just for her. She spent her whole life up at the old Asylum sharing everything with other people. She hardly dared believe it when they took her to her new home, she couldn't help feeling afraid they might change their minds, make her go back. Why else would they search for her here?

The precinct, with the post office was the only place she came to collect her pension, after which she bought her weekly food at the Co-op opposite the library. How they would know that she couldn't imagine.

The young man came back out of the post office, looked over towards the library where Mary watched for any signs of danger. As he began to walk over to the library she knew if she left now she would walk right into him.

She turned to the back of the row of books, hurried along to the bottom of the staircase to the second floor climbing the steps to take refuge on the open plan reference floor with a view of the ground floor.

Once up there, she stood back as he entered the library, watched him walk across to the librarian's desk where she knew the bell with the notice 'Ring for Attention!' sat. She heard it ring noisily as he pressed it with irritation to summon the librarian. A peel of childlike laughter rang out across the library from the corner. She saw him glance over towards the children frowning.

The librarian appeared from out of the door behind the librarian station, a middle-aged stern faced woman with hair scraped back from her face and piled on top in a bun. She couldn't hear her but knew she would ask in a low quietly spoken voice "Can I help you?" Mary heard this question every time she came here.

"Were you working here....?" the man began in a loud voice only to be hushed by the librarian into lowering his voice. Mary knew the librarian didn't like anyone to raise their voice; you must speak quietly almost in a whisper.

The scowl again from the man in the suit told Mary he didn't like being hushed. She prided herself on the fact that the librarian never hushed her into speaking softly. Mary always spoke quietly, usually people asked her, "What did you say?" having to repeat anything she did say. The librarian had not once asked her to repeat anything Mary thought she must have finely tuned hearing working in a place devoid of noise. It was one of the reasons she loved the library, the peaceful atmosphere as well as the smell of so many books in one place; it gave her familiar comfort she remembered.

She looked behind her whilst the man in the suit talked to the librarian. Upstairs there were rows of old scuffed wooden tables with leather chairs where people read the books they called 'reference' because they couldn't be taken home. She often came up here to sit at a table stacked with someone's discarded books, old leather bound tomes with ornate writing and swirly letters she could only partly understand until she realised the letter f should be an s which made more sense. She read the words of Voltaire and others only brief passages, wanting to take the story of Candide home to give her more time.

The man below coughed bringing her attention back to his new quiet entreaties. She watched as the librarian shook her head not hearing her whispered reply. She saw the thin stern man in the suit move off back to the external door stopping briefly to look sharply over as the group of young children laughed once again at the young woman who continued to read acting out the parts in the story.

She eventually ventured down to the desk, got her books stamped out for another week, then scurried off home keeping an eye out for the circulating people who disappeared behind the shops to the entrances of the flats above. Mary managed to avoid any encounters with them and saw no more of the stern man in the suit.

CHAPTER 16

"What on earth?" gasped Terri catching sight of Brendon with his arm in a cast held in place across his chest by a black arm sling. "Did he do that?" She questioned immediately. Gossip was rife around CID about the way Brendon saved Fiona Devonshire from another assault by her husband. "Bastard!" she cried, being unlike Terri. "Why didn't you tell me when I phoned you?" Terri's bombarding Brendon with the distress of Taylor's call flooded back to her. Offloading it on Brendon had eased her guilt a little after Taylor accused her of negligence at the disappearance of both Fiona Devonshire and Jocelyn Phipps her Nanny.

"Well...." Brendon began to wonder what on earth to tell everyone, his thoughts were only about Michael's aggressive attack which he'd rather no one knew about.

"Sarge," Terri went on. "You have to put in a complaint; he shouldn't be allowed to get away with this." His hesitation allowed Terri to talk jumping to the wrong conclusion, making it harder to admit it was his own son's out of control temper responsible, not the blow inflicted by Bernard Devonshire.

Harvey came out of his office at this point, saw Brendon's sling which stopped him dead in his tracks.

"Oh! I was going to suggest we get together to discuss the Devonshire complaint and how to deal with it." Harvey announced shocked at the sight of Brendon. "Never mind, come with me!" he ordered as Brendon followed him out of the CID office along the corridor, then up the back staircase to the command suite. He hung back trying to formulate the words to admit the truth.

The longer Brendon put off telling Harvey about his injury the worse it got for Brendon's conscience. Did he really want people to hear about his son completely losing control, cracking his forearm because of his temper? Before he could resolve this inner debate, Harvey rushed off ahead of him leaving him behind.

Detached from the reality of what he watched, he heard Harvey reporting to ACC Ackroyd how Bernard Devonshire caused his broken arm when Brendon intervened taking the blow intended for his wife.

The chance moment for confession came and went. The embarrassment now of correcting Harvey in front of the ACC was too great for him to go back on; he could no longer tell the truth. He heard himself telling the ACC his forearm was only slightly fractured which didn't lessen their perception of the situation. He felt the whole thing was surreal.

Later he sat at his desk in the CID office as Harvey took the morning briefing updating everyone on the new developments. The missing Nanny and mother of baby Phoebe were recorded, their images transferred to the crime case board alongside the facts of her abduction.

Brendon sat feeling his distress accompanied by the ache from his fractured arm because now the paracetamols had worn off. After the briefing Harvey sent Brendon home on Health and Safety grounds, telling him not to come back until his arm was mended; he ought, he said, to bring his own complaint against Devonshire.

The Chief Constable thought differently. In order to contain the situation he suggested to Bernard Devonshire in light of his Detective Sergeant's injuries he ought to drop his own complaint against him as his officer's condition was medically well documented.

The Chief didn't see the expression on Bernard's face when he put this to him talking as they were on the telephone. Bernard believed none of it, he didn't like losing, not in business or in any other area of his life. His hatred for Brendon Flannery, therefore, moved up a notch.

"What about my missing wife and Nanny?" Bernard demanded of the Chief. "What are you doing to find them?"

The Chief assured him enquiries were continuing across all areas, they would get back to him just as soon as they knew something definite. The Chief didn't like being put on the spot. He placed pressure on his ACC to bring him some news, the sooner the better. The ACC turned this pressure onto Chief Inspector Harvey who kicked his officers into action.

As a consequence Taylor-Smythe went out for the day already feeling frustrated; bad enough he kept coming up with nothing from his enquiries without this. So far he'd been unable to interview the little old woman, Mary Mundy, who always seemed to be out when he called on her. He began to entertain the idea he was given the wrong address, so he went back to the post office to double check where the postmaster thought she lived.

The postmaster, Amar Sandhu, confirmed once again the sheltered housing flats although he hadn't got the number suggesting he check with the warden. As he left the post office he noticed how the library across the road had a direct view of the front of the Co-op store. He knew how quiet libraries could be especially on a week day with everyone either at work or at school.

His frustration of the day grew when he began his enquiry, by the librarian telling him to lower his voice. It didn't help his mood as the library appeared to be empty except for a group of very small children over in the corner. They were making a noise, laughing and chattering loudly although the librarian didn't seem overly bothered by their noise.

He drew a blank when she haughtily assured him she neither possessed the time nor the inclination to gaze out of the windows and no, she wouldn't have noticed who entered the Co-op or see a pram parked outside. She would have been, likely as not, in the back office dealing with a delivery of new books cataloguing them by inputting them on the computer system. Everything these days being computerised, even their lending books were marked off against the integrated library system which automatically catalogues, tracks circulation being an inventory of the library's assets. She grew rather short with him delivering this reprimand in a severe whisper, Taylor being fascinated by the tautness of the pull of her hair away from her forehead which smoothed it so much so that her eyebrows rose making her look permanently shocked. He said nothing just left.

Thoughts of Brendon Flannery annoyed him even more now since becoming the instant hero for defending the missing baby's mother. To him Flannery was a joke, your typical inept copper with no real talent for the job, but managed nonetheless to get promoted to Sergeant whilst he, Taylor-Smythe, was never likely to get a promotion within CID, even after taking his Sergeant's exams, at least not whilst Flannery sat blocking his way.

It put pressure on the rest of them now, him being off sick and languishing at home, making Trevor more determined to find the baby. Now here they were with two more missing people, vital to the enquiry, to find as well as a snatched baby. To make things worse Wilson let them leave not even bothering to establish where they were staying.

As he got to the library door, the group of children burst out laughing watching the young woman pulling faces; he felt like they were laughing at him trying to do his job. After the negative response at the library he decided to go up to the golf club to establish who Fiona Devonshire's friends were.

CHAPTER 17

Once back at the almost deserted CID office Terri began to interrogate the force computer systems for any information they might hold on Jocelyn's boyfriend Dorian Drover. Whoever Dorian Drover was at least he didn't have a criminal record or been linked to any kind of incident. She tried the electoral register without knowing the age of the Devonshire's Nanny. Jocelyn Phipps looked quite young, she thought, guessing she would likely have a boyfriend her own age or slightly older. If he was eligible to vote it didn't automatically mean he would be registered.

The name Dorian suggested to Terri he might be someone well to do. You were unlikely to get anyone called Dorian living on a council estate. She laughed. From her own experience as a kid being brought up on a rough council estate she knew you could get a lot of stick with a name like that. Of course, he might be a student living with other students in some rough accommodation.

The search revealed a Dorian Xavier Drover, the son of James Ellis Drover and Frances Matilda Drover at an address on Blackheath Avenue. Terri thought, *"This can't be right,"* this is where the Devonshire's live. She walked over to the white board to check out the number, saw Bernard and Fiona Devonshire lived at number 58 Blackheath Avenue and now she knew James and Frances Drover live at number 27 with one son registered at the same address.

She tried to visualise how close to each other they were from her recollection of walking the length of the road, realised the properties on the Avenue were all different, making it hard to place how they were set out. She remembered checking them out as she walked along to the precinct timing herself as she went.

Cancelling her 'days off' Terri came into work because she felt guilty after Taylor took her to task for losing sight of the two women. Brendon having been sent home by Harvey made them one man down, leaving them short staffed. If Bernard Devonshire's aggression could break the Sarge's arm, it showed just how hard he hit, which justified her actions in safeguarding both Fiona Devonshire and Jocelyn Phipps.

She wanted to make amends nonetheless by doing what she could to find Jocelyn who hopefully remained the key for information enabling them to get baby Phoebe back. She thought if Jocelyn's boyfriend lived just up the road she should be the one to find her. She left the empty CID office to make the journey back to Blackheath Avenue, leaving without being able to tell anyone where she was going.

She found number 27 on the other side of the road further up the hill to the Devonshire's house. It looked like one of the older traditional houses, unlike 58 over the road they were smaller, less ornate and closer together. She thought them less pretentious than the Devonshire's house with its fancy porch. These had old fashioned front doors with coloured glass insets.

The house at 27 didn't look particularly well kept, badly needing some external redecoration as well as new windows and doors. The path leading up to the front door was overgrown with weeds growing in the cracks in the concrete driveway. *Not gardeners*, she thought as she negotiated some of the taller ones.

She rang the bell hearing nothing, so she rattled the letterbox, waiting. Of course being a week day most people would be at work. She felt tempted to go around the side of the house, to knock on the back door, but rattled the letterbox again.

She turned to leave just as the front door opened with a gap revealing a face peering out; it was a middle-aged woman who neither spoke nor smiled.

"Mrs Drover?" Terri asked.

"Yes," the woman answered quietly.

"Sorry to bother you," she said. "Is Dorian at home?"

Mrs Drover's look changed to puzzlement as she stared at Terri's uniform through the gap where the safety chain looked securely in place. Terri's radio, attached at her shoulder, made a sudden static noise making the woman jump.

"It's nothing to worry about Mrs Drover, I'm trying to locate his girlfriend," she explained.

"Dorian doesn't live here," Mrs Drover made no attempt to take off the chain.

"Oh, okay," Terri said. "Can you tell me where I can find him?"

Frances Drover abruptly shut the door without a word which surprised Terri until she heard the rattling of the door chain. The door opened again to reveal the slight frail frame of a middle-aged woman dressed in a crumpled robe, wearing fluffy pink bedroom mules slightly dingy and worn.

"Sorry about the chain, it's just.....well you can never be too careful," she made no attempt to ask Terri in. "My son lives in town with his band." She still didn't smile. Terri assumed she probably never did.

"He's a musician?" Terri surmised. She looked at Terri as if she didn't quite understand the question, "You said he lives with his band." Terri reminded her.

"Yes, most of the time, when they aren't travelling around," she said. "But he doesn't have a girlfriend." She added. Terri thought she sounded like a computer with a time lag, taking time to process each question.

"You've never met his girlfriend?" Terri asked.

Frances Drover shook her head, "Like I said he doesn't have a girlfriend." She now eyed Terri with suspicion.

"When did you last see your son, Mrs Drover?" At this she seemed to withdraw into herself the strain of trying to remember showing on her face, once again reminding Terri of a computer, at least the force computers, which were slow at the best of times.

Terri waited watching her face as it contorted moving through a range of expressions, reacting to each piece of information as she passed it. Terri felt self-conscious standing silently watching. The embarrassment reminiscent of listening to someone with a severe stutter trying to form words, you wanted to intervene, say something for them. She knew she mustn't, needing to be patient.

Eventually her moving features grew still, "I'm not really sure," she admitted.

"A while ago then?" Terri wanted to ask her if she knew Jocelyn Phipps who lived down the avenue; something told her not to raise it. Frances Drover's vagueness didn't seem quite right. Instead she asked, "If you could give me the address where he lives when he isn't touring with his band."

Frances Drover turned towards a hall table, opened one of the many draws which Terri could see contained a lot of assorted items including pens, note pads, plastic charity clothes request bags, take out menus and an abundance of randomly discarded items. She selected a small card, picked it out handing it to Terri.

"If you could write it down, it's the only one I have," she explained which made Terri feel even more perplexed, would you really need a business card for your son, you would know where he lived.

Terri took out her black police note book with its attached pen, transferring the address printed on the card. She noted his name was the same as the electoral register but no mention made on the card of his band. She handed it back to Mrs Drover who returned it to the messy draw.

As she walked away she could see just how close the Drovers lived to the Devonshire's dismissing any likelihood of social mingling, the only link being the Nanny and the Drover's son.

CHAPTER 18

Even squashing the pillow over both ears, the screaming came through the thickness of the trapped feathers inside. High-pitched piercing screams I couldn't block out, it made me afraid. It stopped abruptly giving way to silence making me lean forward searching for any other sound to replace it. It began again with the next wave of pain getting shorter with silence in between, until the screaming went on without stopping.

I knew it was the girl, the little mite, by the screams; it was the cries of a young 'un. I've heard it all before although I didn't let mine out of my head, I wouldn't let them hear me. I think they could tell because I screwed up my face to help my screams stay in. They know the pains hurt. They keep yelling at you to 'push' like they did to me. The nurse forced her face into mine commanding me, "I want big pushes from you!"

I didn't understand what she meant, but the pain made me want to force it away so I held my stomach tightly just like my eyes to hold in the screams while I tried to force out the pain in my belly by squeezing hard.

The girl's screams went on for hours making me want to yell at them, "Help her make the pain stop!" They can I know, with a big bottle of something that hisses when they let it out. They make you breathe it through a rubber cup they put over your mouth and nose, letting it hiss into your mouth. It smells funny like the rubber cup does. That's when the pain drifts off somewhere above you. It's still there but bearable so you can concentrate on what they say.

Why don't they let the girl have it, I know it would help her to stop screaming. If she got the nice nurse it would be alright, but the old fat one with the angry face I know likes to hear you scream, it made me more determined not to let it out. I heard her say, "serves them right, it'll teach them right from wrong!" You could tell as she leaned in pushing her face at you she liked to frighten you, "come on push girl, don't take all day or we'll have to get it out another way!"

I knew what she meant because I heard the others talking about it, "ripped her right open to pull it out," and how the stitches they used went septic. I had to do something quickly, so I grabbed the table with my hands, gripped hard to squeeze my baby out into the world. It felt so hard. I held my eyes so tightly shut I never saw her except the one arm as they took her away, and I heard her crying for me. I always think of my baby as a girl.

I can hear the young girl Jenny screaming, then nothing, not even a baby crying, just silence as I wait for the cries, they don't come.

They will tell her anyway her baby died. They tell all the 'mental defectives' so we all know it's our fault. That's what they told me, only I heard my baby girl cry, knew she wasn't dead because I saw her waving at me.

*   *   *   *

Mary made it back to her flat as fast as her painful legs and hip could carry her. These days she hobbled with a shuffling gait, her hip toying with her balance as she went along giving a lopsided effect. Once inside her flat, shutting the door behind her with a slam, she engaged the dead bolt, then putting the door chain into its slot. Next she took off her wool mix coat, hung it up on one of the hooks in the hallway. Taking her books into the kitchen where the clock already showed eleven twenty-five. The time for her morning cup of tea with two arrowroot biscuits had long gone.

The delay in the library interfered with her daily routine making her feel irritated. She felt sure the man in the suit was searching for her to take her away from this safe place. She flicked on the kettle having put in enough water for her teapot, she prepared it before she went out to the library – just enough for two cups.

As she stood waiting for the kettle to boil, the baby began to cry again sounding around the room, echoing off the walls. Mary looked upwards to the ceiling, as if she would catch a glimpse of a tiny pink arm waving at her from up there. Was the baby trying to warn her about the man in the suit? Or maybe frightened because she left her back at the Asylum on her own when they found her this place?

The noise from the kettle got louder as it came to the boil blocking out the cries for help. Eventually, the steam flicked the switch off stopping the kettle from boiling. Mary waited as they showed her until the very hot water stopped moving around in the kettle. *"If you pick it up too soon to pour it out you could get scalded,"* she remembered them telling her, so she always counted up to seven to be on the safe side. Mary's lips moved as her head wobbled and the numbers mounted.

She listened for the baby; could only hear faint music coming from one of the upstairs flats. She poured the water on the leaves she left in the small teapot, covered it with a knitted tea cosy to keep the heat in and carried the tray with a cup, saucer, small milk jug, three biscuits this time on a tea plate, into the front room setting them down next to her chair with the comfy footstool for her feet.

Fetching the library books from the kitchen she quickly looked through the new pile she now had, reading the titles randomly selected at the library. She finished Charlotte Bronte's Jane Eyre the day before. A sad story but she found it finished well liking the happy ending. Now a book by another Bronte called Emily with a strange title of Wuthering Heights she hoped would be as good. She chose this one, sat down in her chair to read the opening lines:

1801— I have just returned from a visit to my landlord—the solitary neighbour that I shall be troubled with. This is certainly a beautiful country! In all England, I do not believe that I could have fixed on a situation so completely removed from the stir of society. A perfect misanthropist's heaven: and Mr. Heathcliff and I are such a suitable pair to divide the desolation between us. A capital fellow! He little imagined how my heart warmed towards him when I beheld his black eyes withdraw so suspiciously under their brows, as I rode up, and when his fingers sheltered themselves, with a jealous resolution, still further in his waistcoat, as I announced my name.

'Mr. Heathcliff?' I said.

Mary drank her tea escaping into another world.

CHAPTER 19

Taylor drove slowly down the approach road leading to the golf club where a row of impressive properties faced onto an expanse of freshly mowed grassy practice putting greens, currently being used by one or two club members. The houses he passed were all of different styles and sizes giving the impression they were built at different times to exclusive designs.

He could see no one around at any of the premises and no cars parked out in front of them. He kept going catching sight of the clubhouse set back behind a car park. The last two houses were a pair of small semi-detached quite ordinary properties he guessed built in the 1960s, unremarkable compared to the other homes. They seemed out of place even though they were probably the first to be built.

The small car park at the front gave access to a larger one at the side of the clubhouse sparsely filled with an assortment of cars. He parked as close as he could get to the clubhouse in the second row, giving him less distance to walk as it began to rain heavily.

He killed the engine, sat for a while watching two people pulling golf trolleys walk in front of his car from the direction he'd just driven. The young man he noted wore maroon golfing trousers with a waterproof jacket high at the neck to keep out the bad weather. The woman's clothes were designer; her coat unzipped giving a tantalising view of her figure underneath which he could tell by the young man's glances he also noticed.

They stopped at a car parked in front of his own in the first row. The woman released the car boot as the young man lifted it to open the back. He helped her in with her golf bag collapsing her trolley he folded it up, with one easy movement, to accompany it. Taylor noted the action appeared to be showy and well-practiced. They stopped to speak, Taylor surmised in a coy way he thought it revealed a new relationship. She looked embarrassed with her hand creeping up over her face. Taylor could spot the young man's approach he'd seen it all before and watched him coming on to her.

He felt like a voyeur watching an amateur video, knew if they were inside somewhere instead of standing out in the open in the rain, Mr Flashy would have tried harder, moved it on a pace to a more physical level. He watched as he raised his hand, moved hers away to stroke the back of his finger across her cheek. He could almost hear him telling her how beautiful she was. She smiled nervously, her head lowering to hide the blush as she grew hot with the attention.

Taylor could tell by her face the approach wasn't rejected, she stood too long letting it happen as smiling she nodded, then turned getting into her car. The young man continued to the clubhouse pulling his trolley as the rain came down harder.

Taylor waited until she drove away before getting out of the car, not wanting her to see he'd sat there watching them. Somewhere, he knew, a woman like her would have a husband who was totally oblivious to his wife's new suitor.

He ran to the main door passing through the foyer he walked along by the wall with glass cabinets exhibiting an array of trophies. They were spread each side of a commemorative notice board showing year on year presidents and captains of the club. He stopped reading down the lists of names noting the lady captain's list began much later in time and was much shorter; *"sign of the times"* he thought, *"nothing's sacred anymore!"* Fleetingly he wondered what Terri Wilson would make of it all, knew she would cry 'sexism' or if she knew what he did about golf Club memberships, even 'racism'.

He turned away approaching the golf pro shop on the opposite corner, where a corridor veered off at right angles. It looked open for business, although currently empty of any customers. It was crammed full of racks of clothes and an assortment of equipment. The door stood open with no sign of anyone serving inside. The whole place looked deserted.

He turned right down the interconnecting corridor walking past another notice board pinned with an abundance of sheets of paper with lists of tournaments inviting names and signatures for entry. The ladies side of the board segregated from the men's in the middle of which was a section advertising social functions.

He caught sight of the Men's changing facility down on the right; pushing open the door he heard someone running a shower. He entered the toilet section to avail himself of the facility. He could still hear the water running as he washed his hands before he left; moving back to the main foyer he took the ramp up into the bar area.

Apart from two elderly golfers sitting at the far end eating a bar meal, the place was also deserted. No one stood behind the bar where he could read the lunchtime menu at the top end chalked on a blackboard. There was no sign of anyone taking food orders either.

He began to feel irritated again, another huge frustration, to add to the rest that foiled every effort to get on, eager to get himself a promotion, yet he found it difficult to shine or be noticed. It didn't help being surrounded by a collection of useless fellow officers all content to move at a snail's pace. Everywhere he went he drew a blank, thwarted by someone else's stupidity. He wouldn't be standing here if Wilson had done her job properly.

The two golfers eyed him with suspicion leaning in mumbling quietly to each other. He left the bar to wander back into the golf pro shop. He needed a new glove so might as well look around before he went. He could see the shop well stocked and quickly found the gloves picking his way through the pile.

He inserted his hand into one, trying one on (he was a right-handed golfer) when he heard, "Excuse me, are you a member?" from somewhere behind him.

When he looked up the voice belonged to the young man he'd seen in the car park earlier, only he looked less affable if the scowl was anything to go by. A heavy whiff of shower gel wafted his way as he walked over, Taylor recognising who had been taking a shower (maybe a cold one if his earlier observations were anything to go by).

"Actually, no," he coolly replied. "You are?" Taylor was in no mood to be challenged or to attempt to be polite.

"I'm the golf pro," he sounded short.

"Is there a name to go with the title?" Taylor reached in his inside pocket of his jacket, pulled out his I.D showing it, he made no move to get nearer to him to give him a better look. "D.C Talyor-Smythe," he announced authoritatively.

"Oh!" The golf pro said. "It's Peter Thompson, how can I help you." Taylor noted how quickly he backed down and put his attitude away, even though he kept an eye on the golf glove he held in his hand.

"They are very good quality - reasonably priced," the golf pro said, not wanting to miss an opportunity to make a sale. "Are you here officially D.C. Smith?"

"I am," Taylor took his hand out of the glove, "The name is Taylor-Smythe." He sounded severe; he hated it when someone got his name wrong, especially when someone called him 'Smith' as a few people did to rile him.

Peter Thompson could see he vexed him which made him smirk recognising he'd hit a nerve. "How can I help you?" He asked smugly.

"I believe Fiona Devonshire is a member here?" Taylor watched as the smirk instantly disappeared from his face. Peter Thompson neither confirmed nor denied it, he remained silent. "Well? Is she?" Taylor prompted irritably ready for the denial. The answer wasn't what he expected, but knew a diversion attempt when he heard one.

"You would do better to speak to the ladies captain or the membership secretary. Unfortunately I don't know all the club's members, full or associate."

Taylor eyed him curiously, "I would have thought in your key position you would be familiar with most people." Taylor recognised a brush off when he heard one.

"I'm working on it, detective," he sounded a little haughty Taylor thought. "I've only been here a short while. Let me give you their numbers as neither of them are here today."

He walked over to the shop counter as Taylor watched him consult a list of names at the side of the till writing them down on a piece of paper which he handed him when he came back. Taylor glanced at it briefly saw the two names and numbers.

"So are you having it?" Peter Thompson asked pointing at the golfing glove in Taylor's hand. He put it back with the others on the shelf.

"I'll think about it," Taylor replied, certain he would be back to speak to him again after his performance in the car park with the woman, he knew there was something fundamentally not quite right about this character.

He turned away towards the door depositing the piece of paper into his jacket pocket as he walked away. When he got to the main exit door he turned to look back, Peter Thompson stood in the doorway of the shop watching him leave.

CHAPTER 20

Terri found the terraced house in the middle of an uninspiring block of similar three storey houses with an assortment of brightly coloured front doors. Each of the houses accumulating a variety of wheelie bins outside their front doors, there being no access to the back yards except through the house made the street look less desirable than they really were.

A couple of the front windows were draped in brightly coloured purple or cerise netting indicating proudly the inhabitant's ethnic origins to the world. These were sandwiched between the severe white net curtains of those demonstrating the 'respectable' working class families. The one she wanted had dingy, almost grey vertical blinds that exposed the inside by one or two broken slats hanging down in what announced a student squat. It gave a dilapidated appearance suggestive of little money and even less enthusiasm for their surroundings. Their bins overflowed with takeout cartons intermingled with empty beer cans.

This being number five Terri knocked, expecting no answer, as Frances Drover indicated her son and the band were often on tour. When the door opened it revealed a young girl who blinked blurry-eyed, her short kimono robe loosely tied as if hurriedly put on, her heavily made up eyes smudged with black mascara across her face indicating she had slept in her makeup. Her long blonde hair uncombed and messy convinced Terri she had just woken her up.

"Hi," Terri began. "I'm looking for Dorian Drover, does he live here?"

The girl didn't answer, just turned zombie-like walking off leaving Terri standing at the open door. She stepped inside taking the action as an invitation to come in. Terri found herself in a large hallway with a black and white mosaic floor, a huge battered dresser stood to one side on which various piles of mail, an abundance of circulars and take out menus were scattered in uneven disarray.

Stairs led off the hall to the two other floors. She could see a couple of closed doors off the hallway and a passageway leading to the rear of the house through which the girl just disappeared. She followed the passageway through to the back into a kind of sitting room with a well-worn couch, two arm chairs in the same dingy jacquard mustard coloured fabric and a dining table surrounded by hard backed dining chairs. Everything about the room told Terri the house had seen better days although certain features indicated a once respectable family home.

She heard a toilet flush from somewhere further on. "Hello?" Terri called. "Are you there?" She expected the girl to come back. Instead a tall thin afro-Caribbean youth with dreadlocks escaping from a slouch Rasta beany hat emerged from the back dressed in a hippie shirt in a loose fitting colourful fabric over faded denims; his feet were bare.

"Who are you?" he asked casually.

"Terri pulled out her I.D card, "P.C Wilson," she said. "I'm looking for Dorian....."

The man waved his hand back the way she'd just come walking off mumbling, "First floor, second door." Before Terri could thank him he disappeared.

She went back out to the hallway to climb the stairs. At the first floor the landing gave way to three doors before the stairs turned up to the third floor. She knocked on the second door, could hear nothing moving inside, so she knocked louder. This time she heard a muffled incoherent gruff voice from within; she knocked again, even louder this time yelling, "Dorian Drover?"

When the door opened, a tall delicate-looking man in his early twenties dressed in a black t-shirt with matching black boxers stood yawning; his collar length hair messily flopped over his eyes. It was clear he had also just woken up.

"What do you want!?" he demanded grumpily. His eyes fell on Terri's uniform which made him angrier, he stepped forward pulling the door partially to behind him. "Who the hell let you in?"

"Your mother told me you lived here," Terri hoped it might smooth his ruffled mood if he thought she knew his mother. If anything it made him worse.

"Did she now?!" he snapped. "What do you want?"

"I'm looking for Jocelyn Phipps. I understand she's your girlfriend staying with you." Terri watched as his already frowning face smoothed briefly then furrowed even more.

"What?" he said sternly.

"Is she here?" Terri asked.

"No, she isn't here and is someone I met....maybe one time," Terri thought he sounded condescending as if he were talking to someone feeble minded and needed to stress every word.

"She told me you expected to see her on her day off, could come here to stay overnight....." Terri now began to doubt herself again, trying hard to recall how the conversation with Jocelyn went.

"Look," Dorian Drover spoke slowly. "The band did a gig yesterday; it went on late....it's why we're sleeping this late in the day!" He said to emphasise her having woken him up.

"She came here yesterday....." Terri persisted perplexed by his negative reaction.

"I just told you the band did a gig up in Manchester," he explained sounding irritated. "We were travelling to it yesterday......it didn't finish until after midnight," he faded off as he thought about it. "Then we travelled back stopping at the services in the early hours for something to eat."

Terri left, muttering apologies with a nervousness which compounded with her existing guilt at not getting definite details. She had been so convinced Jocelyn intended to join Dorian Drover for the rest of her day off.

She sat in her car outside the station going over what happened once more in her head. She took out her force mobile searched for Brendon Flannery's number pressing it into life; surprised at how quickly he answered.

"Sarge?"

"Yes, Terri, where are you?" Brendon asked which took her by surprise; she half expected a reprimand for telephoning him on his sick leave.

"Sorry to phone you like this," she began trying to decide how to tell him she'd messed up.

"What's wrong? Are you okay, you sound upset," Brendon could hear the catch in her voice as she apologised.

"It's just...." She took a deep breath to tell him how she'd found Dorian Drover via his mother. "He's denying being Jocelyn Phipps' boyfriend."

"Look, get back to the station," Brendon suggested.

"I'm already at the station outside in the car park, Sarge," she replied.

When she walked in to the department she found Brendon sitting at his desk, his arm no longer contained in the sling he'd been given at the hospital.

"Should you be here, Sarge?" Terri asked concerned.

"It's only a hairline fracture, no big deal." He shrugged the comment off feeling guilty for letting everyone believe he got the fracture from his confrontation with Bernard Devonshire. As hard as he tried he couldn't just sit at home whilst his absence depleted manpower essential for the initial enquiries; time being crucial in these kinds of cases. Harvey took him to one side, told him he ought to be off as Health and Safety required he comply with duty of care as his supervisor. Brendon played the whole thing down promising he would take his time, if necessary just provide office back up support to the investigation wherever he could.

He thought Harvey looked a little relieved, knowing there would be a great deal of pressure from the ACC, complicated by his run in with Bernard Devonshire. When Taylor got back to the station Harvey called a briefing to update on the progress of the enquiries. He could already see this one going dreadfully wrong if recent events were anything to go by. The last thing Harvey wanted, being so close to retirement, he couldn't mess up at this stage of his career.

Harvey stood in front of the evidence board where a picture of baby Phoebe sat between photos, one of her mother Fiona and the other her father Bernard Devonshire. Taylor began to update on his enquiries at the library. He had to admit that so far he had been unable to talk to the old woman leaving the Co-op at the time Jocelyn Phipps entered after leaving the baby in her pram outside. He believed her name to be Mary Mundy.

"If we hadn't been side-tracked by arresting the father we probably wouldn't have lost our key witnesses," Taylor-Smythe glared at Brendon when he said it being surprised to find him in when he got back. He knew he would have played it differently.

"...well if Bernard Devonshire hadn't assaulted his wife, broken the arm of one of my officers, Taylor, we might not have been side-tracked at all!" Harvey's tone stopped Taylor from taking his comments any further. He could see the 'blue-eyed boy' was even more in favour. The last thing he needed was to get on the wrong side of Harvey, it wouldn't help his promotion.

He carried on with his update, "I've been out to the golf club trying to locate Mrs Devonshire." He caught sight of the photograph of Fiona Devonshire now pinned to the board. "Is that her?" he asked getting off the desk he was perched on; he walked over to the board for a closer look.

He could see the picture was taken at a social function by Fiona Devonshire's evening gown, a different image to the one he saw recently of her standing in the rain, a young golf pro running the back of his finger down her cheek.

"Did you say her husband hit her in the face?" Taylor asked squinting at the picture.

"He caught her just under her eye," Terri confirmed. "It broke the skin bruising almost immediately, it was quite a hit. I think he may have been holding something in his hand, like car keys....."

Taylor ignored her as he usually did, "I saw her this afternoon up at the golf club with the golf pro, I think having a golf lesson, just leaving as I got there...."

"Didn't you think to stop her?" Brendon demanded indignantly.

"I didn't have the advantage of knowing what she looked like!" Taylor snapped back. "Curious though," he went on. Everyone waited for him to expand on his comment. "When I went inside to speak to the golf pro," he flipped his pocket book open for details, "Peter Thompson denied he knew her, he said being new he hadn't met everyone yet."

Taylor fished in his pocket for the piece of paper Peter Thompson gave him, "He gave me the ladies' captain and the membership secretary's phone numbers." He handed it to Harvey who glanced at it holding it out to Brendon.

"See what you can find out will you?"

"Sir," Brendon took it immediately dialling one of the numbers turning his back on the others he talked quietly into the phone.

"It's odd though," Terri Wilson said. Everyone looked at her making her feel self-conscious having actually spoken her thoughts out loud. "How everyone is denying knowing everyone else."

"What do you mean?" Harvey asked.

"Well Mrs Drover says Dorian doesn't have a girlfriend, Dorian says he only met Jocelyn the once, yet she told me he was definitely expecting her yesterday, it made her angry about the shopping errand. She rushed to get back, leaving the baby in her pram for speed, so she could get back quickly to meet him, only he says he went to an evening gig with his band, they were travelling during the day."

Terri now regretted her caution at not asking Frances Drover if she knew Jocelyn, after all they live a few houses from each other. Jocelyn would have walked past the Drover's house to get to the precinct.

Brendon turned back to the briefing as Harvey waited for him to speak.

"Curious Gov," Brendon began. "I just spoke to the ladies captain who tells me she hasn't seen Fiona Devonshire for a few days. She apparently entered a ladies tournament yesterday but didn't show up, let someone down she was paired with, but heard on the grapevine about the baby, so they understood."

"Yet she managed to have a lesson today?" Terri queried. "Are you sure you saw her?" She asked Taylor who bristled at her doubting his word.

"I watched Peter Thompson stroke her across her face where you say she got hurt – I was too far away to notice the actual facial injury, but not too far away to see it was her!"

Terri heard his anger and knew he directed it at her. She could tell Taylor had some problem with her. She felt like hitting him across the face; instead she countered, "You don't play golf when your baby gets snatched – do you?"

The room suddenly went silent, the atmosphere you could cut with a knife.

"Right!" Harvey yelled making everyone jump. "Get the golf pro in, now!" He walked off back into his office shutting the door loudly.

CHAPTER 21

"What do *you* want?" Bernard Devonshire glared at Terri Wilson as he opened the front door catching sight of her uniform. He couldn't have known how much nerve it took just being there. He had no concept of just how intimidating he was.

"I wanted to see if you were okay, sir," She thought about him hitting his wife, tried to accept he would have been charged up by the shock of his missing baby and seeing his home invaded by so many police officers milling about the house. "I wondered if you've heard from Mrs Devonshire or Jocelyn."

Bernard woke up with his temper fuelled on alcohol and feeling annoyed his latest business deal hung in the balance. He needed to focus his attention having drunk half a bottle of scotch the night before waking with a blazing headache, although without the alcohol he wouldn't have slept at all.

"What do you mean have I heard anything?" He yelled. "Where is she, where have you taken her?"

"We haven't Mr Devonshire," Terri began, guilt welling up again, "Your wife left to go to stay with a friend...."

"What friend?" he demanded. "She doesn't have any friends!"

Terri thought it a curious thing to say, "She said a golfing friend." Terri prompted.

Bernard Devonshire let go of the front door he'd been holding onto, more to keep himself balanced than to prevent Terri from entering. He looked unsteady turning towards the hall table he held on to it to steady himself before he slowly made his way into the front room and the safety of one of the armchairs.

Terri followed him in without an invitation looking concerned.

"Can I get you anything, sir?" She asked slipping easily into her liaison role, "Shall I make you a drink?"

He seemed to grunt a reply which Terri took as an affirmative going off to the kitchen to make some tea like before. When she got back he sat holding his head in his hands but took the proffered tea.

"I don't understand," he said, no longer the aggressive bully Terri saw previously. "Fiona doesn't play golf." He raised his head looking enquiringly at her.

This case completely mystified Terri. She could almost believe a mother wouldn't necessarily know if her son has a girlfriend, after all they didn't live in the same house. To have no idea your wife played golf didn't seem possible given they did live together. If she really didn't play golf then Taylor must be wrong about seeing her putting a set of golf clubs into her car boot; not an easy mistake to make. The lady captain believed Fiona Devonshire entered herself in a tournament which seemed to refute that idea.

"Are you saying your wife isn't a member of the golf club?" Terri asked.

She saw Bernard Devonshire look up at her sharply, "I just told you, she doesn't play golf!" he repeated.

"Do you play golf Mr Devonshire?" she asked trying to make it sound as friendly as she could knowing just how angry he could get.

"No, I'm far too busy to spend my time doing those kinds of things," he snapped. "What makes you think Fiona does?"

She felt cornered needing to be careful what she revealed about Fiona Devonshire. She began to realise the vast age gap wasn't the only gulf between them.

"Oh I thought she mentioned she was going to stay with a golf friend – it may have been a 'girlfriend', she added quickly which seemed to perplex him even more.

"As far as I am aware, young lady, she doesn't have any particular girlfriends."

"What about relatives, mother maybe?" Terri remembered Fiona saying there were none locally when she asked her where she could go.

He slowly shook his head, "Her mother lives in Wales. They haven't seen each other for....." he paused, thinking about how he met her when he advertised for a personnel assistant, "....for a good few years."

Well that fitted at any rate. She remembered Fiona Devonshire looking thoughtful when she made her reply to a similar question.

"Have you any idea where she might have gone, Mr Devonshire?" Terri asked straight out. None of this conversation made her feel repentant about pushing Fiona Devonshire to leave before he got back to the house it had been quite rightly for her own safety.

Again he shook his head.

"What about Jocelyn, Mr Devonshire, have you ever met her boyfriend?" Terri asked.

"Has she got a boyfriend?" He looked completely mystified. "I rather assumed Fiona took her on because she didn't have a boyfriend – one of the things we required – there should be no distractions."

"You mean it was a stipulation to get the job?" Terri tried hard not to sound disapproving knowing how far the police had moved away from asking these kinds of personal questions, as part of an equal opportunity policy. She'd heard in the past you could even ask a female applicant if she intended to have children. She focussed her thoughts back on Bernard Devonshire.

"Not exactly," he offered. She thought she saw a sudden sly side glance at her to gauge her reaction. "It's just you hear about Nannies not being able to travel on holiday with a family, because of being away from someone." He said. "We didn't want any complications; well Fiona didn't." She noted how he put all the emphasis on his wife in her absence.

"Were you planning a holiday Mr. Devonshire?" Terri didn't see his relationship as being stable enough to spend time together on holiday. He'd just indicated he didn't have time to indulge in golf, being away from his business to go on holiday didn't strike the right chord.

"No not really," the sly look flicked across his face again. "I have to be away a lot on business. Fiona used to travel with me." He didn't elaborate further on her previous role as his secretary/personal assistant, merely added, "Having Phoebe is a complication if you haven't got someone to depend on to look after her."

Terri almost winced at him calling his daughter a 'complication' suddenly wondering what on earth Fiona Devonshire saw in this man.

"I see," she said simply. "So you took Jocelyn Phipps on because she had no 'complications' of her own," She realised how critical it sounded, "to enable her to travel with you."

"Yes," Bernard Devonshire didn't miss the jibe. "And because she convinced us she wanted to travel – in fact, she hoped we wanted her to."

"You mean she told you she didn't have a boyfriend?"

"I'm not sure she specified exactly," he tried to summon up her exact words. "She told us she wasn't married and had no close relatives. We took her at her word," he added in justification.

"Did she have any references?" Terri now began to wonder about Jocelyn Phipps whom she previously thought of as a frightened vulnerable girl, someone you could overlook in the chaos of the moment.

Bernard Devonshire got to his feet unsteadily, walked over to a bureau tucked away in the corner of the room. He lowered the desk lid, pulled open a draw searching the contents bringing back two pieces of paper. He handed them over to Terri who could see they were two separate letters from, she imagined, people Jocelyn Phipps once worked for.

"Can I take these Mr. Devonshire, I'll let you have them back," she promised. He waved his hand as if he didn't care one way or the other.

When she left him to go back to the station she now had several more nagging doubts related to both Jocelyn Phipps and Fiona Devonshire. Her preconceived idea about Bernard Devonshire, the bombastic bullying husband had taken a knock; there seemed to be another side to him which obviously drew someone as young as Fiona Devonshire to marry him in the first place. For Terri, no amount of money would tempt her into a relationship with someone she couldn't love for themselves.

She thought of Taylor-Smythe and shivered, not in a million years.

CHAPTER 22

I knew the moment the sour-faced nurse told me to wear my best dress it was going to be the big day. The only time all year they make us wear one. Usually most days, unless they give you treatment, we wear work clothes. She yelled at me to clean myself up because I looked dusty from working in the gardens. Some of the jobs are messy. Today we put down fertilizer they call it.

Shit is shit however you spread it around. It comes from chickens, stinks like nothing else; they don't waste anything here. Chicken shit spread out on the soil to grow the vegetables makes them grow big, so they say.

Nurse makes me wash, scrubbing my hands till they hurt. They're always red and sore. I can still smell the stuff anyway, no matter how hard I scrub. I don't think I'll ever get used to it.

We walked the big corridor to the top. At least I know it isn't treatment this time. My best dress is blue but nothing special. I have no idea who had it 'afore me. At least it's clean making me look what nurse calls 'spectable' or something like that but I think it means clean.

I was right though. She took me into the big office, the one with lots of books. Three people were sitting in a line behind the big table in there. She made me sit in a chair facing them. I watched her move to stand in the corner behind me. She frowns at me for looking her way nodding her head to make me look back at the three people who are ignoring me anyway. They are reading the huge leather bound book in front of them, that's where they keep all stuff about us patients. It fills the desk looking thick and heavy. I can't imagine holding a book as big as that, let alone carrying it. I can see there are lines all the way down on both sides of the pages opened. At the top of the page a small square of paper is stuck in, I know that is a phot'graph. I remember them taking it when my parents brought me here. It was the first thing they did 'afore they cut off my hair and made me look like all the others.

I know the man in the middle of the three is the big doctor in charge; his name is Dr Roberts someone told me, although he never told me it. The woman at his right side is matron, she's fierce, she tells the nurses what to do. I don't know the other one; every year I come here it's always someone different.

Matron says, "This is Mary Mundy doctor, one of the mental defectives now in her seventh year with us."

The doctor reads down the lines of hand written notes about me. He looks up at me studying me with his staring eyes. He looks really serious and doesn't smile.

"Any problems?" he asks Matron as he watches me.

"No doctor, she's no trouble, works well in the gardens."

The man on the other side leans in handing the doctor a piece of paper which the doctor reads.

"Ah," he says looking at me again. "Mary I have to tell you your father died." He comes straight out with it staring at me again with his strange fixed stare. It took me all my will power not to let him see me react. I knew right then I couldn't show just how happy hearing it made me feel. If I did let on they would give me treatment. I wanted so much to raise my arms and shout for joy. The old bastard is dead, hurrah!

"Do you understand Mary?" the doctor asks me, obviously I'm not making the right reaction so I nod lowering my head (just in case a smile escapes) – they would expect me to be sad but not too sad otherwise you get the electrics for being too sad.

He picks up an ink pen to begin to write in the ledger, I could hear the pen nib scratching against the page. "Works well in the gardens you say?"

Matron nods as I watch him write it down on one of the lines. "I will make a note we told her about her father." They all agree. He looks at me again as I peer up through my eyelashes. "Keep up the good work, Mary," he says in a slightly louder voice, maybe he thinks I'm deaf, then he nods to the nurse in the corner who comes to stand at the side of me.

"Say thank you to the doctor Mary," she tells me. She always says that, so I mumble a "thank you" then get up to leave. I do wonder why I need to be there, they could have done it without me getting in my best dress.

My annual reviews are always the same, except for this one because they told me about my father. It makes me glad, I want to shout it out, tell everyone about him and why my parents left me here. At least putting me here stopped him doing those things to me. I was so afraid he might hurt my baby, but they took her away anyway. I never saw her again.

*   *   *   *

"Are you in there Mary?" Terri's voice carried through the door gently after she knocked twice hearing nothing.

Mary could see through the spyhole a police officer in uniform; a woman. She sounded nice, Mary thought, but she was still one of them, probably come to take her back to the Asylum.

"I just want to ask you some questions about the baby?" Terri assumed Mary Mundy to be at home, after speaking to the warden she bumped into on site who told her Mary hardly ever went out, only to do some shopping or go to the library.

Mary heard the word baby, thought about her baby girl and wondered how this police officer knew. No one ever asked her about her baby or even mentioned her again once they took her away. Sometimes she wondered if the whole thing ever happened. Yet here was this policewoman wanting to talk to her about it.

Terri heard a rattling of the door chain and the door begin to open slightly. An anxious face, a sweet old lady's face peered out, eyes starring wildly at her.

"It's okay Mary," Terri said smiling. "There's nothing wrong I just need to talk to you about Tuesday."

Mary's face looked puzzled, "You said about the baby," Mary reminded her,

"Yes, about the baby," Terri confirmed.

Mary took the door chain off to let her in. She led Terri into the kitchen where she could see she was busy making herself a cup of tea.

"It's my tea time," Mary told her without looking at her.

"You carry on," Terri became intrigued watching her cutting open two tea bags with a pair of scissors, and also the way her head wobbled much like the Indian head shake she'd seen in documentaries. She found it fascinating.

"I can make some tea for you," not so much an invitation, more a statement Terri realised.

"No thank you, I just had some," Terri lied not wanting to put her off her routine.

Mary looked relieved not to have to make it for two people, although she thought she would be able to. She poured the boiling water into the pot looking up at Terri whilst she waited for the tea to mash, her lips moving slightly as she counted. Terri wasn't a very tall person but Mary Mundy being small of stature made her feel tall, her slight frame more girl-like than an elderly woman.

"I think you went shopping at the precinct on Tuesday," Terri began.

Mary felt the same old fear rise again, felt sure they still watched everything she did. Her head wobbled as Terri waited for her reply. "Yes, always on Tuesdays when it's pension day, I get my shopping then." Mary waited for Terri to tell her if she did something wrong; a bad thing to get her sent back. They told her at the other place if she couldn't look after herself she could always go back, or get more help. Mary poured her cup of tea hoping she did it right. She eyed the police woman to see if she looked critical.

"Shall we go and sit down?" Terri asked. She felt tired, from lack of sleep worrying about Fiona and the Nanny wondering whether she should have done it all differently.

Mary took her tea leading the young policewoman into the lounge where she settled down in her comfy chair to wait for the bad news to come. She watched as the policewoman looked over her window sill with her ornaments, she looked strained knew by her eyes there was something wrong.

"They're nice, Mary, do you mind if I call you Mary?" she asked quietly. Mary's head wobbled. "You keep everything so tidy," Terri commented taking the action as agreement.

Mary thought it might be a trap although she learnt it was better to say nothing until you were asked a straight question. If you said the wrong thing or something they didn't like, they might get cross, make you do some extra work or even move you out of the garden. Once she got out of the laundry she didn't want to go back.

Mary sipped her tea.

"When you went into the Co-op on Tuesday did you see anyone?" Terri asked.

Mary's alarm grew, how did she know that she went into the Co-op, she knew a trap when faced with one? "You mean like the man, the young one who did my shopping?"

"Well yes, apart from him – what about other customers like when you were leaving?"

Mary thought back, "A girl in a hurry, she nearly walked into me – when I put my money in my purse, I didn't see her until she stepped to the side."

"I need you to think carefully," Terri said. "Did you see anyone else - they could have been next to the pram?"

"Pram?" Terri watched the puzzled frown appear on Mary's face.

"What about a large coach built pram outside, near the door?" Terri prompted as Mary's head moved slowly from side to side.

"I put my purse into the carrier bag and walked straight back here," Mary explained. She sat thinking for a minute about the girl she saw, "She was too young to have a baby."

"You mean the girl who nearly walked into you?" Terri asked surprised at her comment. Mary nodded her head. "How old did you think she was?" Terri asked, perhaps they were both talking about someone else, not Jocelyn Phipps. "What did she look like?" Terri asked conjuring up an image of Jocelyn Phipps as she remembered her: Small, slightly built with short brown elfin cut hair feathered onto her face, large brown eyes and high cheek bones. She particularly remembered her cheek bones, she thought her pretty – no actually beautiful in a very natural way that she envied. She on the other hand thought herself rather solid, with her mixed race favouring her father not her mother's delicate traits; she tried not to sigh at the thought of it.

"She looked like they all do," Mary assured her. "Very young, too young to have a baby, they never let them keep their babies...." She sighed deeply her mind off in another world.

The answer confused Terri, "Who wouldn't Mary?"

Mary went on ignoring the direct question, "She was tall, she nearly walked into me, she swerved out of the way."

Terri felt deflated remembering how small Jocelyn is, "What about her hair?" she asked hoping at least their descriptions would have some similarity.

"Hair?" Mary's frown broadened. "They all have the same hair," Mary's unexpected declaration carried an underlying hint of frustration which worried Terri.

"What was it like Mary?" She encouraged gently trying not to upset her.

"Cut short because they said it's easier to keep clean," Mary seemed to focus her gaze on something although not in the room; her mind moving back in time to the young girls like herself. "We weren't allowed to keep it long, less for the head lice to get in, they said it took too long to dry after washing it," her voice sinking to a whisper as she absently scratched at her scalp, "or when they gave you the treatment...." Her gaze moved back to Terri's face and the room in which they sat, "water jets, hot then cold and often baths for hours...."

Terri shivered at the horrific image she brought back for Mary to face again by asking such a simple question which inadvertently took her back in time, she supposed, to the Asylum. It seemed to Terri everything she did or said these days made things worse somehow, "I'm sorry Mary I didn't mean to make you remember."

Mary looked straight at her like she didn't understand.

"You said you wanted to talk about the baby," Mary reminded her.

"The one taken from the pram, outside the Co-op," Terri assumed everyone would now be aware of the case, there were continuous news bulletins with televised press briefing held by the Chief Constable.

Mary gaped non-comprehending, that's when Terri looked about the room noticing Mary didn't have a television.

"You don't have a TV," Terri stated. "Do you listen to the radio?" She couldn't see anything like a radio in the room either.

Mary picked up a book from the coffee table to show her, "I have books, I get them from the library," she said briefly looking contented.

Terri noticed she seemed not to retain her attention on the conversation for long, her mind moved to the next part of the conversation or her own inner thoughts.

"The baby, the girl left outside the Co-op asleep in the pram," Terri reminded her. "Did you notice the pram as you left the shop Mary?"

Mary's head moved from side to side again it looked almost like a wobble. It stopped when Mary looked up to the ceiling as Terri watched her listening intently. Then she looked back at Terri, "I thought you wanted to talk about my baby?" she said.

"Your baby?" Terri checked the room again for any evidence of the presence of a baby but found none.

Mary scowled, thinking about the girl who nearly walked into her at the shop. "The girl left a baby outside the Co-op?" She suddenly said in amazement.

"She says for only ten minutes whilst she went inside to do some shopping," Terri found herself defending Jocelyn Phipps. "Did you see anyone outside after the girl went inside?" Terri tried again to get her to focus.

Mary's head wobbled again, "I never talk to anyone I don't know," she said. "I come straight home."

Realising she would get nothing out of her Terri made her excuses to leave. She heard the chain being placed back on the door before she walked away.

CHAPTER 23

Taylor's dislike of him took some hiding as he watched Peter Thompson through the one way glass partition in the interview room. He sat at the table picking at his fingernails, pushing back the cuticles on a well-manicured hand, one Taylor knew hadn't ever seen a real day's work. It galled him he would never have to dirty his hands in manual labour.

Talk around this old obsolete police station speculated it had been put on the list of police premises to be sold off; this interview room was the only concession to modern day policing they'd so far managed to achieve. Times were tough with the year on year reduction of police budgets that now required desperate measures to achieve meeting their policing needs.

Interview room one, where the golf pro sat, doubled up to provide an I.D. parade resource because a witness could view a line up behind a one way glass partition without being seen. The only problem, someone discovered, they forgot to sound proof it. The story doing the rounds described that one potential suspect, having been told to stand in position three, the sound carried and overheard by the eyewitness who then picked him out. A leak from someone inside the police to the press blew that particular case out of court.

Today, however, the golf pro came in following his denial at knowing Fiona Devonshire after Taylor saw them together in the car park at the Golf Club. Harvey and Taylor-Smythe left him for half an hour whilst they watched silently through the partition, drinking coffee, mindful of how any sound would carry into the room.

Peter Thompson recognised the younger cop immediately they entered the room, rounding on him with, "I've no idea what you expect me to add to what I've already told you," he protested as they sat down opposite him. They both observed how irritated he became at being kept waiting.

Mike Harvey introduced himself adding, "You have already met Detective Constable Taylor...."

"Exactly, I've answered all his questions....." he interrupted.

Mike Harvey threw a brown envelope onto the table which Thompson eyed suspiciously as he settled in his chair.

"You told him you hadn't met Fiona Devonshire, Mr Thompson," Harvey reminded him.

"Because I haven't been there very long....." he put in defensively.

"Isn't it the golf pro's business to get to know all the club's members?" he suggested.

"Well, yes, I suppose so, but mostly specific members who take golf lessons or need help with equipment," he clarified. "We do have in excess of 1,000 members. It's a lot of people to remember. Of course, not everyone is a frequent visitor or joins in with the social side, there's bound to be people I'm less likely to meet."

"Yes, indeed," Harvey conceded.

Taylor kept quiet, watching him squirm a little, until he could hold his tongue no longer, "Tell us about two days ago." Taylor demanded.

Although initially shocked, Peter Thompson tried to recall, it being the day he met this strange cop in the pro-shop. "Just a typical day except the weather was foul if I recall with only a couple of people turning out on the practice green due to the rain."

Taylor recollected the way the pair were dressed as he squinted through the rain running down his windscreen, not wishing to give himself away by flicking his wipers because of the noise they made, would have drawn their attention. Seeing how intense the moment between the pair seemed, he felt oddly aroused, fascinated by his voyeurism watching the golf pro's finger as it stroked the woman's cheek. It was like watching a porn movie, anticipating what would happen next, what he might have done. Taylor grew mindful of the effect their behaviour had on him seeing the obvious deliberate 'come on' the young pro made.

"Go on, Mr Thompson," Harvey encouraged as Taylor sat silent making no attempt to move the interview on.

"It was hardly worth my while getting wet putting in an appearance," Thompson complained. "There were only two people attending...."

"Usually there's more?" Harvey prompted.

"Usually," he glanced over at the chirpy cop he remembered trying on the golf gloves. "It's a practice range for pitching," he added for clarification. "But raining heavily so we gave it up in the end because it got too dark, the rain interfering with.....look what is this about?" he asked running out of patience. "I do have things to do!" He sounded peeved.

Harvey opened the envelope in front of him, took out the picture of Fiona Devonshire in an evening gown taken they thought from some local Sunday supplement at a formal gathering of the Rotary Club. He turned it to face Peter Thompson pushing it over to him.

He glanced at it, then looked up eyeing them directly one after the other. "Who is it?" he asked.

Taylor sighed heavily, sat slightly back in his chair giving away his feelings. It didn't go unnoticed by Harvey who flicked him a side look to keep quiet.

"Why don't you tell us Mr Thompson," Harvey said calmly.

Peter Thompson looked again, picked up the picture studying it, his focus not wandering much beyond the tight fitting dress with a tantalising glimpse of soft firm breasts overflowing the low cut neckline.

"Nice," he commented. "It doesn't look like the kind of social event I've had the privilege of attending," his sarcasm feigning modesty.

Taylor knew golf club functions were equally as flashy if the ones he'd been to were anything to go by.

"Do you recognise her?" Taylor's patience snapped. His dislike of this overconfident smarmy privileged man overtook him. He felt Harvey's hand briefly on his arm indicating for him to shut up.

Peter Thompson sensed his hostility in the interchange between them. "Look she seems vaguely familiar, but no, I've no idea who she is, maybe you could tell me what this is all about?"

Taylor's anger welled up again; he hated the confidence someone this young exuded, knew it came from a wealthy privileged background.

"This is Fiona Devonshire, who you say you haven't met. I saw you with her after your class at the golf club," Taylor blurted out.

Thompson looked genuinely puzzled, peering once again at the photograph, this time taking in her face. "Oh!" he sounded surprised. "She's the woman in the car park." Taylor was taken aback by the admission.

"Also at your golf session, Mr Thompson?" Harvey asked.

"Err, no, only the two - like I said - only they were elderly gentlemen members, I can give you their names if you need them, they will confirm it with you."

Taylor remembered the two elderly members who eyed him suspiciously when he went in the bar, "I saw you with this woman in the car park...." Taylor began which made Harvey scowl at him to shut up.

"I just said," Peter Thompson emphasised. "I saw her in the car park as I passed through to go back to the clubhouse, looked to be struggling with a bulky set of golf clubs in a trolley – I helped her with them, put them in a car she stopped beside...." Taylor could see a slight smirk appear on his face. "I assure you she wasn't dressed like this." He picked up the picture openly ogled the form of Fiona Devonshire, "Lovely!" he commented.

Taylor wanted to wipe the smile off his face.

Peter Thompson frowned, "She didn't look this happy either," his finger rose to his face reminding Taylor of the way he stroked Fiona Devonshire's face. He touched his own cheek just below his eye, "Her face was swollen, with bruising; she had a cut just here." Thompson remarked. "I asked her if she was okay - if I could help, but she seemed in a hurry to be off. I put the clubs then the trolley into her car boot and she left." He said simply.

Taylor tried to remember if what he saw could be interpreted that way.

"But you didn't know her?" Harvey repeated.

"Never seen her before," he deliberately turned to Taylor, "Like I said I don't 'know' everyone yet." He sounded peeved, knew Taylor was in for a dressing down, so he wanted to add to his discomfort. "Anything else?" he asked them.

"No, Mr Thompson that will be all," Harvey said picking up the photograph inserting it back in the envelope.

Peter Thompson turned to Taylor again, "Be sure to let me know if you want the golf glove....." he mocked with a grin.

Taylor got up and left the room without acknowledging him.

CHAPTER 24

Harvey tried hard to gain his composure as his anger flared leaving him feeling unusually out of control. He'd spent years conditioning himself to avoid such feelings, now in the space of one short interview his resolve was demolished and his barriers breeched.

"What was that all about, Taylor!?" he yelled.

He admonished Taylor loud enough for it to carry into the CID office where Brendon Flannery and Terri Wilson sat with the other detectives listening whilst pretending to be engrossed in whatever they were doing. Glances were exchanged as they heard the rare outburst from their leader unleased. They knew him only as a mild mannered man, calm in the face of most things.

Trevor Taylor knew he'd lost ground, "So I got it wrong," he conceded. "The point is who would stroke the face of a total stranger..... if you believe him?" He knew the action he observed held more intimacy than Thompson admitted to.

"No, Taylor, the point you're missing is what was Fiona Devonshire doing at the golf club the day after her baby had been snatched, don't you think?!" Taylor recoiled from the level of his boss's anger. "Maybe we'll never find out now, Taylor, having been side-tracked by your 'interpretation' of events!" he yelled. The truth being the pressure from ACC to find the baby and the missing two key witnesses had intensified, whilst they seemed to be getting nowhere.

"Sorry Boss," Taylor said giving a rare apology. "He just makes me so angry by his smugness." The irony of the statement seemed to evade him.

Harvey got hold of his temper, stood up moving to the door he walked out to the anticipated briefing he called earlier.

"Right you lot this has gone on way too long without as much as a lead on anything - the Chief Constable wants answers," he stood in front of the evidence board waiting for everyone's attention. "Do we have anything, no matter how unusual?"

People fidgeted a bit with no one looking inclined to speak.

"Okay," Harvey sighed at the lack of response. "Let's start again shall we?" He took a deep breath beginning with, "Bernard Devonshire went off to work at his usual time on Tuesday, he didn't see his daughter, but he did hear her before he left the house. We also understand Jocelyn Phipps got the child ready before they left the house about nine o'clock that morning to go to the precinct. It was meant to be her day off having arranged, she told us, to meet her boyfriend Dorian Drover in order to spend the day with him. She left the pram outside the Co-op with the baby asleep, she says for only ten minutes. It wasn't until she arrived back home they discovered the empty pram." He paused in his summing up.

"It's odd though, isn't it boss?" Terri Wilson asked filling the pause. She sounded almost critical as she went on, "she didn't check on the baby when she came back out of the shop I mean."

Taylor frowned at the comment, "Why is it?" he countered scathingly. "She wasn't gone long, she says ten minutes, the baby didn't cry, why would she...... having to do the shopping was intruding into her day off."

Terri resented his persistent criticism, all she ever got from him. She stared at him defiantly retaliating with, "it's what you do when you're responsible for a baby as young as Phoebe is!" Taylor wanted to snigger at the response, clearly he'd rattled her and it rather pleased him. "The baby didn't cry," she retaliated wanting to wipe the smile off his face, "because she wasn't in the pram!"

Brendon Flannery could sense the conversation moving dangerously close to hostile.

"Where could she have gone if she isn't staying with her boyfriend?" He threw in trying to divert attention away from a head on collision.

"That's another thing," Terri continued, "She spoke confidently about being expected by Dorian Drover, her *boyfriend*, yet he denies it."

Harvey intervened, "You definitely got his name right?" he checked.

"I'm sure of it - I tracked him down through his mother," she reported. "It's too much of a coincidence they live a few houses down from the Devonshire's."

"Really?" Brendon's surprise reaction reflected everyone else's in the room.

"His mother says he didn't have a girlfriend even though he doesn't live with them."

"Where does he live?" Taylor asked his tone reflecting his irritation at her having achieved more than him so far.

"He lives in a house in town, near the station, with members of his band," she informed them. "He claims they were away doing a gig in Manchester and wouldn't be expecting her."

"Weird thing to say though," one of the other detectives commented. Everyone looked over to him, "Don't you think?"

"What is?" Terri asked.

"Well telling you he went on this gig, is sufficient, he already said he didn't know her, but to actually say he wasn't expecting her – why say that?" Silence followed leaving him feeling embarrassed at raising it. "You wouldn't say you were not expecting someone you didn't know." He emphasised. He could see everyone else didn't find it weird, so he shut up.

"Maybe she's just a groupie," Taylor suggested the snigger back on his face. Terri wanted to slap him as she felt her temper rise.

Taylor saw her seethe at his comment, not wishing to be outdone he added, "I've identified where the old woman lives, the one leaving the co-op when the Nanny went in," he looked over at Terri Wilson who seemed to be staring hard at him. "She has a flat in a sheltered housing complex not too far from the precinct, but hasn't been at home when I've called round."

"Her name is Mary Mundy. She lives at flat 6. She always goes out on a Tuesday to get her pension at the post office doing her shopping at the co-op after," Terri filled in as she saw Taylor's anger well up once again at her interruption. "Although once a week, usually on a Thursday, she goes to the library to exchange her books."

Harvey looked from Taylor to Wilson then back again trying to work out what the dynamics were between the two of them, the animosity clearly there for all to see.

"I think Mary Mundy is one of the ex-mental patients from the old Asylum when it closed down," Taylor inserted not wanting to be outdone by a 'uniform'.

"She's not good with people," Terri explained ignoring him. "She was very reluctant to let me in at first until I mentioned the missing baby; strange though how she wanted to talk about the baby. I found out she hadn't noticed the pram outside when she left the shop. I got the impression she deliberately hurries back home so she can avoid having to talk to anyone."

"She let you in?" Taylor's surprise was evident, although now greatly peeved to hear it.

"It's not personal to you Taylor, she genuinely dislikes talking. I really think she can't bring herself to speak to men in general, avoids it you might say," Terri explained.

"So if she didn't see the pram how did she hear about the missing baby, did she see it on the TV news?" Brendon asked.

"No she doesn't have a T.V.," Terri said, "But seems to be focussed on the missing baby – well more about finding a baby. She looked once or twice as if her mind kept wandering off somewhere else. I couldn't keep her fixed on Jocelyn Phipps and the pram."

Taylor felt the need to pull something back as attention focussed solely on Terri Wilson's endeavours - he didn't like it. "Maybe we ought to bring her in for questioning," he suggested, "after all she is a potential eye witness."

The thought of Taylor interviewing Mary Mundy horrified Terri; she felt he should be the last person to go near her. Before she knew it she'd already protested, "No!"

She knew she was in great danger of alienating herself completely from Taylor but didn't care. Everyone stared at her outburst.

When she didn't go on, Harvey asked, "Wilson?" waiting for her to explain herself.

"I get the impression her previous life was far from good, sir," she began. "She has a great fear of official people. She appears to me to be very vulnerable – I think we need to consider this, take it into account in our approaches to her."

Brendon could see how upset Terri appeared, he felt drawn towards helping her. "Perhaps we could go back to her place if she feels more comfortable there," it sounded feeble so he added, "Maybe she has a social worker or someone else who might be available to help us understand her history."

Terri stared at him as if seeing him for the first time, surprised he stood up for her like he just did. She looked over to see how Harvey took Brendon's suggestion.

"I still think we should bring her in here," Taylor protested. "If she knows something...."

"Okay," Harvey interrupted ignoring him. "If you think she would respond better with someone she knows with her, see what you can find out."

Terri heaved a sigh of relief glancing briefly at Taylor to assess his reaction. Taylor sat inwardly seething; he hated they ignored his opinion. He noted also the apparent bond he saw existing between Brendon and Terri immediately jumped to the wrong conclusion, seeing them in a close relationship meant only one thing. He sniggered knowingly.

CHAPTER 25

Brendon spent the night in fitful sleep. He could hear Nancy's low snoring at the side of him, for the first time it began to annoy him. The sound seemed to mock his insomnia, *'look at me I'm sleeping the sleep of the righteous.'* He got up, went into the bathroom, the hole in the door once again reminding him he needed to fix it. So far his fractured arm kept him from doing it.

"Not really," he thought, *"just little enthusiasm for anything domestic."*

He wandered down to the kitchen where the large American fridge, Nancy insisted they bought, beckoned him. His usual habit when he couldn't sleep, the cupboard where she kept the crisps and chocolate being his first port of call.

He opened the fridge door where the light from inside seemed brighter in the dimness of the kitchen. Nancy had obviously filled it that day with their week's shopping, the shelves were full.

The leftover spaghetti bolognaise sat in a plastic box begging to be reheated, normally he wouldn't think twice about having it. Today he felt his age and the excess weight he knew he'd piled on. Eating leftovers compensated for *feeling so unhappy* he thought. The extra pounds made him thicken out in the middle, often encouraging Nancy to remind him about getting fat. She took exercise classes, if anything looked thinner now, almost bony in comparison to how she once looked, *"in comparison to me"* he thought.

His hand hovered over the pasta then moved on taking some cold chicken. He left the door open whilst he flicked on the kettle to boil for coffee. The fridge began to beep impatiently; he murmured "alright!" as he found the light switch kicking the door closed with his foot.

He knew the coffee wouldn't help him sleep, drank it anyway sitting at the kitchen table eating the chicken, his thoughts moving back to the missing baby. *"Who would do something like that to a young mother?"* he thought. No ransom demand made so far, which indicated that maybe someone wanted a child desperately, not being able to have one of their own, or more likely someone who just lost their own impulsively taking the baby from the pram to ease their pain. Risky in such a public place, surely someone would have noticed? Although by all accounts Phoebe Devonshire wasn't usually seen out at the precinct as Fiona's groceries were delivered and the Nanny normally took the baby to the country park.

Brendon knew the park, would never forget the day he lost sight of his own daughter Rosie when quite little. The Park was in the opposite direction to the precinct although just as likely to be where someone local would see the distinctive coach built pram, recognising it parked outside the Co-op.

The logistics, he thought, of taking a baby out of a pram in the intervening ten minutes, leaving it covered exactly as they found it so no one would notice until they arrived back home, couldn't have been an easy manoeuvre. The only way within the time available would be to lift the pram cover at the bottom, pull the baby down through the length of the pram, hoping she wouldn't cry, then stretch the cover back over the edges. All this whilst holding a baby who could wake with the movement, suggested it was the act of someone who already decided to take it when they approached the pram.

"All very well," Brendon thought, *"but how would they see a teddy bear in there with the baby?"* Maybe the baby held it in her hand, came out of the pram clutching it. Brendon tried to think whether a three month old child was capable of clutching something like a

teddy bear. He remembered Rosie at the same age holding tightly onto his thumb, so he guessed she could. Searches of the area around the Co-op found nothing associated with the pram or the Nanny.

So far the only person anywhere near the pram or the Co-op within the specified time frame was Mary Mundy coming out of the shop. How could she not notice a pram parked outside? If as Terri said Mary Mundy knew about the missing baby – how could she? Finding out would be tricky, take patience with, hopefully, the help of someone familiar with Mary's history, might be possible. He could see Terri's alarm at the thought of Taylor interviewing her with all the finesse of a police door ramming device they used to break the locks when entering properties during raids.

Thinking about Taylor made him frown. The way he sounded angry when talking to Terri Wilson he'd noticed once or twice before. She seemed to upset him for no apparent reason. He could tell Harvey had noticed it today by the way he intervened. Brendon was pleased Harvey listened to her, being a good copper she had the makings of a detective he felt sure. She didn't mind putting in the effort and had sensitivity with people, to pick up the clues whilst talking to them; just the right person to interview the old lady. He'd have a word with Harvey to see if he'd let him go back with Terri.

This thought made him realise why he couldn't sleep. It was the first time since he got married he thought about another woman – it made him restless. He now admitted to himself that he liked her. She had integrity, didn't play games or try to catch him out or make him look stupid and he began to compare her to his wife.

Nancy always picked fault with him. He could still remember the time he could do no wrong in her eyes. It had all changed. Now she seemed to criticise him, finding any fault she could see or invent. Terri Wilson looked up to him, showing him respect, often asking his advice which made him feel…. he had begun to have feelings for her beyond his role as a mentoring Sergeant.

He began to see her as a very warm attractive woman, which made him feel ashamed just thinking it, but most of all he felt sorry for himself. The pain in his arm didn't help. He took a couple of painkillers with the last of his nearly cold coffee before he went back up to bed.

He turned towards Nancy slipping his good arm around her body hoping she might wake up like she used to do and give him a little much needed comfort. He felt her stir at his touch as he stroked her shoulder; she shrugged off his hand moving closer to the edge of the bed away from him. He turned over towards the edge on his side of the bed to try to go back to sleep.

CHAPTER 26

I hear the creaking noise above my head. I'm sitting in the big chair writing my daily thoughts. At first it sounds like an echo, some far away noise, like people passing through the long corridor where I found the door to this room.

I sit still listening to a muffled grunting noise. It's faint at first then it grows louder just as the light comes on. It isn't the one near where I'm sitting. Luckily I didn't put it on today because the sun is shining through the window, slanting down across the cabinet where I'm sitting in the big chair.

I'm petrified. If I stay here surely I'll be seen by whoever is coming down the steps. There's just enough time to slip down onto the floor, to crawl behind the chair into the corner; it's partly hidden by the wonky cabinet. I feel certain I will be found out. I push my paper and pencil underneath the cabinet where it's raised off the floor. By pulling my knees up I can just about tuck myself into the tiny space as tightly as I can manage. I hold my breath, my hand across my own mouth.

I can hear someone dragging something across the floor grunting under the strain of the burden. Then a muffled noise, it sounds like it's being made by a person, someone who is panicking. I can hear the noise get louder as they get nearer.

"Shssh!" a man's voice hisses so close I almost gasp.

I try to make myself even smaller, I want to scream, "Go away this is my place!" but keep the sound in with help from my hand across my mouth in case it tries to escape me.

I can feel movement in the cabinet as if something catches it a resounding blow, the movement pushes me forward a little. As I turn my head I catch sight of two people through the gap between the cabinet and the big chair.

I see the nurse who works on one of the wards where they put the new mental defectives like me. His hand is over a young girl's mouth and nose, her face looks red as if she is trying to breathe through a gap between two of his fingers, "if you don't..." he says fiercely, then I see him cover her mouth and nose entirely until her eyes stare wildly, move up behind her eye lids. He releases his hand as the young girl loses consciousness slipping down onto the bed in a heap. It is one of the old broken ones just to the side of the cabinet, I feel it move again.

I don't want to look so I pull backwards when I catch sight of him undoing his belt around his waist. Back behind the cabinet now I am unable to watch, knowing what he's going to do. The same as my father did to me before I came to this place.

I can still hear the nurse, first the rustling of his clothes, then the noises he makes doing that thing to her. The girl must have woken up because I can hear her crying, yelping with pain as his grunts get louder, he moves faster until he stops abruptly with an awful, "ahh!" noise they make when they stop, that's when the pain stops.

The young girl is still whimpering. I can hear the nurse rustling his clothes again. "If you tell anyone," he warns her, "I'll make your life so bad you'll want to end it yourself!"

She stops crying becoming completely silent. I lean forward to get another glimpse as they cross the room, I watch them moving up the stairs; she is being pushed by the nurse prodding her in the middle of her bony back.

The light above me goes out.

*   *   *   *

Today, being Tuesday, Mary made her shuffling way to the precinct and disappeared inside the post office. She could see the bright plastic toys lined up along the shelf to one side of a long queue of people waiting for their turn to be served. She didn't like waiting in line, it reminded her of all the years up at the Asylum, waiting for one thing or another, for medication or food. Sometimes a nurse stood there with a comb that she would dip from time to time in a metal dish of pungent Dettol.

She hated that one because if the nurse found some head lice she would shout, "This one!" push her towards another nurse who then shaved off all their hair, dusting the head in foul smelling powder which would sting in the cuts if the razor caught the skin.

Mary left the queue to go to examine what the post office displayed along the shelf today. The gap in the queue closed up as she lost her place. It meant she would take longer today to get back home, but she didn't mind when she saw some new ceramic figures, not the usual animals this time, but an assortment of figurines looking like angels. One particular one drew her attention; a lady holding a baby swaddled in a blanket with only its face peering out.

Mary stroked the tiny baby imagining one of its arms would suddenly reach out of the blanket trying to stroke the tip of her finger.

She tilted the figure upside down to look underneath for a price, knew it wouldn't matter how much it cost because Mary needed to have this one. She needed to have it because it was another omen just like the baby crying; a sign showing her baby still looked for her.

She looked back as the queue began to move faster. She took the lady with the baby taking it to re-join the line at the end. She knew better than to try to get her place back, people could be really mean, she knew it to her cost.

When she got to the counter ten minutes later she thrust her pension giro with the figure into the dip under the window waiting for the man to serve her. He smiled at her as if they were old friends, reached behind him for a box with a picture on the front which he compared to the figure. He showed Mary the price stuck on the side of the box for her approval.

Mary nodded her acceptance watching him count out the money from her giro into a pile, took out the price of the figure to one side, and placed the rest, with the figure now in the box, back under the window. Mary took them moving away from the window.

She put the money in her purse and together with the box into her shopping bag before she left the post office.

It didn't take her long once inside the Co-op to find all of her shopping. She rushed being eager to get back home to rearrange her treasures with her new purchase to be given pride of place, without disrupting the others too much, because Mary liked them as they were.

She wanted to place this mother and baby somewhere she could see it when she looked up; a prominent position which would allow her to see it from any angle in the room, but particularly from the armchair where she sat reading her books.

She found the ideal place for it on the shelf over her gas fire spending a good deal of time looking at the way the mother held the baby, imagining herself rocking her baby in her arms in the same way when the baby cried, although not often. She could feel it in her arms and moved them gently until the cries stopped. She heard the faint music from above, opened her eyes, took up her book and went back to her reading.

CHAPTER 27

Bernard Devonshire sat on the bed trying to shake off the fuzzy head, regretting he'd over indulged once again. It became the only way he could fall asleep at night. Usually quite disciplined, with a single focus when it came to his business interests, he never allowed anything to interfere with it. All diversions were strictly controlled, home, family, leisure even drinking excessively. He couldn't concentrate, without Fiona to attend to the everyday things.

He tried a number of times to telephone her, wishing he'd demonstrated a bit more self-control. After all she must be as distraught as him to have Phoebe taken. All aggression really achieved was to chase her away and it hadn't made him feel any better. He knew she didn't love him, how could she? He possessed no illusions about what he looked like, but then he possessed a lot of things that women really wanted in money and status, she seemed only too eager to comply.

He gave her as much as she asked for, even turned a blind eye to what he knew she thought he wouldn't notice her taking (Bernard wasn't a successful business man because he took his eye off the game); he'd always been meticulous about every detail when it came to money.

He talked to himself, severe thoughts passing through his alcohol soaked brain, telling himself to *'get a grip'* or lose everything. He was well aware he would never cope as a single poor man. He would find it difficult to attract anyone unless he had money.

He shook his head, felt the dull ache of his hangover rising, walked over to the bathroom finding the painkillers in the cabinet over the sink, he took two dry swallowing them. Wincing at the rising pain he took two more realising the headache would be fierce.

The shower helped as he stood letting the hot water run over him. Revived he dressed casually in beige slacks, and a blue polo shirt leaving bending to put on his socks until later when the sick headache would begin to settle.

He stood in the doorway of the kitchen, a place he only ever saw looking pristine and sparkling – one thing Fiona did do, although until now he'd not appreciated it.

The mess of stacked takeout boxes, micro-wave 'ping' meal wrappings, dirty cups and plates of uneaten versions of the said take-out 'ping' meals made the kitchen look like a disaster area. He sighed heavily beginning to do what he hadn't done for decades, clear up his own mess. During the process his head gradually returned to normal; well not normal, more a numbed state of functioning he could deal with.

He scraped, washed and stacked the dishes in the dishwasher, throwing all the debris into the large flip top waste bin with the black bag liner to throw away all the evidence of his first ever show of weakness. He saw the past few days of sinking into self-pity – weakness.

He, Bernard Devonshire, had never been a weak man, he told himself. *"I didn't get where I am today...."* He thought, *"Who said that?"* He was right to remind himself of it.

He stood surveying the sparkling kitchen which seemed unreal, like looking at a magazine for the first time noting every feature, every labour-saving gadget he bestowed on Fiona together with the rest of the immaculately furnished house. He felt the beginning of his suppressed anger threatening to rear up to take hold again.

"NO!" he told himself voicing it out loud this time. "You will not beat me!" he vowed although his determined threat, directed at no one in particular, could easily have applied to his destructive anger. He knew it wasn't the way to go.

"Don't get angry, get even," he thought. He would begin with whoever took his precious Phoebe. Her face rose in his mind, sweet smiling Phoebe, giggling at the faces he pulled to elicit a smile in those rare moments when, in her cot late at night, he would go into the nursery to spend moments with his sleeping treasure. She would wake looking up at him with those innocent baby eyes. She would gurgle trying to speak back as he whispered, "My precious girl" stroking her cheek whilst pulling faces to make her laugh.

His darling Phoebe was the only person who didn't seem to mind how ugly he looked, and the only one who looked back at him with absolute 'real' affection. Unconditional love he prized above anything in his life. The only person who asked nothing of him other than the attention he bestowed on her. She would yawn, purse her lips, her eyelids would flutter as she fell back to sleep.

He stood in the doorway of the nursery room where the empty cot, he noticed, had several smudges on the white surfaces, the changing table, even the chest of draws also. He frowned until he remembered the dusting powder used by the police forensics. It puzzled him. What were they looking for?

Bernard Devonshire had to be an intelligent man to be able to amass the kind of money this house represented and more which he had secretly stashed away. It didn't take many minutes for him to work out the police were looking for any signs of foul play – but why here when they took her from her pram outside the co-op where that stupid girl left her alone?

He could see something further back on the floor under the cot. He walked over bent down feeling blindly underneath. He grasped something soft between his first two fingers and pulled. The tiny teddy bear, Mr Cuddles, he brought her back from one of his trips away, discretely hidden in his brief case. He remembered giving it her during one of his nocturnal visits; the tiny bear with the blue chiffon bow became her favourite even at this age because he used the bear to talk to her to make her giggle.

He looked down at the bear in his hand waiting for it to speak, to tell him where to find Phoebe, or to tell him why he wasn't with her in her pram when she went out. Of course the bear couldn't do that. Bernard smiled, walked back to his office, put the bear into his brief case once again, it was all he had left of her. He knew sometimes words were not necessary.

CHAPTER 28

Mike Harvey arrived back home, another late night feeling utter frustration at the flagging case. With a missing baby, one as young as Phoebe Devonshire, there was usually some kind of a lead, a sighting of someone seen by a member of the public or at least a ransom demand, but so far nothing. Forensics on or around where the pram stood outside the shop drew a blank.

The only finger prints of any note were those of her mother or the Nanny in keeping with the impression they held of Bernard Devonshire's absence in the care of his daughter.

Harvey slumped into an armchair in his living room of the flat where he lived alone, totally fatigued by yet another long frustrating day. He flicked on the T.V as he sipped another coffee, the first thing he did when he arrived back. Whilst he waited for the kettle to boil he slipped two slices of bread into the toaster, put on the cooker grill whilst slicing pieces of cheese from a block in the almost empty fridge. He spread them randomly onto the lightly browned toast when it popped up putting them under the grill to melt the cheese. He topped the cheese with tomato ketchup from a squeezy bottle on the side, retired to the comfy armchair to watch the 10.00 o'clock news whilst he ate his meagre meal.

Times like these he felt relieved living alone. He didn't always feel like that. In the beginning, after his divorce, he missed the closeness of belonging. The shock came late one night when his wife Shirley declared her intention to leave him. "What's the point," she said calmly, "in being married to someone who is never here?" He was married to the job whilst she was so very lonely.

He didn't put up much of a protest, he couldn't argue with anything she said, even when she stood still at the door as she left, "At least you haven't made any half-hearted promises to change because we both know it isn't ever going to happen."

What could he say? Except after his girls left home there just didn't seem like there was anything left. It all wound down like a tired old clock, they had both kept ticking until the last one left home. Somehow the clock ticked on for a while in a last but dying way until it stopped altogether. Coming home ceased to be the biggest part of his life. The job took over completely until it became his whole life. Coming home becoming just a place where he slept for a few hours until it was time to go back to work again.

Mike Harvey's eyes drooped as he ate his cheese on toast watching the news moving from one world crisis to another. He fell asleep as he did most nights in the same chair. The glow of the screen finally dying as it went into sleep mode, cutting off any light in the room, which plunged the half eaten toast and half-drunk coffee into the semi-gloom of what little light filtered in through the vertical slats of the blinds against the one window.

Outside the street lamp would eventually plunge the whole room into pitch darkness as it cut out like most of them did these days to conserve energy to meet council precepts.

When the burring sound of his phone woke him up Mike found himself in total blackness unable to work out where he was. He could feel the vibration of his mobile phone against the lining of his trouser pocket as it continued to make the 'burring' sound. He moved his body trying to extract it.

When he flipped the leather cover the light penetrated the gloom. Mike recognised the shape of his wood burning stove, knew he'd fallen asleep again after coming home. The cold cheese on toast with his teeth marks lay on the coffee table, testament to just how quickly he succumbed to the need for sleep. His head held a dull ache as he squinted at the mobile screen. He didn't recognise the number nevertheless he pressed it into life, knowing no one would phone at this hour for a social reason.

"Hello?" he said as he answered.

"Central control room here, is that Chief Inspector Harvey?"

Mike felt the inevitable sinking feeling being on call for the night.

"Yes, Control, what's happening?" he asked with great reluctance. The one thing he needed above anything else was a good night's sleep free from interruptions.

"Uniform got a call out to a drugs overdose they are requesting CID," the control room operator heard Mike groan, "They think it looks suspicious," she added.

"Okay," Mike replied reluctantly, "Where?"

The operator relayed the directions to an alleyway at the side of 'Speed Dial' one of the towns more popular nightspots that Mike knew maintained a history of drug related activity, one which he heard the drugs squad threatened to have closed down having raided it a number of times.

When he arrived at the scene having driven there with his window open despite the cold night, it was nearly half past two in the morning. He could see a number of the club's revellers hanging around the main entrance with the heavy door operatives trying to move them on. He watched a group of young girls scantily clad seemingly oblivious to the biting cold night swaying on wobbly legs, shouting loudly at each other, the worse for drink. One girl in a short skirt held another girl's long hair back as she threw up against the wall of the nightclub.

Mike thought about his own girls, briefly wondered what kind of things they might get up to. He always thought of his eldest Gilly quite the serious studious one; although he had confidence she was nothing like these girls. But then, what did he know? He hardly ever saw them these days. Bethany, his youngest, being the rebel of the two, so who knew what she would be like.

As he walked down to meet the uniforms he tried to put them out of his mind, not wanting to think this young girl could be one of his daughters; being a cop you never knew whether you would get a call out to someone you might know, let alone be related to you.

The constable waiting at the top of the alley spotted him as he got nearer to him.

"Guv," he greeted.

"Evening," Mike said realising the hour made it strictly the morning but he didn't correct himself. "What have we got?"

"It's a young girl, sir," he began. "Found by a couple who were….let's just say getting better acquainted." He blushed as Mike looked down the semi-dark alley. "It's quite a popular place at kicking out time." He knew it also served as a place where the revellers could secure an assortment of recreational drugs from various dealers who turned up to service their needs.

Mike could see the forensic doctor already examining the body kneeling alongside the prone figure. Mike knew the Forensic pathologist having met him on a number of occasions in the past although he was surprised to see him dressed in a dinner jacket with a bow tie under his chin; always a smart middle-aged man, he felt it somewhat excessive.

"A bit overdressed Jim," Mike greeted him without smiling. The pathologist looked up scowling at him.

"Rotary dinner," he said also not smiling.

"Bad luck," Mike commiserated. "I nearly got a night's sleep." He didn't smile either. "What can you tell me?" he asked as he watched him turn the body over.

"Hard to say, uniform thought it an overdose given where she's been found," he picked up the arms to check for track marks finding them clear. He turned the girls head facing forwards from where it flopped to one side and heard Mike gasp when he saw the face as the shock registered. "You recognise her, Mike?" he asked peering up at him.

"Err, yes," Mike said. "Her name is Jocelyn Phipps who is the Nanny of a missing baby case I've got –she was also reported missing."

Mike sat down squatting on his heels peering at the face of the young girl he interviewed briefly only a short time ago. "How did she die?" he asked.

"Can't say at the moment, although there are some marks on her neck and she has blood in her hair. I can't tell you if it could be an overdose given where we are."

Mike stood up turned to look at the alley where several large rubbish bins stood. The body had been hidden behind them lying slumped on the ground.

"She looks very much like she may have been dumped here," Jim commented. "Face down."

"You mean if it is an overdose she would probably be sitting?" Mike asked.

"Or at least lying face up," he said. "Just a thought."

They were joined by Taylor-Smythe who walked up to them yawning.

"Is it for us?" he asked looking down at the body. "Pretty girl." He observed casually.

"This is Jocelyn Phipps, our missing Nanny," Mike told him.

"Bloody hell," Taylor exclaimed. "What happened?"

"We don't know yet," Mike said.

Taylor looked around the alley, "How did she get here?"

Mike Harvey stood up, "It's an interesting question. This place is known for its drug dealing activity, perhaps she came to buy, might have got herself into some sort of trouble." he suggested without much conviction. "Find out if she has any transport will you Taylor?"

Taylor scratched his head. Harvey could see the puzzlement on his face. Mike Harvey being no less stymied by this sudden turn of events, turned going back up the alley to where the uniform officer he spoke to earlier stood talking to the young couple he assumed found Jocelyn Phipps' body. He sighed knowing it was going to be a long night.

CHAPTER 29

The CID briefing next morning kicked off early despite Mike Harvey only managing a short two hours of sleep after the call out; he'd tried to revive himself with a hot shower. He made no attempt at breakfast, a habit he long since succumbed to, *"why bother,"* he thought, *"when there's a bread shop just up the road"* that did a roaring trade in take-out bacon or sausage baps?

The large metal tea pot stood on the side already made waiting for everyone to arrive. One of the young DCs having gone out for a shipping order to the Crusty Cob on the corner was busily dishing out the white bags whilst taking in the coinage for each one. When Harvey emerged from his office he was already chewing on his breakfast. Someone handed him a mug of tea.

"Okay, let's start," he called watching as everyone settled down for the briefing. "I expect you've all heard we were called out to the alley behind the Speed Dial nightclub about two o'clock this morning by uniform. The body of Jocelyn Phipps was found by a couple of clubbers who were using the alley," here he faltered and coughed, "let's just say to get better acquainted."

A raucous giggling ensued then someone said, "Bet that put them off their stroke!" Mike Harvey scowled at the comment. He couldn't remember the last time he got close to a woman since he split from his wife Shirley, having given up on that side of his life, burying himself in his work. It took the edge off the ache of the loss.

He noticed everyone staring as his thoughts drifted. He told himself to get a grip, he carried on, "We don't know how she got where we found her. She was meant to be visiting her boyfriend Dorian Drover who denies being her boyfriend and all knowledge of seeing her." He looked over at Terri Wilson as if seeking backing for the remark.

"I've given it a lot of thought sir," Terri responded to his non-verbal cue, "She definitely said Dorian and seemed quite agitated by not meeting him earlier."

"Do you suppose he expected her to go with the band on their gig?" Brendon asked. When Mike met his gaze he added, "We've only got his word for it he wasn't seeing her."

"You mean he could have murdered her in a fit of anger because she turned up late," Taylor sarcasm undeniable. "It's a bit farfetched."

"According to Dorian they were travelling during the day for the evening gig....." Terri began.

"Yes, how long would it take to get to Manchester for an evening appearance?" Terri asked.

Harvey interrupted the turn of the briefing, "It's all speculation," he said. "What we need is some facts, get verification of the gig....let's start with Dorian Drover - bring him in, he did by his own admission meet her. Taylor take it will you?"

"What about Mr Devonshire, sir?" Terri asked.

"Yes Terri," Harvey agreed. "Let's find out where he was last night. Can you take the post mortem please Flannery, get uniform to take you." Brendon nodded. He wore his frustration at his limitations clearly visible on his face. "I don't want you anywhere near Bernard Devonshire," Mike warned.

At the mention of his name Brendon looked away, he felt guilty he'd allowed everyone to believe his fractured arm happened because of his set-to with Bernard Devonshire. He'd even tried to convince himself the first blow to his arm caused a weakness, maybe the beginnings of a hairline fracture which his son made worse. Maybe....

"When I returned to Blackheath Avenue," Terri said. "Bernard Devonshire seemed a different person."

"How?" Harvey asked.

"He seemed quite vulnerable, very subdued - he isn't coping well on his own."

Brendon looked up sharply, "I wouldn't let it fool you!" his sharpness revealed his dislike. "He's capable of anything."

"What? Killing his Nanny?" Taylor said once again mocking. "I suppose you think he's killed his wife as well?"

Whilst Taylor's comments were meant more to ridicule than make positive suggestions, Harvey had become increasingly irritated by his detectives squabbling amongst themselves.

"Can we PLEASE get back to some old fashioned detective work? I want facts not speculation – we're getting nowhere and the clock is ticking on our kidnap case. Now this!" He stormed off back into his office leaving his officers stunned by his outburst.

CHAPTER 30

Still smarting from Harvey's obvious annoyance at his comments Taylor watched as Terri and Brendon left the CID office to call at the North Road sheltered housing complex. They failed to see his curious stares as his eyes followed them through the door. He still felt the need to have Mary Mundy fetched into the station for interview being the one remaining witness.

Instead, he'd been tasked with bringing Dorian Drover in and he was reputed to be nowhere near the precinct when the baby disappeared. A phone call to the on duty uniform section took care of it leaving him free to make a few on line enquiries via his computer to check out the golf pro Peter Thompson to see what he could discover about him. He thought him suspicious, there was something not quite right about his story, denying knowing Fiona Devonshire when he clearly saw them together with his own eyes, wouldn't you at least introduce yourself under those circumstances? The signs were there of some kind of intimacy as he'd watched them together.

*   *   *   *

Terri Wilson drove Brendon via a circuitous route which raised an enquiring eyebrow from her Sergeant. He sat quietly contemplating his disturbed night from thoughts of her, now feeling uncomfortable in her presence. He was glad of the diversion when he realised they were off course for Mary Mundy's place.

"Where are we going?" He asked his curiosity peaking.

"Blackheath," Terri replied.

"Err, I'm supposed to avoid all contact with Devonshire," he reminded her. "You heard what Harvey said, it's not like him I know…. he wasn't himself today." Brendon felt alarmed at his outburst, having worked with him for a lot of years, he never once saw him this rattled, even when his wife left him.

"No, Sarge," she replied, "I wouldn't do that to you." She noticed just how close No 27 was to Bernard Devonshire's house and knew what the repercussions would be if Brendon met with him for round two. "I want your thoughts on Frances Drover, Dorian's mother," she sounded cryptic. "She's not quite right." Terri couldn't explain what she meant, just felt there was something wrong so she wanted Brendon to meet her to assess her statements.

They could see down the road the ornate electronic gates of 58 Blackheath Avenue, firmly closed against the handful of news media still congregating outside.

They got out of the car, stood observing what little activity still remained, most of the Nationals having long since departed, losing interest in a baby snatch where there was no ransom demand or obvious domestic confrontation. A few of the locals stayed clinging to the hope of a late ransom demand coming in. Clearly the news of the Nanny's death hadn't filtered through yet.

Terri turned away from the sight of them, her attention on the Drover house which once again seemed deserted. She rang the bell again having forgotten it didn't seem to work, so rattled the letterbox again. Brendon raised his eyebrows shrugging. They heard the clatter of the door chain watching the crack in the door open to the full extent of the chain.

Frances Drover peered out like last time, recognising Terri from her previous visit she said, "I told you Dorian doesn't live here."

"Yes, I know Mrs Drover, I found him at the address you gave me," Terri said. "We just need a word with you, if you would spare some time."

Frances Drover sighed, took the chain off the door and reluctantly let them in. Fully dressed this time it didn't lend any substance to her, Terri thought, she looked even frailer than the last time she saw her; quite undernourished, like a gust of wind might knock her over.

She led them into a sitting room with poor visibility, the curtains being closed against the sunlight. It smelt of stale tobacco and the room was thick with a smoky hazy atmosphere.

Frances Drover sat down in the one armchair in the room but didn't invite the police officers to sit; they did anyway.

"What is it you want?" she asked sharply.

"I wonder if you've noticed the activity down the Avenue a little way?" Terri asked.

Frances Drover stared at Terri, reached across towards a coffee table where they could see a large ash tray full of cigarette butts almost overflowing. She picked up a pack of cigarettes from beside it, took out a cigarette placing it in her mouth then lit it with a lighter from the inside of the pack. She inhaled deeply like it was the first hit of the day slipping the lighter back in the pack before she placed it down next to the ash tray again.

Terri was just about to repeat her question when Frances Drover answered, "I don't go out," she simply said. "I can't...." she stopped as if any more words would hurt her.

Brendon looked at Terri to assess her reaction.

"At all?" Terri queried.

Frances Drover slowly shook her head, "It's hard...." She began to explain getting no further with it.

"Take your time Mrs Drover," Brendon spoke up seeing how hard she found it.

She looked over at Brendon as if seeing him for the first time, sensing the sympathy in his words drew encouragement from them and tried to continue, "It just got harder every time I went out....you know, shopping...." They both nodded. "I would rush back here in panic to find I'd forgotten what I went for," she looked anxious thinking about it, gazing off into the distance as if seeing something they couldn't or to find what she meant to say next, whilst the pause grew.

She looked back at them, a slight twitch indicating she had forgotten they were there seeming surprised seeing them sitting together on the couch. "Sometimes I couldn't take a step over the doorstep," she said reliving whatever nightmare vision it brought back to her. "Then one day I just stopped going out there at all. The terror I felt inside eased off eventually until I didn't feel it anymore. I never tried again."

As she finished Terri wanted to shiver but managed to control her reflexes. She felt absolute sadness for the poor woman's plight.

"Do you see anyone who can help you with it Mrs Drover?" Brendon asked. He'd heard about agoraphobia although never met anyone with it, he knew how totally debilitating it could be. He felt pity seeing her very much as a prisoner in her own house. Terri regarded the overflowing ash tray thinking no wonder she smoked so much.

Frances Drover shook her head again, "Even if I knew who could help me," she kept Brendon's eye contact. "How would I be able to go to see them?"

"What about your doctor, Mrs Drover?" Terri saw the woman sigh; she looked almost fatigued by the questions.

"Doctors don't come out to see you anymore, if you can walk they expect you to go to the surgery.....I can't...." The words didn't come; she looked like the effort might finish her off.

"But surely if your condition...." The sharp stare from Frances Drover cut Terri off from finishing the sentence. It sounded like a Catch 22 situation, although she wanted to add, "...*prevents you going out, a doctor would come to you?"* It seemed obvious yet she felt it might be a naïve thing to say.

"For which you need a diagnosis," she said with just a hint of exasperation, "To get one you need to see a doctor...." She shrugged which summed up all of her frustrations in one final acceptance. She continued to take a lungful of cigarette smoke, exhaling a cloud to add to the general fug in the room. Then in a small voice devoid of any emotion but racked with fatigue she added, "Can you imagine what it's like to be confined to one small world with no means of escape?"

Terri and Brendon couldn't imagine living like this, understanding the chain smoking as they watched her stub out the cigarette in the overflowing ash tray then immediately taking another with the lighter from the pack, lit it once again concentrating on the first deep inhalation, closing her eyes as she did.

"I take it your husband....." Terri referred to the black police book she took out of her pocket, "James?" she queried. "Does all the shopping for you?"

Frances Drover flashed a quick piercing look that Terri missed by once again looking down at her note book. Brendon caught it in passing.

Frances Drover didn't reply, instead she asked, "Why have you come?" as if she just noticed them again.

Terri looked back up meeting her steady stare, "We are making house to house enquiries," she lied. "Do you know the Devonshire's at number 58 down the road?"

Frances Drover's forehead creased slightly indicating she was contemplating the question, and then her head moved from side to side once again.

"I don't go out," she repeated as if it were sufficient an explanation which she'd forgotten she already told them.

They found themselves walking away from the house both deep in thought, both thinking how devastating it must be to someone's life if they couldn't take one step over the threshold everyone else took for granted.

Neither of them at this point considered asking her if she knew Jocelyn Phipps who was supposed to be her son's girlfriend. As they got to the gate they looked back down the Avenue seeing increased activity outside the ornate gates where a fresh surge of media activity and mobile units were arriving and once again blocking the entire road. A police traffic car rushed past as they stood there, its blue light flashing a warning of its approach.

The news of Jocelyn Phipps' body being found had finally been released.

CHAPTER 31

Sitting at his desk Taylor-Smythe scratched his head; so far his computer enquiries had drawn a blank. That is apart from a superficial confirmation of Peter Thompson's live-in golf pro role. Trevor assumed he lived in one of the two unremarkable semi-detached houses closest to the club house. Being a golfing person himself, Taylor felt better placed than most to know about the workings of golf clubs.

His next moved him to the internet where he searched for the Golf Club's address, fetching up their website he found it surprisingly well established. The one he belonged to had just recently computerised and was not nearly as accomplished being work in progress as it stated when you logged into it.

This one he found most informative, noting that whoever designed it must be a newcomer to computing as they hadn't yet learnt about privacy settings. He knew you could limit access to the general public or certain sections of the membership allowing, for example, only members to view photographs taken at social functions. This website lay open to anyone who cared to view it.

He pressed on 'social activities' fetching up a list of previous social functions, and also dates for future events. He brought up the last Christmas' dinner/dance with a synopsis of the event as it played out, obviously whoever maintained it fancied themselves as a bit of a blogger and an amusing one at that.

Just about to press his cursor against 'photographs' the telephone on his desk began to ring.

"Taylor-Smythe," he sounded irritated being disturbed.

The on-duty custody sergeant informed him Dorian Drover, brought in by 'uniform', now sat in Interview Room one waiting his attention. Trevor sighed as the first pictures of the golf club's festive function loaded onto his screen. *"Bloody timing,"* he thought reluctantly closing his access to the Golf Club website, he hadn't expected quite such a rapid response from uniform. He knew from his own experience of fetching someone in, it could easily develop into a 'jolly', or an impromptu café break.

He tentatively knocked on Harvey's door to inform him of Dorian Drover's arrival, hoping Harvey would now be in a better mood and not still irritated by him.

"Come!" he heard Harvey yell registering from the tone of it, no such luck.

"Dorian Drover is in interview room one, sir," Taylor announced. He thought Harvey looked drawn as if he hadn't slept properly for days.

He didn't normally notice such things, as people's wellbeing didn't register high on his radar, except it did on this occasion because he thought Harvey didn't like him. To Taylor-Smythe this wasn't something that would ordinarily be of any concern to him. What people thought of him rarely affected him anyway, so focussed was he on his own career.

On the other hand he reluctantly conceded Harvey to be instrumental in his future career prospects. His sole focus being to portray himself as the modern skilled detective with the most potential for promotion.

So far he had to admit it was slow going, mostly down to Flannery whom he regarded as the 'blue-eyed boy' blocking his way, and felt totally out of date and inept. At least it ticked along, until the uniformed Wilson girl stuck her nose in. Her handling of the baby snatch witnesses showed her more qualified to be a social worker than a copper; he had little time for social workers.

Everything seemed to be going her way. Getting an interview with the old woman whilst he couldn't, showed just how lucky she was.

"Is Wilson around?" Harvey snapped as if he read Trevor's mind.

It startled him out of his thoughts, "Err, no sir, she's out somewhere with Flannery," he said seeing Harvey frown he took it to mean his annoyance must be caused by her absence. In fact, Mike Harvey yet again picked up the tone Taylor used; his reference to his sergeant as 'Flannery' showed a blatant disrespect Harvey was tuned into.

He snapped back irritably, "I'm sure Detective Sergeant Flannery will be 'out' following up my instructions...." He wanted to add, *"Whereas you have been sitting at your desk all morning,"* but Harvey bit his tongue saying nothing. He wasn't sure whether his concerns about Taylor-Smythe's attitude, especially his behaviour towards his colleagues were real, or a direct reflection of his frustrations with his own non-working life.

Harvey, usually a cautious man, liked to assess all information before he acted. He had a reputation for never making rash decisions, for collecting all the evidence, dotting every 'i', crossing every 't', before making an arrest or charging someone. In so doing he accrued an exemplary record of convictions and successful prosecutions.

Likewise as a Chief Inspector, a manager of staff, he wouldn't act on gut instinct if faced with a staffing problem. There would be no come back on him for getting it wrong. He backed off, "Right!" he stood up resignedly, "Let's go talk to this Dorian Drover, see what he has to say about Jocelyn Phipps."

Taylor breathed a sigh of relief as he followed Mike Harvey out of CID.

CHAPTER 32

Brendon immediately became fascinated by Mary Mundy, watching her as her head wobbled. Averting her eyes she never once met his own although once or twice they paused on Terri's face. He let Terri take the lead feeling instinctively the old lady would respond more easily to her questions. He noted the frailty of this woman highlighted by having just left Frances Drover; he could see the similarity in their circumstances. He knew, of course, Mary Mundy did go out otherwise she wouldn't have nearly collided with Jocelyn Phipps on Tuesday outside the Co-op.

"Mary," he heard Terri once again speaking interrupting the image of Frances Drover replaying in his head, "This is Sergeant Flannery." Mary neither looked at Brendon nor acknowledged his presence, her head Brendon noticed wobbled a little faster. "I wonder if you could tell us again about meeting the girl outside the Co-op."

Mary's face turned to Terri with a look of puzzlement on it, her head stopped wobbling.

"Girl?" she asked genuinely curious.

"You told me about a girl who nearly bumped into you when you came out of the Co-op with your shopping," it concerned Terri the old woman might actually be in the first stages of Alzheimer's, something she hadn't noticed before but knew about from her own Gran's condition before she died.

"Oh, that girl," Mary said. Terri sighed with relief. "The one you told me left her baby outside?" She queried with disapproval Terri noticed.

"Yes, Mary," she confirmed. "Can you tell us what she looked like?"

Mary frowned, "I didn't see her baby," she said simply.

"No, not the baby, Mary....what did the girl look like, the one who nearly bumped into you?"

Mary's head began its slow movement as they watched her thinking about the question.

"They are all small and frail," Mary began. "They all look the same."

Brendon gave an involuntary cough which caused Mary Mundy to flinch, her eyes flicked sideways towards him, her gaze not making it to his face.

"Take your time Mary," Terri encouraged soothingly.

"Short hair," Mary looked up into the face of Terri for the first time with a steady real-world focus, her hand coming up to her own head waving at her forehead she added, "Cut delicate around her face making her look really young, but she's older than most of them."

"How old would you have put her Mary?" Terri asked gently seeing her focussed on Jocelyn Phipps.

"Maybe twenty," she said. "But she's tall."

"Did you notice what she was wearing?" Terri asked having read the statement from Fiona Devonshire she knew her Nanny wore denim jeans, a green t-shirt with a black cotton jacket.

Mary frowned again as her memory searched for the image of the girl, "Not the usual dress," she said as if the memory disturbed her.

"Usual dress?" Terri prompted.

"The ones they made us all wear, they were fawn," she looked at Terri for confirmation of the word, "light brown," she added.

Terri recognised her mind once again slipping back in time to the Asylum days and wished she'd waited for the social worker to arrive.

"The girl you met outside the Co-op wasn't from the hospital Mary," Brendon's voice sounded deeply resonant against the quietness of the room. Mary jerked slightly as if his voice made her jump pulling her thoughts back from a different time. She looked at Brendon for the first time.

"I know that," Mary answered. "She reminded me of the young girls with the swollen bellies, poor mites."

"How was she like them, Mary," he went on whilst he'd got her attention.

Without hesitation she said, "She looked frightened – they all did when they arrived. I used to care for them." Mary almost smiled but didn't quite make it. She looked from Terri back to Brendon. "I used to sing to them like my mother used to sing to me if I had a bad nightmare."

"They were very lucky to have you there," Brendon said although he knew Mary hadn't been lucky to be there at all. His mind wanted to use his voice to shout his anger at what he knew they did to her in those days.

They were interrupted by a knock on the flat door. Brendon realised they had forgotten to warn Mary about her social worker coming to the interview. Mary tentatively got up to answer it leaving Brendon and Terri together for a moment.

"The poor woman," Brendon whispered. "What the bloody hell did these places do to patients?"

"According to her social worker when I arranged this," Terri told him. "They put young unmarried pregnant girls in Asylums to hide the shame to their families, then took their babies away because they were deemed to be mentally deficient therefore not able to care for them." She saw the stark anger on Brendon's face.

"The bastards!" Brendon spat under his breath just as Mary appeared back in the room leading a young stocky woman who bustled in red in the face.

"So sorry!" She gushed. "Traffic – there's some sort of incident blocking the road – had to turn back, divert to another route....." She seemed flustered and obviously out of breath from hurrying.

"Never mind," said Terri reluctant to interrupt the interview now it began to go well. She feared they would have to start all over again losing momentum. "You're here now," she placated the woman who sat down unzipping a large black leather file case, searching through the contents for a specific file which she took out and proceeded to scan the contents.

"We were just asking Mary about a young girl she almost bumped into last Tuesday outside the Co-op supermarket," Brendon recapped watching the social worker ignore him.

"Who is this lady?" Mary asked.

"She's your social worker," Terri reminded her.

"Well actually I'm not," the woman said. "Mary's social worker is away on sick leave. I've been given the case whilst she's away," the woman sounded frantic, "adding yet another case to my already impossible workload."

Brendon's hackles rose, more because of hearing Mary referred to as a 'case' than the fact she obviously hadn't caught up with Mary's history, knew nothing about her.

"The point of you being here is to give Mary someone who knows her," Brendon tried hard to keep his cool and not allow his anger to overflow.

The social worker looked abashed, fussing over the folder in front of her. "Her social worker," the woman emphasised with underlying tones of frustration, "is off sick due to sheer pressure of this job which puts even more pressure on the rest of us."

Terri could see the interview slipping away, "Look let's leave this, Mary doesn't need this kind of disruption."

The social worker stuffed the file back into the leather document holder, stood up to leave. "I'm sorry," she said turning to leave without a word to Mary.

Brendon and Terri exchanged glances. Mary leaned towards them saying in a whisper, "The other lady is nicer, very caring."

"I'm glad to hear it, Mary," Brendon said. "I would hate to think you were given someone who wasn't."

Mary smiled again. She pointed at Brendon's plastered arm. "Does it hurt?" She asked.

Brendon looked down at his plastered arm as if it belonged to someone else. "Not so much," he assured her.

Terri could see Brendon made a connection with Mary, "Our job can also be a difficult one," She commented.

Mary's eyebrows rose in surprise but she said nothing in response, instead she asked, "Is the girl in trouble for leaving the baby outside?"

"No Mary, not really," Brendon said. "Could you hear the baby crying when you left the shop?" he asked.

Mary shook her head, "If she had been, I would have noticed."

"You told me you didn't see the pram," Terri reminded her.

"No I didn't, I always rush back home once I've got my shopping," Mary said. "It's nearly my morning tea time, y'see."

Mary glanced up, her vision seemed to focus on something off in the distance as Brendon and Terri saw their interview slip away.

Mary focussed on the shelf over the gas fire; it settled on a figurine of an angel holding a swaddled baby in her arms

Mary's head slowly wobbled.

CHAPTER 33

Dorian Drover was another arrogant sort Taylor instantly detested.

"Why have you brought me here?" he demanded rudely as Harvey and Taylor came into the interview room. He stood leaning against the wall seeming to spring into life immediately the door opened. Harvey winced as he lunged forward.

"Sit down!" he yelled fiercely to their surprise.

Drover stopped in his tracks retreating instantly at some perceived underlying tone in the command. Harvey gained his composure adding in almost a whisper, "If you would please, sir," he added politely.

The incident left Harvey a little alarmed at his own reaction, the feelings momentarily rising in him were totally alien to him. He rarely felt intimidated by the people he dealt with, mostly feeling only a sense of pity for them. On this occasion he put his feelings down to lack of sleep or the pressures this new murder enquiry placed on him. Why it should, given the number of cases he often had in the past, didn't occur to him. He needed a reason why he felt as he did, one easier and simpler to explain it.

"Mr. Drover," Harvey calmed himself, then looked at Dorian Drover for the first time, pausing as he took in what he could only describe as an over-privileged 'fop'. *Where the hell did that thought come from,"* ran through his head as he took in this tall rather delicate looking man – no boy – his inner voice corrected him, *"he's only a boy."*

Mindful of both Dorian Drover and Taylor-Smythe staring at him, his gaze fell on Taylor, noticing his smart suit and fancy tie for the first time. *"Two peas in a pod"* he thought assigning them both to the same 'foppish' type.

He shook his head to rid himself of both images making the inevitable connection.

"Mr Drover," Harvey began again, "I understand one of my officers came to see you?"

Dorian Drover found Harvey strangely intimidating. All the frustrations he felt whilst waiting for him to arrive disappeared to be replaced by a growing fear. A fear born out of numerous conversations in his student days when his political views centred on anti-establishment and police brutality, something he spent much of his time protesting about.

He flicked back the heavy fringe of hair that flopped into his eye as it often did, his head giving a subtle yet effeminate tilt Taylor caught instantly.

"Would you like something to drink?" Taylor found himself asking, interrupting his boss who looked somewhat startled by it.

Dorian Drover also seemed alarmed. He had heard about police tactics, 'good-cop'/ 'bad cop' being a ploy he recognised from watching police dramas on TV which fuelled his disquiet.

"Err, no thank you," he responded hesitatingly waiting for the older man, he thought of him as the 'nasty' one, to intercede with some hard line. "What is this all about?" he finally dared to ask. "I did have a visit from a police woman looking for a girl I met once."

"Who was she?" Harvey asked fully back to himself once more.

"I can't remember her name, or even if she gave it to me," he replied. He remembered the young police officer but couldn't remember whether she even said her name being woken so suddenly and half asleep at the time. "She was black though."

Harvey straightened in his chair picking up some underlying yet vaguely masked feelings attached to the one word 'black' which raised an alarm and which he let ride on this occasion.

Now if Taylor had said it he would have had to deal with it. However, the moment drew Mike Harvey's attention to the emerging idea that the animosity he noticed between Taylor and PC Wilson could have deeper origins. He tried to put it out of his mind.

He involuntarily shook his head again to clear it only making him look impatient as he said, "No Mr Drover, not the police woman, the name of the girl she asked you about!"

He watched the pained expression on Dorian Drover's face as he searched his memory for the person who was meant to be his girlfriend.

Eventually he said accusingly, "She woke me up," as if it were relevant. "No I can't remember." He shook his head.

"If I'm not mistaken, the girl is someone you went out with," Harvey reminded him.

Dorian jerked to attention sitting up straight in his chair as if Mike Harvey just struck him lightly across his face to prompt him.

"That's what the police woman said," he added crossly, "Or rather suggested she is my girlfriend!"

Harvey began to feel this interview was surreal.

"You are Dorian Drover?" He asked with a deal of sarcasm.

"Yes, Inspector, I am," Dorian replied wanting to laugh out loud at his previous thoughts about police brutality, but he only managed a kind of smirk which Harvey found distasteful, mocking him.

"Then answer the bloody question!" He yelled being provoked once again as his anger flared. "....and it's Chief Inspector!"

Dorian flinched as if he'd actually been hit this time.

Taylor-Smythe, so far remaining silent, was quite mystified by the whole interview making him feel uncomfortable.

"It's a simple question Mr. Drover," he put in calmly. "What is the name of the girl the P.C came looking for?"

"Josie," he replied. "Or Josephine, I really can't remember."

"She is meant to be your girlfriend," Taylor sounded frustrated, about to lose his temper at the whole turn of events. He expected some kind of denial but this was much stranger.

Harvey suddenly tapped Taylor's arm to indicate him he shut up.

"That's right!" he suddenly declared. "She asked me the same thing."

Harvey watched the flick of his head where the piece of hair that had fallen over his eye, moved out of the way. He stared into the cool blue eyes of Dorian Drover, clear blue innocent looking eyes.

"I told her I didn't have a girlfriend but she kept insisting I was meeting her," Dorian Drover looked from Taylor to Harvey, back again. "I went with the band to Manchester, for a gig," he said. "Check it out!" he challenged looking quite agitated.

"Yes, we will!" Harvey declared and for the second time in two days he stood up leaving the room whilst Taylor-Smythe stared open-mouthed.

CHAPTER 34

"What's going on, sir?" Brendon asked standing alone in front of Mike Harvey in his office. He'd returned to the station after his two interviews with a feeling of nervousness hovering under his usual calm determination. Dealing with two frail vulnerable women brought back the old memories of helplessness he saw in his own mother. A strong need to protect merging with a hopeless lack of opportunity to defend them both against....well he wasn't sure what they needed protecting from.

When he defended Fiona Devonshire from her husband's assault he reacted instantly it being the obvious thing to do. The two women he just met lived in different worlds, both isolated from the 'real' world yet somehow inextricably linked.

When he arrived back in the office, the underlying buzz going round was talk of Harvey's second abrupt withdrawal from an interview that caused his concern and resulting unease to heighten. He'd known Mike Harvey a long time. They were cut from the same cloth, with Brendon thriving on Harvey's lead and quiet strength to put away the perpetrators of some horrendous crimes. A role model Brendon admired and sought to emulate.

These days Mike Harvey appeared a different man, somehow smaller, weak and powerless sitting at his desk with his head in his hands, elbows leaning against the surface of the wood he looked like an apparition of quiet despair.

He peered up at Brendon as if he'd only just noticed him, his face a mask of weary fatigue.

"Sir?" Brendon queried again wanting to ask, "Good heavens what's wrong?" but only stood helpless in front of him.

"Flannery," Harvey said in a quiet matter-of-fact way.

"Sir?" Brendon repeated.

"This is all wrong," he admitted. "It's like watching a play where none of the characters seem to fit together, you can't work out what the plot is all about."

It was the last thing Brendon expected to hear having spent so many years with Harvey always able to fit any case into a clear precise pattern. It was the first time he heard such an open admission from him. Where he, Flannery, failed to see the truth, Harvey always grasped it and ran with his hunches to extract all the evidence.

"Sir?" Brendon had no idea what to say in response to Harvey's admission which matched his own disquiet making him feel the old powerlessness he felt as a boy.

"I believed him Flannery," he admitted quietly before Flannery could ask again, "I believed Jocelyn Phipps wasn't his girlfriend."

Brendon felt the sudden split loyalties; did it mean Terri got it wrong? He could only think of Taylor's sneering face delighting if she had. Here was yet another female he wanted to protect from the consequences, from any comeback and certainly from Taylor's vindictive jibes.

Harvey observed Brendon's troubled face saying, as if he could read his mind, "Yet I believe Wilson got it right."

"But..." Brendon began about to add *how could she have?*

Harvey held up a hand to stop him, "It's not a name she could have pulled out of thin air, is it Flannery?" The question seemed to put a little life back into him; he sat upright in his chair looking to voices only he could hear.

Brendon almost tempted to repeat, "Sir?" again, held back not wanting to interrupt Harvey's train of thought because he could see that old look in his eyes, the one Brendon used to see, he felt the old confidence in it leading somewhere. He wanted to shake him, to jump start the old Harvey who lately seemed like a clockwork version of himself, winding down just before it stalled.

"Well, whoever Dorian Drover really is he put the fear of God into Jocelyn Phipps," Brendon declared.

"What?" Harvey's head jerked up, his gaze penetrating. "Drover's a wimp!" he scoffed. "He wouldn't scare anyone, ask Wilson. I bet she sussed him." Then he remembered Brendon hadn't met him. "Trust me....what makes you say that?"

Brendon suddenly became flustered stuttering, "Err, Mary Mundy said Jocelyn Phipps looked scared when she went into the Co-op...."

Harvey sat with a puzzled expression, "Did she now?"

"Maybe she was scared of Devonshire," Brendon added without much conviction.

Harvey shook his head, "The timing's all wrong."

Brendon conceded, "So who was she scared of?" he asked.

"Not Drover, take it from me," he said. "Maybe a what," he added. Now Brendon looked puzzled. "If not a person.....then she must have been afraid of something else." Harvey said out loud, "Something caused her to end up in an alley in a place you wouldn't have expected her to be."

This, Brendon thought, sounded more like the Harvey he knew.

"We need a briefing!" Harvey announced, jumping up leaving Brendon sitting in his office as he left the room.

CHAPTER 35

Harvey stood waiting in front of a bemused CID gathering. Taylor wasted no time updating anyone who would listen about Harvey's erratic behaviour. Unlike Brendon most of them were new to CID therefore less familiar with Harvey's methods; they held no preconceived ideas about him.

"Right you lot," Harvey barked. "We still have a snatched baby to find," he pointed at the picture of a smiling 3 month old Phoebe Devonshire pinned to the board. A picture that resembled a typical advertisement for baby nappies or baby formula of a smiling contented child looked back at them. "We also have one very dead Nanny who left the child in her pram outside of a shop for only ten minutes whilst she popped inside."

Terri felt a brief surge of anger for anyone who would be so stupid whilst Brendon's thoughts flicked to Bernard Devonshire when Harvey uttered 'dead Nanny', even though he knew Bernard Devonshire went home after being released from custody. His arrival back home appeared all over the evening news media. He'd watched that awful man's face as police officers helped him run the gauntlet of the press to ease himself through the gates of his own property. He felt sure it would have been recorded if he left again later.

"It's weird though, sir" Terri Wilson's voice cut into the pause left by Harvey from where she sat at the back of the room.

Harvey whirled round to face her. "What is?"

"Jocelyn saying Dorian Drover is her boyfriend when everyone else unanimously denies it, who should we believe?"

"I believed Drover when he said he didn't know her, what did you think Taylor?" Harvey turned to face Taylor.

"I don't think the Nanny would be Dorian Drover's type," he managed with a sneer.

Everyone in the room went quiet at the inference. Taylor looked into a sea of shocked faces. He grinned nervously seeking confirmation from Harvey.

"You think he's gay?" Harvey asked reassessing his own impression; he had to admit he wasn't a typical ladies' man.

Taylor shrugged, "Well it would account for his mother's belief he didn't have a girlfriend."

"Although she admits she doesn't see much of him, sir," Terri added, "Him being gay would account for her certainty."

"Did you get that impression of him Wilson?" Harvey asked.

Terri remembered a very angry Dorian Drover she woke up from sleep. "When I met him he did seem angry because someone let me into the house," Terri recalled. "And I did wake him up after he got to bed late after the band gig the night before."

"But did you believe him Wilson?" Harvey asked.

"Well, yes sir, I did. I also woke a girl she let me in.....I have no reason to disbelieve him," Terri said.

Sudden silence stunned the assembled officers as they watched Harvey's pained but thoughtful expression. No one dared interrupt him having heard about his recent erratic behaviour, not wanting to put themselves in the line of fire by saying something out of turn.

Harvey in a whisper, as if speaking to himself, murmured, "So who is Dorian Drover?"

"Sir?" Brendon asked mystified by the comment.

"The other odd thing is how close Dorian Drover's parents live to the Devonshire's, don't you think?" Terri Wilson asked. Harvey nodded to Terri to go on, his hand moving to silence anyone else's

167

challenge as the murmurs began again. "She made no mention of activity along the Avenue, asked us nothing about it."

"Would she see it given she doesn't go out?" Brendon recalled the darkness of the smoke filled room with closed blinds to block out the daylight.

"It's on all the news channels," Terri countered.

"She didn't seem to me like someone who would watch the news," Brendon said. "In fact quite the opposite if she's afraid to leave the house." Terri nodded in agreement.

"Not likely to have murdered our Nanny, leaving her in an alley in town then," Taylor quipped, mocking their line of thought. "Does she know Jocelyn Phipps," he asked.

Brendon looked over at Terri seeing the confusion on her face, "She seemed adamant Dorian didn't have a girlfriend," Terri confirmed once again realising her failure to ask her the question.

"No, Wilson, did you ask her if she knew Jocelyn Phipps," he persisted. Terri's momentary silence brought a sneer to Taylor's face.

"We didn't ask it directly," Brendon replied. "The woman kept reminding us she didn't go out and being a prisoner in her own home would have no opportunity to meet them." Brendon chose his words carefully and heard a self-satisfied grunt from Taylor.

"I think she would have known if the Nanny was her son's girlfriend, she may have visited...."

Taylor's voice was cut short by angry shouts from Harvey who exploded suddenly with, "Make your mind up, Taylor, either he's gay or he isn't!" he stormed back into his office without waiting for a response.

Taylor shrugged rolling his eyes mockingly to endorse what he'd been telling everyone about Harvey's unpredictable behaviour. Brendon glared over at Taylor resisting the urge to wipe the smug smile from his face. There was definitely something troubling his boss which bothered him greatly.

"Taylor!" the yell came from the inner sanctum of Harvey's office. The smile died on Taylor-Smythe's face to be replaced by a scowl as he opened Harvey's door and went inside.

The ensuing shouts were indecipherable as Harvey laid into Taylor giving vent to some deep-seated frustrations of his own, taking them out on Taylor.

Mike Harvey would have described himself as a fair manager, one more of arbiter than antagonist, but on this occasion his venting proved cathartic. He made it clear to Taylor if his future aspirations were to remain in criminal investigation he needed to learn to get along with his fellow officers, one's he suggested who were showing more aptitude for the job currently than him, "What have you brought to this enquiry so far?" he yelled. "Absolutely bugger all! So get out there and find something!"

Taylor left his office and CID without a word to anyone.

CHAPTER 36

Bernard Devonshire didn't believe in coincidences. As a man of many businesses he knew you made your own connections. When you wanted something badly that you couldn't have, the 'wanting' wouldn't budge. To tip the balance to have it, you gave a gentle nudge somewhere else, then stood back watching it all fall right into your lap. Not exactly illegal, otherwise he would not stand up to scrutiny. He on the other hand has always been found without a blemish. No, just a helping hand here, a few well-placed welcomed payments of encouragement there. He knew anyone could be bought. The skill came from knowing when to do it.

The first time he did it was completely by accident when, one night whilst entertaining some visiting clients he took them to a new local casino. He wasn't much of a gambling man himself, at least not in the sense of throwing his money at a croupier or some large bosomed blackjack dealer. It fascinated him to watch those who gambled; the people around the roulette table mesmerised by a tiny bouncing roulette ball as it tumbled from pocket to pocket.

You could always spot the fevered gambler with sweat-soaked brows eagerly licking their lips. This was just how he chanced upon his first 'domino' as he called the unfortunate pawns in his own game. Someone he discovered to make to tumble first after which everything else would fall into place. When the ball stopped tumbling he saw the sickened fear on his 'domino's' face and knew he owned him. This was his very first 'legal', not so legal, planning application for an unpopular development achieved on the turn of the roulette wheel.

Of course, there was no real way of tracing any wrongdoing back to him because it was all done through the eager casino owner only too happy to oblige if it meant he got what was owed by the customer. He couldn't let his new business go under at this stage or afford to play it through a long drawn out court process. Money flowed one way whilst opportunity or favours moved the other.

In those early days of small fry transactions the game was miniscule; the unwanted noisy night club gave way to the more lucrative hotel complex developments he got involved in, some of these in the most glamorous of settings. Bernard Devonshire's properties were avidly sought by rich powerful people. Whilst he retained his modestly wealthy lifestyle, his finances grew in abundance within many offshore accounts he knew were safely untouchable.

Of course, he meant to stop once he secured enough. Always 'just one more' and the last development which would do it, he would then stop. But to Bernard Devonshire the lure for him was always about the game, never the profit, which led him down routes his shrewdness wouldn't have otherwise allowed him to venture.

Doing deals with dangerous people became a side-line to his developments; his contracts the means of channelling money other people needed moving for whatever reason. Those reasons he did not need to know about. Profits from drug dealing, the 'human' leisure trade he managed to ignore, even though he was a family man, he needn't know or understand the murky depths of providing arms he knew went to somewhere in the world.

None of it he really understood, for his role lay in the 'movement' of funds in the guise of over-priced development contracts. All he needed to do was to build something somewhere in the world allowing a conduit for other people to channel what then became legitimate money. He was in reality an overtly 'quality' building developer even though in practice he was a dubious multimillionaire and a very successful one. His lifestyle hid much of his worth.

The icing on Bernard's cake being his long awaited daughter Phoebe, yet another arrangement he sought and bought losing her along with her mother. This was not the deal he entered into. He didn't believe his beloved Phoebe had been taken by some passing chancer who the police were looking for. In time he would receive the clue to who took her, he knew the 'why' would be a ransom demand or at least some kind of request for his particular skills.

Fiona voiced it when she lost control suggesting in front of the coppers that it was his fault, hinting his contacts were behind it. So he hit her to shut her up. It got him arrested delaying any approach being made and was now a question of damage limitation. He would do anything to get his precious Phoebe back; having to wait was killing him.

Bernard's temper flared momentarily when he heard his front doorbell's sharp chimes which startled him dragging his thoughts back to reality. How anyone managed to get as far as the front door under the current circumstances baffled him. The mob at his gates, carefully controlled by the police presence, would dissuade any nosey chancer from attempting it.

He peered cautiously through the porch window spotting the policeman, the Chief Inspector who came here when the other copper, the fat one, arrested him for hitting Fiona. He searched around the hallway for his mobile in case he needed to phone his solicitor, but realised he'd left it in his office on his desk.

Just for a moment Bernard thought he would have to come clean, admit just maybe Fiona might have a point, some low life played him at his own game, taking his precious Phoebe as collateral in a much bigger game.

The doorbell sounded again. Glancing towards his gates he could see a diminished crowd of paparazzi outside in the street, they looked more orderly, less congested than he remembered on his return. The chief Inspector (Bernard already forgot his name) moved to one side looking up at the front of the house for any signs of life revealing a smart, stylish but gaunt young man with him who wasn't here with the others searching his house; *at least not the fat one then.*

Bernard's heart began to pace faster feeling instinctively they were here to deliver news, which would be bad news to bring out the top ranking one, not the bit of a girl who liked to make tea and deliver sympathy. Bernard moved automatically over to the front door, his mind repeating, "*Not my Phoebe,*" over and over again in his head.

He opened the door to them and they both took a step closer. The Chief Inspector tried for a smile which faded as Bernard scowled. The gaunt copper made no attempt, confirming for Bernard they were there to deliver bad news.

"Chief Inspector Harvey," Mike Harvey flashed his I.D card, "Can we come in Mr Devonshire."

Bernard was beyond manners, his temper having long departed, he just stood back to let them enter, closing the door behind them. He hesitated for a minute then led them into the library office; his thought moving across a spectrum of issues, wondering if it looked tidy, or if he'd left anything incriminating on his desk, then thought, "*Who the fuck cares!*" if the news they came with is about his precious Phoebe it would be bad!

Mike Harvey asked Bernard Devonshire to sit down, saw him move to sit at his desk shakily.

In a weak feeble voice, Bernard said, "Please, not my Phoebe?" his breathless question the first real emotion Harvey caught from him.

"No, Sir, I have no news about your daughter," he said quietly but firmly waiting for some angry outburst from Devonshire.

His eyes fixed searchingly on Harvey's face, *"he looks like a man about to be served the death penalty"* He thought he had his full attention, "It's your Nanny," Harvey began watching the sheer puzzlement begin to cross Devonshire's face.

"Who?" Bernard managed to say, wanting to ask, *"What the fuck are you talking about?* He sat dumbly waiting for the rest of it.

"Jocelyn Phipps?" Harvey queried making sure he understood who he meant, "the body of Jocelyn Phipps has been found," Harvey watched as first relief then total bafflement appeared on Bernard Devonshire's face.

"The Nanny?" he asked as if a complete surprise to him: he hadn't registered the name of his Nanny. In Bernard's head an array of emotions fought for supremacy; *'not Phoebe'* he wanted to yell out loud which gave him immediate relief, then replaced by conflict and confusion, *"who would want to kill the Nanny?"* He hadn't shown relief or spoken it out loud as the two detectives watched his reaction to the news; a game he knew most of them played. 'A body found' doesn't necessarily mean foul play his self-survival voice reminded him.

He managed, "She's dead?" wanting to ask if by an accident but not daring to show his own inner thoughts, he chose, "I don't understand...." He trailed off.

"At the moment Mr Devonshire we are treating it as a suspicious death but haven't got a definite cause of death yet."

"Why would anyone want to kill her?" Bernard stood unsteadily, staggered over to his whisky decanter, poured a hefty measure, swallowing a mouthful. He turned, stared disbelievingly at the two detectives trying to interpret their penetrating stares. "You think someone killed her?" he said disbelievingly. The real question running in his head, *"Why would they kill the person who left his precious Phoebe alone for them to take, unless......"* His thought took only the form of a frown followed by a look of stark disbelief, then slowly a neutral expression slid smoothly across his usual wrinkled contours. It was his long practiced business face (some would call it a 'poker player's face'), the one he used at crucial points in his often dirty dealings and one no one could interpret or fathom his thoughts. For Bernard now began to understand or he thought he did, that this slip of a girl was somehow tied up in the plot to snatch his daughter, this proved it.

His blank face stared back waiting for a reply, "well?" he prompted.

"We don't know at the moment," Harvey said. "As I said we...."

"Yes, yes!" Bernard interrupted looking impatient, felt his anger stir, wanting to be released, "there's always so much you don't know!" he said critically. "You people are always so quick to jump on an innocent man....not so good at finding the truth!" He could feel himself getting out of control again, more from his own frustrations at what he believed the whole situation to be about. He saw the other copper sitting riveted to the spot looking bewildered. He felt like hitting his ineffectual face to hammer some life into him, to jerk him into some sort of action, to find his Phoebe.

"What about my baby?" he yelled. "What are you doing to finder her?!"

Harvey stood up when he saw Bernard Devonshire's anger rising, he didn't want to feel at a disadvantage if he should suddenly strike. Mike Harvey being much taller than him increased his advantage should Bernard Devonshire prove to be as violent as he already witnessed.

He merely walked back around his desk to sit down shaking his head, "This doesn't make any sense," he said.

"Exactly," the quiet voice of Taylor cut in. "Have you got any idea why someone would want to hurt your Nanny!" Taylor asked with just a hint of accusation in his voice making Harvey look sharply his way.

Bernard heard it too and glared at him, "You think I...?" he wanted to say "....*killed her?*" He stopped himself as they didn't say whether she had been 'killed' only she was dead. Bernard couldn't think straight or even begin to work out 'why' they would want to kill her. He took it as some kind of warning to him to tow the line when their demands came as he fully expected them to do. But 'who' were 'they'?

He heard Harvey's voice intercede quickly in his thinking.

"No, no, Mr. Devonshire," he put in to stop any sudden violent outburst, "we don't think so. We don't have the exact time of death yet, but believe she died between six o'clock and midnight." Harvey wanted to confirm part of the time he had still been in custody so it gave him an alibi.

Bernard Devonshire seemed to calm again having puffed up in an aggressive stance he deflated as if some of his hot air had been released, like a deflated balloon the surface of his face resumed the pizza crinkle reminiscent of the cellulite on a woman's thighs. Taylor's mocking thoughts made him want to laugh at the analogy he watched in fascination.

Bernard saw him smirk taking offence to being laughed at.

"You find all this amusing?" he threw at Taylor with the hidden threat in his words not going unnoticed, followed by the same look he gave Brendon Flannery at his release from custody. Taylor also picked up just how dangerous this man could be.

Bernard Devonshire didn't find any of it amusing. He felt considerably relieved when they both went. He sat in his office thinking about this new development, trying to place it into the context of his business dealings trying to work it all out whilst he waited for the ransom demand to come.

CHAPTER 37

Mike Harvey woke up in a panic, his nightmare still vivid - the face of a smiling three month old baby crumpling into one of distress as she screamed. It was a cry of pain that instilled fear into him. The feeling of despair remained as the face of the baby faded.

It mingled with his own deep seated melancholy, grown over the years but more especially since his own daughters, Gilly and Bethany left home, as he knew one day they would, his wife Shirley would give up on him. That's how he saw her inevitable departure always knowing he would end up on his own. Despite his own parents he'd always felt alone, without bonds, *"what a curious thing to think"* echoed around his brain. He did have those early ties yet felt adrift on an endless ocean where only the motion of the water with its ups and downs kept him afloat.

He thought perhaps he married Shirley to give himself someone to anchor himself to in this huge nothingness called life; even his choice of profession deliberately made. Whilst solving the puzzles of other people's lives and their misdeeds, it distracted him from trying to work out his own or more precisely why he felt so much alone.

For Shirley, with both parents dying in a senseless car accident when they were still young must surely be part of why she felt the need to belong to him. Learning about her pain he held no sympathy for anyone caught drink-driving. He avoided as far as he possibly could any part of the force like traffic policing, feeling bad about the man who, she told him, had been three times over the legal limit, when he lost control of his vehicle careering into the oncoming traffic which just happened to be her parents car after they dropped her off at college and were set for their own work day.

The euphoria of being taken out of college, given a ride in a marked police car, ultimately gave way when she learnt about her parent's death. She already knew about loneliness when they met, about detachment and not belonging. These were the kinds of things you learnt about in the care system and her eager need to have a feeling of attachment so she chose him because he seemed to understand.

Shirley, of course, had been the first girl to show an interest in him. She told him once he seemed so vulnerable, she wanted to care for him identifying something appealing about him, a look of 'little boy lost' she found deeply attractive. Who wouldn't fall for a person who told you that when all you ever wanted yourself was to feel you belonged? So Shirley, his first 'love', in truth his only love, made his life wonderful for a while, giving him someone to belong to at last.

She gave him two beautiful daughters making his family complete whilst in return he gave her a secure home in which to nurture them. The perfect happy family home, at least for a while enabling him to work hard at his police career to sustain it. The empty feeling never left him, it merely moved a little farther away inside, a little deeper but never hidden, never too far away he could forget it completely.

Shirley blossomed, all her attention transferred from him to their daughters, who were, of course, initially quite vulnerable with need of her total attention. By the time they became self-sufficient she was unable to shift it back to him. She began to complain he cared more about his job than he did about her. Maybe he did, he couldn't really say because he only worked like he always did to provide her with a secure home and to provide himself with something that would reduce the huge empty chasm he felt inside.

The picture of Phoebe Devonshire began to fade as Mike drifted back to sleep in his usual armchair. There was really no point in going to bed, it just reinforced how empty his life had become.

CHAPTER 38

Brendon stared at Mike Harvey, his face always craggy with lines from his lifelong dedication to cigarettes, looked pale and drawn. *He looks ill* Brendon thought as he handed him a mug of tea together with the inevitable white bag from 'The Crusty Cob' on the corner. "Sausage with brown sauce," Brendon announced which didn't raise the usual smile. It was always sausage with brown sauce and only once he'd said 'tomato ketchup' for a laugh, but his boss only frowned, he didn't have much of a sense of humour.

"What am I missing Brendon?" Mike asked without anxiously looking up having inspected the contents of the white bag, by lifting the bread roll to examine the sausage, then nodding approval. If he'd looked up he would have marked the shock on Brendon's face.

"That's the first time you've called me that," Brendon noted.

Absently Mike replied, "Called you what?"

"Brendon," said Brendon now certain something really concerned him. "You always call me Flannery, boss."

Mike Harvey looked puzzled, "Do I?" He took a bite out of his sausage bap, closed his eyes as if he were savouring haute cuisine. He felt totally exhausted needing the sustenance of food inside him.

Brendon watched him eat, his mouth moving automatically as he chewed, showing none of the signs of real enjoyment in this action, unlike Brendon who delighted at every bite of food he took. He noticed how thin his boss looked; never an overweight person, he was verging on skeletal. He lost weight over time, since his wife's departure Brendon realised, whilst his had crept on pound after pound giving Wendy something to continuously nag him about, to watch his weight, whilst her efforts to give him healthy food came to nothing. She had no idea what he ate outside of home especially during working hours.

"You should take better care of yourself boss," Brendon dared to comment, letting his thoughts spill out of his mouth. Harvey's eyes snapped open glaring at Brendon. He never encouraged familiarity and this comment bordered on intimacy.

"What am I missing Flannery," he asked again correcting himself this time to avoid any invitations for further personal comments.

"Maybe you aren't missing anything," Brendon replied lamely. "If it's not been seen yet, you couldn't have missed anything." He knew he sounded cryptic and stood thinking of another way to put it.

A knock on Harvey's door gave way to the head of Terri Wilson appearing as it opened.

"Sir?"

"Come in Wilson," Harvey motioned with his hand now feeling slightly giddy which wasn't like him. He carried on eating his breakfast, beginning to feel the rumblings in his stomach as it reacted to the food. Brendon raised his eyes at Terri as a loud noise emitted from behind Harvey's desk. Harvey looked embarrassed at the loudness of his stomach rumbles, "I think I might need this, Wilson, excuse me continuing eating?"

It was Wilson's turn to look embarrassed, "Of course," she whispered.

"What have you got?" Harvey asked between chews seeing her holding a piece of paper in her hand.

Terri consulted the sheet, "I thought I would do some background digging," she sounded almost apologetic as if she just confessed to skiving. Harvey took another bite, chewed with little interest beyond necessity; he nodded for her to proceed. "I started with this," she handed the paper over to Harvey. "It's the birth certificate for Fiona Devonshire."

Harvey scrutinised the document, "Fiona Evans," he read from the birth certificate, "father, Alwyn Evans, miner, deceased." He looked up at Terri, she nodded for him to read on, "Mother, Alwen Evans, housekeeper."

Terri stood expectantly whilst Brendon looked on trying to keep his mind on the conversation but failing badly. He could only think how lovely she looked.

"Place, sir," she prompted.

Harvey looked back at the certificate again registering Clwyd, Wales.

"Didn't we already know she has no relatives close by?" Harvey asked.

"Yes, sir," Terri went on enthusiastically. "We did - I traced her mother to Clwyd in Wales, there are a great number of country houses in this part of the world," she enthused; they could see she enjoyed the whole fact finding exercise. "I believe she may have once been housekeeper in one of them although it's a little vague."

"How does...." Harvey began wanting to yell "get on with it Wilson" or "how does this help us?" He realised his impatience was a result of how he felt because he felt like shit.

"Sorry Sir," Wilson quickly cut in, "I traced Alwen Evans to a small cottage in Clwyd although I've no evidence how long she lived there. She was registered....." Terri saw Harvey's face frown again as she lapsed into detail. If he got bored she would never finish her update. "She lived there with her daughter." Terri pointed at the birth certificate, "who is our Fiona Devonshire, the address matches....." Terri stopped revealing how she got to it, she could see Harvey was in no state to sit listening to it all.

"So are you saying we have her mother's contact details to check with her if she's heard from her daughter?" Harvey's face brightened realising this could be one bit of news he'd been waiting for.

"No, Sir," Terri said quietly watching as Harvey deflated. "She disappeared about three years ago."

"Disappeared?" Harvey sounded frustrated. "People don't just disappear, unless you suspect foul play....."

"No sir!" She cut in not wanting to mislead him. "She just....." She stopped, once again on the verge of repeating 'disappeared'.

"There is usually some trace, they remarry or die!" His bombastic school teacher lecturing voice lost any authority, "Don't they?" he asked.

"None of those, sir and no postal voting or...." She wanted to show him the extent of her search, but could see he was in no mood to listen to it. "There is nothing after 2009, she did receive some community care, then it just stops," Terri's previous enthusiasm began to wane. *If he only knew how hard I worked to get this!* "I thought maybe someone could go to Wales to have a look....."

Harvey abruptly stopped eating. He threw his remaining sausage bap into the metal bin with a loud thud stood up and walked out of the office.

Brendon Flannery looked shocked, saw the sudden anguish appear on Terri's face. He wanted to rush over put his arm around her, comfort her.

"He thinks I'm looking for a jolly!" Terri's anger flared, it being the last thing on her mind.

"No!" Brendon reacted, "He isn't like that.... he wouldn't think it of you!"

By the time Terri composed herself they had returned to the main office. Harvey stood in front of the assembled CID officers ready to start the morning briefing. He held a new cup of tea in one hand.

"Right!" he yelled for order. "It looks like we may have a new lead, although a fairly tenuous one."

Terri and Brendon watched as he explained her tracing of Fiona Devonshire's mother to Wales then tasked two of the detectives to go to Wales to follow it up. There were no negative comments or even a hint of the Alwen Evans disappearance which amazed Terri even more than his previous erratic behaviour.

Brendon looked on as Mike Harvey revealed the new lead and gave his instructions, curious about his obvious strange reaction to the part about Alwen Evan's disappearance. To someone like him, who had known Mike Harvey for years it was indeed bizarre.

Of course, no one knew just how this finding by Terri affected him so personally at the time; no one knew because he shared nothing of a personal nature with anyone.

CHAPTER 39

Taylor's dislike of Peter Thompson grew every time he observed him and as his dislike grew so did his 'observations' which began to take on an obsessional quality. What he didn't like the most was the way he held himself with an air of smugness that Taylor believed wasn't practiced; but born out of a genuinely well-to-do background. He knew it because he spent hours trying to adopt a similar air of sophistication. Hours in front of a mirror as a boy trying to change himself and his appearance from the weedy boy at the start into someone people, especially his peers, would be proud to choose as a friend.

In the early days it wasn't so much to attract girls, although he knew girls liked 'a bit of class'. He supposed it was because like him, they held high hopes of leaving their roots behind them, escaping the mishmash of the council dwellings where they grew up submerged in poverty.

You were either 'rough' or popular 'aspiring' to survive. Being delicate of looks with a slight build made you a sitting duck to be bullied and abused by the tough elements who dominated his everyday living nightmare.

They were ever present around the walkways of the concrete construction of council dwellings, experimental at the time they were built. They quickly became an eyesore; an amalgam of rotting homes with their interconnecting communal stairs quickly falling into disrepair and being a far cry from the intended community project. Their more colloquial nickname 'Colditz' placed all who lived there into a stigmatised group of losers.

Everyone he remembered, held the one ambition to get out, even those at the top of the pile, who took away any power they could dominating the rest into a collective miserable submission.

When Taylor thought about his roots he would shiver; it made him feel physically sick to his core. Every time he saw Peter Thompson it brought it all back to him, now years later from where it was once confined in the deep caverns of his memory where he deliberately placed it. Hidden in some honeycomb cell, sealed up over the long years of effort to escape to be the person he wanted to be.

He created Trevor Taylor-Smythe to facilitate his escape, leaving Billy Smith, a delicate persecuted memory back there in the decaying pile of experimental boxes that were later demolished together with his memory buried within a new wave of regeneration. He changed his name, his appearance and his status through long hours of night school study with dishwasher jobs to fund it, leaving Billy Smith back there in that concrete coffin.

Peter Thompson, the young confident golf-pro made it all come flooding back just like the wrecking ball that eventually demolished the 'project'. He smashed the tightly concealed roots exposing with his false smile, that easy charm with the image of a finger stroking the cheek of a pretty girl, that symbolised he could have her if he chose to. Taylor remembered the gesture well; bullies always picked over the hottest girls who were also powerless to refuse them.

Taylor started off observing Thompson from his deep seated conviction he was basically trouble. Although, he had no particular reason to justify this assertion, only his own newly released feelings born out of old prejudices. He was a 'suspicious' character, Trevor Taylor-Smythe knew it and would prove it.

Taylor applied for membership of the club citing his need to move clubs for geographical proximity reasons, to be nearer to where he worked. He sat back waiting for the long slow process to grind on. More often than not he 'sat' waiting in the clubhouse where he became a familiar figure, where he met and befriended a handful of the more sociable members who even asked him to 'guest' in a few rounds of golf.

Sometimes he would spend his off duty time at the club, whilst often he 'popped' in for a cloaked official look around should anyone at work enquire until the difference between the two became a blur, at least in the mind of Trevor.

He came to be a feature of the place even Peter Thompson accepted; after all he sold the copper a new golfing glove, who knew what else he might buy from his pro-shop? Very quickly the weird gaunt copper became just another member and in Trevor's case 'potential' member whom he accepted fading into the background with the rest of the punters.

CHAPTER 40

Another typical Sunday afternoon for Brendon Flannery, after a large satisfying roast dinner, he snored loudly in an arm chair in the front room. His fondness for roast beef, Yorkshire puddings with roast potatoes and all the trimmings followed by reading the Sunday newspapers, always made him nod off before he got as far as page three of the first broadsheet.

Today something he read just before he dozed off prompted him to have a particularly vivid dream. A dream in which the story making news headlines about a woman kept prisoner by her parents for thirty years mingled with his own thoughts of Frances Drover as he remembered her. She seemed to also be held prisoner in her own home just a few hundred yards away from where a baby mysteriously disappeared and where the baby's Nanny went missing and then was later found dead in the alley behind a nightclub in the city.

His dream misinterpreted the newspaper article's vivid descriptions of a helpless woman's plight, being tied to a bed, bound and gagged in a solitary room. In the dream the woman appeared as France Drover with her tiny frame, thin body and frightened face, only the mouth gag having slipped, she inhaled deeply the cigarette held precariously between her lips whilst the ash on the cigarette grew longer as she smoked it.

Eventually the cigarette dropped onto her dress where at first it smouldered then eventually caught the fabric alight. Brendon woke with a start just as the flames grew brightly. He sat bolt upright in his chair where he had previously slumped finding himself quite alone. The door to the hallway and to the kitchen both stood open.

He could hear no sounds of activity from the kitchen, no tell-tale swooshing or gurgling of the after dinner dishes being cleaned by the dishwasher.

He supposed he'd slept a long time from the dimness of the light filtering in through the window, guessing it to be late afternoon or early evening with no sign of his family.

The image of Frances Drover rose up invading his thoughts, together with his sudden solitary state, gave him a sense of foreboding. Feeling his mouth dry he was barely able to swallow, he supposed sore from snoring loudly which drove his family out of the house.

He went into his neat tidy kitchen to quench his thirst taking a clean glass from the cupboard he let the cold water run colder.

He pressed off the dishwasher lights showing the cycle completed, he opened the door a piece to feel the level of heat inside; cool meant he slept a long time now feeling ashamed at having driven his family away by his selfishness. Whenever he felt himself or his behaviour open to criticism he usually punished himself by wondering what someone he held dear might think of him.

The image he summoned up was mostly of his wife Nancy. If closer to a work situation then usually he thought of his boss Mike Harvey imagining what he might say about his lack of leadership qualities or detective skills or whatever he perceived his own failings to be.

Today he thought of neither of them. He looked down at his ample belly full of Sunday roast whilst his thoughts were mostly of Terri Wilson who recently took him to interview Frances Drover; her image tied to a bed would not leave him. '*A prisoner without a jailer*'. The thought rose up so suddenly it stopped him mid-gulp of water. He leaned over the sink toying with the concept of being imprisoned somewhere you couldn't leave although totally alone. What about Mr. Drover?

The question came so suddenly it took Brendon completely by surprise. He couldn't even remember hearing Terri talk about a Mr Drover and couldn't even place whether his name had been mentioned.

Once inserted into his thoughts it mingled with the frightened face of Frances Drover staring back at them through the crack in the door, now intertwined itself with another voice, of Mary Mundy, "She looked frightened," she said referring to Jocelyn Phipps.

His own unease grew to a level that made him feel perturbed about being alone in his deserted house.

As he rushed through the hallway from the kitchen he grabbed his casual jacket from the rack in the hall, took his car keys out of the dish where they sat alone and where Nancy usually kept hers, they were missing but he didn't notice. He left the house, got into his car and drove away.

His reactions were automatic, programmed like a robot, they were inevitable. He drove straight to Terri Wilson's home. Being late on a Sunday afternoon, he neither thought about what such an action might look like nor even considered whether she would be there. He drove like someone on autopilot.

When he reached her street he found the narrow road lined with many cars, a street where only one or two houses possessed a garage. The Sunday accumulation of vehicles left Brendon cruising slowly along trying to find a parking space which gave him sufficient time for his doubts to kick in, which they inevitably did, mingling with his thoughts about the urge that brought him here. He hoped it wasn't just the loneliness he felt from the unusually quiet house.

He saw a gap at the kerb, reversed quickly as the headlights of another car appeared at the top of the road, flashing him giving him the right of way down, there not being enough room for two cars to pass each other. He ignored it tucking in tightly behind a battered Vauxhall Astra.

He consulted his mobile phone, flicking a couple of screens to identify the number of the house he knew Terri lived in. He smiled fleetingly more from relief than anything else; he knew Wendy's reaction would have been finding himself over the road from his destination, it would have been a scornful "typical!" making it clear as always he needed more exercise than he ever took.

He got out, walked over to the house catching a glimpse of the other car crawling along like he just had. He knocked boldly trying to crush his creeping doubts wanting to ask, *"Why are you really here?"*

He saw a light come on inside. When the door opened a middle-aged white blonde haired woman stood smiling at him, dressed to go out or just come in, her coat buttoned up, she wore a handbag strapped across her body hanging down at the side of her.

"Hello?" she said when Brendon didn't speak.

"Ah," he blurted surprised at seeing her. "I may have the wrong house - I'm looking for Terri....Terri Wilson? I'm Sergeant Flannery."

The woman stood back to let him in, still grinning, "Yes? Go in," she pointed at a door along the passage showing him where to go, then she yelled, "Terri!"

The beep of a car horn from the street drew Brendon's attention to a taxi just pulling up outside blocking the road.

"Go in!" She said again as Brendon stepped into the hallway, she left shutting the door behind her.

Brendon made his way into what turned out to be an empty front sitting room. He felt like an intruder into someone else's space giving him that uneasy feeling of having no right to be there; it always set him off on a back foot when visiting the public.

When the door opened Terri gave a surprised barely audible gasp then smiled broadly like the woman who just left which he recognised as a family trait. The blonde woman must be Terri's mother.

"Sarge?" Terri said expressing her surprise.

"I...I..." he stammered. "The lady who just left let me in....."

"Ah," Terri laughed, "My mother you mean." She knew very well how surprised people were when she introduced her mother to them, "Before you say anything she doesn't look old enough to be my mother!" Terri laughed again noticing how edgy Brendon seemed. "What's up Sarge?" As he looked so nervous she indicated to him to sit down. She sat opposite him waiting expectantly for him to tell her why he came.

"Can we get rid of the Sarge?" he asked by way of delaying the conversation, happy just to look at her. He needed a way of expressing how he felt. It didn't help as she sat there waiting, grinning at him and he tried to remember if he ever noticed before how her face lit up when she smiled; she looked so beautiful.

"Okay, S...Brendon," she said.

With nowhere else to go he began, "I fell asleep," he stopped trying to summon up the words, "this afternoon....oh, lord this is hard to explain!" He added in exasperation.

"It's okay, tell it as it comes," she encouraged being really surprised to see him like this.

"This will sound crazy," he took a deep breath before he went on, "I had a dream....no, I read an article in the Sunday's, the one about a girl whose parents kept her prisoner?" he asked for clarification if she knew about it.

"Oh, I think I read about it, wasn't it awful?"

He eyed her noticing how relaxed she looked off duty, not at all the nervous novice she often came over as, but then she had a lot to put up with, especially the likes of Taylor he'd noticed. He made a mental note to do something about him.

"Yes," he said. "Then I must have nodded off to sleep and began dreaming. My dream was based on the pictures in the paper," he looked up. "You know? Of the room they kept her in...only in my dream she had Frances Drover's face, with a cigarette in her mouth," Brendon waved his hand towards his own face.

Terri laughed again, "She is rather a chain smoker isn't she, Sarge?" She realised what she just called him, corrected quickly testing it out, "Brendon."

"I suppose the dream doesn't really matter because it wasn't real," he admitted. "I think Frances Drover made a bit of an impact on me, or rather her circumstances being a prisoner in her own home." Thoughts of his mother slipped into his mind, he quickly pushed them away. He waited for any reaction from Terri.

"Yes, I feel for her living like that....it must be awful."

Brendon sat quietly homing in on his own disquiet, "I don't know Terri, there's something really wrong about her situation. I think it's how frightened she sometimes appeared to be, if you caught the look...." He thought of his mother all those years ago, with the same look, the same fear.

Terri sat staring at him, scrutinising him whilst he told it, "Yes I agree, go on." She urged.

"As I woke up from my dream all I could think about was what Mary Mundy said about Jocelyn Phipps looking frightened when she saw her."

Terri sat considering as the quiet grew.

"I wondered if you've met her husband?" He asked suddenly.

Terri's head snapped up looking at Brendon anticipating some kind of criticism.

"No, he hasn't been there when I've called round, I'm afraid I made the assumption he would be at work," she admitted. "Have I failed you?" she asked.

Brendon's hand automatically shot over to hers and he grasped the back of it. "Absolutely not," he placated. "I'm at fault for not thinking about interviewing him..... I don't even know his name...."

"James Ellis...." Terri cut in. "I never thought to ask her given how fragile she seems."

They heard a sudden cry from somewhere in the house which made Brendon immediately alert. Terri jumped up muttering, "Excuse me," She rushed out of the room.

CHAPTER 41

Another day's briefing without one hint of a clue into either the baby snatch or the unexpected death of her Nanny, Jocelyn Phipps, left Mike Harvey feeling out of control of his cases. It mirrored his feelings about his own life, he knew the one fed the other, compounding his perceived inability to do his job or live his life as he saw no way of separating the two.

The new unexpected need to withdraw marked this decline. He had no idea why this urge for flight suddenly came upon him. He had always stood up to face whatever crisis came his way in his usual stoical way. Why now of all times to lose it? The more it happened the worse he felt until he no longer identified with himself.

Fight or flight always a two-edged sword, until now, when this....he began to see them as panic attacks....started to happen. He preferred to run rather than attempt to explain himself, or his feelings, it's a longstanding 'fault' (did he see it as a fault) of his to bottle up his own fears whilst providing an ear to other people to offload their problems always gave him the breathing space enabling him to crush his own.

Who knew what he managed to stifle all these years? What hidden issues he crushed burying them deep within his compartmentalised memory? He'd always been a master at the art of suppressing his own feelings.

Something triggered this current state which he was powerless to stop its progression. He felt like a runaway train picking up speed down a steep incline, brakeless, unable to stop it before he hit – he had no idea what lurked at the bottom of the slope or whether he would be able to stop 'it' happening when he got there.

"Sir!" Mike looked up from where he sat in the station's canteen startled at finding himself sitting alone at one of the tables with not even a cup of tea in front of him. "Are you okay, Sir?" The voice belonged to Ashley Stevens one of the two detectives he'd actioned to follow up on Fiona Devonshire's mother.

Mike felt his temper rise, "I thought I sent you to Wales!" It wasn't so much a question as a reprimand his irritability flared up on his face.

The detective coughed feeling exposed, vulnerable, "You did Sir," he blurted out confused by the question. "We went yesterday, I wanted to report back."

The shock on Mike's face confused Stevens even more than the unprovoked reprimand. With no idea how to deal with this strange encounter, he chose to ignore it and carry on with his report.

"We discovered where she...I mean Alwen Evans used to live," he took out his police notebook glad of the distraction to consult it briefly. It was not the time he thought to make mistakes. "She seemed quite a well-known person, knew everyone in the area having lived there most of her life." Mike Harvey recognised how nervous he seemed and indicated for him to sit down. He carried on, "People remembered her as housekeeper on one of the big estates around the Clwyd area before she moved into the 'tied' cottage where she raised her daughter Fiona Evans."

"This 'tied' cottage belongs to the estate where she worked?"

"Yes, Sir. It's one of those old fashioned arrangements," Stevens saw his boss's puzzlement so he hurried on, "usually they are given to employees as part of their wages settlement, free or peppercorn rent, in exchange for low wages with unlimited hours of service."

"So Alwen Evans used to be the housekeeper with her own cottage?" Mike still looked confused.

"Yes, well no, sir, she lived in the 'big house'," he grinned at the quaint way people spoke of the large manor houses, "When she was housekeeper. She only moved into the cottage after she left her job - it's where her daughter was born."

"So she got married to Fiona Devonshire's father and they lived at the 'tied' cottage on the same estate she used to work for?" Mike frowned. "Is it some kind of redundancy package?" he asked sarcastically, he knew it sounded comical put in those terms. Stevens thought so anyway because he grinned broadly at the idea.

"I don't think so, at least not for anyone in 'service'," Stevens thought about it adding, "Well not impossible I suppose."

Mike's confusion grew giving rise to irritation so he urged, "Go on."

"She lived there with Fiona until her daughter left to go to University, after which alone until 2009 – the latter part of this she got some assistance from community services after some kind of stroke left her unable to manage totally."

"What about her husband 'Alwyn' Evans, it's confusing with them both having the same sounding name," Mike Harvey asked.

"We found no one who could tell us anything about a husband." Stevens admitted, saw Harvey scowl again so hurried on, "In fact, there is one local, some yokel ex-game keeper who scoffed at the idea she was ever married. In fact, he hinted at trying his luck to woo her himself, but got knocked back."

Harvey looked shocked, "What about Fiona's birth certificate? It does say 'deceased' father which means he died before Fiona was born."

Stevens shook his head, "According to my amorous yokel there were rumours there that Alwyn Evans was her mother's attempt to legitimate her daughter's birth."

"Unusual choice of name though," Harvey stated.

"Who?"

"Well it's the male equivalent of her own name."

"Without a father she would have been both mother and father to Fiona," Steven's insisted.

Harvey shrugged, he didn't find the woman's plight remotely amusing, "Go on," he demanded abruptly.

Stevens caught the renewed irritation once again, "There's not much more to tell, only Alwen Evan's community service input had been cancelled by her daughter, recorded as Fiona Devonshire in 2009, which is when she vacated the tied cottage."

"No forwarding address I take it?" Harvey asked half optimistic.

Stevens shook his head, "No."

"You mentioned rumours," Harvey said, "What were they?"

"It's just local gossip really so not very reliable. We stopped at the village pub for something to eat, the locals knew we were 'job', believe me some of them were well dodgy." Stevens remembered they considered them to be the lunch time's entertainment once they knew why they were there. They threw a lot of stuff at them that seemed to taunt their mission, some openly laughing at them.

"There can be a lot of truth in gossip, Stevens," Harvey chided. "You can't dismiss any of it – give!"

"There is one 'rumour' that Alwen Evans got pregnant by one of the sons at the Manor so had to leave her job," Stevens didn't sound convinced.

"Well it does explain the tied cottage, a payoff to get rid of her, to keep her quiet – check her finances, see if there were any regular payments," Harvey looked at Stevens, "She must have lived on something," he said.

"According to the locals she took in washing," Harvey looked doubtful as Stevens went on, "She did a few cleaning jobs."

"Not a huge money spinner, are you sure?"

Stevens remembered one of the locals voicing, "She did housework…. my missus used her, the lazy cow!" He told Harvey.

"Still check her finances anyway Stevens." Stevens got up to leave as Harvey added, "Get me a tea and a scone before you go will you?"

Harvey sat back contemplating until Stevens returned with his order, he made no attempt to give him any money for the order having slipped back into thought mode. As Stevens walked away too embarrassed to ask Harvey for money he shouted after him, "What's the name of the family Estate?"

Stevens stopped, took out his note book again, flicked over a few pages and his face turned bright red with embarrassment.

"Drover, sir!" he said.

Harvey had just taken a bite of his scone; a crumb stuck in his throat which caused him to choke. Stevens scurried off.

CHAPTER 42

I thought this will never end! Even after hearing talk from the others about how long they kept you inside for, it goes on and on. Every time someone comes I want to scream "Let me go!" as they pour in hot water then the ice. My hands are held by straps each side of the bath to stop me escaping.

After a while my only hope is to slip into sleep. The ice cold numbs me making it easier to feel nothing, to slip away. Then when the hot comes again it wakes up my whole body, I can feel it on fire, the pain eases back into throbbing hot aches, panic creeping over me.

I shut my eyes tightly even when I hear them call my name, I won't let them hear me scream, I keep it inside my head where only I can hear it. If you let them see how you feel they will do much worse things than this. It helps you to learn to survive here though there is no hope of ever getting out, unless they take me to the place next to the laundry – no one ever comes back from there.

I have learnt the lesson, I repeat over and over in my head, "I must not ask where my baby is....I must not ask where my baby is...."

*　　　*　　　*　　　*

Mary lost herself in the wonderful world of the Yorkshire moors and a secret garden. The magical story about a girl also called Mary whose parents both die in India where they all live. She is brought to England to live with her Uncle Archibald Craven at his isolated house on the moors, Misselthwaite Manor.

She heard the knock as she read on, her cup of tea cold at the side of her, too engrossed in the story to drink it. The second knock came louder more impatient than the first. Mary seldom showed annoyance, but this intrusion came at the wrong time, the Robin was just about to show Mary the hidden door behind the overgrown greenery where she knew a wall ran along the garden. Mary pushed her hand through......*knock, knock!*

Mary Mundy's head bobbed and her face became fierce, "What?" she muttered, putting the book mark between the pages, closing it she stood up stretching her stiffening frame.

When she got to the door she looked through the spy hole seeing the angry face of the gaunt young man in the business suit once again. She heard his fist pound against the wood and could see the accumulated frustration of his many other visits.

She quietly took the chain off, now resigned to having to meet this Manager she knew wanted to take her back there, to the place of her awful memories and nightmares. She had another one of them last night and knew when she woke up it had been an omen. The dream being about the only time she ever asked the nurses about her baby, when they did those things to her to make her forget.

Mary opened the door just as the young man's hand moved forward about to hit the door once again with his fist. She flinched as the punch hit the empty air between them. She managed to move back away from it, her heart pounding.

Almost losing his balance with the momentum, his face still fierce, turned a red shade as his embarrassment coloured his cheeks.

"Oh!" he said seeing Mary's tiny frame with her frightened face. "I'm sorry I was about to knock!"

"Yes, I heard you." Mary's quietly spoken voice made Taylor-Smythe regret losing his temper so easily.

"I've been before," he offered in justification for his lack of patience.

Mary said nothing; she wasn't about to admit to knowing, years of experience with these people told her to offer nothing.

"Can I come in?" Taylor asked forgetting protocol in his flustered state. He was aware the gesture with his fist would look bad if Mary Mundy decided to complain about him or worse, if he had been caught on camera. He looked furtively about him, down the length of the corridor looking for any sign of CCTV devices. Of course, his fevered knocking could have drawn other attention from the neighbouring flats, someone who might have seen him through their own spy holes.

"Who are you?" Mary Mundy heard herself ask; from somewhere she found the nerve. Perhaps the assertive and stubborn Mary Lennox gave her the encouragement. She knew her namesake wouldn't have let anyone do anything she didn't want.

"Oh!" Taylor said again flustered, realising this time he hadn't introduced himself. He reached for the inside pocket of his jacket, thought he saw Mary flinch ever so slightly. "I'm D.C Taylor-Smythe," he pulled out his I.D card turning it towards Mary to examine the likeness of his picture. Mary's head bobbed as she tried to understand, but failed.

"You're one of the new Managers come to take me back," it wasn't a question Taylor heard, but a declaration which held years of fear culminating in abject resignation at her plight.

"No! No!" he hurriedly reassured her, "I'm a policeman," he blurted knowing for once he had got this visit completely wrong.

All he could think about was Wilson's entreaty for Mary Mundy to be treated differently, *"She has a great fear of official people, it appears to me she is very vulnerable"* Didn't Terri Wilson say she shouldn't be brought to the station as it would terrorise her?

For the first time in his career Taylor bottled it, he held up his hands in resignation, muttered, "Sorry to have bothered you," incredibly she watched him rush off down the corridor.

Mary peered around the door frame as he disappeared through the external door. She shrugged, stepped back closing the flat door.

Back once more in her comfy chair she sat considering the strange man in the suit – he didn't look much like the other ones – he still seemed more like the managers up at the Asylum than a police officer.

Overhead the baby began to cry pitifully as if on cue. Mary looked upwards towards the ceiling and not for the first time wondered if her baby was trying to warn her. She knew her baby still needed her.

The mother angel with her baby in her arms stared back at Mary from the shelf over the fire while Mary began to cradle her imaginary baby in her arms gently rocking back and forth as her head wobbled in time to the motion. Eventually Mary picked up her book The Secret Garden to continue to read on.

"Surprising things can happen to anyone who, when a disagreeable or discouraged thought comes into his mind, or just has the sense to remember in time and push it out by putting in an agreeable determinedly courageous one. Two things cannot be in one place. Where you tend a rose ... a thistle cannot grow." (Frances Hodgson Burnett – The Secret Garden)

CHAPTER 43

Brendon sat waiting alone in Terri Wilson's front room, feeling astonished he'd come there so impetuously. Nothing he told her so far seemed urgent enough to rush right over on a Sunday afternoon. He felt his embarrassment spread over him in a surge of heat.

The sitting room door opened slowly to reveal a child with braided hair twirled into tiny knots stuck up all over her head. She wore Hello Kitty pink pyjamas and carried a long-legged soft white rabbit, holding it by its ears. Brendon recognised the fluffy bunny tail. The girl blinked at Brendon looking like she just woke from sleep. Although her dark hair if released from the tight knots would be naturally afro-textured like Terri's, her face was pale with delicate features showing none of her characteristics, they were more like the woman he met on his way in.

"Hello," Brendon said as the child stood mesmerised by him. The little girl smiled coyly. Brendon pointed at the rabbit, "Couldn't he sleep?"

"Silly!" the girl chided, "It's a toy!"

Brendon grinned placing her at around four years, he knew from experience the phase when everything became literal and the magic of fantasy began to pale.

The door opened wider revealing Terri holding a glass of water, she offered it to the girl who took it but remained staring at Brendon.

"Go on!" Terri urged, "Back to bed." The child ignored her standing her ground until Terri placed a hand behind her head to guide her from the room with a gentle push.

"Bye," she called to Brendon.

"Nite, nite sweetie!" Brendon offered being reminded of his own daughter Rosie. Always the curious one with no natural fear of any stranger, Rosie looked about the same age when she wandered off at the park. For some frantic moments he believed someone had taken her, led her away when, in fact, feeling thirsty she went over to the drinking fountain which she could barely reach to get a drink of water.

This flood of memory made Brendon even more uncomfortable reliving the awful scene afterwards as he confessed it all to Nancy expressing his worry over Rosie's fearless streak. Nancy ignored him and never forgave him for letting it happen.

"How could you be so stupid!?" she yelled at him.

It was how she saw his momentary lapse of concentration, caught in a daze thinking about a work related matter which he'd long since forgotten. Not so the sheer scorn of Nancy's rebuke, her sharp tongue setting the timeframe for when she came to blame him for everything, never again calling him 'stupid' but implying it ever after.

"Sorry about that, Sarge," Terri came back into the room and stopped abruptly seeing the awful pain on Brendon's face. "What's wrong.....Brendon?" She enquired.

Brendon couldn't answer her, to tell it would open himself up to being seen by Terri in the very same way Nancy saw him. Terri was one of the few people who showed him respect and he couldn't risk losing her regard.

"Beautiful child," he offered instead.

Terri laughed, her natural cheerfulness echoing in the room.

"Nosy," Terri admitted seeing the painful expression slip away. "She must have heard us talking; she's at a curious age.

Brendon stood up afraid of intruding into her life on such a whim because of his own solitary feelings after waking from a bad dream. He felt foolish, "silly" the childlike voice reminded him, and he should never have come.

"I'm intruding on your time off," he muttered. "This can wait until tomorrow."

Terri stood up not wanting him to leave, "No, it's okay, you're not," she said realising it didn't make much sense. "Intruding I mean. I wasn't doing anything particularly." Her mother's departure to work meant another long lonely night on her own. "Truth is it is rare for me to have a chance to talk to anyone...." Terri could hear herself admitting her feelings wanting to carry on, to let it all out – all the years of bottled up emotions she'd kept well controlled whilst she achieved her dream of becoming a police officer. She wanted to tell someone how she sacrificed her own needs to do it and once achieved she now wondered at the single-focussed ambition and whether it had been worth it.

Brendon watched as she stood letting her thoughts play inside her head, the expression so pained he could identify with it; he sat back down without a word.

"She's mine," Terri confessed so abruptly it startled Brendon.

"I wasn't sure," he said tenderly. "I thought maybe your sister? I saw your mother ....she does look young enough...."

"It's how she wants it to look," Terri admitted. "....easier...well for her...." He could see her struggling with the idea.

"But not for you?"

Terri looked ashamed, "At being at school at the time. I think Mum saw it as lessening her shame.....and easier to move away, present Olivia as her own, as my sister."

"You didn't though?" Brendon asked.

"Oh, yes," Terri interjected. "I always wanted to be a police officer...it meant I could finish school then follow my dream....." she smiled showing all the feelings she felt for her mother. "I have nothing but gratitude for her sacrifice....."

"Does Olivia call your mother....?"

Before he could finish Terri shook her head, "She calls Mum, Nan," Terri's eyes flashed to indicate it was a sensitive subject. Brendon found it hard to read her thoughts, but before he could ask any more questions Terri's guilt showed. "We haven't really explained one way or the other," she said. "Soon when she starts school, we'll have to decide what to tell her."

"Doesn't she already ask?" Brendon didn't want to upset her, he knew from his own children just how curious they were at that age.

"She hasn't so far," Terri explained, "Before you ask she calls me Terri, like Mum does."

"She's lovely," Brendon smiled suddenly feeling foolish for his earlier thoughts, after all he was hardly on his own he had a wife and two children.

He thought about his own mother suffering years of living with his father whilst trying to protect him from a drunken lout, taking his moods and alcohol induced beatings year after year. He felt all his early pain having to hear her sobs, being too powerless to help her. The tears welled up hot, stinging his eyes. He rubbed them away with his hand. He felt Terri's eyes on him, watching him.

"Mother's sacrifice an awful lot for their children," his declaration strange sounding in the silence of the room. "Maybe not always true, but yours and mine are the special kind." It brought her back to life speaking about her; he didn't correct himself, just let it lie.

He saw Terri's subtle nod in agreement, "Maybe we don't appreciate them enough," she said. He knew she meant herself, not him. "I suppose they have to make decisions they wouldn't ordinarily have to make, when necessary." She sounded more like she was trying to justify what her mother did for her. She often wondered what it would have been like if she'd just left school to become a full time mother herself. She knew she wouldn't be sitting here having this conversation with Brendon Flannery without her police career.

"What about you?" She asked him.

He seemed to pick up on the direction of her thoughts, "I really don't know whether I would have become a police officer if...." He stalled unable to imagine an early life without the violence, being part of a 'normal' family, although he tried so hard with his own to make it as normal as he could without having an earlier role model.

He just aimed at doing the opposite of his own experience, not easy given the cases he came across in his working life. It made him self-reflecting and certainly self-critical. He blamed himself when Nancy turned on him after the Rosie incident, he should have taken more care of her, not let her wander off, a good father wouldn't have let it happen, she was therefore right to be critical of him.

There were times more recently when he thought he should never have had children with always the fear of passing on his familial genes. Michael already showed the violence of his grandfather, what if Rosie took after his own mother, became the accepting victim in her own abusive relationship?

"You okay Brendon?" Terri asked. He merely nodded unable to shake off the inevitability of the outcome.

"When does Olivia start school?" he asked thinking it wasn't too late to admit her parentage. "The time flies by." She could sense a deep sadness in Brendon, but reluctant to say anything to deepen it. "The problem with schools," he went on, "is the teachers try to equalise everyone – like each child ought to have a mother and a father, it's in all the learning material isn't it?" He remembered the stories of such wonderful loving 'normal' families but was unable to identify with them.

"It's changed a bit these days," Terri said not wanting to emphasise the difference in their ages, "There are some very different set ups these days. I'd say there are more one parent families than there used to be, same sex parents as well."

Brendon doubted there were many storybooks denoting the latter, well many included in the official curriculum. He sighed at his own cynicism even though he didn't voice it.

Terri heard a soft sigh wanting to raise the mood. "You were asking me about Mr Drover," Terri reminded him. "Do you think it important to interview him?" She asked trying to divert Brendon's mind away from the place she could see caused him so much distress.

Brendon's thought once again passed over his waking dream of Frances Drover trapped in a room tied to a bed.

"Yes I do," although he couldn't say why. "Let's go to find him first thing tomorrow." Brendon stood up to go, his sudden need to find his own family uppermost in his mine. "See you tomorrow," he said absently leaving Terri sitting there.

CHAPTER 44

Taylor, late for the Monday morning briefing, slipped quietly in at the back of the CID room where he sat listening to the report back by Stevens fresh from discovering the Drover Estate in Wales where Alwen Evans once worked.

He couldn't help himself from asking, "Isn't it a bit of a coincidence?"

Harvey glared at him, "You don't say, Taylor!" He wanted to say "No shit Sherlock!" but either way his sarcasm echoed in the silence of the room. "Has anyone heard from Flannery or Wilson today?" He searched the blank faces as he scanned around the room catching the smirk on Taylor's face, "You have something to say, Taylor?"

Taylor-Smythe immediately thought the two of them were skiving somewhere together; he couldn't help himself or his facial expression revealing his thoughts.

"Maybe they're on leave," Taylor suggested although no one would miss his implied 'together' somewhere in there. Nobody grinned or laughed, they were focussed on Harvey's obvious dislike of the comment, all of them wondering what he would do about Taylor. No one had missed the growing tension between the two of them.

"You think I wouldn't know if he requested leave?" For a moment Taylor forgot the protocol, requiring Flannery's line manager to give his consent for leave; especially at the moment as all leave was cancelled with the crucial investigative work going on. Taylor went quiet bowing his head.

The CID office door opened as Brendon Flannery came in on cue, he looked slightly pale if not a little green of face, "Good, I'm glad I haven't missed the whole briefing," he announced. "I got an early call, Gov, about Jocelyn Phipp's post mortem first thing this morning so I went. I didn't have time to let you know, it seems like the pathologist has a heavy workload so he started early knowing we needed it as soon as possible.

"Okay, Flannery," Harvey said slipping back into his formal address. Brendon noticed the switch. Once again he could tell Mike Harvey wasn't himself at the moment. "Do you know where Wilson is, did she go with you?" He could see Taylor suddenly alert at the back of the room.

"No Gov, we were on our way to make enquiries about Dorian Drover's father," he waved his arm to indicate he still couldn't drive. His temporary lapse the night before, when he drove his own car to Terri Wilson's house, warned him against trying it again, he nearly wrote his car off from lack of movement in his arm. It convinced him not to attempt it again, "So Wilson dropped me off at the mortuary then went off to seek out James Drover."

Harvey looked over at Taylor to see his reaction to this news. Taylor's face showed his anger, not for the first time Harvey's dislike of him rose without warning. He knew he must do something about Taylor; he didn't want either him or his attitude in his unit.

"We've just found out Alwen Evans was once housekeeper on a large country estate in Wales, owned by no less than the Drover family." He could see from Brendon's surprise he found it more than a coincidence. "Is there a way we can tell Wilson what we found in Wales, give her a heads up on the Drover link?" would you do that Brendon, then we'll hear about the post mortem."

Harvey left briefly disappearing back into his office as Brendon took out his mobile to call Terri Wilson. Taylor watched him press a couple of buttons, grinned gloatingly seeing her number there on speed dial. He saw it as an indication he wasn't wrong about the two of them. He watched Brendon talking, then press again as he went over to pour himself a badly needed cup of sweet tea.

Brendon hated post mortem duty. Standing watching someone being carved up with a scalpel or that dreadful buzzing saw they used around the head to open the cranium to take out the brains disturbed him. He didn't understand some of the ritual removals with all that weighing of organs in any case.

Harvey came back in carrying his mug, he saw Brendon fetching himself a cup from the tea table, "Any luck contacting Wilson?" he asked.

"No, Gov, but I left her a message," he said certain Terri would listen whenever she could, it being from him. There had been a slight awkwardness that morning when she picked him up having to detour to the mortuary he didn't have the time to sort it out.

When the briefing settled down again Brendon took a few sips of his tea then he filled them in on Jocelyn Phipps post mortem.

"She died from strangulation," Brendon began trying to forget the more routine procedures, "Evidenced by the bruise marks on her neck and depression of the trachea it is expected the brain will show absence of oxygen caused by strangulation." He paused briefly before going on, "although, there is a head trauma, where someone may have knocked her unconscious before they strangled her." He paused slightly before going on, "There is no evidence of any track marks to arms or any other part of her body from taking drugs – the alley is recognised for being a drug hot spot," he reminded them. "However, samples have been sent off to toxicology for any substance abuse either in her bloodstream or the contents of her stomach," Brendon looked over at Harvey adding, "He thought it unlikely from his cursory look....."

Brendon suddenly paled at the thought of the stomach contents with the inevitable smells of a mortuary where bodily fluids mingled with the heavy odour of formaldehyde. He gulped a mouthful of tea then carried on, "There is, however, evidence of a lot of bruising on her arms, as if she had been held tightly – these were pre-mortem, maybe an indication of some violence."

Another sip of tea as the memory of the young girl he'd seen at the Devonshire house came back to him. He'd seen her naked dead body having the indignity of being hacked and prodded. He knew he wouldn't ever get used to it and couldn't help but imagine how it might feel if a body turned out to be his own daughter cold on that same metal slab.

He shivered but went on, "There are no indications of any recent sexual activity or abuse," he lowered his gaze from the staring faces in the room, "although she wasn't a virgin," he muttered quickly without qualifying it technically, embarrassed at having to reveal such intimate details whilst his own daughter lingered in his thoughts.

"Right, thank you Brendon, as stated we have ourselves a murder to investigate," Harvey said, sensed his difficulties knowing their job required them to do although they never got used to it despite a 'gung-ho' attitude towards anyone's first time. They always laid bets on who would pass out and how long they would last before fainting. It went no way towards lessening the horrors they had to endure.

As a young copper he prided himself on lasting a full hour before he hit the floor which put him near the top of the score board his unit kept – there was always someone who made it through unscathed.

"Anything else?" Harvey asked.

"Not yet, sir," Brendon said forgetting he never called Harvey 'sir' always 'gov' or 'boss'; he sat down feeling wobbly on this feet.

CHAPTER 45

Bernard Devonshire's uncharacteristic lack of concentration on his businesses he knew couldn't be allowed to continue indefinitely. For him to take his eye off the game for too long would result in dire consequences. He couldn't allow himself this dreadful feeling of powerlessness that had crept over him to continue.

Why did no one call? To be left waiting for so long baffled him, unless they wanted to make him sweat, become more malleable. He felt scared not knowing what their demands would be. He hadn't given his associates much thought whilst they remained faceless. Why wait when the whole thing would be a paperless exercise of just moving money through legitimate sources to....wherever, he didn't need to know the specifics being a kind of 'middle' man.

He couldn't work out why they took his baby if it wasn't for a substantial ransom.

How they would know he prized Phoebe above anything else, his most precious possession (it never occurred to Bernard people weren't really possessions) as he kept his private life separate from all his business contacts. That's why he had a financial associate to do it for him. The big question now, that he didn't understand, having taken her why then would they take his wife and his Nanny before seeking any payment?

The telephone in his office began to ring stopping him mid-swallow of yet another mouthful of whisky; his resolve to get himself together, to stop drinking, lasted as long as it took to rid himself of one more headache, one more hangover. The phone kept on ringing.

His stomach churned, this must be the long awaited call when he would find out how deep he would be dragged into this seedy world.

His hand hovered over the telephone, his fear not allowing him to grab it away from its cradle. He gulped the last mouthful, his already perspiring brow allowing trickles of sweat to run down his hot face. He grabbed the phone raising it to his ear listening. His face immediately relaxed.

"Where are you Jed?" he asked his financial advisor of long standing. In itself a relief just hearing his voice, he'd been trying to get hold of him for days. He held in the temptation to ask, "*Where the hell have you been?*" in his usual rude manner, but part of his abrasive forcefulness disappeared when this weak powerless man he had become appeared.

He listened as one of the key figures in his business life spluttered out some feeble excuses. He felt his temper flare once again but wouldn't allow it to interfere, not when he needed help.

He quickly gave him instructions ignoring totally anything he'd told him about his own family problems, he didn't much care how other people lived, his total focus currently centred on himself. With luck he thought, in salvaging the latest deal he must offer his apologies for having to cancel the meeting due to family issues.

"Did you get that?" he snapped into the phone; the very phone he expected to receive the ransom demand on. "Get on with it!" He cut the call off abruptly transferring the handset back to its cradle, feeling better he asserted himself once again. It made him feel more in control; gave him back a little of his lost power.

He opened his brief case at the side of him on the desk, revealing the tiny teddy bear with the blue chiffon bow. He picked it up. The bear stared back at him, its tiny face looked fierce, he noticed for the first time how ridiculous the chiffon bow contrasted with the look. He flicked it with his thumb, undoing it taking the ribbon from around the tiny neck.

The miniature bear looked back, its eyes fixed staring fiercely he almost expected it to open its mouth to show a range of sharp spiky feral teeth. Why did he think that? This is Mr Cuddles that his daughter loves, how could he see him any other way than loveable?

He took the ribbon attempting to tie it back, to make the bow like before; although not quite the same, it would have to do. He tossed it back into the brief case and closed it.

CHAPTER 46

"Any news from Wilson?" Harvey asked Brendon as he stood in front of his desk fidgeting nervously; he'd come in to check on Harvey's state of mind which currently exhibited uncharacteristically erratic traits. At the moment he was too concerned about Terri to take on board any problems Harvey might have.

"Err, no boss," he said pleased he didn't have to raise it first. Brendon spent the last couple of hours trying to contact her as she didn't return his original call it worried him.

Part of the time he tried to figure out what he'd done or said that might have upset her. He knew he left pretty abruptly the night before mostly due to his own embarrassment at impetuously charging over there on a Sunday afternoon. It prompted the whole conversation maybe Terri would have preferred not to have confessed her long since buried secrets.

"And you say she went back to see Mrs Drover?" Harvey asked.

Brendon nodded, "We both were meant to initially, to catch Mr. Drover early before he went off to work." They arranged it so they might still make the morning briefing after.

Of course, it being one of Brendon's 'feelings' he had no idea what to ask when he met up with James Drover. At the time it seemed the lesser of the two evils, not taking her to the post mortem he tried not to subject her to the whole gruesome ordeal. He now felt ashamed allowing Terri to go there alone.

Of course the arrangement had been made before Stevens' visit to Wales, before he knew about the potential connection to Fiona Devonshire's mother that cast doubts over her parentage.

"The thing is, boss, I'd go over....." he looked frustrated by his plastered arm preventing him from driving, he felt like ripping it off; although it hurt a fair bit still.

Harvey could see his agitation, "Just check again to see if the control room has heard from her, if not, get Stevens to get a pool car and go over there, see if you can find her." Harvey thought he must be getting soft in his old age, but he could see something in Flannery's face, he still rated intuition especially from a seasoned detective. "We'll sort the paperwork out later."

Brendon didn't need telling twice, he rushed out of Harvey's office over to his desk to pick up the phone. He caught sight of Taylor grinning his toothy grin. Brendon glared at Taylor who looked away as he turned his back waiting for the control room to answer. As he suspected they had received no notifications from her.

"Just hold on Sgt Flannery, I'll give her a shout," the control room operator put him on hold; it seemed the longest minutes of his life. "P.C Wilson isn't answering," the operator came back at him breaking the silence making Brendon jump, "Maybe tied up somewhere." The latter didn't try hard enough to hide the doubt.

"Can you keep on trying, get back to me?" Brendon asked already a tiny bit of fear beginning to creep into his mind.

"Stevens?" Brendon called across the room to where D.C Stevens sat at his terminal interrogating his computer. Stevens joined him having picked up a print out from the communal printer.

"Sarge?" he said. Brendon held up a finger to silence him as he spoke once again into the telephone. "Brilliant, we'll be right over." He turned to Stevens, "We've got the last pool car," he breathed a sigh of relief. "Go get the keys would you meet me out in the car park?" Stevens rushed off picking up his jacket on the way.

Brendon switched off his computer, turned to leave, his way blocked by Taylor who nonchalantly sauntered into his path holding a cup of tea he'd just poured himself; his grinning face irritating Brendon considerably.

"She's probably off skiving somewhere *Sergeant* Flannery," Taylor emphasised the Sergeant revealing his own problem with him having the rank.

Brendon eyed his ginning face, then deliberately down at the cup in his hand he said uncharacteristically, "Well if you were to do something useful in this case, *you* might make the rank, Detective *Constable* Taylor!" He swerved around him and rushed out.

His fears were straining to be let loose into outright panic, blaming himself for letting her go alone. *Why ever not you knew something wasn't right otherwise why dream about Frances Drover in the first place?*

The pool car bay was empty except for one small Ford Focus which Stevens sat in. Brendon knew it to be the car most cops preferred not to get allocated on a trip out of force; the bigger more powerful cars were all out, he preferred to drive the Mondeo if he needed to do a trip out somewhere.

"Bummer!" he managed a smile as he eased himself into the passenger seat.

"As long as it goes," Stevens replied philosophically. Starting the engine he held his breath until it caught. He raised his eyebrows at Brendon who looked on when the ignition didn't catch the first time. "Where to?" Stevens asked convivially backing the small car out of the parking bay beginning the climb up the hill to the main gates as Brendon filled him in on the destination of the Drover's of Blackheath Avenue.

Stevens listened intently until he'd finished, fished into his jacket pocket one handed for the sheet of paper he took off the printer earlier.

"Funny you should say that," Stevens passed it to Brendon who cast his eye down the sheet. "I did some ferreting into the Drover's of Clwyd."

Brendon read a potted history of the family tree, turned the paper over as if searching for something.

"Where is this from?" he asked wondering just how reliable it was, he couldn't see the source.

"It's one of those sites, like Burke's Peerage, with a list every noble family wants to get onto; only these days everyone's at it, the internet is full of such things," he looked over at Brendon who clearly didn't surf the net like he did. "There's a whole industry of genealogy experts tapping in to trace their family trees to prove they are of Royal birth!" he laughed. He knew because he did it himself. "It's a great source of information on all kinds of people." Brendon looked at him with renewed interest. "It's all a question of knowing where to look, there's no shortage of information on the 'haves', there's a sort of battle to be included in the most prestigious levels of society." He laughed out loud, "Of course they are really good at hiding their skeletons or darkest secrets which I think is why Fiona Devonshire's birth certificate is very much a fake one."

"Being because there is no Alwyn Evans?" Brendon asked.

"Exactly," Stevens replied triumphantly. "Although it is still not clear who the father really is." He nodded at the sheet.

Brendon read on picking out the appropriate dates in the 80s/90s when Alwen Evans occupied the housekeeper post at the Drover's Country Estate – actually more a Hall than either a castle or a stately home and definitely acquired with 'new' money.

Brendon stared out of the car window as Stevens chatted on about his Welsh trip, describing the area where the Evan's cottage sat surrounded by beautiful landscapes situated just inside the grounds of the large country estate owned by the Drover's.

"Inside the grounds?" Brendon's head snapped back peering at Stevens.

"Yep," Stevens replied. "More of a gatehouse really," he corrected himself, "Like they wanted to keep her as close as possible."

Is that normal Brendon thought having one of his strange feelings again. He thought about his own mother, tied to his abusive father and reined the thought in. Alwen Evans left her job only to move as far as the end of the drive, to the gatekeeper's cottage, just as much a prisoner as Frances Drover was confined to her house. Similarly, Mary Mundy confined for years up at the Asylum, limited by her years of institutionalisation, moved close by into sheltered housing.

"Where are you going, Stevens?" Brendon suddenly asked unable to hold his tongue after trying to identify where they were. Stevens showed no sign of being lost, he took the next right instinctively.

"You said Blackheath Avenue," he looked at Brendon for confirmation. "I just checked the route – it seems like the bottom end is still blocked by press vans around the Devonshire's place. I thought it best to go round the other way."

"Ah," he said having forgotten the paparazzi's renewed interest, he guessed since they found the body of the murdered Nanny.

Brendon glanced at his watch saw the morning creeping on when he knew, after the Chief gave a press conference mid-morning, this activity would be the result.

Stevens turned in at the top of Blackheath Avenue cruising slowly down the road gazing casually at the houses as he passed, looking for number 27.

Brendon busied himself with searching the sparse row of parked cars for Terri's blue Astra, the one he knew she drove because she picked him up in it earlier. He couldn't spot it and felt disappointment well up again.

"Just there," he pointed to a space between a white van and a battered green Citroen with a lot of rust spots.

Stevens pulled in, checked the number of the house and once satisfied he switched the engine off. Brendon could see farther down the road where a larger crowd of news reporters, photographers and chance freelance snappers were vying for position outside the Devonshire's house again. He could see Stevens was right to come this way.

As before the house looked deserted with all the windows at the front blocked by pulled curtains; Brendon visualised Frances Drover sitting in the smoke filled sitting room chain smoking. He could see no lights through any chinks in the curtains. It being a grey day with threatening rain clouds, he knew it would be gloomy inside with all the natural light blocked out.

They got out of the car, moving to the front door.

"Looks like no one's at home," Stevens said.

"There is," Brendon assured him. "Frances Drover is extremely agoraphobic." Stevens looked enquiringly. "She doesn't go out."

"Oh?"

"Over the years she says it got increasingly difficult," Brendon told him. "She finds it much easier if she doesn't try."

Stevens arrived first on the doorstep, leaned in to ring the doorbell. He looked at Brendon when he heard nothing.

"I don't think it works," Brendon said simply. Stevens rattled the letter box loudly making Brendon wince imagining the effect it would have on a very nervous Frances Drover.

The same two minutes silence elapsed before they heard the door chain being taken off. The door opened a crack revealing the anxious face of Frances Drover who recognised Brendon then looking at Stevens asked bluntly, "Who are you?"

Stevens fished reluctantly for his ID card which he pushed towards her. It shocked him when a hand shot out snatching it out of his hand halfway through his announcement, "D.C Steve……" His face made Brendon want to laugh.

Frances Drover scrutinised the ID photograph looking at Stevens to match it up. She mumbled, "You need a new one it looks nothing like you," she pushed it at him out of the gap handing it back; Stevens took it quickly conveying it to the inside pocket of his jacket.

Brendon said, "You may remember me….."

"Yes," she confirmed.

"….I came with the other female police officer." She nodded. "P.C Wilson came to see you this morning?"

She shook her head as she muttered, "No." Brendon could tell she looked nervous opening or even standing near her front door was extremely difficult for her.

He went on quickly, "She hasn't been here this morning?" His underlying concern notched up a degree.

"No, as I just said," Frances Drover seemed more annoyed.

"Okay, sorry to have bothered you," he backed away from the door leaving Stevens alone on the step looking mystified. He stared at Frances Drover who shut the door in his face.

When he caught up with Brendon his comment, "She's rude. That was a bit weird," which stopped Brendon before he could open the passenger door to get into the car. He stared at Stevens for an explanation.

When one didn't come he snapped, "I told you she suffers from agoraphobia."

It irritated Stevens, he hated being misunderstood, "Yes I heard," he replied. "My Nan had it once...."

Brendon wasn't in the mood to discuss the finer points of the condition, so he left it. His concern for Terri Wilson got the better of him now threatening to take him over, he pulled out his mobile trying her number again whilst he ignored Stevens.

Stevens reached out to push Brendon's mobile down to gain his attention.

"Agoraphobia doesn't automatically make you unable to leave your house...."

Brendon's anger rose suddenly, "It's the fear of open spaces....." he began.

"Yeah, yeah also crowds," Stevens replied. "Odd though," he pointed back at the front door. "She was sweating....."

"....probably about to have a panic attack!" Brendon suggested, "And why I left quickly to enable the poor woman to go back inside. If you could see how she lives in there you would have more sympathy."

Stevens shrugged. He could tell Brendon wasn't receptive to anything he might have to say. He pointed down the road at a much larger crowd outside the Devonshire's, "I'll go to check on what's happening down the road whilst we're here," he said walking off briskly before Brendon could instruct him differently. He fumed at the delay to finding Terri.

He took out his work mobile again to telephone the control room glancing over the road whilst waiting for them to answer. In the garden of the house opposite an elderly man with a pair of garden shears in his hands stood clipping at loose sprigs of privet from his front hedge whilst watching Brendon intently.

Brendon stopped listening pressing his phone off; he walked over to the old man flashing his ID quickly but didn't give his name.

"Morning," Brendon greeted him.

"Aye, it still is," the old man threw back, looked at his wrist watch adding, "just."

"I wondered if you noticed anyone around here earlier?" Brendon asked.

"Hard not to, wi' that lot yonder," the old man pointed down the road. He growled, "Like Piccadilly Circus, comings 'n' goings all day!"

"Mostly press," Brendon had some sympathy for the chaos the media always caused. "I meant here, or over there," he pointed at the Drover's house.

"Oh, them!" the old man shot back. "Weird lot they are!"

"Weird?" Brendon queried. "Who are 'they'?" He found it an odd statement given how quiet he found the Drover's house - it grated on him he used the same word as Stevens, but then he'd only met Frances.

"Shouting 'n' screaming at all hours!" He looked intently at Brendon. "I may be 'owd but I'm na deaf!"

"Who does the shouting?" he couldn't imagine Frances Drover raising her voice, she was a timid mouse.

"'er an' 'im," he said. "An' that weird hippy son when he's around."

"Do you mean Mr and Mrs Drover shout at each other?" Brendon asked.

"Aye used to," he said, "afore he went."

"Mr Drover doesn't live there?"

The old man scowled, "I told the other coppers all this," he growled. "Don't you lot talk to each other?"

Brendon sighed, "What other coppers?" he asked.

The old man gave a cynical laugh, "Them as come the other day," he said.

Then Brendon realised he meant the door to door when Phoebe Devonshire went missing. He made a mental note to check the door to door reports for anything significant.

"Have you seen a uniformed police woman around here today?" he asked.

The old man shook his head, "I'm not stood 'ere all day tha knows," he replied indignantly. "No copper."

Brendon decided to give up on the grumpy old man as he saw Stevens walking back up the hill.

"Just her driving off in her car," the old man yelled after him. Brendon raised his arm waving believing he wasn't a very reliable witness. "I never knew she could drive," he added half shouting half muttering to himself.

Stevens reached his car, got in as Brendon walked around to the passenger side, looking back over the road he saw the old man had gone.

CHAPTER 47

Bernard thought he was still dreaming. His dreams were becoming more vivid each night as his drinking crept back up to full throttle. The voices he heard were muffled with an occasional louder word, usually his name, being shouted above the rest.

He opened his eyes. The room spun making him feel giddy. The shouts he heard were coming from outside where once the press were camped just outside his gates. It took some considerable effort to sit up. Nothing wanted to stay in one place as the room swam around him at a dramatic speed. *Never again* he vowed for the umpteenth time, his promise of sobriety having slipped away at the behest of his enforced imprisonment.

Eventually, by small steps he managed to get to his feet moving over to the bedroom window. Through a crack in the heavy drapes (which these days he didn't bother to open) he saw his front gates once again besieged by the paparazzi. At least the world seemed to care about his missing daughter and his wife and Nanny.

He remembered the Nanny, but temporarily forgetting her name? His mind slipped a notch leaving most things hard to remember these days. His Nanny was dead? The idea made him feel sick to his core. If they could kill his Nanny what would they do to his precious Phoebe? Why take Fiona? Would these types of ruthless people want her to look after Phoebe? Why go to such lengths? All these questions flooded together in one surge.

He peered again at the crowd outside his gates, spotted a man walking slowly down the Avenue to where a lone uniformed police officer stood trying to keep the crowd in some semblance of order, stopping one of them every so often from attempting to scale the gates.

He watched the young man draw something out of the inside of his jacket chatting to the police officer. They both turned to peer at the house. He ducked behind the curtains holding his breath as if breathing would draw their attention. When he dared to look again he saw the young man making his way back up the hill while the policeman once again tried to control the hordes.

His curiosity short lived was interrupted by the telephone ringing and forgetting his delicate condition he turned too quickly towards the sound nearly falling over in the process.

"Easy, easy," he told the room as he made his way back over to the bed, taking hold of the bedside telephone, he held onto the cabinet to steady himself for the next big thing, the ransom demand.

He raised the telephone slowly to his ear, "Hello?" It came out like a throaty whisper.

The quiet pause as he strained to listen produced nothing, only the sound coming from the mingled shouts outside.

"It's me," his financial advisor said, "Jed."

His sigh of relief, almost a hiss, was loud as Bernard Devonshire collapsed sitting down hard on the bed.

"I thought...." He began, but didn't continue. Not being certain just how much Jed knew of his darker dealings made him cautious. "....some news about my daughter."

He couldn't make out the sound that came back, it got lost amongst the cries coming from outside.

"Is there any news?" he heard faintly before he realised he held the telephone against his right ear, the one with slightly impaired hearing. He switched the telephone to the other ear automatically.

"Say again," he demanded sharply frustrated by the call tying up the line on which he felt certain the ransom demand would come.

"Do you have any news about your daughter?" The words were now clear and if anything too loudly shouted as Jed raised his voice.

Bernard moved the hand set away from his ear slightly, sounding deflated he replied, "No, I'm still waiting for them to call."

"Them?" Jed asked tentatively.

"Whoever's taken my baby," he wanted to yell it down the telephone, *"Are you stupid?"* Instead he said, "And my wife," as if an afterthought.

"They've taken your wife?" Jed echoed down the phone.

"Yes!" Bernard's reply fell just short of a scream. He heard another phone, a mobile tinny sound begin on the other end of the line.

Just then his doorbell rang and he heard an engine revving outside. *What the bloody hell*, he thought

Jed said, "I've got to go – another call, I need to take it."

Bernard slammed the phone down in anger, stood shakily making his way down the stairs holding tightly to the bannister as he went. Once at the front door he thought *who the bloody hell has the copper let through*, he opened it to reveal a builder (the words Safe Building Contractors displayed on the side of a battered two tone, rusty red van parked alongside his porch). The man wore dirty overalls whilst a second man similarly dressed began taking boxes out of the back of the van.

"Who the hell are you?!" Bernard demanded angrily.

"If I could just step inside, Sir," he said showing no emotion, "I will show you my police I.D," he delivered in a deadpan voice. "We are here to set up recording equipment to monitor your telephones in case of any ransom demand."

For once Bernard felt lost for words, this was the last thing he needed although he meekly stepped back letting him in. Immediately the second man followed the first one in carrying two large paint splattered boxes of equipment. Once inside they showed Bernard Devonshire their I.D badges.

*   *   *   *   *

Jed heard the crash of the phone against the cradle cutting off the call to Bernard Devonshire. His mobile persisted, he caught it just before it went to answer phone.

He yelled, "What!" and listened. "What have you done?" he demanded. "I'll get there as soon as I can, just don't go anywhere!"

He cut the call.

CHAPTER 48

Mary listened to the baby crying again, no longer able to concentrate on her book she felt almost relieved to be able to break off from reading it. This book revealed such a dark sad story it set her mind to thinking back over her early life. There were too many people dying, too much grief and hatred. She liked stories mostly about love with happy endings like when Jane Eyre came back, married Mr. Rochester and together with their children they lived happily ever after.

She knew it wasn't real, even though her life hadn't been like that, it had been sad with the exception of the baby, they told her died, but she knew it existed out there somewhere in the real world. She wanted her happy ever after.

The baby's demanding cries reached down to her from the ceiling, followed by the light music from the flat above as the baby's cries faded away. Mary closed the book, it being the first one she didn't want to finish; the ending, she felt sure would finish unhappily. Some lives were like that, not meant to end happily although finding herself here in her own tiny flat probably represented her very own happy ending.

*   *   *   *

She swapped one unhappy fraught existence at home with her parents who were meant to care for her, for the even harsher cruel regime of the Asylum.

She learnt long ago her father's abuse wasn't the normal thing a parent did to their child, despite the many uttered assurances, "You know I love you, don't you Mary?"

She eventually told her mother about what her father did to her not expecting her mother to become angry, or to call her dreadful names. A reaction she wouldn't have believed possible from her own mother; her father used it as a threat after that to keep her quiet whenever he did it again.

He also stopped being gentle and kind. He saw her telling her mother as a huge betrayal of what he said they did together. If she tried to resist afterwards he taunted her with, "Who's going to believe you?" He called her bad names like "slut", "whore" and began to slap her. She could see by his face he enjoyed it as she slipped away into a safe place inside her mind where such things never happened and where she could close off those words altogether, just lay silently still until he stopped and went away.

He no longer told her he loved her or called her "his little princess"; initially the taunts of "who is going to believe you" stopped also. Mary knew by the way her mother changed towards her she didn't believe her. After that whenever she got irritated or was displeased with her, she also called her names like "wicked" or "liar", so she stopped trying to seek help withdrawing into herself to a safe place inside her head.

After a while there was a doctor at the big place whose voice carried other words she didn't understand, like "mental defective" which she heard from the safety of her mind. She stopped going to school about the same time her belly began to swell, having to endure the same doctor prodding her whilst her mother wailed "the shame of it" and cried a lot. She remembered the day they took her to the Asylum, it was the last time she ever saw them.

She remembered only the one moment when she stood in the Asylum doctor's office with her parents whilst his strange melodic voice filled the room with his assurances they would take good care of her. "Mental defectives," he told them, "do not have the capacity to understand about morality. We will take good care of the 'little situation'. Mary will receive 'treatment' for her condition; you needn't worry she will be safe with us."

Her mother took a step closer to her, looked like she might put her arms around her, tell her everything will be all right, perhaps to comfort her. She hesitated; stopping with an outstretched hand hastily pulled away by her father who stepped forward, took her mother's arm pulling her away out through the door, his leering face the last she ever saw of them. Mary remembered standing alone in the huge office whilst the doctor fetched the nurse.

The room crammed full of books, the only other memory left after she chose to forget the faces of her parents. She took comfort from the shelves full of leather-bound volumes with the smell of the old mildewed yellowing pages giving testament to the length of time of their endurance. She pulled herself up proudly standing tall like the rows of book shelves, silent, strong and enduring.

*   *   *   *   *

Mary looked down at the closed book across her lap. A book someone wrote long ago, which she knew couldn't have been easy pouring out all that sorrow and woe to produce what after all became one of the classic books of all time.

She opened it once again to read it out of respect for their sacrifice. If they could finish writing it, she could finish reading it, no matter what thoughts it brought forth from her past hidden deep inside her.

CHAPTER 49

The CID office was cloaked in darkness with just the glow of the computer screen emitting sufficient light to highlight the surrounding desks. It made an eerie picture as the changing screens caught Taylor-Smythe's face set in fierce concentration. He preferred the office empty of the other detectives this early in the morning because he found he could concentrate without any of their inane banter and prying eyes.

Today Taylor woke up from a strange dream. He knew the dream had been prompted by his many visits to the golf club where he observed the young golf-pro Peter Thompson. The dream, a typical social gathering like the ones he attended on many occasions at his own club, where the well to do mingled with the aspiring like himself. He knew it to be a place where social climbers gathered to get themselves noticed, to meet influential people if they were really lucky enough to climb the social ladder. Taylor's desperation had grown so much he wanted to do just that, to prise himself away from his humble roots. This he thought provoked his subconscious into dreaming about his advancement.

His rise made possible by his own endeavours, at first as a casual employee at his golf club, tending bar, and waiting at tables in the restaurant he worked until he amassed sufficient money to actually join the club. He also knew how hard it could be to get on the first rung; needing to be supported on his application by an existing member, preferably a distinguished one willing to oblige, being the hardest part of it. People in his world just weren't members of golf clubs. He fortunately spotted this job opportunity enabling his long desired plan to take off. 'Bar staff wanted apply to the Social Secretary for an application' caught his eye in his local newsagent's window providing him with the opportunity to begin his long desired social climb.

A barman was one of those faceless humans most people could never really describe but which the lonely alcohol dependent's spent hours talking to about their fears, their sorrows and mainly the people they hated the most. On a slow shift where the bar became devoid of more interesting members, Taylor remembered, a lone '19th holer' provided the in-house entertainment between serving the odd drink or two to a handful of similar loners.

You could learn from them about the same people he so badly aspired to be. Over time they began to call you 'Trev' like a long lost friend, an abbreviated name he hated the most. However, such a small sacrifice to hold his sharp tongue, not to rebuke the deliverer of the hated abbreviation, and given sufficient fuel to fade their memory, they were more than willing to sign as sponsor on his golf club application. Trevor Taylor-Smythe, his new chosen name, embarked on his upwardly mobile life style.

His dream encompassed much of his latent memories, replaced after years of acceptance, by the small out of the way club at the start of it all. When he woke it sparked the forgotten memory of searching the records of Peter Thompson's club with the many photographs of the social events the web-site included.

He got up dressed hurriedly that morning leaving for work before the sun came up, hoping the web-site manager (he wanted to think all main tasks would be undertaken by the men's side) with their amateur blogging chat, would still be oblivious to the privacy settings.

Once installed at his terminal he delighted in finding it to be the case. Not for the first time it reminded him to get a computer terminal at home, and after taking all the training courses he could get himself on at work ready now to own one. Even so, in this case, evidentially it was better to use the force systems as something at the back of his mind reminded him he must.

He found the social events part of the web-site intriguing, a veritable wealth of valuable information. If only he knew who everyone was, he thought as he scrolled down the many pictures. To think someone takes all these at every gathering. There were people posing in pairs with tags like 'Captain with friend' or Mr and Mrs somebody social secretary, year on year for as long as the website existed. Someone back in time, loaded existing photographs laboriously tagging each one, dated in chronological order. Someone, Trevor assumed, whose life revolved around the golf club with little else in it.

Every so often he found a group sitting at one of the many formal dinners, jolly people around large round tables drinking, eating and laughing in merriment on an alcohol induced festive occasion; wine bottles on each table. The further back he went the differences emerged; the equality of the sexes disappeared. Gone were photographs of mixed social evenings with the appearance of 'male only' events captured for all time were commonplace; Trevor sighed for the loss of those days.

He remembered working on a few of the very last ones to be held as a barman knowing just how rowdy they could get without the presence of their womenfolk to keep them in check.

He stopped, staring at the screen where a wide shot of a few male only tables, revealed large numbers of men in dinner jackets holding up their glasses in an obvious toast to something. He peered at the nearest one to the camera; between the tables he could see one or two waitresses passing carrying bottles to replenish the glasses for the toast.

In this shot he recognised a young Fiona Devonshire dressed in the standard black skirt and white shirt of a waitress. She looked up at the camera smiling as she stood between two of the seated guests while someone snapped the picture. He leaned in further, the photograph being slightly grainy but clear enough to see the shadowy arm of one rather ugly man extended behind her, no doubt patting her behind if his memory of such events served him well.

"Well, well, well," he muttered. "If I am not mistaken…."

He got up from his chair went over to the evidence board took down Bernard Devonshire's photograph bringing it back he held it against the screen and smiled. He printed off the photograph from the screen and carried on his search for anything he could find related to Peter Thompson.

CHAPTER 50

Taylor stood in front of the Golf Club notice board, the one exhibiting the club's previous captains and honorary life members. He couldn't help likening this established practice to an obituary list like the military ones you saw for service men and women killed on active duty or missing, lost in action. The idea of someone lost in action on a golf course whilst chipping out of a bunker made him chuckle.

"Can't keep away?" a voice behind him asked; the statement carried a measure of sarcasm. Peter Thompson drew level with his elbow also staring at the board.

"There is something curiously amusing about being made an honorary life member," Taylor announced philosophically, "especially I imagine most of these are long dead." He nodded towards the board.

Thompson scrutinised him closely for any tell-tale signs of a trap, "I wouldn't know," he said. "I haven't been here very long."

Taylor recognised his attempt to be consistent with his previous statement, as they looked at each other they laughed in recognition of it.

"There wouldn't be much point in showing you an old photograph to see if you recognise anyone then," Taylor's statement was a feeble attempt at justifying his being there so early in the day.

"Not if they're a long gone honorary life member," he said provocatively.

Taylor glanced at his face to see if he was making fun of him. He took out the grainy black and white photograph that had lost quality from the initial scanning onto the system, made worse by copying it on the police photocopier which wasn't exactly state of the art. He handed it to Thompson to look at, if only to prove he did have a photograph.

"I take it this is another attempt to see if I recognise the woman you keep harping on about?" he nodded at the picture.

"Well....?" Taylor began.

"I take it she works here, not an actual member," Thompson asked.

It threw Taylor by his honesty wondering for a moment why he had been so critical of him. He didn't trust himself to say anything, just waited for his reply.

"The ball gown threw me," he glanced at the photograph. "She obviously waits table." He tapped the picture at where Fiona Devonshire stood looking at the camera, "Although this is an old picture of her, I have seen her at more recent social events."

Taylor's head snapped upwards to stare at him, "You mean as a guest?"

Thompson's head moved from side to side, "No, she still waits at table, not very often mind. I forgot when I saw her with the golf clubs.....kind of assumed her to be a playing member," he smiled adding, "one I hadn't met before."

It stunned Taylor to imagine after everything he heard or read about Fiona Devonshire's life style, she should still work there, "Are you sure it's the same woman?"

Thompson looked at the photo again, nodded, "Yep, although I can't remember what you said her name was?" He could see the shock on Taylor's face. "I don't know the names of all the waitresses either; they use one of those 'silver service' agencies for the bigger occasions so they aren't technically golf club staff."

Taylor, floored by his candour and just how helpful he was being asked, "Recognise anyone else?" trying to maximise on his co-operation, maybe he got him wrong first time they met.

Thompson studied the picture again tapping his finger against it. Taylor expected him to recognise Bernard Devonshire. He saw Thompson laugh, "He's an honorary life member," he smiled at the irony given their previous conversation, "only still alive." Taylor leaned in to look pointing at Bernard Devonshire.

"Him," he asked tapping his image noticing once again Devonshire's sneaky arm around Fiona the waitress.

Thompson shook his head, his finger pointed at the man to his left where Fiona stood between them. "James Drover....I'm sure it's him, although this doesn't do him justice," he said.

"Why?" Taylor asked.

"In reality he looks younger, he's quite the handsome noble sort," he looked thoughtful. "Well I always imagine him being by the way he speaks and acts."

"Oh!" it wasn't exactly what Taylor expected.

"They made him honorary life member, I think, because of his connections rather than his service to the club."

For someone as new as Thompson claimed, he surprised Taylor by his knowledge assuming family connections and familiarity with the wealthy gave him such an insight.

"You have family connections?" Taylor asked tentatively.

Thompson suddenly laughed so raucously it surprised him, "Err, no!" He could hardly speak for laughing, "You have to have been brought up on my manor to understand you are well off the mark!" His chuckling took a while to subside. "Not to say I can't spot someone from a privileged background and his is definitely one."

Taylor's opinion of Peter Thompson took a 180º turn reversing his previous opinion of him. About to leave with his photograph he stopped to ask, "What about him," he pointed at Bernard Devonshire.

Peter Thompson looked puzzled, "What do you mean?"

"Do you see him around here?"

He studied the picture again shaking his head, "No, I haven't seen him before, but then……" his infectious smile appeared once more on his face.

"…you haven't been here very long," Taylor finished for him also smiling. He started to walk away waving his hand in a friendly gesture.

"I thought of that too," Thompson called after him.

He stopped turning back towards him, "What?"

Thompson grinned again, "Becoming double barrelled," he waited for Taylor's attempt at denial.

He watched the smile appear on his face and nodded acknowledging they both had a lot in common, but mostly to lose their roots.

CHAPTER 51

Harvey and Taylor, together with a few of the detectives, stood in front of the evidence board where earlier Taylor drew in the links between the Devonshire's and the Drover's before he explained his findings. The new photograph they pinned to the board between them.

"Of course," Harvey said. "Just because they were sitting at the same table doesn't mean they knew each other well."

"Unlikely they wouldn't...." Taylor knew from his own experience placement at tables could be random before people imposed their own seating preferences.

"These were the days before women influenced the mix," Taylor saw Harvey scowl at him expecting a politically incorrect declaration to follow it. Taylor swallowed hard, "You joined the golf club not just for the sport," he suggested, "Also for career or business purposes – to make connections in order to further your own position. You wouldn't waste an evening's opportunity by sitting with just anyone."

Harvey looked at him with renewed interest, "Are you saying they were more likely to be business contacts?" Harvey asked.

"Or even 'potential' business associates," Taylor said. "More deals are done on such occasions than not. I expect one of them probably encouraged someone financially to place them at the table."

Harvey wasn't a golfer. He never saw the point of whacking a tiny ball for yards trying to get it into a small hole. However, he was lost for words, more at this show of knowledge from Taylor than anything else. The other detectives stared at him in amazement.

They were interrupted at this point by the office door bursting open to reveal Brendon Flannery red in the face and out of breath rushing in.

Harvey looked concerned, "Flannery?"

It took Brendon a minute or so to get his breath back, "Boss," he gulped. "I'm really worried about Terri....."

Harvey turned to Taylor, "Get Brendon a drink," he turned back offering him a chair then noticed the plaster on his wrist ripped away from his hand. "Take your time Brendon to get your breath back before you tell us."

Brendon revealed how after Terri dropped him off at the mortuary she was meant to go to interview James Drover at Blackheath Avenue but according to Frances Drover she hasn't seen her.

"Maybe she didn't make it," Taylor suggested, "her car broken down or...."

"She's not answering her mobile or work phone, the Control room can't raise her on her radio," the concern in Brendon's voice unmistakeable. "I went to her house to see if she went home but there's no one in." He couldn't explain how he knew her mother and daughter ought to be there because it was personal to Terri so knew he shouldn't reveal it.

Taylor raised his eyebrows saying nothing; clearly the admission supported his thoughts on their relationship.

"Unlikely if she's supposed to be working," Harvey suggested deliberately ignoring any implications.

Stevens also arrived back in the office, "Ah, there you are," he said returning from taking the pool car back. "Is there any news?"

The look on Brendon's face told him the answer to the question, so he moved quietly behind the others looking at the board with Taylor's golf club picture.

Harvey brought Brendon and Stevens up to speed. "If the gossips are correct, then James Drover could very well be Fiona Devonshire's father," Stevens suggested.

"Are you certain?" Harvey asked.

"Well no, not really, it's just gossip, common knowledge at the local pub about Alwen Evans being given a home on the estate."

"Then what do we know about this picture," he tapped it with a finger, "Fiona Evans married Bernard Devonshire, but once waited table at a function where James Drover is seated next to him – let's pursue it. Find James Drover .....Bring...." Harvey began.

"Sir," Taylor interrupted. "She still does according to Peter Thompson." This admission must have slipped Taylor's mind partly because he felt it unlikely given her marital status and her husband's wealth, but mostly he felt Harvey might ridicule the whole idea.

Harvey, stunned into silence, stared at Taylor in amazement making him wince under the scrutiny; even though he expected it he braced himself for the backlash.

Brendon Flannery interjected, "What do you mean?" he asked sharply. "She's rich – it's hardly likely she works especially with a new baby...."

Taylor resented his condescension, "I'm aware of all that!" he snapped indignantly. "Why would he lie, he had no idea who she was OR make the connection between the waitress and the woman in the car park.....the one with the badly bruised swollen face," he emphasised.

"You've changed your tune!" Brendon accused suddenly angry at Taylor's defence of Peter Thompson whom he'd obviously previously disliked.

Taylor bristled at the personal attack, "I'm merely reporting what I've been told," his anger at the challenge being great, he turned to Harvey, "Apparently the golf club hire in a waitress service, one Fiona Devonshire *still* works for occasionally...." He emphasised the still. "It is strange, although he did say not recently...the baby is only three months old," he finished feeling unsure about having raised the matter.

Stevens said, "I'm sure we could verify it one way or the other don't you think?"

"I haven't been able to follow it up yet I'm just about to...." Taylor put it at the top of his list of things to do for after the briefing.

"Would you do it now please Taylor?" Harvey asked politely without one bit of animosity.

"Sir?" Taylor queried not sure of his thoughts on the fact.

"This is the first real lead on Fiona Devonshire," he said quietly almost to himself. "She's a bit of a mystery..." he looked up at the detectives all staring at him, "Quite strange she disappeared just after her baby was taken."

"Sir?" It was Brendon this time looking for an explanation.

Harvey looked to be deep in thought before he realised Brendon had spoken.

"Why would a kidnapper of a baby take the mother later?" he asked the room. "It doesn't fit any normal profile." He echoed the question Bernard Devonshire had just asked himself.

"Maybe they aren't connected," Stevens suggested.

"So where is she then?" A little bit of Taylor's earlier animosity tinged his words. "She must have been upset at losing her baby surely?"

Harvey glanced at Brendon trying hard to recall their earlier interview with her.

"What did Wilson tell us when we arrived at the house, Flannery? Harvey asked his face perplexed remembering he'd shouted her down at the time.

"She said Fiona Devonshire was really upset," Brendon began. "No! She said distressed at telling her husband and you told her she would be...."

"More agitated at having to face her husband when he got back," Harvey remembered her face when she heard him in the hallway, "she actually shook with fear then he burst into the room." The detectives sat in stunned silence, "She lost control, shouted at him.........do you remember what she said about him Flannery?"

Harvey searched Brendon's face for help.

"Something about him being upset the dinner party was ruined," Brendon recalled.

"Yes, but she began to say 'you don't think he'll still'....she thought he might still expect it to take place!"

"I did think it odd she would even think it," Brendon agreed.

Steven's looked on puzzled, "Are you saying she didn't once mention her baby?"

"No, she did ask 'Who could take a baby?' didn't she boss?"

Harvey nodded, "She accused her husband of being responsible – or rather the people he does business with."

"....which was when he hit her!" Brendon said excitedly. He remembered it well looking down at his half plastered injured arm certain now it got weakened when he intervened between them, when he caught the first blow of the day to it.

Harvey shook his head, "Let's see what else we can find out about Mrs Devonshire, can we?" His gaze fell on Taylor who nodded, "Steven's see if you can trace her mother, she must be somewhere, in receipt of benefits, a pension, or something." Steven's nodded this time.

"Can you come into my office Brendon?" Harvey asked quietly. He moved away with Brendon Flannery following behind him.

CHAPTER 52

The shadowy figure hidden by the dense greenery moved furtively, reaching forward one arm parted the leaves slowly so as not to attract attention, allowing sufficient view to reveal the young slightly built girl moving along the pathway towards this concealed hiding place.

She laboured behind a large silver-cross coach built pram which she seemed to be having trouble pushing up the incline towards the shrubbery. She stopped just short of the patch the figure hid behind, where an ornamental bench with elaborately scrolled metal arm stood, the framework securely fixed to the ground, supported a wooden bench seat. It displayed a commemorative plaque inscribed with someone's name who died many years ago.

The young girl stopped as she approached it, patted her short cropped hair blown aside by the wind, back against her forehead. Bending down she engaged the brake on the pram before she sat down on the bench, taking out her mobile phone. She began to flick a few screens as she read the messages.

The arm holding the branches of the shrubbery pulled it further apart watching as the girl pressed the screen, stopped and waited. A low muted buzzing sound carried as far as the seat where the young girl sat. Suddenly alert at the faint sound she raised herself upright looking around her for any sign of the origin of the noise, saw no one and relaxed.

The arm released the bushes, extracted a mobile from inside a pocket, and brought it up to eye level pressing the screen to life where the name read 'Josie' then a message popped onto the screen.

"Hi, Dor, meet on Tuesday at yours? Day off J xx"

The hand pressed the 'reply' symbol and quickly tapped in:

"Ok house to myself 10.00 don't be late! D"

The thumb pressed 'send' and 'message sent' appeared, as the message added to a list of previous messages. The mobile switch off, the hand pushed back the undergrowth once again revealing the empty bench. The girl had moved on.

*   *   *   *

"Boss?" Brendon asked closing the door behind him having meekly followed Harvey into his room. He felt a low level sickness in the pit of his stomach; sure Terri Wilson's silence was ominous.

He knew by her face when she dropped him at the mortuary she felt something for him; he dared to hope her feelings matched his own. She gave him a long hard look not requiring any words although he'd still said, "We'll talk later" hoping he would find his voice to be able to tell her how he felt about her.

She nodded silently having spent the night since Brendon left her trying to justify her own feelings for him, a married man. She always promised herself never to get involved with anyone already married; she wasn't a home wrecker and had no aspirations of becoming anyone's 'bit on the side', no matter how much she cared for them.

Yet when she saw the look on Brendon's face her resolve began to weaken, so with the promise to 'talk later' she would settle the matter one way or the other. As he sat staring at her, he looked like he might lean over to kiss her. How would she feel if he did?

He leaned slightly forward towards her making her feel hot panic creeping up her spine, knew she wanted him to. Instead he stretched his hand behind him, caught hold of the car door lock to release it. He turned as the fresh air hit her through the open door, then he slipped out leaving her sitting there.

Harvey's telephone rang loudly bringing his thoughts back to the moment. He heard Harvey say, "Yes! Harvey," briskly into it. He followed it with several "yes" replies as he listened intently then once he queried, "Valium?" in a puzzled question. "Do we have any idea....okay I see." Harvey returned the phone to its cradle and sat silently staring at it.

"Boss?" Brendon interrupted the silence standing like a statue in front of Harvey's desk.

Harvey waved him to a chair his face looking perplexed.

"That was Jim at the mortuary," he said. "Apparently Jocelyn Phipps had been hit over the head, strangled, but also her stomach contained a large quantity of Valium...oh and tea."

"Tea?" Brendon queried.

"Yes," Harvey suddenly looked up sharply. "Making her death I would imagine possibly nearer to the time she left the house at Blackwell Avenue."

"I thought she died much later?"

Harvey shrugged, "She was drugged with Valium in tea....you remember Wilson made tea whilst we talked to Mrs Devonshire?" Brendon nodded his agreement. "Wilson might be able to confirm whether the Nanny drank any of it..." he wanted to add, 'when we find her' but realised from Brendon's face how concerned he felt about her absence.

"So what actually killed her?" Brendon asked to cover his own agitation.

"Logic supposes she was drugged first, obviously," he said trying not to sound too pompous. "The blow to her head, Jim thinks being sufficient to knock her out, but he doesn't think it would have killed her – so the strangulation finished her off which is curious as the marks on her neck are consistent with a good deal of force, likely delivered by male hands by virtue of the thumb marks on her neck, whereas the blow to her head took less strength although sufficient to render her unconscious."

Brendon scratched his head, "So are we saying whoever killed her got progressively more violent?"

"Or there was more than one person involved," Harvey looked for agreement.

"Did he find any other injuries – defence wounds or torture?" Brendon asked.

"None whatsoever, suggesting whoever intended to subdue her, rather than kill her."

"Can the contents of her stomach place the time any closer?" Brendon asked.

Harvey shook his head, "It contained nothing else, no breakfast or other subsequent food, just tea with Valium."

"Would she likely have a prescription for Valium?"

"Good point Flannery, but unlikely she would be prescribed it given her age," Harvey added. "But find out will you?"

"The alternative is it was used to calm her," Brendon said. "Why? Why not just kill her if you intend to do it?"

"Motive being the key." Harvey toyed with the M.O in the Nanny's case and could only come up with, "She must have seen something incriminating about the baby being snatched."

"Really?" The idea surprised Brendon.

"I understand from hers and Mrs Devonshire's statements they were shocked at discovering the pram was empty.....she actually screamed," Brendon remembered reading.

"It doesn't mean she didn't see anything or recall something significant later," Harvey explained.

"You mean like nearly colliding with Mary Mundy?" Brendon suggested noticing Harvey flinched at him mentioning it which he ignored saying, "Check the prescription query would you?"

Brendon took it as a dismissal and turned towards the door.

"Send Stevens in will you?" Harvey asked as he passed through the door.

CHAPTER 53

Bernard's pacing drew more agitated across the bedroom where the curtains closed out the daylight apart from the one inch strip at the centre where they didn't quite meet. The gap cast a silent star wars lightsabre across the carpet. Every once in a while he stopped, peeked out between the narrow gap displacing the lightsabre and letting in the bright light. He had no idea what to look for but knew 'they' were out there somewhere watching him.

It wasn't easy when the new horde of journalist news hounds appeared in response to the Chief Constables press bulletin after the discovery of the Nanny's body but especially since the 'builders' turned up to tap his phones. The people watching him were way too smart to be deceived by it.

He wanted to scream, "Who the hell has building work done when their wife and baby were missing?" The kind of people he dealt with wouldn't be fooled by it for one minute; it only delayed the ransom demand. The longer it went on the more he feared for his Phoebe's life.

He let the curtain go to pace across the lightsabre once again, he felt like pulling out what little hair he still owned; never a vain man he'd seen more hairs on his comb that morning than should have been there indicating the stress beginning to take its toll.

Through the gap in the curtains he assessed a much thinner crowd outside this morning, "They're getting bored," he muttered. "Why don't you just go away – all of you?"

He watched as the gates opened sufficiently for the uniformed police officer to let two figures through the gap. He took a step closer to the window focussing on the approaching figures, recognising the Chief Inspector who witnessed him attack his wife.

"What the bloody hell does he want?" he hissed scrutinising the other younger man who looked remotely familiar. "Not the fat cop!" He almost salivated at the thought, he would know the one who arrested him anywhere, knew they had unfinished business. He heard the doorbell ring, going to answer it, he sighed heavily.

When he found them they were sitting in his lounge waiting, no doubt let in by the other coppers tapping his phone. He felt an initial surge of anger at their audacity although they rose to their feet as he entered.

"Make yourself at home!" He growled, "This is absurd! You have taken over my home completely."

Harvey inwardly sighed in resignation of this truly repugnant man. "I'm sorry for the inconvenience of all this, but it's essential if you receive a ransom demand Mr Devonshire I assure you."

"Building work, Chief Inspector?" Bernard's sarcasm grew with his temper, "Who the hell would carry out building work under these circumstances? Who is it going to fool?" Bernard walked over to his sideboard to pour himself a drink. He whirled around, "They have taken over in my office!" He wanted to mention them helping themselves to cups of tea but even he thought it petty, so he bit his tongue.

"I understand you haven't heard anything, Mr Devonshire?" Harvey persisted ignoring his complaints.

Bernard slumped unexpectedly into an armchair looking exhausted, now a completely broken man. Suddenly unable to speak he shook his head wearily. He didn't trust himself to answer feeling more like crying.

His head raised as if a thought just occurred to him, scrutinising Stevens standing beside Harvey, "You!" his anger now back at full force, he felt safer behind the protection of anger, "I saw you yesterday outside," he just remembered the man walking down the road who spoke to the uniformed officer outside.

Harvey shot a glance at Stevens surprised by what he said registering Stevens looking sheepish.

"Just checking on the media presence Sir, to see if we needed more uniform here," Stevens said thinking fast on his feet, unsure of how much he should reveal about their missing colleague.

"Why are you here?" Bernard asked, "What are you doing to find my daughter?"

Harvey was surprised at his question which he'd asked for the first time.

"I assure you we are doing everything we can to find both your daughter and your wife," he forced himself to be civil given his lack of concern for his wife, "And of course who murdered your Nanny."

Bernard paled at the declaration, "It's definitely murder then?" he managed. He didn't dwell on her death, he didn't want to hear what the kidnappers were capable of, after all if they could do it the once, they could do it again.

"Not everything, otherwise you would have found them by now...."

"It's one of the reasons we are tapping your telephones, sir," Harvey felt his own temper rising at this so obviously stupid man. "How about helping us Mr Devonshire, you must have some idea who might do this. Mrs Devonshire seemed convinced it's someone you might know," Harvey reminded him surprising even himself at his own audacity and not normally his style to antagonise people unless they were the villains or he didn't have any respect for them.

It surprised Bernard Devonshire as all the cops he'd met so far always tried the fawningly nice approach which he never responded to. All except the fat copper who arrested him, the one he intended to personally return the favour to one day. His mouth took on a sneer momentarily, then faded.

"I have no idea what she meant by it, Inspector," Bernard retaliated, demoting Harvey by his address, "My business clients have no reason to do something like this…"

"Like what Mr Devonshire?" Harvey cut in, "What do you think *this* is?"

Bernard stared at him in disbelief, "How do I know, my daughter hasn't been taken before."

"And I assume your wife, Mr Devonshire," Harvey reminded him, "You did report her missing." Harvey's deliberate jibe didn't go unnoticed by Stevens who stared in disbelief at the interchange. What little he knew about Harvey, he wore his tact and diplomacy at all times like a medal, this just wasn't like him.

"Where else would she be?" he shouted, his temper taking over once again. "Gone on bloody holiday whilst her own baby is missing?"

Stevens sat between them listening to this exchange knowing it wasn't getting them anywhere. The doorbell rang as Harvey and Bernard Devonshire glared at each other.

"I'll get it, sir," Stevens jumped up, glad of the opportunity to escape.

He came back into the room followed by a smartly dressed man in a business suit, his longish dark hair slicked back off his face giving him an Italian look. The anti-thesis to Bernard Devonshire being younger tall, slim and well groomed.

It was hard for Harvey to interpret whether Bernard Devonshire welcomed his new visitor or not, as he sat silently waiting for him to speak.

"I'm sorry if I'm interrupting," he began looking at Bernard for any signs of disapproval.

"And you are?" Harvey asked rudely even though he felt sure he recognised his face.

"This is my financial advisor," Bernard jumped in quickly feeling some alarm at having him there. "What do you want?" he intervened abruptly. "This is not a good time is it Chief Inspector Harvey?" Harvey looked at him suspiciously.

"Can I ask if there is any news, Bernard?" The visitor asked hesitantly.

"Apparently not," Bernard replied. "But these officers are expecting me to get a ransom demand so they've set up taps on my phones."

"I did wonder why you haven't contacted me lately," he eyed Bernard closely.

"I'll phone when I can Jed," Bernard assured him. "Or come to see you soon, okay?"

"Yes, right," he said backing off towards the door. He was followed out by Stevens to see him out.

Harvey found Stevens standing on the porch steps gazing as if in a trance; the last of the paparazzi still held vigil at the gates.

"What are you doing, Stevens?" Harvey asked lowering his voice to almost a whisper.

The builders van stood to one side of the main steps up to the door as Stevens gazed in the opposite direction.

"Watching him walk up the hill – I expect he's parked away up the hill," he nodded towards the incline as Harvey followed his gaze but could see no one. Stevens turned to Harvey, "I'm trying to place where I've seen him before." He shook his head as if the motion would help his memory to return.

They both heard the front door slam behind them as they moved off to find their own car.

CHAPTER 54

Brendon sat pensively at his desk, his face a picture of stark frustration. The surface now covered in the scattered papers once contained neatly in the evidence file in front of him.

"What are you doing, Sarge?" The voice belonged to one of the computer staff who worked on the collation of the door-to-door interviews. She tried hard not to sound too peeved by his disembowelling of her neatly collated manual evidence file.

"Looking for a particular interview, Poll," Brendon sounded so disheartened she wanted to laugh at him.

"Why don't you look it up on the system Sarge?" she asked pointing at his terminal.

Silence followed her question revealing as she already knew, not all the detectives took the basic computer course relying heavily on her instead.

She sat down next to him on the extra office chair and walked it closer to him. "Shove over, Sarge, let me!"

Brendon wheeled his own chair aside with his feet letting her take over his terminal. She waited as he looked blankly at her.

"Name?" She asked politely.

"Ah, I have no name, just that he lives opposite the Drover's on Blackheath Avenue," he said.

She waited for him but nothing more came. She tapped lightly on the keyboard reminding Brendon just how inept he had become since his plastered wrist only let him rip it off sufficiently to drive his car. His initial concern for Terri had now given way to panic with so many people disappearing, and one found dead, he knew he had to find her quickly.

"Okay, odds or evens," Poll asked patiently.

"Evens," he said then as she typed Blackheath into the computer he added, "Higher than 58."

More tapping revealed an emerging list of rows of names with addresses, "I don't think it will work, he's an old guy, probably lives on his own, probably easier to go back there...." His voice faded as he watched the list get bigger with names grouped together at each address. "Wait he cried seeing one a single name, Brown, amongst the rest. He pointed, "Try that one." He tapped the screen against it.

She selected it bringing up his interview; when Brendon read it, he looked excited. "Can you print it?" he asked.

"Yes, Sarge," she tapped again, after a slight delay Brendon heard the office printer jump into life; he rushed over taking the one piece of paper out of the printer tray.

When he returned to his desk she began putting the loose pages back in order.

"Sorry," he mumbled realising he had caused her extra work. Waving the sheet he said, "Thanks for this," He rushed off.

He popped his head through Harvey's door, found the room empty, hovering for a moment he hesitated, then made a decision yelling over at Polly, "It's easier just to go round," leaving her with the unenviable task of placing the pages back in order in the file.

Brendon didn't relish the task of talking to the old man again as he knew he would be awkward.

"You again!" The old man greeted him grumpily. The hope he might be a bit forgetful and not remember the last time they spoke faded. The old codger grinned, "Knew you'd be back."

"Can I come in Mr Brown?" Brendon asked pocketing his ID having flashed it at him.

"Aye, reckon," the old man stood to one side as Brendon stepped inside to be led into a back room of this very large house on Blackheath Avenue.

"These houses are much bigger on this side of the street," Brendon observed conversationally.

"Nowt wrong with yer eyesight anyroad," the old man quipped.

Brendon grinned. He could see he had been hasty to write him off, there was nothing wrong with his memory.

The untidy room they walked into Brendon thought wasn't too unreasonable for an old man living alone. He sat down on an old sofa covered with a crocheted blanket that probably had seen better days. The old man sat down in a chair at the side of which a large dog lay curled up in a dog basket. It looked to Brendon like a black Labrador. The dog's head rose as the old man's arm reached over the side of the chair stroking the dog's ears. The dog's tongue appeared, licked the man's hand as he mumbled words of comfort to it.

"'Owd, like me officer," he said to Brendon. "We've not got long as like as not." He looked over at Brendon waiting.

"I read the statement you gave to my colleagues from the door-to-door interviews," he said.

"Aye, I gev one," he confirmed. "Toad you that last time."

"Have you lived here long," Brendon began.

The old man began to laugh which turned into coughing. Brendon could hear a faint rattle in his chest and knew his previous assertion to be probably correct; a giveaway for the one-time miner if he was as old as he looked. He noticed an old pipe rack on the mantle-piece containing old pipes and pipe cleaners and thought *that won't help his condition.*

When he stopped coughing he launched off about how long he'd lived there with dates that Brendon knew would be accurate.

"The ha'sus were original ones," he continued. "I remember when there were green fields ovver yonder." He pointed in the direction of where the other side of the Avenue would be.

"So you'd remember when the Drover's at number 27 came?" Brendon asked.

"Aye, it's an easy one," he laughed. "She came...." The old man stopped to think. "Aye last year....the end of last year it wor."

Brendon looked surprised, "Are you sure, the place looks a bit dilapidated, like it's been neglected."

"Aye, were empty for a long time - she's done nowt to it since." He said.

"Don't you mean 'they', what about her husband?"

The old man began to laugh again and Brendon feared it might set him off coughing.

"I toad yer, he don't live there," for the first time he sounded a little impatient.

"I thought you meant the son," Brendon suggested.

"'ee comes 'n' goes I reckon."

"So the son doesn't live there either," Brendon asked, caught the glare of the old man's stare, "you mean he never has?"

"Not for long, reckon he can't stand his mother either," the word 'mother' he pronounced like 'bother' making Brendon smile at his accent.

The dog in the basket at his side snorted. Brendon could see it shaking, its legs trembling with the claws catching the side of the basket as it twitched. The old man reached down, "Dreamin'," he explained, "Chasin' rabbits I reckon."

"So Mr Drover doesn't live with his wife?" Brendon recapped.

"Like I said, I reckon he just dumped her there and ran, he's a reet poncey git, one of them toffs."

Brendon nodded. The old man waved his hand down himself, "Posh suit the works," he continued. "Pretty looking like that deadbeat son of his, two peas in a pod if ever I saw," he said screwing up his nose as if he could smell something bad. "Never done 'ard graft either of 'em."

Brendon looked down at the print out sheet of his first interview, "You said she drove," he read.

"Not much.....didn't know she 'ad her own car, don't see her much, since she came like."

"But you saw her driving recently?"

"Aye, day afore, I toad yer," he said impatient again.

"Do you remember what kind of car?" Brendon hardly dare ask.

"Ah, can't say what it wore, I don't do cars me sel," Brendon let out the breath he'd been holding. "It were blue though.....and small." He added.

That confirmed he'd seen Frances Drover driving Terri Wilson's blue Astra.

CHAPTER 55

Brendon's legs felt heavy as he staggered away from his interview with the old man. He felt sick at the thought Terri might meet the same fate as Jocelyn Phipps although he couldn't rationalise where the Drover's fit in to it.

He made it to the gate where the neatly trimmed privet hedge looked shaved evenly on either side of the gate whilst, he noticed, the rest of it all the way around the garden didn't get the same attention by its nosy owner who used it as an excuse to spy on his neighbours.

Brendon's telephone buzzed in his pocket bringing him alert once again. He stopped, leaned against the gate for support whilst he took the call. When he answered it the force control room made his heart flip giving him the sinking feeling you get on a big dipper at the fairground as it launches you down the steepest incline.

"Flannery," he managed, listening as the operator informed him they found PC Terri Wilson's car in the car park at the country park just down the road from where he now stood.

A uniformed officer from Traffic called the control operator who relayed the message, about a suspicious car reported by one of the Country Park's employees.

"Right," Brendon glanced over at the deserted looking Drover house, his mind assessing just how close it was to the country park at the bottom of the hill, close enough to drive Terri's car there and walk back. He considered whether it could be possible for Frances Drover with her condition. He remembered Stevens saying

"*Agoraphobia doesn't leave you unable to leave your house*...." he knew it because his grandmother once had it. *Could it be cured?*

Brendon fought the urge to rush over the road to break the front door in searching for Terri. Instead he walked briskly up the hill to where he left his own car away from the Drover's house.

He sat behind the wheel, fighting the urge to get back out and storm up to the Drovers' door. His instincts told him it would be a mistake if the old man had been mistaken, and what he saw wasn't Frances Drover but Terri herself. The image of Frances Drover as the pitifully frail woman still wouldn't leave him.

On impulse he started the car, did a frantic turn around on the Avenue then pelted down the hill. He noted the few media outside number 58 as he passed by which slowed his speed in the 30 mph limit to much closer to it. He took in huge gasps of air to try to calm his erratic breathing as he reached the entrance to the Country Park's main car park. He hadn't been back here since the fateful day he misplaced his own daughter Rosie, somehow it symbolised the decline of his marriage.

He could see the car immediately as most of the spaces were empty, just one or two others dotted about he assumed to be employees of the Park or maybe dog walkers. The 'Police Aware' sticker hit him first. He looked around for any evidence of a Traffic car, obviously long since gone. *Routine* he thought, even where the car is one of their own, it was just another car to them like the dozens stolen by joyriders who abandoned them although they usually left them burnt out.

What if Terri came here with her daughter? Is it likely she would have just disappeared during a working day to take her sister/daughter to the park? Brendon got out, cupped his hands to peer into the car trying not to touch the side, he couldn't remember what the inside looked like, although he thought it still the same. He spotted the fluffy white rabbit on the back seat seeing the little girl in the Hello Kitty pyjamas once again dragging it around by the ears, remembering his comment about it not being able to sleep; the very grown up four year old Olivia who called him "Silly" because it was only a toy. A little girl too old for her years who didn't even know her 'sister' was in fact her mother.

He tried hard not to think about what she would do without her if anything happened to her 'nan'. He pushed the thoughts away getting back into his own car. He phoned Harvey's number waiting for his boss to answer gruffly with "Harvey?"

"Boss, Traffic just found Terri Wilson's Astra at the Country Park," he announced hoping he wouldn't say anything to set him off panicking again.

"Where are you, Flannery?" *All business like using his second name again* Brendon registered.

"I'm sitting in my car next to it," he said. "It's definitely hers."

"Okay," Harvey instructed. "You stay there...."

"You need to know the Drover's neighbour opposite saw Frances Drover driving away in a blue Astra yesterday......"

"Stevens just identified James Drover who visited Bernard Devonshire whilst we were there earlier," Harvey said.

"According to the neighbour, Mr Brown, James Drover doesn't live with his wife whilst the son comes and goes, but doesn't stay for long," Brendon took some more deep breaths. "I think we ought to...."

"It's okay, Flannery, I've actioned a search, got firearms unit back up with a warrant to search the house just in case Fiona Devonshire and the baby are there – I'll explain why when we get there. Stay where you are it's the rendezvous point.... I'll get Forensics on to the car." Harvey's phone line disconnected.

Brendon sat with his head in his hands behind the wheel considering how long all this would take; he feared they would be too late for Terri let alone Mrs Devonshire and the baby.

The rap of knuckles on the window at the side of him made him jump. The man peering at him, dressed in some kind of uniform, stood glaring at him. Brendon pressed his window down.

"What are you doing?!" The man growled.

Brendon was in no mood for petty officials, "Sitting in my car, who are you to ask?"

The man grew red in the face, "This is a private car park to the Country Park and that car," he pointed at Terri Wilson's Astra, "shouldn't be here either."

Brendon feared he might just lose it altogether with this 'jobsworth' so he reached his hand inside his jacket which alarmed the man sufficiently to make him jump back away from the car window. Brendon noticed he carried a two-way radio.

"I'll call the police!" he threatened raising it to his mouth ready to speak into it.

"Whilst you're calling your mate tell him D.S Flannery…." He pulled out his ID badge, "said, hi!"

Just then they both heard the screeching of tyres together with a burst of a police siren somewhere outside near to the Park. Two seconds later a procession of assorted police vehicles including the firearms squad and forensics appeared at the entrance to the car park filing through parking randomly across all the vacant spaces.

"No need to bother," Brendon said. "They're already here."

Harvey's car appeared with Stevens beside him, they got out. The firearms squad followed by a forensics van turned in at the entrance to the car park, filed through adding to the chaotic parking.

The Park keeper looked on in amazement as a squad of armed officers all dressed in black wearing body armour and helmets got out of the van grouping together, their PSU leader met Harvey as Brendon walked over to them.

He listened whilst Harvey filled everyone in about James Ellis Drover, whom Bernard Devonshire called Jed his financial advisor, also likely to be his wife's father.

Steven's added, "It's only gossip back in Wales but he is definitely one of the sons from the country estate back there where Fiona Devonshire's mother worked. Apparently she was brought up there," he told them. "Actually, having met him he looks too young to have got her mother pregnant but he did seem mighty interested in any news about the investigation."

Brendon looked confused, "He doesn't live with Frances Drover according to Mr. Brown opposite, never has."

"Except he came to see Bernard Devonshire today and walked off towards Number 27," Stevens added.

Brendon was becoming quite agitated again for Terri, "Can we just do this," he urged Harvey.

The PSU leader opened out a street map giving instructions in a clipped concise way before everyone jumped back into their vehicles leaving the forensic officer to process Terri Wilson's car.

A very surprised Park Keeper stood beside Brendon's car as he approached it.

"Look..." he began in a more conciliatory voice.

Brendon walked up to him, poked him in the chest, "No you look!" he spat harshly. "If you are in the habit of challenging people let me give you some advice. Firstly, this is a public car park attached to a public park. Secondly, if you don't reconsider your person skills I will tell you one day you will come across someone not as amenable as me and I guarantee your employment will be terminated along with yourself I shouldn't wonder."

He got into his car to follow the others out back up Blackheath Avenue.

CHAPTER 56

I just came in from the garden with the others; we are dirty from kneeling in the soil all day my 'coolie' hat is still on my head. It's what nurse Bryony always calls my straw hat when she yells, "Put your 'coollie' hat on Mary Mundy, we don't want to take any chances, it's hot out there today!" I always remember it anyway and today I had it in my hand ready.

Coming back in I didn't have the chance to take it off because we are hurrying along as it is nearly time for tea, and being Saturday we are promised jam for tea. I don't want to miss that. We always have jam for tea once a week instead of dripping with salt. I do like dripping especially if I get to scrape the bottom of the dish with the tasty brown jelly which I love. Someone said it was meaty essence or something, but it tastes fine to me reminds me of Sunday dinner back home with me Mam and Da again, a big joint of pork with crispy crackling, the pork dripping poured off into a side dish for tea later when it sets.

I must have been dawdling or dreaming of how good pork crackling used to taste soaked with gravy because when I look up the others have gone and I'm all alone in the big corridor just along from the spur that goes to the chapel at the end.

I can hear my baby yelling, a long plaintive cry I know means hunger. I know she wants feeding, so I follow the sound.

*   *   *   *

Mary heard the baby crying quietly against the silence of the room. She had just made tea and toast, trying to decide whether she really wanted eggs for breakfast. Thinking about it being Saturday and how they always gave you jam on a Saturday at teatime up at the Asylum. In the shop she noticed a basket of little jars of jam. Tiny pots of all kinds, not just the raspberry she used to get, but strawberry, apricot, damson and blackcurrant. She assumed they were new. They sat in a fitment next to the big jars of jam she always looked at when she did her shopping on a Tuesday for her usual things. On impulse she took three out putting them in her hand basket looking carefully at all the flavours.

The baby yelled, its voice moving away from the kitchen where she stood going out into the hallway; she followed the sound as it moved. She opened the flat door in a trance, listening intently to the baby's cries moving along the corridor as she followed the sound through the next fire door, walking past the slatted door where the communal bins sat in rows behind it.

Mary spotted the lift to the upstairs floor of the complex. The light next to a button shone green. Mary's hand reached out to it pressed, the door slid noiselessly open making Mary jump backwards away from it.

She peered inside as if she might find her baby there, her heart beating fast. She was tempted to step inside, saw the panel with more buttons suddenly feeling afraid, her mind slammed back to the Asylum once again.

*   *   *   *

She was strapped to a table like the time when she pushed her baby out, she had her ankles tied at the bottom each side while her arms were strapped to her side by the leather strap across her tiny body, pulled tight it dug into her. She couldn't move. There was no point in fighting it being surrounded by people busily doing things.

She turned her head to look over her shoulder where all kinds of gadgets sat on a bench table behind her and the figure of a doctor, she recognised from her annual meeting in the big office with all the books, now checking the equipment. A red light shone brightly from a dial at the front of the metal box showing an array of numbers with colours above of green, yellow or red squares segmented off; a hand like on a clock was moving slowly up through the numbers.

"Mary?" She heard a voice at her side say. She turned to see a nurse standing with an injection needle in her hand. She knew it was like the ones she had before many times, more when she first came or when she got too emotional or cried a lot, then they gave her an injection which hurt her, sticking them in her arm until everything went dark.

The nurse took a step nearer, "This won't hurt you, Mary," she lied; they always told you that and it always hurt. "Why bother saying it," she thought resigning herself for more pain. "This will just make you more relaxed, Mary." The nurse said sounding not one bit convincing.

Mary closed her eyes waiting for the sharp needle to enter her arm; it always hurt because being so tiny with such small veins they pushed the needle right through, then pulled back to find the right place. Mary held herself stiff keeping in the scream, it reverberated through her head but she made sure she didn't let it out.

She drifted in a haze, as the shadows of people hovered all around her. Someone pushed something like hard rubber across her lips parting them with the instruction, "Bite on this, Mary," so she did.

She drifted again until she felt the pressure of two pads one each side of her head at the temples, heard the sound of something whining behind her where she lay. A loud voice, this time the doctor ordered everyone, "Stand back!"

Her head exploded with a surge of pain making her body quake then lift her off the table, it arched in the middle but the straps held her down stopping her falling right off the table. She shook as the surge of electricity cursed through her body sending it into violent fits of pain then motion, lights, more pain, darkness and light as she moved in and out of consciousness. Mary's tiny body convulsed with violent heaving, diminishing down to fading judders until she stopped altogether unconscious.

The doctor checked her eyes lifting each eyelid in turn to peer with a light shining directly onto her pupils. The nurse dabbed cotton wool against her lips taking out the round rubber block with teeth marks. A trickle of blood from where she'd bitten her lip the nurse mopped up with more cotton wool.

"Okay," the doctor said as a man moved forward to wheel the trolley they placed her on away to the next room to recover.

Eventually she opened her eyes to a nurse's face peering down at her. "Okay Mary, we will take you back to the dormitory where you can sleep," she heard the nurse say.

The fear she felt seemed less, in fact she couldn't remember what scared her in the first place. She tried to think harder but it wouldn't come, so she lay still as they pushed her back. She felt intermittent hot then cold air whenever they passed an open door catching the draught. The lights above were dim for most of the journey until she got back to the ward where the glare of the long strobe lighting made her close her eyes tightly.

Trying hard to remember something on the edge of her conscious mind, she slipped from the real world hearing only a voice quietly whisper, "She'll forget about the baby after this," then waves of darkness with intermittent light. Finally she heard a baby crying plaintively for its mother and then lastly her own voice, but inside her head calling out, "I'll find you, my darling, I'll find you."

She slept for a long time.

*　　　*　　　*　　　*

Mary found herself back standing in front of the open lift doors with the panel of buttons. Too afraid to enter, she turned to the side where another door with an oblong window revealed a stairway going up to the floor above. Mary entered the stairwell where she could now hear the baby's cries much louder.

271

She began to climb upwards holding onto the bannister for support, her painful hip complaining as she took each step.

"I'm coming my darling..." she thought trying to convey the message to the baby, trying to stop it feeling frightened and alone.

She made it up the stairs by using her right leg each time, pulling up her left leg behind her as she met each step in turn. She moved through another fire door giving way to a corridor exactly the same as her own on the floor below and momentarily lost her bearings. There was just the closed lift door, no communal rubbish bins here like on the ground floor. The Warden had shown her this part of the building when she first came here.

The rest of the Warden's speech that day she had long forgotten because Mary wasn't very good at listening and thinking at the same time.

The bin cupboard reminded her of the large bins up at the Asylum as the Warden showed her the different coloured bins inside. She only listened as far as 'garden rubbish' falling into daydreaming about picking the ripe pea pods, the smell of the earth running through her fingers and white butterflies fluttering past.

"Mary?" a voice beside her brought her back to reality once again. "Are you looking for the day room?" The kindly face of the Warden stood beside her smiling.

She listened but could no longer hear the baby crying while the Warden, whose name she couldn't remember, pointed down this new corridor gesturing for her to follow, "Come let me show you.

Mary followed her. She could see where her flat would be on the floor below. Another corridor led to the communal lounge, with a sign above the door. The warden pushed it open to show her a large empty spacious room filled with tables, chairs and towards the top end sofas with easy arm chairs next to low coffee tables. Around one of the walls were many shelves filled with books, boxed jigsaws with colourful pictures on the lids; other boxes of games, dominoes and packs of playing cards stacked together.

Below in a large box she noticed children's toys thrown together as if cleared up in a hurry and left with just one clown's face peering over the side looking straight at her with open black circled eyes, wild orange frizzy hair giving it a surprised look.

Mary pulled back as if afraid it might jump out at her. The Warden took a step backwards letting the door swing closed she took another two steps across the corridor to two more doors; the first clearly marked as 'Laundry room'.

The Warden opened the door, reached round to flick on a light switch, "No windows," she explained, "So you will always need the light on." Mary stared as if transfixed to the spot whilst the Warden rambled on, "It's got everything you need for washing, drying or ironing your clothes." She looked at Mary who uttered not a sound. "It is very cheap, you can get any change you need from the change machine," She pointed past the door next to the laundry towards a square box attached to the wall. She heard Mary gasp looking frightened.

She watched her turn away scurrying back along the way they came in a most unusual gait, half skipping, half running in that strange way she had whilst outside, needing to get home without having to meet or talk to anyone.

She didn't look back, not even when she found the door to the stairs, she just disappeared through it leaving the Warden bemused by her reaction. Only when Mary reached her own flat, slammed the door securely behind her leaning back against it did she calm her breathing. The beating of her heart slowly returned to normal from its wild 'thump', ' thump', she felt in her temples. She reached a hand up rubbed the side of her head.

When she went back into the kitchen her tea and toast stood on the work top. She felt the tea pot underneath the crocheted tea cosy, still warm she poured it into the cup at the side, picked up the tiny blackcurrant jam pot, twisted the lid open, and smelt the sweet fruity smell of the jam.

All thoughts of the door next to the laundry were forgotten, sealed away somewhere in her mind with the thoughts of 'the place next to the laundry' no one ever spoke about.

CHAPTER 57

The long line of black clad AFO's wearing dark helmets with hard body armour carried Heckler & Koch MP5SF semi-automatic carbines across their chests lining up either side of the tall hedge at number 27 Blackheath Avenue. Once again the house appeared closed down with all the curtains pulled tightly against the world. The Team Leader assessed, gestured with his hand as each officer crouched moving through the broken gate in sequence to the perimeter of the garden.

The remaining group of officers huddled together, all wearing routine Kevlar protection including Harvey, Stevens and Flannery with the AFO Team Leader. An officer carrying the official 'door knocker' to gain entrance to the premises quickly to allow them the element of surprise, stood waiting. The group moved quietly up to the front door as the AFO's lined up against the house ready to enter.

"Let's do it," Harvey said. The officer carrying the knocker stood in front of the door waiting for the signal whilst the AFOs moved closer as the order came, "Now!" he swung it back letting the impetus take it hard against the lock. The door burst open crashing back hitting the wall behind it with a resounding bang.

A shout, "Police! Stay where you are!" as the AFOs led them swiftly through the broken door where they split up beginning the systematic search of all the rooms.

Frances Drover sat in her usual chair in the semi-gloom of the lounge, a semi-automatic pointing at her, she held her arms up above her head; she stared blindly into space not looking at the AFO or anything else in the real world.

Brendon and Harvey found the scene faintly disturbing standing in the doorway; she made no sign of recognition or express any form of protest at the intrusion. They could hear the tramping of feet with the inevitable shouts of "clear!" from far away above them. Brendon's heart beat faster waiting for the tell-tale, "here!" which did not come.

Harvey moved towards Frances Drover whose ominous silence began to give him an unsettling feeling, the scene reminding Brendon of Bernard Devonshire's burst of brutality when he arrived home; he was beginning to panic.

"Mrs Drover?" Harvey moved closer to her, if she heard him she made no sound. Her head remained still as she sat impassive staring into space. "Where is your husband?" he asked. A slight frown appeared across her forehead as it wrinkled. "Mrs Drover?" he repeated.

Her head moved slowly around to face him. "He doesn't live here," she answered, her voice steady and not one bit afraid.

It brought Brendon over from the doorway where he stood watching. It wasn't what he expected from her, even worried the raid might have finished her off completely making her sink irretrievably into her fears. How wrong could he be, she showed no sign of actual alarm.

"Where is P.C Wilson?" he asked shakily. He felt Harvey's arm rise to hold him back in an attempt to shut him up.

"Who?" she asked looking genuinely puzzled.

"She came to see you again to ask you about Mr Drover," Brendon could see Harvey begin to get angry. Frances Drover looked away, her gaze settling back into space again.

The AFO Team Leader came to the lounge door. Harvey and Brendon searched his serious face as he slowly shook his head from side to side indicating they found nothing.

"You were seen driving her car!" Brendon's voice raised an octave in panic shouting at her.

She looked back at him defiance flicked across her face briefly then vanished. "I don't go out," she replied in a firm voice, unemotional with just an undertone of mockery Brendon picked up on.

"Right!" Harvey appeared about to lose control of himself once again, "Stevens!" he yelled as loudly as he could.

Stevens wasted no time getting to the lounge door. "Sir?"

"Take Mrs Drover in," he glanced over at the AFO standing pointing the gun, "Armed escort!"

Frances Drover looked vaguely puzzled, "What are you arresting me for?" she challenged calmly.

Brendon stared in amazement at how different she seemed now thinking about Steven's words, *"My Nan had it once,"* knew in this moment Frances Drover didn't have Agoraphobia or any other phobia, what she did have, it certainly wasn't as debilitating as she wanted them to believe.

The AFO clutching his semi-automatic moved towards her stretching out his other arm to help her up from the chair, "This way," he said as she slowly got to her feet.

"Let's start with obstruction, see how we go," Harvey hissed back at her. Frances Drover wasn't the vulnerable female he expected.

"Do I get a telephone call?" she asked calmly.

"All in good time Mrs Drover, you'll certainly be given the chance of a solicitor," he said. "Perhaps you would give me your husband's address before we leave?"

Frances Drover smiled benignly, "of course, no problem," she said stopping as she passed the hall table she opened a draw which action brought the AFO a step nearer raising the gun to waist level.

She grinned at the action, reached into the draw taking out a business card which she handed to Harvey, then moved out through the front door following Stevens.

Harvey stood at the side of Brendon Flannery looking tragically after her, "She's dead, isn't she?"

"Who?" Harvey replied almost trance like following her progress.

"Terri Wilson," he peered at Harvey's face for his reaction.

"I wasn't sure whether you meant Mrs Devonshire," Harvey explained.

The AFO team leader stood beside them, "no sign of anyone else, particularly there are no signs of the baby, not even in the kitchen or the fridge," he informed them.

"I didn't get it wrong....." Brendon protested as Harvey walked away leaving him still standing at the front door.

Brendon followed him down the pathway to the gate, stopped to watch the convoy of cars pulling away. The marked police car with Frances Drover in the back with an armed escort slid slowly past Brendon. Frances Drover's eyes moved upwards to stare into space somewhere behind Brendon's head, her lips curled into a faint smile.

Brendon shivered, glanced over the road, saw the old man, Brown, standing watching the spectacle from the vantage point of his front gate, making no attempt this time to disguise it as anything other than voyeurism.

"Rum do, eh lad?" his voice loud above the noise of the disappearing vehicles.

Brendon walked over the road feeling irritated at accepting his word for anything, trying hard not to let it show. He felt deflated, incensed by him now for trusting his word and believing there was some hope of finding Terri Wilson.

The old man emerged from his gate to join him on the pavement both standing gazing at the house opposite.

"Mebbe the kafuffle will stop now," he said.

Brendon followed his gaze, "What do you mean?"

"All yon comin' an' gooin', shouting 'n' the like," he nodded over the road.

"But she lives there on her own," Brendon reminded him firmly.

The old man nodded his head again at the house, "a lot of noise for one person t'mek!" He said.

Brendon followed his gaze taking in how deserted it looked. All the curtains were closed at each level and higher up the round window at the top apex glinted in the sunshine. For a moment he saw Frances Drover's face as she slid past in the police car staring past him at the house and smiling.

CHAPTER 58

"Oh, my god!" Brendon yelled which shocked the old man making him jump. He took out his mobile, "Get inside Mr Brown!" he yelled gently pushing the old man through the gate. He listened as Harvey's mobile rang in response to his speed dial. After several rings he expected the answer phone.

"What!" Harvey yelled as the line engaged.

"He's still in there!" Brendon's voice above a whisper just in case it carried across the road.

"What are you talking about, Flannery?" Harvey's patience now hanging by a thread,

"I just saw movement at the attic window..."

"Hold! Harvey instructed leaving Brendon crouched behind the hedge, waiting; he could hear low level talking. "Where are you?" Harvey's voice sounded clear business like.

"I'm over at Mr Brown's house...."

"Just stay where you are, we've no idea whether he's armed..." Harvey began.

"What!" Brendon grew agitated at the thought of Terri being held in the attic by someone armed, *anything could happen.* He saw himself as the young boy unable to protect his mother flash before his eyes; all the pain, the frustration of having to watch his bully of a father beating her helpless before his eyes.....the image drifted giving way to rising frustration . He hated his father, it mixed with the fear he felt putting a surge of life into him.

He saw the old man hovering just within his vision, "Get inside!" he yelled loudly as he charged through the gate running across the road towards number 27. In the distance he heard police sirens getting closer but he didn't wait for them.

He ran full speed at the broken front door someone tried to put back into the frame temporarily securing it, charging it like a stampeding rhino slamming his full weight into it. For a second time it hit the hall wall with a loud bang sounding like it might shake the foundations of the house.

The noise brought him momentarily to his senses warning him of the need for caution. He crept quickly up the stairs unsure of how far that one sound would carry. He peered over from the stairwell onto the empty landing, then upwards at the ceiling where he would have expected the attic hatch to be. The painted ceiling showed no sign of a trap door. *Hell,* he thought, *where's the entrance?*

The doors leading off the landing were all standing slightly ajar after being searched – *not too well* the unexpected criticism flittered through his head. The window on the stairs, he assessed to look out onto the side of the house let sufficient light in to illuminate where he stood. He listened for any noises from above. The utter quiet challenged his judgement once again. *Did he really see some movement at the attic window?*

He heard a faint scraping sound that spurred him on. He began systematically to search each room, this time looking for a break in the ceiling where there could be an entrance.

Nothing.

He went back into the master bedroom, the largest of the three bedrooms and the only one with an en suite shower room, compact and nicely tiled. It looked more recently installed, the only improvement made, the rest of the house's rooms looked older. He found it tucked into one corner partly concealed by the shower, a door Brendon assumed to be an airing cupboard. He gently opened it revealing a completely empty space except for some wall hooks on which hung two dressing gowns, one a woman's negligee which surprised Brendon, he couldn't see Frances Drover, the long suffering mouse of a woman wearing something so frivolous. He ran the silky fabric through his fingers looking puzzled.

The other hook held a man's heavy fabric robe in dark burgundy with a contrasting shiny brocade collar also looking out of place sitting alongside the other in a defiantly anachronistic silence.

The scrapping sound again brought him back to reality, coming from just above where he stood. When he looked up he found a thick cord with a rubber stopper at the end, hanging just above his head firmly fixed into the ceiling. He knew immediately it wasn't a light pull. Brendon surmised it was once a built-in wardrobe, converted to give access to the attic.

"....*we've no idea whether he's armed....*" Momentarily re-ran in his mind, if anything it triggered him into action.

He reached up pulled the cord, felt the initial resistance until he applied sufficient pressure and watched as part of the cupboard's ceiling began to descend, and the short steps to move downwards. He stepped back saw the waiting lock fitment bolted into the floor, to secure the steps with a click.

The sound of approaching sirens cut off he supposed as a precautionary measure, he could make no judgment on how close the backup was, only that you would hear the sound of the sirens from the vantage point of the attic.

"*What if he kills her?*" he thought as if hearing their approach could trigger someone sufficiently to panic them.

Once secured in place he began to mount the steps into the attic wishing he was armed like the others. Of all the random thoughts he admonished himself for not taking a firearms course or applying for one of the special units, PSU/AFO. It had been a rational choice when the kids came along of course. Later when they were older, he was also older not fit enough to meet the selection criteria, so it ceased to be an option.

He crept noiselessly up the steps until his head appeared over the ceiling and he could see into the semi-dark space running the width of the house; the only light slanting in from the one round window he saw from outside over the road. The bright sunshine cast a beam of light across the attic floor like a spotlight leaving parts of the attic in shadowy corners. The shadows were made worse by the amount of things stored up there; long since discarded or broken, bits of unwanted furniture, boxes tied with string to keep their contents from spilling were piled up on top of each other.

He heard a sudden clear moan from somewhere deep to the side of him, where large shadowy objects sat outside the beam of light from the window. Then the scrape again as if in reaction to it, he saw a crouching figure rise up to peer through the window at the top of the attic. He could see a man, the one he'd seen from across the road.

Brendon scanned him quickly trying to calculate if he was armed, whether he could make the distance from the steps to where he stood at the window, in time for him to draw a gun, aim and fire.

He reached his arms up either side of him to give himself some leverage moving his hand along one of the beams he hit an obstacle and as his weight against it increased a light in the attic came on – he accidently caught a light switch!

The man, James Drover turned his head sharply. Brendon recognised him from the one photograph pinned to the evidence board; tall, thin and delicate looking with collar length hair heavy at the front flopping over his forehead.

"Armed police!" Brendon cried, "Hands above your head!" He saw James Drover stand up to his full height raising his empty hands. "Put them behind your head!"

Brendon eased himself through the hatch of the attic confident that he still wore the routine Kevlar protection, he felt he could take James Drover; he moved quickly over to him.

"Down on the floor!" He ordered watching him first kneel then lie flat, "arms out!" He kicked his wrist to move one of his arms out away from his body, leant down quickly patting him down to search for a weapon.

He heard a clattering of feet on stairs and saw the armed AFO's burst into the attic where Brendon stood over a prostrate James Drover. He moved quickly to one side slipping back along the attic searching the discarded items behind which he found Terri Wilson bound and gagged lying on an old disused mattress. He bent down this time feeling her neck, found a slight pulse just as he saw Harvey appear.

"Here, boss!" he yelled.

Harvey rushed over, "An ambulance is on the way, Brendon." He said not adding his thoughts on having sent for one not knowing whether they would be taking a body away.

Everything happened in double quick time and all a bit of a blur to Brendon. He stood outside watching the paramedics taking Terri Wilson away in the ambulance and the somewhat dazed James Drover away in a marked police car.

Out in broad daylight where he could see him clearly he looked a bit of an effeminate sort Brendon thought, certainly not the aggressive kidnapper he expected.

A voice at the side of him said, "Aye, rum do, lad," the old man stood next to him watching the activity. "All this kafuffle."

CHAPTER 59

The interviews with James and Frances Drover turned out much differently than Harvey expected. His assumption, under the circumstances of their discovery of Terri Wilson, led him to believe they were working together despite her statement they didn't live together; nothing could have been further from the truth. James Drover fearing he would be charged became only too willing to explain the whole 'sorry mess' as he put it.

Go on Mr Drover," Harvey, encouraged now as he sat with Stevens opposite James Drover in interview room one, watched him squirm at the side of his solicitor. Harvey observing him noted his mannerisms and appearance resembled those of his son, Dorian. In fact the similarity didn't stop there, he reminded Harvey that the word 'fop' had come to him at the time he interviewed Dorian Drover.

James Drover looked much younger than his years; they could have been brothers or even twins. He spoke with a 'public school' accent he knew came from mixing with similarly privileged people – the huntin', fishin' and shootin' set. Moreover he could imagine Bernard Devonshire eagerly seeking him out in his pursuit of acceptance by the golf club crowd because Bernard Devonshire as a self-made business man lacked the privileged background necessary. It was a background he would never be able to shake off.

"Tell it from the beginning," Harvey said to the nervous fop James Drover.

*   *   *   *

James Ellis Drover, one of two sons grew up on the same Welsh country estate his father inherited from several generations of a privileged family. His father developed the belief in its preservation, together with the inherited wealth created by a line of wealthy entrepreneurs set in a similar mould, becoming even richer.

His older brother, was the modern day classic version of his father, and also loved the idea of the lineage. He married a nice aristocratic minor daughter of another wealthy family who were eager to offload her. Things began to go wrong when they discovered they couldn't have children. The heir his father needed for the succession in the inheritance game began to crumble as time moved on.

He, James, having shown little interest in the female sex, became the one to fulfil the family need for an heir and also for educational aptitude. He loved the public school life he was subjected to seeing a clear future ahead of him in the financial dealings of investment within the big city life. The pressure from his father came later after the taste for his bachelor life took hold.

*   *   *   *

"Don't get me wrong, Chief Inspector," he droned. "I loved the ladies!" he grinned almost salivating as if he were describing a juicy steak tartare he once ate. "There was always an abundance of damsels, only too willing, to choose from and have sport with, if you didn't look too closely at their pedigrees."

Harvey found himself shiver at the way he spoke about women becoming suddenly impatient as his temper flared, "Go on Mr Drover perhaps you would like to fill us in about Fiona Evans!"

James Drover's face darkened at the name; he looked like someone biting into a rotten apple but too polite to spit it out in company. He continued.

*   *   *   *   *

For much of his childhood he attended public school before he went up to Cambridge. Whilst away he heard rumours of a scandal with one of the servants back home, the house keeper he thought although at the time he paid it little heed having too much fun of his own. He learnt later they installed her in the gatehouse cottage where she gave birth to a daughter.

*　　*　　*　　*　　*

"It surprised me," he interceded in his story. "I would have expected father to take care of it, you know in the normal way" His solicitor shifted in his chair at his comment.

"What do you mean, Mr Drover?" Harvey stared stricken by the turn of the conversation.

"It's what most genteel folk do, keep it quiet, terminate the pregnancy," he showed no sense of morality on the subject.

"Abortion?" Harvey managed although Stevens could feel him tense sitting next to him.

"Well yes, if they get themselves pregnant they should have to face the consequences....don't you think?"

Much to Steven's surprise Harvey's reaction was unexpected, he stood up as if choking, storming out of the room leaving Stevens to officially close the interview, retrieve the tapes and return the prisoner to his cell.

Stevens found Harvey in his office standing at the window staring out as if fixed to the spot. He coughed trying to gain his attention.

"Are you okay, sir?" he asked when he didn't acknowledge his presence.

Harvey spoke quietly, "You would think after all these years," he turned his head toward Stevens, "I've seen a few things I can tell you – I once worked 'Child Abuse' early on in my career – it's not for the faint hearted," he assured him. "But this man's blasé upper class drivel......" he faded off as if choked into silence.

"Would you like me to finish the interview, boss?" Steven's offered.

Harvey remained quiet for several moments whilst Stevens thought he might seriously be contemplating the offer.

"No, Stevens," he said after due thought. "Let's leave him to stew. He deserves all the hospitality we can offer him."

"His solicitor won't like it sir....."

"Fuck his solicitor!" Harvey growled much to Steven's surprise as he'd never heard him swear before. "He's another privileged upper class tw....." Harvey trapped the next expletive before he could finish it. "....person who can go stew," he turned completely around. "This is a murder case, Stevens - we still have two people missing, one of them a baby which James Drover puts little value on!" His voice having risen failed him on the last word.

He sat down at his desk with all the signs of the fatigue he felt. "Let's have a coffee," he looked up at Stevens, "Mine's strong, black, no sugar," he grinned or tried to, it looked more like a leer, "Then we'll go to see what Frances Drover has to tell us about her husband – will you set it up please?"

Stevens left the room to fetch coffee.

CHAPTER 60

"Chief Inspector Harvey and Detective Constable Stevens, interview with Frances Drover and her Solicitor...."

"Duty solicitor Simon Reid," The young man impeccably dressed in a grey suit, white shirt formally tied at the neck with what looked to Harvey to be a rugby club tie, had little in the way of facial expressions.

Fucking hell, he thought, *another one!* Instead he finished with, "Interview timed at 11.45."

Mike Harvey observed Frances Drover for the first time since her arrest, his first assessment being she was a strange woman. She sat, wearing an oversized t-shirt with sweat pants several sizes too big; her own clothes having been sent for forensic examination.

She looked a frail agitated victim sitting beside the duty solicitor they obtained for her. She agreed to him because she said she couldn't afford to appoint one of her own.

"I need a cigarette," her tiny voice sounded timid.

"You can't smoke in here, Mrs Drover," Harvey said.

"Where can I smoke?" she asked her voice a little stronger as her body swayed slightly.

"I'm afraid these buildings are smoke free zones for Health and Safety reasons," he said without much conviction, once a smoker himself finding it hard to give up he was glad of the ban. He caught a glint in her eyes like a caged animal assessing her surroundings for danger. "I'll see what we can arrange later – the FME could prescribe you a nicotine based substitute," he added to offer her some compromise.

She looked up at her solicitor studying his face; he glanced away not wanting to engage in the conversation, he didn't feel it part of his remit.

"Right, Mrs Drover, maybe you can tell us why you kept PC Wilson prisoner in your attic." Harvey fully expected a long drawn out tale of an overbearing abusive husband who made her go along with his plans.

"She didn't fool me!" Frances Drover exclaimed so suddenly Harvey sat up with the force of the change in her. She leaned onto the table, "Kept coming round looking for Dorian she did, telling me about the other bitch being his girlfriend! Huh!" She spat. "He hasn't got a girlfriend I kept saying. I don't care if SHE came looking for him either!"

"Who Mrs Drover....who came looking for Dorian?"

"The Josie girl – and she said she was Dorian's girlfriend...." Frances Drover went red in the face, she stared at Harvey accusingly. "Dorian is gay! He wouldn't have a girlfriend, most likely another of James' floozies – there were plenty of those!" She hit the table with her fist making everyone jump by the sudden action. "Year after year I've had of it! After he got his son that is! It's all he wanted ME for. There was no way I would give him any more children – I made sure!" She sat up grinning maniacally, a wild look that had now become completely insane.

"I think that's enough...." The solicitor began to protest recognising his client's condition and not wanting any part in what he knew would inevitably follow.

"Err, no it isn't," Harvey's authoritative voice sent the solicitor back into silence.

"What about Jocelyn Phipps...or Josie you called her?"

Frances Drover smiled sweetly. She seemed to change once again into her former subdued self, although she rocked gently back and forth in her chair.

"She came to find Dorian so I asked her in, thinking maybe she was a friend of his until I realised she meant James." Her face changed again with a flash of venom. "Can you believe it? He told her *his* name is Dorian, aaah!" She screamed. "My James! She sat there telling me they were meant to meet about a baby!" Her face became wildly contorted. "I thought she had his baby." She rocked even faster. "Do you know he bought me a house just up the road from his other floozy. Fiona! She has a baby. He told me his father made him see her because she's his sister!" Frances Drover shrieked with hysterical laughter. "His sister!"

"Okay Mrs Drover let's talk about what happened to Jocelyn Phipps, can you tell us?" Harvey asked.

She bowed her head going silent. Harvey opened his mouth, about to repeat his question when she raised her head slowly.

"I gave her some tea, put my Valium in it, just a couple to relax her, let her talk. I wanted to hear about the baby, to find out if James got – has another brat tucked away somewhere. It's all they care about, keeping the family line. James tried to tell me his father wanted to find out about the baby...."

"Do you mean Fiona Devonshire's baby, Phoebe?" Harvey interrupted.

Frances stared at him in amazement, "Josie's baby!" she yelled, "She sat there telling me she lost her baby and was looking for Dorian for somewhere to stay. My Dorian – but she meant James!"

Harvey could see Frances Drover mixed everything up in her mind, but he didn't want to miss the opportunity to find out what happened to her.

"What happened next Mrs. Drover, after you gave her the tea," he prompted.

"She tried to leave. I couldn't let her because I needed to know about her baby, so I hit her over the head with the poker from the hearth when she tried to leave, it was the only thing I could do to stop her," she looked a little ashamed at this point. "She stumbled being only a bit dazed because I didn't hit her hard enough," she explained. "She kept shouting for Dorian expecting him to be there," She sat with her head bowed again as if the effort of telling it had become too great for her.

"What did you do then, Mrs Drover?"

Frances Drover raised both her hands peering at them as she held them together Harvey could see her hands shaking.

"For the tape Mrs Drover is looking at her hands – what did you do Mrs Drover?" he asked watching her miming squeezing her hands together.

She looked up at him, "I didn't mean to kill her, just to shut her up, squeeze her neck to stop her calling for my Dorian….. he's such a sweet boy, he doesn't need a girlfriend, he has his band," she said. As she sat thinking about her son, her face grew fierce again. "James put pressure on him," she said in disgust, "Always telling him that it was his duty to get married, that he needed a girlfriend - to have children." She laughed a weird shrill cry, "To produce an heir like he'd done – his duty! It's all I was – his duty!"

"So what did you do, Frances," Harvey spoke her first name encouraging her, wanting to hear her say what they all needed to hear, whether she intended to kill Jocelyn Phipps.

Her face slipped to sly with a smile on her lips as if her actions were an unfortunate accident, "I squeezed too hard - I only wanted her to keep quiet." Then as if she knew what he wanted her to say, "I didn't mean to kill her," she said again.

Harvey paused letting her sit for a moment. His next question in his usual business-like manner, "What did you do next Mrs Drover, what did you do with the body?"

At this point the Duty Solicitor intervened again, "I think we could have a break, Chief Inspector," which incensed Harvey just as the interview gained momentum.

He glared at the man, "We'll have a break when I say so!" He carried on asking, "What did you do with Jocelyn Phipps' body Mrs Drover?"

"I called James, of course," she said calmly becoming her subdued simple semi-rational self, the helpless woman again. "His phone rang - I could hear it in the hall as he came in."

Harvey looked at Stevens puzzled.

"He was already there in the house, Mrs Drover?" Harvey asked. "Does he live with you?"

Frances Drover frowned at the question trying to work it out herself, "No he was just coming in as I telephoned him," she clarified as if explaining it to herself, "like he expected her to be there.....he wouldn't be coming to see me...." she seemed to be trying to rationalise it all. "You think he knew she would be there?" She stared wildly suddenly realising, "he arranged to meet her there only...."

"...only she thought his name was Dorian, her boyfriend?" Harvey finished for her.

Frances Drover looked shocked. Harvey could see she was neither too angry, nor deranged that she couldn't work it out for herself.

"No!" She said shaking her head, "He has his son, his heir, my Dorian."

"But Dorian would never have children of his own would he Mrs. Drover? Maybe if he had another child...."

Harvey's line of questioning stopped abruptly as Frances Drover's final hold on sanity exploded in a violent outburst requiring Stevens to press the emergency strip along the wall to summon help, but not before her Duty Solicitor unfortunately got in the way of her flailing arms suffering a bloody nose when one hit him full on.

The FME doctor who attended her was shocked by her condition. He made arrangements for immediate psychiatric admission having to give her medication to calm her down for her own safety. Reporting back to Harvey he commented, "I can't believe you were interviewing her in her state."

"I didn't," Harvey replied, "I think she finally succumbed after years of living in a dysfunctional family."

CHAPTER 61

"How is she?" Harvey asked as Stevens came into his office carrying a single sheet of paper which he placed in front of Harvey. He read it briefly then looked up at Stevens. "Maybe I should have stopped when her solicitor asked me to," Harvey admitted looking completely deflated.

"I don't think so, sir," Stevens replied. "We still have a baby to find. At least we know what happened to Jocelyn Phipps. Then there's Fiona Devonshire still missing, sir," Stevens added reminding him. "We still have James Drover's interview to complete….the Custody Sergeant wants me to remind you the clock is ticking…." Stevens debated with himself all the way up to Harvey's office how he might deliver the message with Harvey in the mood he found him.

Instead of reacting badly as he predicted Harvey seemed to deflate slumping down in his seat at the thought of resuming the interview with James Drover whom he knew he felt like hitting.

Stevens waited wondering whether he ought to offer once again to carry on James Drover's interview alone when Harvey's telephone began to ring.

Harvey grabbed it glad of the interruption, "Harvey!" he barked into it. Stevens watched his face as the stern craggy expression moved into a faint smile, not one he was familiar with.

"Great news, Flannery," Harvey said. Stevens immediately recognised it was news about Terri Wilson. "Let me know when she comes out of it will you?" He put the phone down. "P.C Wilson is stable, Stevens, they've got her sedated at present – giving her fluids to get the drugs out of her system – it looks like we got there just at the right time." He didn't add thanks to Flannery, he just thought it.

He stood up suddenly, "Right," he sounded more determined. "Get uniform to bring Bernard Devonshire in...."

"Is it wise, sir, him being a friend of the Chief Constable's...." Stevens let it slip out before he could think about what he was saying. The rumours were rife around the station. He thought it may only be gossip, he felt it might cause Harvey even more grief than the last time when Bernard Devonshire had been arrested for assaulting his wife.

Harvey bristled at the suggestion. He leaned in to Stevens, "That may be the flavour of the week around here Stevens," he said severely. "Which I am sure is idle chit-chat over the shepherd's pie in the canteen at lunch time, but I don't care if they're conjoined twins separated at birth, Stevens," Stevens stifled a smile at the image, then Harvey hit him with, "Get him here! Like you just reminded me, we have his wife and baby still missing! I for one want to find out why his close business associate, who is involved in his Nanny's murder, seems to be related to his wife and said baby which he failed to tell us!" Harvey stood, edged forward until his face was just a few inches away from Stevens who stood tensely still and took it.

"Right ho, boss," he gulped. He left Harvey standing like a statue in the middle of his office.

CHAPTER 62

The young girl with the elfin haircut tapped lightly on the front door of the terraced house with the dingy vertical blinds in the front window where two of the slats were broken. The dustbin standing on the street at the side of the front door was crammed to capacity, the lid stood up failing to trap all the contents which spilled over onto the ground at its side.

The door opened revealing another young girl, this one with long unkempt dreadlocks, peering out at her.

"Is Dorian here?" she asked her taking a step back at the sight of her. Her heavily made up blackened eyes were smudged giving her a fierce look. She scratched her nose with long black talon, her nails filed to points.

"They've gone to pick up the gear," the girl's tiny voice dispelled the illusion, strangely lost in all the painted on fierceness. "They've got a gig in Manchester tonight," she added as an afterthought suddenly suspicious of this girl she didn't know, not wanting her to think 'gear' meant something other than the band's instruments.

"Oh," She said remembering the message on her mobile definitely saying the 'house' would be empty. "Where's the 'gear' kept?" she asked.

The girl told her Dorian stored it at his mother's house, "Blackheath Avenue, number 27 I think," the girl said quickly slamming the door shut leaving Jocelyn Phipps standing on the pavement.

*   *   *   *

Spending time in a police cell didn't faze James Drover as much as Harvey hoped it would. He met Harvey with a mild plea of, "Can we get on with this Chief Inspector, I can't waste my time here......"

Harvey raised his hand to stop him going any further, "Let's see Mr Drover shall we, just how much 'time' you'll have to waste after you've answered all my questions now having interviewed your wife."

"My ex-wife," James Drover corrected prissily.

"Your ex-wife, Frances Drover, told us a lot of interesting things. However let's leave that for now shall we, you were explaining to us your side of things – would you like to continue, please?" James Drover picked up the hint of sarcasm in his voice looking at his top of the range solicitor at the most expensive end of available solicitors. He leaned in towards James Drover to whisper in his ear. Harvey waited for him to continue.

*   *   *   *   *

James Drover's Cambridge years gave him or rather his father, the family's sort after educational endorsement of a Cambridge educated son although his father would have preferred a first class honours. From his heir, his less adept older brother, his father expected the assurance of a son to carry on the family business.

Meanwhile, James had other ambitions after a taste of the freer wilder bachelor life away from what he saw as the shackles of the crumbling family country estate. Settling down with a wife to produce more Drover progeny he saw very much as his elder brother's role being traditionally the heir. He preferred the more exciting life of London's bright lights; he became used to living on his generous allowance which held him in good stead until he made his name.

*   *   *   *   *

"I didn't go back," he explained. "Why would I with my brother the doting son? The problem being he was 'shooting blanks' or that wife of his couldn't sprog," he said.

Harvey winced at his description now getting tired of his droning upper class accent.

"So, what about Alwen Evans and her daughter Fiona?" Harvey pushed.

"Ah, the family's dirty washing," he seemed only too pleased to oblige him with an answer. "Daddy's a bit of an old dog, I suppose, it's some kind of inheritance," he laughed cynically more at Harvey's facial expression than his own words. "Like father like son, eh?" he boasted. Harvey coughed scowling at him. "Yes, well – he installed her at the gatehouse cottage, more to keep her close," he winked at Harvey, "More to preserve the family name than to see his 'daughter' grow up."

"You were aware Fiona Devonshire is your sister then?" Harvey asked.

"Good lord no! I had no idea!" he exclaimed. "I never went back, sorry – we didn't 'grow up' together if that's what you think," he looked over at Harvey seeing disbelief written on his face. "No, Chief Inspector, I went to the City to build my financial experience, lived on Daddy's allowance until I made my way, only it wasn't enough for him, he threatened to cut me off unless I got me a wife to give him some heirs to carry on the family name."

Harvey began to really hate James Drover, "So when did you realise Fiona Devonshire is your sister?"

"I didn't 'realise' it at all," he said. "Good old Pater found out she'd married only when she went back to get her mother," he could see Harvey looked confused. "She meant it to be secret, taking her mother away somewhere, but the old bugger found out somehow. Something to do with paying for Alwen Evan's care at the time and the carers reported directly to him," he looked baffled. "Something like that.....anyway he traced her (Daddy's not beyond using his money for sneaky things like private investigators) up here after college or University she stayed here. One of those huge coincidences I knew Bernard Devonshire.....” he stopped, looking like there was a nasty smell under his nose. “Awful man....if you've ever met him you would see what I mean.”

“You work for him!” Harvey protested, shocked at the way he spoke.

“I am his financial consultant,” he corrected grandly.

“Did that entail fixing him up with your sister?” Harvey asked contemptuously.

James Drover looked shocked, “What are you talking about?” he asked indignantly. “I had no idea his wife was my sister!”

Harvey turned to Stevens who opened up a folder as if on cue handing him the grainy picture of Bernard Devonshire, James Drover with Fiona standing between them; Harvey pushed it in front of him.

He picked it up and peered at it.

“That was taken when I met him Chief Inspector,” he said handing it to his solicitor. “A Rotary dinner at the golf club, I found him seated next to me – it's how it works, tried to tap me up for.....” he stopped to think what to say. Harvey could see him suddenly look cautious. “Some financial input for his business,” He said.

“So you began to work together?”

“Err, no Chief Inspector, took an instant dislike to the man!” he answered much to Harvey's surprise. “I wouldn't have got involved with him at all – such an uncouth type - dear old daddy discovered he'd married Fiona, my illegitimate sister,” he said with all the contempt he could manage.

“Really?”

He leaned into the table, "Yes, really," he mocked. "I got an ultimatum; you know the age old 'if you don't keep an eye on her I'll cut you off without a penny' kind of incentive." He sneered. "To be honest I can't wait for the old bugger to vacate, then maybe I'll have a reasonable attempt to get my untalented brother to sell that pile of crap, split the proceeds. I have my eye on warmer climes with a bit more of an exciting life."

Harvey found his contempt for the man getting the better of him.

"Take another look at the photograph would you?" Harvey asked with forced politeness. "My apologies for the quality of it, it's taken from the golf club website."

James Drover took it back from his solicitor and scanned over it again, then looked enquiringly at Harvey, "You want me to guess at the date?" he asked.

"No, Mr Drover we have the date it was taken," he assured him. "I'm wondering why you don't recognise your sister standing next to you."

James Drover moved it closer to his face, scowled, took out a pair of spectacles from the inside pocket of the jacket he wore. After he placed them on his nose he looked again.

He seemed quite shocked when recognition took hold, "I had no idea," he sounded more subdued. "Well, well..." He thought for a moment. "It must have been..."

"...where he met your sister whom he subsequently married." Harvey finished for him. "So Mr. Drover perhaps you would tell us what you have done with her and the baby – your niece whom you have been keeping an eye on for your father!"

"I...I...haven't done anything," he stuttered. His solicitor leaned in at this point to whisper again in his ear. James Drover looked annoyed, "Don't be so bloody silly," he rounded on him extremely angry. "My solicitor is advising me to continue with 'no comment' which I have no intention of doing! I don't know what has happened to them Chief Inspector, that's the point of keeping contact with Josie Phipps..."

"Ah, since you mention her Mr Drover, we hear from your wife," he spoke deliberately to annoy him, saw him about to correct him, "Ex-wife, you were seeing Jocelyn Phipps who believed you to be Dorian your son."

"The silly cow killed her out of jealousy!" he yelled. "I found her dead at France's house."

"Where I believe you arranged to meet her?" Harvey suggested.

"Err, no!" Again he sounded indignant. "At Dorian's house because it would be empty," he turned to his solicitor, "My son's band were scheduled to play up in Manchester that night. Josie met me there once or twice, on her days off, she thought I played in the band because she heard them practising once when we were over there - she mixed me up with Dorian who I think she'd only met the once – I just let her believe it. I didn't know she was Fiona's Nanny at first, just thought she was a groupie and a bit of..."

"Yes, thank you Mr Drover!" Harvey cut in sure he wouldn't like the rest of it. "How did she get over to your wife's house?"

"She followed Dorian there - a girl at the house told me when I arrived."

"Didn't it worry you she'd gone to your wife's house?" Harvey had visions of the manic Frances Drover answering the door to someone else asking for Dorian.

James Drover shrugged his shoulders nonchalantly, "We're no longer married, Chief Inspector as I keep telling you, why would it bother me?"

"So why go over there Mr Drover? If you weren't 'bothered' like you say?" Harvey studied his face for the tell-tale signs he knew Frances Drover's mental state.

"She telephoned me," he said simply. "I went there because she asked me to."

"How strange, Mr Drover, because according to Mrs Drover when she dialled your number, you were coming through the front door – she heard it ringing in the hallway."

"Well I wouldn't believe anything she tells you," the contempt for his ex-wife cut the air between them.

"Of course, if we take your keys from those we booked into prisoner property we could at least prove one way or the other your ability to enter your wife's house which would give some credence to her statement," Harvey said.

"Why Chief Inspector, I do own the house; it's likely I would hold keys to the place."

They stared each other out for a moment. Harvey could feel Stevens fidgeting at the side of him.

"Let's leave that one for a moment Mr Drover," Harvey conceded. "What did you do next?"

"What do you mean?"

Harvey sighed deeply at the man's arrogance it positively oozed from him.

"After you found *your* girlfriend dead in *your* house," Harvey emphasised both words deliberately. Just for one moment James Drover looked trapped.

"I found Frances completely panicking....."

"Why wouldn't she, if she just killed someone?" Harvey asked.

"I don't know, perhaps because she thought she was an intruder...." He suggested, beginning to sound less sure of himself.

"You mean someone whom she invited in, gave a cup of tea laced with Valium to? Is it likely Mr. Drover?"

James Drover looked surprised, "She told me she hit her over the head...."

"Yes she did and followed up by strangling her to death," Harvey informed him.

"Frances isn't strong enough...." He began to say. "Did she really?" He asked realising if he pleaded for his wife's frailty he might just put himself under suspicion.

"Like I said Mr Drover, she gave her some tea laced with Valium together with a blow to Jocelyn Phipps' head, it might have given her the advantage," Harvey said. "Or maybe she was still alive when you arrived and *you* finished her off?"

James Drover looked genuinely horrified, "No, no you aren't putting it on me – Frances is completely bonkers, Chief Inspector," he admitted. "She was definitely dead when I got there."

"Did you check for signs of life?" Harvey asked.

He looked trapped. He leaned over to his solicitor and whispered something in his ear. His solicitor whispered back.

He turned to Harvey looking weary, "I believed her to be dead. I couldn't see any signs of life," he said cautiously. "I picked her up, carried her to my car and left her sitting up in an alleyway in town," he finished.

"Why did you pick that particular alley, Mr. Drover?"

"It's one I believe where all the kids go to buy drugs, so I thought it might look like she took an overdose," he suggested.

"Really? We would have needed to find a sufficient quantity of a drug to OD on," Harvey said. "Let's leave that one – you left her sitting in the alley, you say – it's not how we found her Mr Drover." Harvey said.

"Maybe someone moved her later....." he suggested calmly.

"Why would some anonymous person do that?"

James Drover shrugged.

"For the tape James Drover shrugged his shoulders," Stevens said.

"Okay, let's leave it there," Harvey announced. "Let's turn to P.C Terri Wilson."

"Who?" James Drover asked which irritated Harvey.

"She's the person you drugged and imprisoned in the attic at your ex-wife's house – oh, sorry – at *your* house."

"It has nothing to do with me, I....."

"Don't tell me, let me guess – Frances telephoned you again to tell you she had another young woman she plied with Valium in a friendly cup of tea?" Harvey's sarcasm made his solicitor wince.

"She did!" he yelled realising just how much trouble he might now be in. "I was at the Devonshire's house with Bernard when she telephoned, you saw me there!" he gasped.

"Yes, I saw you leaving walking away up Blackheath Avenue. Was this because Frances summoned you again?"

James Drover nodded, "I told you she is completely insane!"

"Yes you did Mr Drover and I'm wondering if you knew she drugged, hit and strangled Jocelyn Phipps you still helped her by leaving the girl's body in an alleyway – why didn't you just report her, Mr Drover?" Harvey asked. "If you had done, PC Wilson wouldn't be in hospital!"

"Lord, Chief Inspector, imagine what my father would make of the scandal?" he asked incredulously.

"You mean, I suppose, it would be goodbye inheritance," Harvey suggested. James Drover looked sheepish. "I imagine being found with a captive police officer in the attic at your wife's house would do it also, Mr Drover," Harvey couldn't resist saying. "So she telephoned you once again for help with PC Wilson?"

James Drover toyed briefly with a 'no comment' but clearly saw it as an admission of guilt which denied him any attempt at extricating himself from any blame.

"Look, she'd just drugged yet another person, I was trying to work out how I could help the police woman when your lot arrived," he said feebly.

Harvey sighed again, "Okay, let's start with how about you tell me how your 'frail' wife managed to get PC Wilson upstairs, then up those narrow steps into the attic."

James Drover shrugged his shoulders again and DC Stevens reported, "For the tape Mr Drover shrugged his shoulders."

"Perhaps you could speak for the tape Mr Drover," Harvey asked. "Was that a 'don't know' or 'no comment' shrug?"

Whether James Drover's arrogance flared once again or whether he saw his inheritance disappearing fast he began to tell Harvey what happened.

"You see my ex-wife is a pathologically jealous woman, Chief Inspector. She reacts the same way to every female who comes near me. She even thinks Fiona Devonshire is my mistress, wouldn't have it she's my sister. Can you believe it?"

"Well you do have a history with the ladies," Harvey mocked his previous admission. "It's quite possible isn't it?"

James Drover frowned, "No, officer, she's quite mad," he repeated.

"Yet you did nothing about her condition, sought no medical help for her, leaving her to harm other people." Harvey was well aware of his spoken condemnation, knew he should stick to the line of questioning, however, James Drover's attitude to most things severely grated on him.

"I think we both know you must have helped your wife to carry PC Wilson up into the attic. I also suspect Jocelyn Phipps was still alive when you took her to the alley which means *you* are responsible for her death because you could have saved her," Harvey's summoning up left James Drover looking stunned.

"I....I....believed..." he stammered. Harvey held up his hand to silence him.

"What I need to know, Mr Drover, is where Fiona Devonshire, your sister, and Phoebe her baby....your niece are?" Harvey watched as he sat upright in shock.

"I have no idea! It's what I need to know – I wouldn't put it past Bernard to have harmed them both!"

For the first time Mike Harvey believed him.

CHAPTER 63

Later Bernard Devonshire sat in the same interview seat James Drover vacated earlier, alone having been offered a call to his solicitor. He declined it saying he didn't need one.

After grabbing a cup of coffee and a cheese sandwich from the canteen, Mike Harvey began to feel really fatigued at the thought of another potentially fraught interview.

He knew Bernard Devonshire wasn't an easy man to deal with but now believed the possibility that Fiona and her daughter wouldn't be found alive.

He took James Drover's word, he saw him very much as an obnoxious privileged bully. All the same, he thought him dreadful at lying, in fact, so far any attempts he made were pitiful because his sort always said exactly what they thought, however disgusting, having little idea how it sounded to other people. He would be failing in this duty if he ignored his words to look more closely at Bernard Devonshire.

"Mr Devonshire, we have reason to believe you may know the whereabouts of your wife and daughter," Harvey had become too tired to play games, he cut to the chase.

He fully expected Bernard Devonshire to explode, would have put money on the likelihood of him becoming violent, consequently he placed a uniformed officer just inside the door of Interview Room one. Bernard Devonshire stared at him in stunned silence. "Well Mr Devonshire," Harvey proceeded, "Where are they? Are they still alive?"

He gaped trying to assess Mike Harvey's words as if he spoke a different language, one he knew little of.

"This is all so surreal, Chief Inspector, I have come here in good faith, expecting either you needed further information from me or at worst you have the bad news which I have expected since you put those people in my house!"

Harvey was taken aback by this new controlled Bernard Devonshire.

"Okay," Harvey sighed wearily, "Let's do it the hard way shall we?" He paused before he continued with, "Why do you believe the phone tap is jeopardising their lives?"

Bernard laughed cynically, "Do you really think the kidnappers aren't watching for any police activity at my house?"

"You think you are being watched?" Harvey sounded surprised.

"If they could take both my baby and my wife in broad daylight, they aren't going to risk being caught are they? For heaven's sake I've seen the bloody builders van parked in front of my house on the ten o'clock news," he pooh-poohed. "Who in their right mind would have the builders in if they'd just had their family abducted?"

This very point Harvey had considered himself, however he didn't comment, but asked, "Did you receive a ransom demand *before* they arrived, Mr Devonshire – maybe someone already contacted you?"

"No! They haven't, but if they're capable of killing my baby's Nanny, how ruthless are these people?"

Ignoring this Harvey decided to change tack, "What can you tell me about James Drover?"

"Jed?" He looked suspiciously at Harvey with this line of questioning he didn't want him focussing on any of his business deals or any of the people he was involved with. He believed they had taken his family; their price would require him to do something illegal. "He's my financial consultant, you already know that," he said.

"How long has he been your financial consultant?"

"Only about a year or so," he said. "Why?"

Harvey nodded to Stevens who produced the golf club photograph of the Rotary dinner. Bernard looked down at it, "Where did you get this?" he asked sounding intrigued as if it was the first time he'd seen it, "I don't remember it being taken."

Harvey couldn't help himself, "Maybe you were otherwise pre-occupied!"

Bernard picked it up off the table where Steven's placed it; he grinned but made no comment.

"But you remember the evening Mr. Devonshire?"

"Yes I do," he said still smiling. "The lady doesn't seem to be complaining."

"Maybe it is something to do with having her hands full," Harvey's criticism made Bernard smile some more.

"Or perhaps I just made her an offer she couldn't refuse," he said.

"You mean to become your wife?" Harvey's morals were getting the better of him again. He couldn't help thinking Fiona Evans looked much the same age as his own daughters, knowing how he might feel about Bernard Devonshire marrying one of them.

"Good lord, Chief Inspector, what do you take me for?" he exclaimed. "I'd only just met her at this dinner! No, she accepted my offer of a job. She just got a degree I needed a secretary, maybe a little over qualified for it but better than her waiting on table for a crowd of drunken old men." Harvey realised he was mocking him. "She became my secretary – well my P.A actually, she's very bright."

"Ah, so she is aware of all your business dealings, Mr Devonshire?" Harvey began to fish for a motive for disposing of her if James Drover was right.

Bernard Devonshire looked him in the eye, "Not exactly, Chief Inspector, that's more the role of my financial consultant."

"Who is also in the photograph," Harvey pointed out tapping the picture on the table.

"Except not then, he wasn't one bit interested," he said staring at the photograph. "And you can't imagine how much the night cost me," he sighed wistfully.

"Well you got your wife and daughter out of it," Harvey reminded him.

Bernard's face showed his characteristic anger briefly, "What are you doing to find them, apart from invading my house as well as trying to place their disappearance on me? You'll be accusing me next of killing my own Nanny. Then I would have to remind you I was here most of the day and later at home with a horde of press at my gates!"

His thunderous look was enough to jerk Mike Harvey into completing the interview.

"Are you aware of who James Drover is, Mr Devonshire?"

Bernard's anger calmed a little, "You mean other than my financial advisor? Why don't you surprise me," he challenged wondering where the conversation could possibly lead.

"He's your wife's brother," Mike Harvey revealed. Bernard burst out in raucous laughter.

"Don't be ridiculous," he mocked. "I introduced them to each other. I assure you they had never met before."

Harvey tapped the photograph, "Well clearly they did meet."

"Apart from that night, I mean," he became thoughtful. "And if I recall correctly, Chief Inspector, after a few glasses of wine he actually tried it on with her, which I doubt even you can call brotherly. In fact, it was how my conversation with Fiona began which led to her needing a job that might be less fraught, not so exposed to such behaviour," he said. "Actually, he doesn't remember the little episode because when I introduced him to my wife after he joined me I am convinced he didn't recall it."

"You are possibly right," Harvey agreed. "It was his father.....he is also your wife's father, who traced her to you."

Bernard looked puzzled, "She hasn't got a father, he died...." He began.

"Have you met her mother, Mr. Devonshire?" Harvey interrupted.

"No, she lives in Wales somewhere, Fiona doesn't see much of her," he concluded.

"Do you know when she saw her last?" Harvey asked.

Bernard thought for a moment looking strained trying to recall, "Can't quite remember, she only goes every once in a while, stays just the one night....Oh, except once when she stayed an extra day; her mother took ill.....look what is this all about?"

"It's about the fact, Mr Devonshire, not only has your wife and daughter gone missing, but also her mother disappeared some time ago from her home in Wales where she lived on the country estate of Mrs Devonshire's father. We do believe, however, your wife removed her from there; where she took her is a mystery." Harvey explained. "Are you aware James Drover has a house a few doors away from yours on Blackheath Avenue?"

Bernard looked aghast. "No Chief Inspector, Jed, has a flat in town," he said. "I think you have this all wrong," he tapped the photograph. "This is Jed," he said.

"I'm perfectly aware of who he is," he turned to Stevens for confirmation.

"We met him at your house, do you remember?" Stevens asked. "I showed him out, watched him walk up the road towards his house." Bernard sank back into his chair deflated by the turn of the interview. "In fact, sir, he is being held, together with his wife for the murder of your Nanny!" Steven's announced.

Bernard Devonshire gaped in amazement, "I don't understand any of this," he complained. "Has he got my baby, my beautiful Phoebe – what has he done?!"

Bernard Devonshire broke down completely and cried like a baby.

CHAPTER 64

Brendon Flannery stood gazing out of the hospital side ward window at the heavy storm clouds gathering overhead, listening to the distant rumble of thunder. Since her admission Terri Wilson had been kept sedated, the intravenous fluids they told him were more to re-hydrate as well as to flush out anything toxic she may have been given.

It seemed like hours since the forensic doctor attended her, taking bloods and examining her together with the hospital doctor for any other injuries. He hadn't wanted to leave her for more than a minute since he found her.

He heard the faint sound from the bed where she lay illuminated by the single light above it necessary for the nursing staff to undertake continuous routine observations at regular intervals.

The lightning flashed as he turned to the sound, he could see her eyes beginning to flutter as she woke up. He watched her come fully awake.

"Hey," he said gently as her eyes eventually settled on his face.

Her first word a croaky, "Sarge?" half caught in her throat, followed by, "Thirsty."

He reached to the table, pulled it across on smooth castors, poured a small amount of water from the plastic jug into an empty plastic water beaker, knowing from experience it would have an awful tang to it.

She lay in the bed half raised so he found the controls, pressed them to help her sit up some more, put the beaker to her lips for her to sip. She winced at the taste of warm plastic water.

"It's horrible isn't it?" he laughed. "I'll get you a bottle from the hospital shop," he promised.

She looked around the room, raised her hand with the cannula inserted into the back of it where a tube attached to the intravenous fluids hooked onto a frame at the side of the bed.

"Hospital?" the one word question. Her face showed greyness under her usual golden complexion which made her look vulnerable.

"We found you at the Drover house?" his statement more of a question which he hoped would prompt her memory of what happened to her. He feared the drugs might have done some permanent damage. Her face frowned as her mind engaged, then realisation as she remembered.

"Her!" she gasped.

"Who Terri?" He didn't want to lead her in any way or to influence her memory. He smiled at himself, *once a copper, always a copper*, something from his own dark recesses of his mind sneered at him in his father's voice. His father always hatred all things law, he realised it influenced him greatly in his choice of careers. His father's disrespect for the police and eventually his fear of them made him determined as a weak powerless boy to become one; the full force of the law behind him to take him down.

"Frances Drover," Terri's voice grew louder, she looked into his face. "She isn't who we thought."

Brendon squeezed her hand, "I know," he said. "All in good time, just take it easy, there's no rush."

"What about the baby, Sarge?"

The lightning flashed illuminating the room.

"No, we haven't found her or her mother," he said not telling her his concerns were more for her safety than theirs.

The door opened just as the thunder boomed overhead and a nurse bustled in followed by Mike Harvey. The nurse began to take obs, wrote them up at the bottom of the bed where the medical notes lay on another high table, "Don't stay too long, she needs to rest." She scowled at Brendon who ignored it.

"Hey, sir?" Terri said. "What's happening? Did you get James Drover?" The nurse peered up scowling once more.

"Yes, Terri, thanks to Flannery here we have them both," Harvey replied.

Terri looked round at Brendon, saw him blush at the acknowledgement from his boss, then back at Harvey, "You do know it's her..?"

Harvey raised his hand to cut her off, "All in good time, Terri, just rest up."

Terri tried to sit up even further, but Brendon's arm moved across taking her hand, "The boss said rest," he added gently as she eased back down again.

"Mum will be frantic," she said almost in a whisper to Brendon.

"It's okay," he winked watching her relax.

He moved away to the door disappearing for a moment leaving Harvey alone.

"Someone will come to take a full statement tomorrow Terri, so try to relax until then," he said gently.

She reached out taking his hand, "How did you find me?" she asked having spent only a few waking moments believing she would never see her daughter or her mother again.

"I have a very determined and I might add experienced Detective Sergeant," he grinned, "Although some might say stubborn or even bloody minded." She saw Harvey laugh for the first time finding it a strange sight.

The door opened again. A four year old Olivia carrying a white fluffy rabbit came through followed by her mother, and Brendon who took up the rear. He watched Terri's face beam with pleasure. She patted the bed at the side of her. Olivia took the cue and ran to her pushing the rabbit onto the bed.

"We brought Topsy to keep you company," she announced as Terri took him holding him close. The little girl nodded, "he will keep you safe," she added.

Terri's mother went around to the other side of the bed and hugged her hiding the tears which she wiped away with one hand. Harvey picked the little girl up to sit on the bed beside Terri who hugged her and the white rabbit with her other arm. The little girl leaned back scrutinising Terri's face as if she were trying to assess how well she was.

"Are you really my mother?" she asked quite calmly.

Terri gasped, looked sharply at her mother's face for an explanation, "It was time." Her mother said.

Terri turned back to Olivia, "Yes I am," she admitted nervously expecting a whole outburst of questions even condemnation. "Is it okay with you?"

The little girl blinked, "'Course, I always knew," she said.

"How?" Terri asked intrigued by her four year old daughter.

"We look the same," she replied.

"Can't argue with that," Terri laughed hugging her closely for the first time as her daughter.

Brendon watched the scene, felt perilously close to tears; it made him think about his own children back home.

"Okay, I'll be going," he said. "I'll see you later."

Harvey moved to join him showing no signs of surprise at the scene he just witnessed, "Just rest for now, P.C Wilson," he said formerly.

Terri mimed, "Thank you" to Brendon as he looked back before he closed the door.

CHAPTER 65

Fiona Devonshire left her front door carrying an overnight bag. She moved swiftly around the side of the house as if being pursued by someone. She pressed the keys in her hand opening the double garage door which glided silently upwards as she approached it. She continued ducking her head underneath the rising door.

Another button on yet another key brought the high pitched yelp of her 4x4 car doors awake. She threw the overnight bag onto the passenger seat sliding into the driver's seat, at the same time engaging the engine in one smooth movement by inserting the keys before she closed the driver's door. She eased the pedals, slid smoothly out of the garage not waiting for the door to reach its maximum position. She shot across the gravel drive releasing the button to open the electric gates, and as they began their full arc she moved into position waiting only for sufficient room to exit. Moving forward into the gap she crawled through when they gave her enough room to manoeuvre.

She glanced once into the back seat where a tiny sleeping baby sat securely strapped to a baby seat. She peered up the avenue, silently slipping out onto Blackheath Avenue turning right she cruised down the hill until she picked up speed.

*   *   *   *   *

Early morning in the dimly lit CID office only a straggle of detectives were illuminated by the glow of their computer screens against a shadowy background helped by one or two of the main lights in the office. Mike Harvey pressed a few more switches on the panel at the door as he came through making the room jump into life. A flash of lightning outside added to the sudden brightness; the storm had raged on and off for two days returning once again with a vengeance adding to his mood and made worse by the summons to meet with the ACC.

"Any reason why we're sitting here in the dark?" he yelled. A few heads looked over anticipating his mood having watched him leave twenty minutes earlier after the telephone call from the top floor.

"No, gov," Stevens replied for all of them. In his absence he filled them in briefly about charging the Drovers with Jocelyn Phipps murder although it was still unclear whether Frances Drover would be fit to plead. He also broke the news about Bernard Devonshire's interview which provoked a debate whether it could be possible for someone not to have met their mother-in-law.

Without any exceptions, the married detectives pooh-poohed the idea. Stevens heard one of them say, "No bloody chance!" whereupon everyone laughed at him. He was known amongst them for his comments or moans, especially after a weekend when it appeared his mother-in-law was a frequent visitor. The office joke every Monday at his expense being, "How's the 'outlaws'?"

Mike Harvey announced, "Briefing in ten," he disappeared into his office after which the room jumped into life by someone fetching the large communal tea pot (the size of a large kettle), someone else rushing out for the previously telephoned breakfast order from the 'Crusty Cob' on the corner.

The white bags were being dished out when Harvey reappeared from his office fifteen minutes later carrying his own sausage cob with a mug of strong tea. No one said it, although everyone to a man observed how drawn he looked.

The room quietened as he perched on the nearest desk, "Has Stevens filled you in about the Drovers?" he asked as if the effort of the question sucked even more life from him.

They all nodded. Stevens asked, "What about Frances Drover? Is she likely to...?"

"Waiting for psychiatric assessment," Harvey admitted glumly. "And we all know what it will mean."

The low muttering was interrupted by the office door opening, and Brendon Flannery coming in, "Sorry gov," he apologised. "Needed to pop to the hospital...." He held up his fractured arm now encased in a detachable arm brace fastened with Velcro straps. "Needed to get rid of the plaster – they wanted to redo it – we came to a compromise."

The truth being Brendon swapped the plaster the day before, he just 'popped' into the hospital to check on Terri Wilson who had been discharged into her mother's care after threatening self-discharge. The sister proclaimed police officers to be the worst patients in her opinion.

"Any news on Terri Wilson, Sarge?" Stevens asked. Brendon looked at him sharply for any signs of criticism; he knew about the police grapevine with its gossip mongers only too well.

Harvey spotted his discomfort at the question trying to head it off, "She's doing well. I believe she is at home."

He saw the relief on Brendon's face making a mental note to speak to him later, to remind him about the pitfalls of office liaisons. He felt suddenly old at even contemplating such a thing but before the idea gelled into a bigger thought the CID office door opened again as Terri Wilson appeared.

Harvey surmised it wasn't a casual visit being dressed in her police uniform which she didn't have to wear on secondment to the CID investigation. She made her way slowly to her allocated desk and stood as everyone stared at her.

"Morning, sorry I'm late, sir," she looked coyly at everyone's shocked faces. Taylor moved over to the tea pot when Brendon arrived, to pour him a cup of tea, turning at her entrance.

"Should you be here, PC Wilson?" Brendon voiced critically, the first one to speak.

Terri grinned, bowed her head trying to hide it, "Err, and you, Sarge?" she asked cheekily noticing his new wrist brace. "Looks swish," she gestured to his arm as Brendon blushed.

Harvey watched Taylor carry two mugs of tea, he gave one to Brendon who took it, muttered a "thank you," he kept on going over to Terri Wilson. He grabbed the back of an empty office chair as he passed by it, pushed it towards Terri offering her the seat as he handed her a mug of tea.

Everyone gaped at this uncharacteristic gesture instead until Harvey said, "Right! We still have a baby and her mother to find."

Terri took the offered cup of tea sitting down on the chair as Taylor made his way back to his own desk. Harvey's shocked face expressed everyone's current thoughts. He coughed nervously rousing himself from his momentary trance, "What do we know about Fiona Devonshire?" he addressed the room, without waiting for a reply he proceeded to go over the details mostly for Terri Wilson's benefit describing the latest developments with the discovery of Fiona Devonshire's birth right and her husband's ignorance.

Stevens glanced briefly at his computer screen having heard the 'ping' of a new e mail arriving; he reached for his mouse to open it, read its contents which brought a smile to his lips.

"Am I boring you Stevens?" Harvey's uncharacteristic sarcasm cut into the silence of the briefing.

Stevens pressed his mouse as the printer sprang into life he stood up, walked over to retrieve the print out which he gave to Harvey going back to his desk.

Harvey's scowl smoothed out as he read it, "Nice work Stevens! This is our first lead on Alwen Evans, Fiona's mother," he announced. "She appears on the list of a private nursing agency."

"What's that?" Brendon asked.

"They are companies you can engage for elderly or ill people who aren't able to look after themselves, they come in twice a day to bathe and dress someone who can't do it for themselves, put them back to bed later, that sort of thing," Stevens replied.

"Do we have an address, Stevens?" Harvey asked.

He shook his head before he finished having anticipated the question, "Not yet but I'll follow it up."

"Anyone else have anything?" Harvey asked although he didn't hold out much hope.

Taylor said, "I think we should talk to Mary Mundy," he saw Harvey wince at the mention of her name, he hurried on, "She is after all the only witness we can place at the scene of the snatch, sir." Harvey bowed his head thinking. He looked like he was trying to keep control of himself. Taylor knew he recently lost a lot of ground with him.

"Maybe I could go back to talk to her again, sir," Terri interceded quickly not wanting Taylor to suggest again she be brought in for questioning she knew how it would terrify her.

After a long pause Harvey took a deep breath, "Okay, PC Wilson, go back see if she remembers anything more," he could see Brendon Flannery about to offer to accompany her and not wishing them to be paired together quickly added, "Go with her, Taylor. A pair of fresh eyes might do the trick."

Brendon Flannery looked peeved he sank down on his chair. "Brendon," Harvey said to distract his attention, "Could you help Stevens try to locate Alwen Evans, it might speed things up," he passed a look at Brendon about to protest. "I can't have too many injured police officers out there at any one time," he offered lamely.

Only too pleased to be doing something worthwhile, Taylor got up following an eager Terri Wilson out of the office. He thought the old woman key to their finding the missing baby.

Brendon watched them leave, a wistful expression on his face.

CHAPTER 66

The 4x4 land cruiser turned into the gates of 58 Blackheath Avenue impatient to be back it moved rapidly around the side of the property where the garage door stood open. It slid into the empty garage coming to a halt whilst the door immediately began to close.

Fiona Devonshire jumped out moving hastily through the side door leading into her expensively equipped sparkling kitchen with just enough time to grab a wicker basket containing a pair of secateurs as she passed through. She crossed the expansive hallway and out through the front door of her house where she stood cutting some choice blooms from the roses growing there, laying them in the bottom of her basket.

She didn't look up, concentrated hard on regaining her breathing as her heart beat swiftly in her chest. Having sufficient blooms for a table centre piece, she turned once again to re-enter the house as her Nanny pushed the pram towards her. "Did you get everything?" She asked.

*   *   *   *   *

Trevor Taylor-Smythe insisted he drove them to the sheltered housing complex which Terri took as an attitude towards women drivers. He showed all the signs of being a male chauvinist and acutely felt his dislike for her.

"How do you want to play this?" Taylor asked breaking the silence. He felt a little nervous about his last visit to Mary Mundy when he inadvertently raised his fist to knock on the old lady's door when she unexpectedly opened it. He saw how it startled her because he heard her gasp which fortunately gave him sufficient time to pull back his arm; otherwise he would have accidentally struck her. Anyone watching the incident might have thought it deliberate. Taylor thought about telling Terri what happened.

"Did we ought to speak to the warden if she's around?" Taylor asked.

"Why?" Terri looked puzzled although a little annoyed because he assumed the warden would be a woman. "Mary knows who I am. Even if she's forgotten me, the uniform is a bit of a giveaway." It sounded curt and a little abrupt which she didn't mean it to be.

"I wasn't sure whether we needed to tell her why we've come," Taylor mumbled unsure of himself now.

Terri hated that she analysed everything he said for hidden meaning. "You can if you want to," she said. "I'm not sure it'll be much use or if she would be able to tell us anything about Mary – she's very much a loner and doesn't mix very well with anyone else, you'll find her quite hard work. It's like every so often her mind wanders back to her previous life. You have to really listen to her because in amongst her ramblings you'll find her quite astute. For example, the comment about Jocelyn Phipps looking frightened when she nearly bumped into her, she threw in as an aside."

"What would she have been frightened of?" Taylor asked.

"No idea unless being late to meet 'Dorian', as we now know he wasn't the real one, so who knows?"

"Hmm!" Taylor said. "How about you go start it, I'll see if I can find the warden."

It irritated Terri but nonetheless she saw it as a bonus getting rid of him for a while.

They entered through the main door where the warden's small office stood at the far end of the recreational room, a plaque over the door reading 'Communal Lounge'.

Taylor found the warden, a plump jovial woman sitting at her desk in the windowless room, clearly impressed by his status and more than willing to spend time in idle chat about the complex, detouring into the kind of social events she organised for the more able residents.

"Of course, Mary Mundy never comes to any of them," she confided. "Not what you might call a social person," she offered. "Then with her past life...." She shrugged her shoulders in resignation. "I thought the odd game of 'bingo' might bring her out of her shell, but she hasn't even come in here," she pointed out into the vast array of empty tables. "Until the other day when I found her wandering about in the corridors," she said.

"What was she doing?" Taylor's ears pricked up at the comment having let her babbling wash over him.

"I'm not sure really," she replied. "At first I thought perhaps she might be looking for the facilities," the warden then launched off into a long winded description of the 'facilities'. Taylor-Smythe felt a certain amount of sympathy for the residents as a captive audience to her ramblings.

"And was she?" Taylor interrupted into her diatribe.

"What?" The woman asked.

"Looking for any of the facilities?" he emphasised.

"No, I don't think so," she said. "I did show her where everything is again like I did when she first came here." She became thoughtful, "It was really strange."

"What was?"

"Well one minute she seemed okay...I had just shown her the laundry room and about to show her the kitchen next door to it, when she looked afraid...yes, genuinely scared, then she ran off." The warden laughed as she remembered Mary Mundy's odd lolloping gait as she ran down the corridor back to her flat. "It's such a shame," she added suddenly looking sadly at Taylor. He gazed back uncomprehendingly and she went on, "her history?" she prompted.

"What about her history?"

"How as a child she was repeatedly raped by her own father," the warden said lowering her voice in case anyone overheard her. Taylor fell silent shocked by her gossiping matter of fact voice as if it were quite a normal occurrence. "Apparently she got pregnant I guess the scandal of it would be too great, so they 'put her away' in the Asylum; committed her as an 'incompetent.'

Taylor couldn't conceive of a child all alone in an institution, having a baby, "How old was she?" he eventually managed to ask, it wouldn't make any difference to how he felt already about parents or childhood; he had been only too pleased to leave his own back in time.

"I've no idea," the gossipy warden admitted. "Although in those days it wasn't like it is today, with all these young girls, mothers at such an early age – it's quite the norm isn't it?"

"What happened to her baby?" Taylor asked more out of curiosity remembering a lot of the girls from the estate with pushchairs toting round their own babies 'living off the welfare payments and family allowance'.

He heard his mother's harsh criticisms on the subject, usually followed by *"don't let me hear you've got one of them in the family way!"* It usually came with a sharp slap around the head. Taylor grew up with a natural fear of getting some girl 'in the family way'; he mostly shied away from the danger. He saw the whole female sex as a trap, baited by his own desires, lured by the way they dressed or acted. But the idea of locking some child up for life and taking her baby away, that was another matter entirely.

"Maybe it's why…." The warden began looking suddenly shocked.

"Why what?" Taylor asked waiting for some other ghastly revelation.

"I heard her say she could hear her baby crying," she looked at Taylor enquiringly. "She probably still hears it in her head....her own baby crying I mean. They made them have them in those days you know....no such thing as legal abortion."

Taylor knew about it from his own mother's lips and he shivered not wanting to remember the part she played in it.

"I expect you're right," he whispered feeling sick at the whole subject. "Right!" he said firmly, "Thank you for your time," he walked off down the corridor to the stairs leading to the ground floor watched by the warden who would later tell her friend at the bingo all about the story of the strange copper she met earlier in the day.

*   *   *   *   *

Terri Wilson found Mary Mundy in a particularly thoughtful mood being even more subdued than on the previous occasions they met. She hoped it wasn't the uniform which upset her or any of the accompanying equipment she carried with her. The truth being Terri found it quite comforting to wear it.

That morning having dressed in a suit for the CID she suddenly felt exposed; the disquiet grew as she got to the station. It eventually became so intense she found refuge in the female locker room where she kept her uniform stored away in her personal locker. The rising panic inside her only diminished as she opened it and began to change into her police uniform. At its worst she pressed her forehead against the cool metal of the locker breathing deeply, waiting for the panic to subside.

The final strapping on of her radio with the gentle static pulse as it came to life, reporting her sign on to the control room eventually calmed her. It gave her the confidence to walk into the CID office.

Her heart fluttered intermittently until she took the cup of tea Taylor-Smythe offered her, sipped it and listened to the briefing, feeling safe amongst friends.

*   *   *   *   *

Mary heard the knock on her flat door as Terri watched her jump nervously at the sound. Terri stood up quickly, "It's okay Mary, it will be my colleague DC Taylor, he's come with me today, I hope you won't mind." She went to let him in.

She thought Taylor looked abnormally pale as he slipped through the door into the narrow passageway. She wasn't in the habit of looking closely at Taylor, in fact, made a point of not looking at him at all; coming face to face with him it was unavoidable.

"You okay?" she whispered seeing his large brown eyes up close for the first time made her think of a frightened puppy dog. He nodded silently. "Mary seems a little jumpy today, can we tread carefully?" she warned.

"Yes...yes...of course, I'll leave it to you," he said lamely. It wasn't the first time today she'd given him a double-take, he seemed so different to his usual arrogant self.

They joined Mary in her sitting room.

"Mary?" Terri announced hoping Taylor would have heeded her warning. "Mary, this is DC Taylor," she said, then realised she cut his name down, braced herself for the inevitable rebuke of "Taylor-Smythe!" which didn't come.

"Hello, Mary," Taylor said gently when he saw the tiny woman encased in her large comfy chair. His fear she might suddenly scream or accuse him of trying to hit her made his heart beat faster.

"Yes, I've seen you before," she said quietly whereupon he began to sweat. "I saw you at the library," she said.

Taylor looked at Terri for clarification, "I just told Mary the hospital has closed down," she explained.

Mary's fixed stare didn't leave Taylor's face, "You're not a manager then?" she asked.

"Me?" he looked embarrassed, "No, I'm just a police officer like PC Wilson. I did visit the library – I didn't see you there," he said remembering how it was empty except for the school children listening to the teacher reading them a story.

"No," Mary explained. "I thought you came to take me back, so I hid upstairs." She looked around her sitting room, over to the bay window with her collection of treasures. "I like it here," she said to justify hiding from him.

"Yes, it's nice," Taylor agreed. "I wouldn't want to leave it either," he said. "No reason why you should," he reassured her.

Mary stared at him. Terri watched the interchange in amazement.

"We're sorry to have to bother you again," Terri cut in. "You must be fed up with seeing us so often, but we still haven't found the missing baby from outside the Co-op the day you were there."

Mary's face grew concerned, "You mean the one the silly girl left outside on its own?"

"Yes in the pram just outside the door," Terri reminded her.

Mary scowled, "I didn't see a pram," she said. "I told you I always hurry to get back for my tea time," she explained.

"You didn't hear the baby crying at all?" Taylor asked, all the evidence suggested the baby didn't wake.

Mary shook her head, "Not then," she said.

Terri sat up in alarm at this new statement, "When did you hear it crying?"

"I heard crying later," she looked around the room, over to the shelf above the fire where the figure of the mother held the child. "I hear *my* baby crying sometimes," Mary said.

Taylor knew Mary's history now having seen the warden. He could sense Terri's alarm at her words. His hand moved over to hers to stop her from speaking.

"How often does your baby cry, Mary?" he asked gently.

Mary's eyes fixed on his large brown sad eyes as she thought about the question, "Only since the girl left the baby alone," she said. "After I came back, but mostly when my baby wants me to feed it," she said.

Mary looked upwards at the ceiling as if searching for something. She heard the gentle far off cry of the baby and her arms drew together as if she was holding her baby; she began to rock.

Taylor looked upwards at the ceiling as Terri's eyes followed, both were listening intently.

CHAPTER 67

The flat above Mary Mundy's was an identical layout to hers allowing a view through the spyhole along the corridor to the next fire door, not to the communal bins like hers, but to the communal lounge and other facilities. Taylor approached the flat from this direction, accompanied by the complex' warden whose name he just learnt to be Molly Saunders; she told him about the lady who lived directly above Mary Mundy.

"She's been with us quite a while," Molly said. "She's one of our more infirm residents – a stroke left her with limited movement – though she does have one of those electric scooters which allows her to join in our get-togethers," the warden looked delighted at the thought of her get-togethers.

"What about visitors, do you have any idea who comes to see her?" he asked, "Or any idea about her relatives?"

"She just has the one, her daughter she comes to see her regularly. She brought her here to be close to her." Taylor suffered the warden's inane chatter again as she began to search her paper files on a very messy desk. She found what she was looking for, "Here we are," she cried as she took out a piece of loose paper sandwiched between other sheets, "Her daughter's phone numbers."

Taylor took it from her writing the numbers down; one main line he assumed to be her home number, the other one her mobile. He took out his own mobile punching in the first number.

After four rings it was answered although no one spoke. After a further click, a sharp in-take of breath followed by, "Bernard Devonshire," Taylor panicked pressing the 'end call' hanging up.

The warden looked surprised, "I usually telephone her on the mobile number," she said. "Actually I've only ever done it the once when Wynn was under the weather, she comes most days anyway."

"Would you give me a minute," Taylor asked walking out of her office into the vast lounge he walked over into the far corner of the room where he telephoned Harvey.

The warden peered at him from time to time through her open office door mindful something out of the ordinary could be taking place.

*   *   *   *   *

Harvey put down his phone looking stunned. He yelled, "Flannery!" as he walked over to the main office, "Stevens!" he called seeing them sitting together huddled around Steven's terminal. He watched both detectives jump up hearing their names.

"We may have found Alwen Evans," he said as they approached him.

"The sheltered housing complex on North Road?" Stevens queried.

Harvey's mouth dropped open forming, "Oh," which didn't make it to any sound.

"We just got it, boss," Brendon said.

"Taylor and Wilson are already there, get over to them will you, we think Alwen Evans might know where her daughter is!" he sounded relieved.

"Aren't you going, gov?" Brendon asked expecting him to want to be in on the find. He could see Harvey looking seriously shaken by the news not understanding why he wasn't eager to find out.

Harvey seemed oddly pensive, "Err, no, I've got to see the ACC," he said as they hovered in front of him, then yelled, "Go! It sounds like Fiona Devonshire might be there; Taylor could hear a baby crying."

They disappeared at a run leaving Harvey to flop down once again in his chair.

*   *   *   *   *

The warden knocked on Alwen Evans flat door, held up her radio to press a number, "Wynn, it's Molly can I come in?" She spoke into her hand set.

After a crackle a thin shaky voice answered, "Use the key," she invited.

Taylor watched as the warden took out a bunch of keys but instead of inserting one in the door lock she used it to open a box attached to the wall at the side of the door in which a key hung on a hook. She took it to open the flat door placing it back inside the box.

"The attendance service use it to get in because Wynn can't let them in herself," she explained. Taylor thought it an excessive rigmarole, but kept his comment to himself.

Molly could see him smiling, "It's up to the resident who has access," she explained taking the smile as criticism. "It's not a prison, officer, but independent living," she quoted from some promotional literature.

Taylor took the chastisement nodding towards the open door to get the warden moving. They found Alwen Evans in the sitting room just like he found Mary Mundy earlier, all alone. The only immediate evidence Taylor found of Fiona Devonshire and Phoebe was a baby's travel cot in the one small bedroom where Alwen Evans slept. A tin of baby milk alongside two empty baby bottles, both clean with their teats inverted inside.

Alwen Evans said, "Ah, you've just missed my daughter and granddaughter, they've just left.

CHAPTER 68

Harvey had to admit to himself perhaps he'd been a bit harsh on Taylor and maybe he'd been right to suspect the golf pro Peter Thompson when he saw him meeting with Fiona Devonshire in the car park at the golf club. They found her staying in the house next door to his, one of the two semi-detached houses nearest to the club house. It was Alwen Evan's innocent mention which raised the alarm. Initially the surprise Taylor felt turned into shock quickly followed by embarrassment that Peter Thompson had duped him.

He wasn't about to let Harvey know of the number of occasions he visited the club even though some were an investment in his application to swap clubs; the rest being a natural suspicion of the golf pro's affection for the ladies. Instead of confessing he remained quiet.

He discovered she divided her time, since she went missing, between the golf club and her mother's flat. He hadn't seen her on any of his visits. It was Brendon Flannery who said, "Surely someone must have heard the baby?" He knew only too well how noisy they were at that age.

"Mary Mundy did," Terri Wilson reminded them, "Only she thought it...." She began as the vision of the tiny woman holding an imaginary baby, rocking it, haunted her memory and felt it would for a long time.

"What about Frances Drover, gov, will she be prosecuted?" Brendon asked as the rest of the detectives waited for an update on his previous statement that she might not be fit to plead.

Harvey hesitated, he knew everyone had worked hard and particularly Brendon in rescuing Terri. They solved the murder of Jocelyn Phipps although Harvey was unable to tell them all about subsequent developments in the case, nonetheless they deserved something.

"She's likely to end up at a special hospital for the criminally insane, I understand," Harvey's nervousness showed. "Right, Brendon, Terri can I see you in my office please?" He walked off leaving the rest of the officers looking bemused. After they followed Harvey as his door closed the room erupted into a cacophony of angry muttering.

*   *   *   *   *

"Sit down," Harvey said waiting until they settled themselves. He stood in silence thinking about what he could justifiably tell them about the orders he received from the top floor.

"It is doubtful whether we have any conclusive evidence on James Drover," he began tentatively as the frown appeared on Brendon Flannery's face. Harvey knew it would take something to pacify Brendon. He felt annoyed at having his hands tied by command.

"Would you say there is any evidence from your point of view PC Wilson to show the part he played in your imprisonment in Frances Drover's house?"

Terri felt embarrassed by the whole incident and annoyed with herself for putting herself in danger. She gave many statements to a variety of people including the Regional Crime Squad who came to apprise her of their intentions; swearing her to silence on the matter.

"I didn't see James Drover whilst I was in the house," she explained more to Brendon than to Harvey who knew already.

She could see it wasn't what Brendon expected. His irate voice cut in, "No way did Frances Drover carry you up into the attic!" he said indignantly.

"Carry on PC Wilson, tell him the rest of it," Harvey requested.

"She drugged me, I have no idea how I got up there," she bowed her head as thinking about it still upset her. "I can't even tell you who gave me the drugs, apart from the cup of tea when she asked me in. I don't have any recollection after, until I woke up in the hospital."

"I saw him up there from outside!" Brendon insisted. "Hell we arrested him up there, where we found you, how could he not know you were there?" He protested indignantly.

"Just think about it Flannery, he's claiming just that," Harvey's voice rose an octave in anger, but not because Brendon persisted to argue, more because of the way the powers that be agreed to deal with James Drover. "The evidence is inconclusive; all we have on him is the possible dumping of Jocelyn Phipps' body," Harvey proceeded. "Even that isn't conclusive...." Brendon grunted in protest. "There is no 'real' evidence to support it. The car used for transporting Jocelyn Phipps' body belongs to Frances Drover – we found it in the garage at the house."

"But she never went out...." Brendon repeated her oft quoted statement. He shut up remembering the claims by the old man, Brown, across the road to seeing her driving. Steven's voice once again playing like a stuck record, *"my Nan had that once,"* came back to him. Even Stevens knew agoraphobia wasn't always a permanent condition.

"There is no evidence James Drover was ever in his wife's car, Flannery, but much evidence Jocelyn Phipps was. With a head wound DNA show her blood on the carpet inside the boot with fragments of her hair and other fibres."

"Did he not admit to disposing of her body? He meant to meet with her...." Brendon persisted. Harvey chose not to answer.

"This is in the strictest confidence, it must go no further," Harvey sat down behind his desk. He'd been standing by his office window like he did on numerous occasions when something troubled him; just looking out at the world somehow helped him. "The RCS are pursuing a bigger case involving mass corruption, money laundering, arms dealing involving the widespread organised trafficking of both adults and children some of which cuts across many boundaries and countries," Harvey began. "I understand one of their 'persons of interest' locally is no other than....."

"......Bernard Devonshire!" Brendon finished for him.

"Yes, Flannery, your friend Mr Devonshire has been up to all kinds of things. Of course, it may only be on the fringes of some of the more 'nasty' stuff. The point is his financial consultant, also his wife, who once used to be his personal assistant both have a lot to contribute." Harvey paused letting the implications sink in. "It is one of the reasons Fiona Devonshire planned her own and her daughter's disappearance – of course, she also planned her mother's removal from Wales, everyone involved believing it to be her need to bring her closer to her to be able to care for her."

"Which is probably true," Terri admitted.

"Yes, she didn't at first link her husband's financial advisor, she knew as Jed, to her Welsh background, in fact she thought by bringing her mother here it would shut off her past altogether. She only discovered the connection accidentally on hearing someone talking about James Ellis Drover. When he showed up as her husband's colleague she knew he was interested in her and more specifically her daughter. I suspect her mother confessed it all to her once away from her former life."

"So are you saying Bernard Devonshire may well get the justice he deserves?" Brendon asked subconsciously rubbing his injured arm.

Harvey gave a big sigh, "It's early days, but yes, we can only hope, although they have their eye on much bigger targets than Devonshire, they hope he might lead them to these."

"So James Drover gets let off his part in a murder...." Clearly Brendon was still peeved at what Terri Wilson went through, which he believed Drover to be involved in. The vision haunting him of one little four year old girl who might never have discovered who her mother really is let alone the chance to have a proper relationship with her; he shivered thinking of what might have happened to Terri Wilson.

"Not exactly Flannery," Harvey replied. "In exposing Bernard Devonshire's illicit dealings I'm thinking he might just expose himself....he is probably arrogant enough to believe he is somehow immune to any consequences, but I doubt it very much, what is it they say? "Give someone enough rope....." he didn't finish the saying not wanting the image of a hanged man to grow in his mind.

"What will happen to Fiona Devonshire, sir?" Terri's voice cut in.

"It already has, PC Wilson," Harvey said. "Let's just say in the interests of justice she, her mother and her daughter...." He smiled calmly. "Disappeared, only this time officially and quietly to assist the bigger picture."

Harvey was not prepared to go any further into it. Neither of them knew anything about how the police went about such matters. Or even Harvey who ceased to have any involvement with them.

"What about Bernard Devonshire, gov, won't he go on bleating about police incompetence in finding his wife and daughter?" Brendon's dislike of the man increased every time he thought about him hitting his wife.

"We'll leave the phone tap in there for a while," Harvey didn't want to think about the actions of the other special units, they told him his investigation would scale down considerably, that he could only deal with getting the evidence together for the Jocelyn Phipps murder. "I'm sure Bernard Devonshire will make his usual overtures, but as they say Flannery 'not my circus, not my monkey'," Brendon smiled at Harvey's attempt at humour. "He has friends in high places, let them deal with it," Harvey said cynically.

Harvey sank back in his chair a sign the discussion was over. The deep crevices in his face revealed the downside to a long career. Brendon and Terri stood up to leave. Brendon's mouth opened once again ready to ask another question, one which he often repeated of late – *"Are you okay, boss?"* His mouth snapped shut, the words unspoken.

They left him deep in thought accepting he hated this situation just as much as they did, maybe even more. Harvey hated letting his staff down; hated anything getting in the way of him doing his job. Now more than ever with the internal politics and the rise in 'specialisms' the job got harder.

His thoughts dwelt on whether the time had come to call it a day. To retire whilst he still had enough life left in him, after all he'd done more than his 30 years, starting as a cadet at 16 he could retire if he chose to.

There was just the little matter of what he would do with his retirement, indeed, the rest of his life. He held no particular ambitions to go into something else to develop a new career. At this moment in time Mike Harvey felt like the proverbial 'washed up' 'worn out' seashell scattered on the shore of some remote isolated beach.

Everything he started out to work hard for had long since moved on; his wife, his home, his two daughters off somewhere forging their own way in the world. Their plans he knew did not include him within their scope.

He took out a key from his trouser pocket, reached over to unlock his desk draws, pulled open the top one he slipped his hand inside. He took out the envelope he'd securely set aside some weeks ago and re-read the one page for yet another time. It dropped onto his desk when his hands opened as if in supplication he bowed his head into them.

That was the thing about time it had a cruel way of taking everything away from you.

The End

Epilogue

Harvey sat in his car mesmerised by the rain against his windscreen, watching long trailing rivulets as they made their way down the glass, his wipers as still as him, having worked twice as fast as usual to clear the heavy downpour when he drove back here once again like on two other occasions.

The lights from the solitary milk float temporarily illuminating the inside of his car makes him flinch turning away as if he were a thief casing his next job. What did it matter if anyone saw him just sitting in his car?

"Old habits die hard," his mother's voice this time sounding in his head, "once a copper always a copper." It carried a measure of criticism, something unusual for her, she never criticised him not even when he knew he neglected going to see her after his Dad died leaving her on her own. It had always been family or the 'job' to keep him away. Then it had been too late and he was sitting by her hospital bed trying to understand the sounds she made that were meant to be words but came out as senseless noise, more like grunts.

Those other words spoken by her in retaliation for his enquiry, "What did he die of?" when he heard about his father's sudden death. It wasn't meant to hurt her, although she took it as criticism.

"People die, Mikey," she told him. "His health wasn't good at the end." The realisation he didn't notice, mainly because he didn't see his father much, what with his own life deteriorating; the all-consuming demise of his marriage as well as the job, always the job that got in the way to keep him away. "He had a heart problem," she said. "It got worse."

He remembered the flare of his temper wanting to yell, "Of course it got worse....he bloody died!"

Was it the moment when he lost control, he certainly felt 'out of control' the majority of the time after that. He blamed his mother for not telling him just how bad his father's condition had been. She claimed she didn't know.

Harvey's guilt grumbled underneath his bouts of temper and when they spilt over into his working life, like an out of control steam engine, they picked up speed hurtling him towards the inevitable crash.

His mother's stroke came suddenly and unexpectedly; as far as he knew she wasn't ill either. Watching her lying in the hospital bed unable to communicate, hit him hard. His mother was the last person in his life who could tell him about his childhood, having no siblings. He held her hand feeling his life, his early life, slipping away with hers.

It was a stark revelation finding himself completely alone with no one to endorse his origins. When it came, her death hit him hard, although the doctors did warn him to expect the worst, it still shocked him. Those last few days spent with her as she tried to tell him something, were the most frustrating he'd ever known. She didn't recover enough to be able to communicate what had been clearly on her mind; he could see guilt in her eyes as she tried right up until she died.

If it wasn't for the Council's pressure to clear her home because they needed to re-let, he felt sure he wouldn't have discovered the truth so quickly. He found the adoption papers amongst all the other papers, birth, marriage, death certificates, together in a leather pouch tucked at the back of the large oak wardrobe. It started the quest to discover who he really was; 'mother unknown' flashing in his mind like a neon sign outside of a brothel, always a possibility.

Here once again, with the torrential rain sliding down his car windows like tears streaming down the face of the little boy with the scraped knees and his father's voice in his ears as clear as day saying, "Now come on son that's no way for a 'big man' to act."

Harvey flicked his windscreen wipers revealing the block of flats intermittently sprinkled with early morning glowing lights as people woke up for the day. He sighed deeply, forced himself to get out of the car and with a burst of energy run towards the outer door where the intercoms were fixed to the wall.

The door opened before he could press for attention as a man appeared holding a plastic milk bottle carrier, muttered, "Morning," allowing him inside the block. He took advantage letting the door close slowly behind him, he moved down the corridor finding the door he needed.

He stood like a statue as years of images of his adoptive parents pushed their way through his mind. After minutes of inertia he raised his arm and knocked; he waited almost daring not to breathe.

The door opened wide to the tiny woman, her head bobbing in an exaggerated way.

"Mary Mundy?" he asked. The head changed direction and nodded but she didn't speak. "I think you are my mother."

The tiny form, dwarfed by his tall gangling frame, looked up towards Mike Harvey's face, "I knew you would come," she said and for the first time ever that anyone could confirm, Mary Mundy smiled.